SEIZURE

Also by Robin Cook

SEIZURE

Robin Cook

Doubleday Large Print Home Library Edition

G. P. PUTNAM'S SONS

NEW YORK

This Large Print Edition, prepared especially for Doubleday Large Print Home Library, contains the complete, unabridged text of the original Publisher's Edition.

G. P. Putnam's Sons
Publishers Since 1838
a member of
Penguin Group (USA) Inc.
375 Hudson Street
New York, NY 10014

ISBN 0-7394-3658-9

Printed in the United States of America

**This Large Print Book carries the
Seal of Approval of N.A.V.H.**

FOR AUDREY

Although her faculty of reminiscence has faltered, mine hasn't; so heartfelt thanks, Mom, for all your love, dedication, and sacrifices particularly during my early years . . . an appreciation made more poignant and profound now that I have a healthy, happy, and rambunctious three-year-old boy of my own!

Acknowledgments

As with many of my novels, particularly those dealing with expertise beyond my undergraduate chemistry and graduate medical training in surgery and ophthalmology, I have benefited greatly from the professional erudition, wisdom, and experience of friends and friends of friends for the research, plotting, and writing of *Seizure,* whose storyline spans medicine, biotechnology, and politics. A host of people has been extraordinarily generous with their valuable time and insights. Those whom I would specifically like to acknowledge are (in alphabetical order):

Jean Cook, MSW, CAGS: a psychologist,

a perceptive reader, a courageous critic, and an invaluable sounding board.

Joe Cox, J.D., LLM: a gifted tax lawyer as well as a reader of fiction, who is conversant with corporate structure, financing, and offshore legal issues.

Gerald Doyle, M.D.: a compassionate internist cast from a bygone mold, with a first-class referral list of accomplished clinical physicians.

Orrin Hatch, J.D.: a venerated senior Senator from Utah, who graciously allowed me to experience firsthand a typical day in the life of a Senator and who regaled me with humorous stories of late Senators whose biographies were a fertile source for creating my fictional Ashley Butler.

Robert Lanza, M.D.: a human dynamo who tirelessly struggles to bridge the gap between clinical medicine and 21st-century biotechnology.

Valerio Manfredi, Ph.D.: an exuberant Italian archeologist and author himself, who magnanimously arranged introductions and my visit to Turin, Italy, for my research into the remarkable Shroud of Turin.

SEIZURE

Prologue

Monday, February 22, 2001, was one of those surprisingly warm midwinter days that falsely prophesied the arrival of spring to the inhabitants of the Atlantic seaboard. The sun was bright all the way from Maine to the tip of the Florida Keys, providing a temperature variation astonishingly less than twenty degrees Fahrenheit. It was to be a normal, happy day for the vast majority of people living within this lengthy littoral, although for two exceptional individuals, it was to be the start of a series of events that would ultimately cause their lives to tragically intersect.

1:35 P.M.
Cambridge, Massachusetts

Daniel Lowell looked up from the pink phone message he held in his hand. Two things made it unique: First, the caller was Dr. Heinrich Wortheim, Chairman of the Department of Chemistry at Harvard, saying he wanted to see Dr. Lowell in his office, and second, the little box labeled URGENT was marked with a bold x. Dr. Wortheim always communicated by letter and expected a letter in return. As one of the world's premier chemists occupying Harvard's lofty and heavily endowed department chair, he was eccentrically Napoleonic. He rarely mixed directly with the hoi polloi that included Daniel, even though Daniel was head of his own department, which came under Wortheim's authority.

"Hey, Stephanie!" Daniel called out across the lab. "Did you see this phone message on my desk? It's from the emperor. He wants to see me in his office."

Stephanie looked up from the dissecting stereomicroscope she'd been using and glanced at Daniel. "That doesn't sound good," she said.

"You didn't say anything to him, did you?"

"How would I have a chance to say anything to him? I've only seen him twice during my entire Ph.D. travail—when I defended my dissertation and when he handed me my diploma."

"He must have some idea about our plans," Daniel surmised. "I suppose it's not too surprising, considering all the people I've approached to be on our scientific advisory board."

"Are you going to go?"

"I wouldn't miss it for the world."

It was only a short walk from the lab to the building that housed the departmental administrative offices. Daniel knew he was facing a confrontation of sorts, but it didn't matter. In fact, he was looking forward to it.

The moment Daniel appeared, the departmental secretary motioned him to go directly into Wortheim's inner sanctum. He found the aging Nobel laureate behind his antique desk. With his white hair and thin face, Wortheim appeared older than his purported seventy-two years. But his appearance did not diminish his commanding personality, which radiated from him like a magnetic field.

"Please sit down, Dr. Lowell," Wortheim said, regarding his visitor over the top of his wire-rimmed reading glasses. He had had a trace German accent despite his having lived in the United States most of his life. Daniel did as he was told. He knew a faint, insouciant smile, which he was certain would not be missed by the department head, lingered on his face. Despite Wortheim's age, his faculties were as sharp as ever and attuned to any slight. And the fact that Daniel was supposed to kowtow to this dinosaur was part of the reason he was so certain of his decision to leave academia. Wortheim was brilliant, and he'd won a Nobel Prize, but he was still mired in last century's inorganic synthetic chemistry. Organic chemistry in form of proteins and their respective genes was the present and future of the field.

It was Wortheim who broke the silence after the two men had eyed each other. "I gather from your expression that the rumors are true."

"Could you be more specific?" Daniel responded. He wanted to be sure his suspicions were correct. He hadn't planned to make an announcement for another month.

"You have been forming a scientific advisory board," Wortheim said. He got to his feet and began to pace. "An advisory board can mean only one thing." He stopped and stared at Daniel with acrimonious disdain. "You're planning to tender your resignation, and you have or you are about to found a company."

"Guilty as accused," Daniel proclaimed. He couldn't keep his smile from expanding to a full grin. A deep red had suffused over Wortheim's face. Undoubtedly, Wortheim equated the situation to Benedict Arnold's traitorous behavior during the American Revolutionary War.

"I personally went out on a limb when you were recruited," Wortheim snapped. "We even built the laboratory facility that you demanded."

"I won't be taking the lab with me," Daniel responded. He couldn't believe Wortheim was trying to make him feel guilty.

"Your flippancy is galling."

"I could apologize, but it would be insincere."

Wortheim returned to his desk. "Your leaving is going to put me in a difficult position with the president of the university."

"I'm sorry about that," Daniel said. "I can say that in all sincerity. But this kind of bureaucratic shenanigan is part of the reason I'm not going to miss academia."

"What else?"

"I'm tired of sacrificing my research time for teaching."

"Your teaching burden is one of the least onerous in the department. We negotiated that when you came on board."

"It still keeps me from my research. But that's not the major issue, either. I want to reap the benefits of what my creativity has produced. Winning prizes and getting articles in scientific journals isn't enough."

"You want to be a celebrity."

"I suppose that's one way to put it. And the money will be nice, too. Why not? People with half my ability have done it."

"Have you ever read *Arrowsmith* by Sinclair Lewis?"

"I don't have much chance to read novels."

"Maybe you should take the time," Wortheim suggested scornfully. "It might make you rethink this decision before it's irreversible."

"I've given it a lot of thought," Daniel said. "I think it is the right thing for me."

"Would you like my opinion?"

"I think I know what your opinion is."

"I think it's going to be a disaster for both of us, but mainly for you."

"Thank you for your words of encouragement," Daniel said. He stood up. "See you around the campus." Then he walked out.

5:15 P.M.
Washington, D.C.

"Thank you all for coming to see me," Senator Ashley Butler said in his usual cordial, Southern drawl. With a smile plastered onto his doughy face, he glad-handed a group of eager-faced men and women who'd leapt to their feet the moment he burst into his small senate office conference room along with his chief of staff. The visitors were grouped around the central oak library table. They were representatives of a small business organization from the senator's state capital who were lobbying for tax relief, or maybe it was insurance relief. The senator did not remember exactly, and it wasn't on his schedule as it should have been. He made a mental note to bring the lapse up with his office manager. "I'm sorry I'm late coming in here," he continued, after energetically pumping the last person's hand. "I've been looking forward to meeting you folks, and I wanted to get in here sooner, but it's been one of those days." He rolled his eyes for emphasis. "Unfortunately, because of the hour and another pressing engagement, I can't stay. I'm sorry, but Mike here is great."

The senator gave the staffer assigned to meet with the group an acknowledging slap on the shoulder, urging the young man forward until his thighs were pressed up against the table. "Mike's the best I've got, and he'll listen to your problems and then brief me. I'm sure we can help, and we want to help."

The senator gave Mike's shoulder another series of pats, along with an admiring smile like a proud father's at his son's graduation.

In a chorus, the visitors thanked the senator for seeing them, especially in view of his demanding schedule. Zealous smiles defined each and every face. If the people were disappointed at the brevity of the meeting and the fact that they'd had to wait almost a half hour, they didn't show it in the slightest.

"It's my pleasure," Ashley gushed. "We're here to serve."

Spinning around, Ashley turned to leave.

As he reached the door, he waved. His home-state visitors responded in kind.

"That was easy," Ashley murmured to Carol Manning, his long-term chief of staff, who'd followed from the conference room at her boss's heels. "I was afraid they were going to hog-tie me with a litany of sad stories and unreasonable demands."

"They seemed like nice people," Carol said vaguely.

"Do you think Mike can handle them?"

"I don't know," Carol said. "He's not been here long enough for me to have much of an idea."

Leading the way, the senator strode down the long hall toward his private office. He glanced at his watch. It was five-twenty in the afternoon. "I assume you remember where you are taking me now."

"Of course," Carol said. "We're going back to Dr. Whitman's office."

The senator shot a reproachful look in Carol's direction while pressing his forefinger against his lips. "That's hardly for general consumption," he whispered irritably.

Without the slightest acknowledgment of his office manager, Dawn Shackelton, Ashley grabbed the papers she held up as he passed her desk and entered his private office. The papers included a preliminary schedule for the following day, along with a list of the calls that had come in during the time he'd been over at the capital for a late roll call vote, plus the transcript of an impromptu interview with someone from CNN who'd waylaid him in the hall.

"I'd better get my car," Carol said after glancing at her own watch. "We're due at the doctor's office at six-thirty, and there's no telling what kind of traffic we'll be facing."

"Good idea," Ashley said, going around behind his desk while glancing at the list of calls.

"Should I pick you up at the corner of C and Second?"

Ashley merely grunted an affirmative. A number of the calls were important, coming from the heads of several of his many political action committees. As far as he was concerned, fund-raising was the most important part of his job, especially since he was facing a reelection campaign for the November after next. He heard the door close behind Carol. For the first time all day, a silence descended over him. He raised his eyes. Also for the first time all day, he was alone.

Instantaneously, the anxiety he'd felt upon awakening that morning spread through him like a wildfire. He could feel it from the pit of his stomach to the tips of his fingers. He'd never liked going to the doctor. When he was a child, it had been the simple fear of a shot or some other painful or embarrassing experience. But as he'd gotten older, the fear had changed and had become more powerful and distressing. Seeing the doctor had become an unwelcome reminder of his mortality and the fact that he was no longer a spring chicken. Now it was as if the mere act of going to the doctor increased his chances of having to face some horrible diagnosis like cancer or, worse yet, ALS—also known as Lou Gehrig's disease.

A few years earlier, one of Ashley's brothers had been diagnosed with ALS after experiencing some vague neurological symptoms. After the diagnosis, the powerfully built and athletically inclined man who'd been much more of a picture of health than Ashley had rapidly become a cripple and within months had died. The doctors had been helpless.

Ashley absently placed the papers onto his desk and stared off into the distance. He too had begun to have some vague neuro-logical symptoms a month earlier. At first he just dismissed them, attributing their appearance to the stress of his work or having drunk too much coffee or not having gotten a good night's sleep. The symptoms waxed and waned but never went away. In fact, they slowly seemed to get worse. The most distressing was the intermittent shaking of his left hand. On a few occasions it had been necessary for him to hold it with his right hand to keep people from noticing. Then there was the feeling of sand in his eyes, making them water embarrassingly. And finally there was an occasional sensation of stiffness that could make standing up and starting to walk a mental and physical effort.

A week earlier, the problem had finally driven him to see the doctor despite his superstitious reluctance to do so. He didn't go to Walter Reed or the National Naval Medical Center in Bethesda. He was too afraid the media would discover that something was amiss. Ashley didn't need that kind of publicity. After almost thirty years in the Senate he'd become a powerhouse and a force to be reckoned with, despite his reputation as an obstructionist who regularly bucked his party's dictates. Indeed, with his advocacy and consistency on various fundamentalist and populist issues like states' rights and prayer in school, and his anti– affirmative-action and anti-abortion stances, he'd succeeded in blurring party lines while developing a growing national constituency. Reelection to the senate would not be a problem with his well-oiled political machinery. What Ashley had his sights on was a run for the White House in 2004. He didn't need anyone speculating or circulating rumors about his health.

Once Ashley had overcome his reluctance to seek a medical opinion, he visited a private internist in Virginia whom he'd seen in the past and whose discretion he could trust. The internist in turn immediately referred him to Dr. Whitman, a neurologist.

Dr. Whitman had been noncommittal, although hearing Ashley's specific fears, he said he doubted the problem involved ALS. After giving a thorough exam and sending him for some tests, including an MRI, Dr. Whitman had not offered a diagnosis but instead gave Ashley a prescription to see if it would help the symptoms. He'd then scheduled Ashley to return in a week when all the tests' results would be back. He'd said that he thought he'd be able to make a diagnosis at that time. It was this visit Ashley was now facing.

Ashley ran a hand across his brow. Some perspiration had appeared, despite the coolness of the room. He could feel that his pulse was racing. What if he had ALS after all? What if he had a brain tumor? Back when Ashley was a state senator in the early seventies, one of his colleagues came down with a brain tumor. Ashley tried vainly to remember what the man's symptoms had been, but he couldn't. All he could remember was seeing the man become a shadow of his former self before dying.

The door to the outer office cracked open. Dawn's carefully coiffed head poked in. "Carol just called on her cell phone. She'll be at the rendezvous location in five minutes."

Ashley nodded and got to his feet. Encouragingly, he had no difficulty whatsoever. The fact that the medication Dr. Whitman had given him had seemingly worked miracles was to him the only bright spot in the whole affair. The worrisome symptoms had all but disappeared save for a bit of hand shaking just prior to another dose. If the problem could so easily be treated, perhaps he shouldn't worry so much. At least that's what he tried to convince himself.

Carol was right on time, as Ashley expected. She'd been working with him for sixteen years of his near-thirty-year senatorial tenure and had proved her reliability, dedication, and loyalty over and over. As they headed for Virginia, she even tried to take advantage of the time by discussing the day's events and what to expect for the morrow, but she quickly caught on to the degree of Ashley's preoccupation and fell silent. Instead, she concentrated on the hellish traffic.

Ashley's anxiety ratcheted upward the closer they got to the doctor's office. By the time he got out of the car, his perspiration had reappeared. Over the years, Ashley had learned to listen to his intuition, and his intuition was setting off alarm bells. There was something wrong in his brain, and he knew it, and he knew he was trying to deny it.

The appointment had been scheduled for Ashley's benefit after the doctor's regular office hours, and a sepulchral stillness hung over the vacant waiting room. The only light came from a small desk lamp creating a dim puddle of illumination on the empty receptionist's desk. Ashley and Carol stood for a moment, unsure of what to do. Then an inner door opened, flooding the space with raw fluorescent light. Within the doorway was Dr. Whitman's featureless backlit silhouette.

"Sorry about this inhospitable welcome," Dr. Whitman said. "Everyone has gone home." He flipped a wall switch. He was dressed in a starched white doctor's coat. His demeanor was all business.

"No need for an apology," Ashley said. "We appreciate your discretion." He eyed the doctor's face, hoping for some softening of his expression to interpret as an auspicious sign. There wasn't any.

"Senator, please come into my office." Dr. Whitman motioned within. "Ms. Manning, if you would be so good as to wait out here."

The doctor's office was a study in compulsive neatness. The furniture consisted of a desk with two guest chairs. The objects on the desk were all carefully aligned, while the books in the bookshelf were arranged according to size.

Dr. Whitman motioned to one of the guest chairs before taking his own seat. With elbows on the desk, he steepled his fingers.

He stared at Ashley once the senator was seated. There was a pregnant pause.

Ashley had never been quite so uncomfortable. His anxiety had peaked. Ashley had spent most of his adult life jockeying for power, and he'd succeeded beyond his wildest dreams. Yet at that moment, he was utterly powerless.

"You said on the phone that the medication I gave you helped," Dr. Whitman began.

"Wonderfully," Ashley exclaimed, suddenly cheered by Dr. Whitman's starting with the positive. "Almost all my symptoms disappeared."

Dr. Whitman nodded knowingly. His expression remained inscrutable.

"I would have assumed that was good news."

"It helps us make the diagnosis," Dr. Whitman said.

"Well . . . what is it?" Ashley asked after an uncomfortable pause. "What's the diagnosis?"

"The medication was a form of levodopa," Dr. Whitman began in a doctoral tone. "The body can convert it into dopamine, which is a substance involved in some neuronal transmission."

Ashley took a deep breath. A sudden wave of anger threatened to bubble to the surface. He didn't want to be lectured, as if he were a student. He wanted the diagnosis. He felt he was being teased like a cat teases a cornered mouse.

"You've lost some cells that are involved with the production of dopamine," Dr. Whitman continued. "These cells are in a part of your brain called the *substantia nigra.*"

Ashley held up his hands as if surrendering. He suppressed his urge to lash out verbally by swallowing with some difficulty. "Doctor, let's get to the point. What do you think my diagnosis is?"

"I'm about ninety-five percent sure you have Parkinson's disease," Dr. Whitman said. He leaned back. His desk chair squeaked.

For a moment, Ashley didn't speak. He didn't know much about Parkinson's disease, but it didn't sound good, and some images of celebrities struggling with the disorder popped into his mind. At the same time, he felt relieved he'd not been told he had a brain tumor or ALS. He cleared his throat.

"Is this something that can be cured?" Ashley allowed himself to ask.

"Currently, no," Dr. Whitman said. "But as you've experienced with the medication I gave you, it can be controlled for a time."

"What does that mean?"

"We can keep you relatively symptom-free for a while, maybe a year, maybe longer. Unfortunately, because of your history of relatively rapidly developing symptoms, in my experience the medications will lose their effectiveness more quickly than with many other patients. At that point, the disease will be progressively debilitating. We'll just have to deal with each circumstance as it arises."

"This is a disaster," Ashley mumbled. He was overwhelmed by the implications. His worst fears were coming to pass.

one

6:30 P.M., Wednesday, February 20, 2002
One Year Later

It seemed to Daniel Lowell that the taxi had senselessly pulled to a stop mid-block in the center of M Street in Georgetown, Washington D.C., a busy four-lane thoroughfare. Daniel had never liked riding in taxis. It seemed the height of ridiculousness to trust one's life to a total stranger who more often than not hailed from a distant Third World country and frequently was more interested in talking on his cell phone than paying attention to driving. Sitting in the middle of M

Street in the darkness with rush-hour traffic whizzing by on both sides and the driver carrying on emotionally in an unknown language was a case in point. Daniel glanced over at Stephanie. She appeared relaxed and smiled at him in the half-light. She gripped his hand affectionately.

It was only by leaning forward that Daniel could see there was a traffic light suspended from above to facilitate a rather awkward mid-block left-hand turn. Glancing at the other side of the street, he could see a driveway leading to a nondescript, boxy brick building.

"Is this the hotel?" Daniel questioned. "If it is, it doesn't look much like a hotel."

"Let's hold our evaluation until we have a little more data," Stephanie responded in a playful tone.

The light changed and the taxi leapt forward like a racehorse out of the gate. The driver only had one hand on the steering wheel as he accelerated through the turn. Daniel steadied himself to keep from being thrown against the car door. After a big bounce over the junction of the street and the hotel's driveway, and then another sharp left-hand turn beneath the hotel's porte cochere, the driver braked hard enough to put significant tension on Daniel's seat belt. A moment later, Daniel's door was pulled open.

"Welcome to the Four Seasons," a liveried doorman said brightly. "Are you checking in?"

Leaving their luggage in the hands of the doorman, Daniel and Stephanie entered the hotel lobby and headed toward the registration desk. They passed a grouping of statuary fit for a modern art museum. The carpet was thick and luxurious. Smartly dressed people lounged in overstuffed velvet chairs.

"How did you talk me into staying here?" Daniel questioned rhetorically. "The outside might be plain, but the interior suggests this is going to be expensive."

Stephanie pulled Daniel to a halt. "Are you trying to suggest that you've forgotten our conversation yesterday?"

"We had a lot of conversations yesterday," Daniel muttered. He noticed the woman who had just walked by carrying a French poodle had a diamond engagement ring the size of a Ping-Pong ball.

"You know what I'm talking about!" Stephanie proclaimed. She reached up and turned Daniel's face toward her own. "We decided to make the best of this trip. We're staying in this hotel for two nights, and we're going to indulge ourselves and, I would hope, each other."

Catching Stephanie's witty licentiousness, Daniel smiled in spite of himself.

"Your testifying tomorrow in front of Senator Butler's Health Policy Subcommittee is not going to be a walk in the park," Stephanie continued. "That's a given. But in spite of what happens there, we're going to at least take the memory of a nice experience back to Cambridge."

"Couldn't we have had a nice experience at a slightly less extravagant hotel?"

"Not in my book," Stephanie declared. "They have a health club, a masseuse, and top-rated room service, all of which we're going to take advantage of. So start relaxing and unwinding. Besides, I'll pick up the tab."

"Really?"

"Sure! With the salary I've been pulling down, I should give some back to the company."

"Oh, that's a low blow!" Daniel remarked playfully, while pretending to reel from a make-believe slap.

"Look," Stephanie said, "I know the company hasn't been exactly able to pay our salaries for a while, but I'm going to see that this whole trip goes on the company charge card. If things go really badly tomorrow which they very well might, bankruptcy court can decide how much the Four Seasons will be paid for our indulgence."

Daniel's smile erupted into a full laugh. "Stephanie, you never fail to amaze me!"

"You ain't seen nothing yet," Stephanie said with a smile. "The question is: Are you going to let your hair down or what? Even in the taxi, I could tell you were wound up like a piano wire."

"That was because I was worried about whether we were going to get here in one piece, not how we were going to pay for it."

"Come on, big spender," Stephanie said, urging Daniel forward. "Let's get up to our suite."

"Suite?" Daniel questioned, as he allowed himself to be dragged toward the registration desk.

Stephanie hadn't exaggerated. Their suite overlooked a part of the Chesapeake and Ohio Canal with the Potomac River in the background. On the coffee table in the sitting room was a cooler chilling a bottle of champagne. Vases of freshly cut flowers graced the bureau in the bedroom and the expansive countertop in the generous-size marble bathroom.

As soon as the bellman disappeared, Stephanie put her arms around Daniel. Her dark eyes stared up into his blue orbs. A slight smile played across her full lips. "I know you are under a lot of stress about tomorrow," she began, "so how about letting me be the tour leader? We both know that Senator Butler's proposed legislation would effectively outlaw your patented and brilliant procedure. And that would mean a cancellation of the second-round financing for the company, with obviously disastrous consequences. With that said and understood, let's forget about it for tonight. Can you do that?"

"I can try," Daniel said, although he knew it would be impossible. Failure was one of his worst fears.

"That's all I ask," Stephanie said. She gave him a quick kiss before breaking away to attend to the champagne. "Here's the schedule! We have a glass of bubbly, then take refreshing showers. Following that, we have reservations at a nearby restaurant called Citronelle that I hear is fantastic. After a wonderful meal, we come back here and make mad, passionate love. What do you say?"

"I'd be crazy to offer any resistance," Daniel said, raising his hands in mock surrender.

Stephanie and Daniel had been living together for more than two years and had developed a comfortable familiarity. They had noticed each other back in the mid-eighties, when Daniel had returned to academia and Stephanie was an undergraduate chemistry major at Harvard. Neither acted on their mutual attraction, since such liaisons were specifically frowned upon by university policy. Besides, neither had had the slightest notion that their feelings were reciprocal, at least not until Stephanie had completed her Ph.D. and had joined the junior faculty, giving them an opportunity to interact on more equal footing. Even their respective areas of scientific expertise complemented each other. When Daniel left the university to found his company, it was natural that Stephanie would accompany him.

"Not bad at all," Stephanie said, after she drained her flute and put the glass down on the coffee table. "Now! Let's flip to see who gets the shower first."

"No need to flip a coin," Daniel said, placing his empty glass next to Stephanie's. "I concede. You first. While you shower, I'll shave."

"You've got a deal," Stephanie said.

Daniel didn't know if it was the champagne or Stephanie's infectious buoyancy but he felt significantly less tense, although hardly less worried, as he lathered his face and began shaving. Having had only one glass, he suspected it was Stephanie. As she had implied, the morrow might bring disaster, a fear disturbingly reminiscent of Heinrich Wortheim's prophecy the day he'd discovered Daniel was moving back to private industry. But Daniel would try not to allow such thoughts to dominate their visit, at least for that evening. He would try to follow Stephanie's lead and enjoy himself.

Looking beyond his lathered image in the mirror, Daniel could see Stephanie's blurred figure through the misted glass-enclosed shower. Her singing voice could be heard over the roar of the water. She was thirty-six but looked more like twenty-six. As he had told her on more than one occasion, she'd done very well in the genetic lottery. Her tall, curvaceous figure was slender and firm as if she worked out regularly even though she didn't, and her dark, olive skin was nearly blemish-free. A mat of thick, lustrous dark hair with matching midnight eyes completed the picture.

The shower door opened, and Stephanie stepped out. She briskly dried her hair, totally unconcerned about her nakedness. For a moment, she bent over at the waist, allowing her hair to fall free as she frenetically rubbed it with the towel. Then she stood back upright, flipping her hair back in the process like a horse redirecting its mane. When she switched to drying her back with a provocative wiggle of her hips, her line of sight happened to catch Daniel's stare in the mirror. She stopped.

"Hey!" Stephanie exclaimed. "What are you looking at? You're supposed to be shaving." Suddenly self-conscious, she wrapped herself in her towel as if it were a strapless minidress.

Initially embarrassed about being caught as a voyeur, Daniel quickly regained his equanimity. He put down his razor and stepped over to Stephanie. He gripped her shoulders and stared into her liquid-onyx eyes. "I just couldn't help but notice how sexy and absolutely alluring you look."

Stephanie tilted her head to the side to get a view of Daniel from a slightly different perspective. "Are you all right?"

Daniel laughed. "I'm fine."

"Did you slip back to the sitting room and polish off that bottle of champagne?"

"I'm being serious."

"You haven't said anything like that for months."

"To say I've been preoccupied would be putting it mildly. When I had the idea of founding the company, I had no idea that fund-raising was going to occupy one hundred and ten percent of my efforts. And now on top of it comes this political menace, threatening to destroy the whole operation."

"I understand," Stephanie said. "Truly I do, and I haven't taken it personally."

"Has it really been months?"

"Trust me," Stephanie said, nodding her head for emphasis.

"I apologize," Daniel said. "And to show my remorse, I'd like to make a motion to change the evening's schedule. I propose that we move up the lovemaking and put the dinner plans on hold. Do I hear a second?"

As Daniel tried to lean down to give Stephanie a playful kiss, she pushed his still-lathered face back with just the tip of her index finger on his nose. Her expression suggested she was touching something remarkably distasteful, especially as she wiped the bit of lather from her finger onto his shoulder. "Parliamentary rules are not going to maneuver this lady out of a good dinner," she remarked. "It took some effort to get those reservations, so the evening's plans hold as previously voted on and passed. Now back to shaving!" She gave him a spirited shove toward the sink, then stepped to the neighboring sink to dry her hair.

"Kidding aside," Daniel yelled over the sound of the hair dryer when he'd finished shaving. "You do look fantastic. Sometimes I wonder what you see in an old man like me." He patted his cheeks with aftershave lotion.

"Fifty-two is hardly old," Stephanie yelled back. "Particularly as active as you are. Actually, you're pretty sexy yourself."

Daniel regarded himself in the mirror. He thought he didn't look too bad, although he wasn't going to fool himself by imagining he was in any way sexy. Long ago, he'd reconciled himself to the fact that he was on the nerdy side of the equation of life, having grown up as a science prodigy since the sixth grade. Stephanie was just trying to be nice. He'd always had a thin face, so at least there was no problem with developing jowls or even wrinkles, save for some mild crow's feet at the corner of his eyes when he smiled. He'd stayed active physically, although not so much over the previous several months, due to the time constraints of fund-raising. As a faculty member at Harvard, he'd taken full advantage of the athletic facilities, using the squash and handball courts regularly, as well as the rowing opportunities on the Charles River. His only real appearance problem as he saw it was the retreating hairline at the upper corners of his forehead and the thinning area of his crown, plus the salt-and-pepper silvering of his otherwise brown hair along the sides of his head, but there wasn't much he could do about all that.

After both of them had finished primping, dressing, and donning their coats, they left the hotel armed with simple directions to the restaurant obtained from the concierge. Arm in arm, they strolled several blocks west along M Street, passing a potpourri of art galleries, bookshops, and antiques stores. The night was crisp but not too cold, with a canopy of stars visible despite the city lights.

The maître d' at the restaurant led them to a table off to the side that afforded a degree of privacy in the busy establishment. They ordered food and a bottle of wine, and settled back for a romantic dinner. By the time the entrees had been served and they both had had fun remembering their mutual attraction prior to their ever having dated, they lapsed into a contented silence. Unfortunately Daniel broke it.

"I probably shouldn't bring this up . . ." Daniel began.

"Then don't," Stephanie interjected, having an immediate inclination of where Daniel was heading.

"But I should," Daniel said. "In fact, I have to, and this is a better time than later. Several days ago, you said you were going to research our tormentor, Senator Ashley Butler, with the idea of possibly giving me some help for tomorrow's hearing. I know you looked into it, but you didn't say anything. How come?"

"My recollection is that you agreed to forget about the hearing for tonight."

"I agreed to try to forget about the hearing," Daniel corrected. "I haven't been totally successful. Did you not bring up what you learned because you didn't find anything helpful or what? Help me here, and then we can put it all aside for the rest of the night."

Stephanie looked off for a few beats to organize her thoughts. "What do you want to know?"

Daniel let out a short, exasperated laugh. "You're making this more difficult than it needs to be. To be truthful, I don't know what I want to know, because I don't know enough to even ask questions."

"He's not going to be easy."

"We already had that impression."

"He's been in the senate since 1972, and his seniority gives him significant clout."

"I'd assumed as much, since he's the chairman of the subcommittee," Daniel said. "What I need to know is what makes him tick."

"My impression is he's a rather typical, old-fashioned Southern demagogue."

"A demagogue, huh?" Daniel questioned. He chewed the inside of his cheek for a moment. "I suppose I have to admit to my stupidity here. I've heard the word *demagogue* before, but to tell you the truth, I don't really know exactly what it means other than its pejorative sense."

"It refers to a politician who makes use of popular prejudices and fears to gain and hold power."

"You mean, in this instance, like the public's concern about biotechnology in general."

"Exactly," Stephanie admitted. "Especially when the biotechnology involves words like *embryo* and *cloning.*"

"Meaning embryo farms and Frankenstein scenarios."

"Precisely," Stephanie said. "He plays on people's ignorance and worst fears. And in the Senate, he's an obstructionist. It's always easier to be against issues than for issues. He's made a career of it, even bucking his own party on numerous occasions."

"It doesn't sound good for us." Daniel moaned. "It rules out trying to convince him with any kind of rational argument."

"Unfortunately, that's my take as well.

That's why I haven't told you what I'd learned about him. It's depressing someone like Butler is even in the Senate, much less having the seniority and power he has. Senators are supposed to be leaders, not people who are there for power's sake."

"What's depressing is that this dimwit has the power to block my creative and promising science."

"I don't have the feeling he's a dimwit," Stephanie corrected. "Quite the contrary. He's been very creative in his own right. I'd even have to say Machiavellian."

"What are some of his other issues?"

"The usual fundamentalist, conservative ones. States' rights, of course. That's a biggie. But also he's against things like pornography, homosexuality, same-sex marriage, and that sort of thing. And, oh yeah, he's against abortion."

"Abortion?" Daniel questioned with surprise. "He's a Democrat and not pro-choice? He's starting to sound like a member of the Republican hard right."

"I told you he's not afraid of bucking his party when it suits him. He's definitely against abortion, although his stance has required some maneuvering and backpedaling on occasion. In the same way, he's been tap-dancing around civil rights issues. He's a clever, conniving, blue-collar, populist conservative who, unlike Strom Thurmond and Jesse Helms, did not bolt the Democratic Party."

"Amazing!" Daniel commented. "You'd think people would have eventually seen him for what he really is, self-serving and personally power hungry, and voted him out. Why do you think the party hasn't teamed up against him if he's bucked them on key issues?"

"He's just too powerful," Stephanie said. "He's a fund-raising powerhouse with interlocking political action committees, foundations, and even corporations run on behalf of his various populist issues. Other senators are frankly afraid of him with the kind of PR money he can wield. He's not afraid or shy about using his deep pockets against anyone who's crossed him when they come up for reelection."

"This is sounding worse and worse," Daniel murmured.

"I did learn something curious," Stephanie added. "It's rather a coincidence, but you and he have a few things in common."

"Oh, please!" Daniel complained.

"For one thing, you're both from large families," Stephanie said. "In fact, you're both from families with nine children, and you both are third in line with two older brothers."

"That is a coincidence! What are the chances of that?"

"Pretty small. One would have to assume you two are more alike than you think."

Daniel's face clouded over. "Are you serious?"

Stephanie laughed. "No, of course not! I'm teasing! Loosen up!" She reached across the table, picked up Daniel's wine, and handed it to him. Then she lifted her own glass. "Enough about Senator Butler! Let's toast to our health and our relationship, because whatever happens tomorrow, at least we have that, and what's more important?"

"You're right," Daniel said. "To us!" He smiled, but inside he felt his stomach ball up into a knot. Try as he might, he could not dismiss the specter of failure that was looming like a dark cloud.

They clicked glasses and drank, eyeing each other over the rims.

"You really are alluring," Daniel said, trying to regain the moment back in the bathroom at the hotel when Stephanie had stepped out of the shower. "Beautiful, smart, and very sexy."

"That's more like it," Stephanie responded. "So are you."

"You're also a teaser," Daniel added. "But I still love you."

"I love you, too," Stephanie said.

Once the dinner was over, Stephanie was eager to get back to the hotel. They walked quickly. After the warmth of the restaurant, the night chill penetrated their coats. In the hotel's empty elevator, Stephanie kissed Daniel passionately, backed him into a corner, and pressed against him erotically.

"Hold on!" Daniel said with a nervous laugh. "There's probably a security video in here."

"Oh, my gosh!" Stephanie murmured, as she quickly straightened up and smoothed her coat. Her eyes scanned the elevator's ceiling. "I never thought of that."

When the elevator opened on their floor, Stephanie took Daniel's hand and encouraged him to walk quickly down the hall to their door. She smiled as she opened it with her room card. Once inside, she made a production out of locating the DO NOT DISTURB sign and hanging it outside the door. With that accomplished, she took Daniel's hand and pulled him from the small foyer into the bedroom.

"Coats off!" she ordered, throwing hers onto a side chair. She then pushed him backward onto the bed. Climbing on top of him with her knees on either side of his chest, she started to loosen his tie. Suddenly, she stopped. She noticed his forehead was glistening with perspiration.

"Are you okay?" she questioned with concern.

"I'm having a hot flash," Daniel confessed.

Stephanie slid off to the side and pulled Daniel up to a sitting position. He wiped his forehead and looked at the moisture in his hand.

"You're also pale."

"I can imagine," Daniel said. "I think I'm having an autonomic nervous system mini-crisis."

"That sounds like medical doctor-speak. Can you explain that in normal English?"

"I'm just overwrought. I'm afraid I've had some sort of sympathetic adrenaline rush. I'm sorry, but I don't think sex is in the picture."

"You don't have to apologize."

"I think I do," Daniel said. "I know you are expecting it, but as we were walking back, I had a feeling it just wasn't in the cards."

"It's all right," Stephanie insisted. "It's not going to make or break the evening. I'm more interested in making sure you're going to be all right."

Daniel sighed. "I'll be all right after tomorrow, when I know what's going to happen. Uncertainty and I have never gotten along particularly well, especially when it involves something bad."

Stephanie put her arms around him and hugged him. She could feel his heart pounding in his chest.

Later, after Stephanie had been motionless long enough for her breathing to deepen in sleep, Daniel pulled back the covers and slipped out of bed. He'd not been able to fall asleep with his mind and pulse racing. He put on a hotel robe and wandered out into the sitting room. At the window, he looked out at the view.

What kept coming back to his mind was Heinrich Wortheim's prophecy of disaster and the fact that it seemed to be coming to pass. The problem was that Daniel had burned bridges when he left Harvard. Wortheim would never take him back and might even try to blackball him at other institutions. On top of that, Daniel had also burned some bridges when he left Merck in '85 to go back to academia when he'd accepted the Harvard post.

The champagne bottle nestled in its cooler caught Daniel's attention. He pulled it out of the water; its ice had long ago melted. He held it up to the light coming from outside the window. There was still almost a half bottle left. He poured himself a glass and tasted it. It was somewhat flat but still reasonably cold. He took a few sips as he redirected his attention out the window.

He knew his fear of having to return to Revere Beach, Massachusetts, was irrational, but it didn't make it any less real. Revere Beach was where he'd grown up in a family headed by a small-time businessman who'd blamed his series of failures on his wife and progeny, particularly those who embarrassed him. Unfortunately, that was mostly Daniel, who had the misfortune of following two older brothers who'd been high school superstar athletes, a fact that had provided a modicum of solace for their father's fragile ego. In contrast, Daniel had been a spindly kid more interested in playing chess and producing hydrogen from water, Drano, and aluminum foil in the cellar. The fact that Daniel had gotten himself into Boston Latin, where he excelled academically, had had no effect on his father, who continued to use him mercilessly as a scapegoat. Even Daniel's scholarships to Wesleyan University and then to Columbia Medical School had changed little other than to estrange him from his siblings for a time.

Daniel finished the champagne in his glass and helped himself to more. As he continued to sip the wine, his mind wandered to Senator Ashley Butler, his current bête noire. Stephanie had said she was teasing when she'd suggested that he and the senator were more alike than he'd assumed. He wondered if she really felt that way, since it was indeed such a coincidence that he and the senator had similar types of families. Way in the back of Daniel's mind, there was a thought that maybe there was some truth to the idea. After all, Daniel had to admit that he envied the power the man could wield in putting Daniel's career in jeopardy.

Daniel put his glass down on the coffee

table and turned back toward the bedroom. He moved slowly in the darkness of the unfamiliar surroundings. He was far from confident that he could fall asleep while his intuition was so actively telling him that disaster was coming, yet he didn't want to stay up all night. He thought he'd get back in bed and try to relax, and if he couldn't sleep, at least he'd rest.

two

9:51 A.M., Thursday, February 21, 2002

The door to Senator Ashley Butler's inner office burst open, and the senator emerged with his chief of staff in tow. He snapped up the paper proffered by his office manager, Dawn, who was seated at her desk.

"It's your opening statement for your subcommittee hearing," she called after the senator, who was already rounding the turn into the main corridor and heading toward the front door of his senate office. She was accustomed to being ignored and didn't take it personally. Since she was the one who typed the senator's daily schedule, she knew he was already behind. He was supposed to have been at the hearing already so it could begin at ten sharp.

Ashley merely grunted after he'd read the first few lines on the paper and handed the sheet behind him to Carol for her to take a peek. Carol was more than Ashley's chief of staff who hired and fired personnel. When the two of them reached the waiting room for his office complex and he paused to say hello and shake hands with the half-dozen or so people waiting to see various staffers, Carol had to herd him toward the door, lest they be later than they already were.

Out in the Senate Office Building's marbled hall, they picked up the pace. It was difficult for Ashley, whose stiffness had returned despite the medication prescribed by Doctor Whitman. Ashley had described the stiffness as a feeling like trying to walk through molasses.

"How does that opening statement look to you?" Ashley asked.

"Fine, as much as I've read," Carol answered. "Do you think Rob had Phil take a look at it?"

"I should hope so," Ashley snapped. They

walked for a short distance in silence before Ashley added, "Who the hell is Rob?"

"He's your relatively new head aide for the Health Policy Subcommittee," Carol explained. "I'm sure you remember him. He literally sticks out in a crowd. He's the tall redhead who came over from Kennedy's staff."

Ashley merely nodded. Although he prided himself on having a facility for remembering names, he could no longer keep up with all the names of the people who worked for him since his staff had ballooned to more than seventy people, and there was inevitable turnover. Phil, however, was a familiar name, since he'd been around almost as long as Carol. As Ashley's chief political analyst, Phil was a key player, and it was important for everything that was going into a hearing transcript or the Congressional Record to be run by him.

"What about your medication?" Carol questioned. Her heels rang out like gunshots as they hit the marble floor.

"I took it," Ashley clipped irritably. To be one hundred percent certain, his hand surreptitiously slipped into the side pocket of his jacket and felt around. As he suspected, the pill he'd put in earlier was no longer there, meaning he'd taken it just before leaving his private office. He wanted a good high level of the drug in his blood for the hearing. The last thing he wanted was for someone in the media to notice any symptoms, like his hand shaking during the proceedings, particularly not now that he had a plan to obviate the problem.

Rounding a turn in the corridor, they bumped into several particularly liberal senatorial colleagues heading in the opposite direction. Ashley paused and slipped easily back into his signature, syrupy, Southern drawl while complimenting his fellow politicians' hairstyles, modish contemporary suits, and flamboyant ties. In a humorously self-deprecatory style, he compared their dapper attire with his own plain dark suit, dark nondescript tie, and ordinary white shirt. It was the same style of clothes he'd worn when he'd first arrived at the Senate back in 1972. Ashley was a man of habit. Not only did he still wear the same type of clothes, he still bought his entire wardrobe from the same conservative haberdashery back in his hometown.

After he and Carol continued on their way,

she commented on the degree of Ashley's cordiality.

"I'm just buttering them up." Ashley sneered. "I need their votes on my bill coming up next week. You know I cannot abide such foppery, especially hair transplants."

"Indeed I do," Carol said. "That's why I was taken aback."

As they neared the side entrance to the hearing room, Ashley slowed. "Quickly review for me once again what you and the rest of the staff found out about this morning's first witness. I've got a special plan brewing on my back burner that I definitely want to succeed."

"His professional resume is what stands out in my mind," Carol said. She closed her eyes for a moment to help mobilize her memory. "He's been a science prodigy since middle school, and he breezed through both medical school and his Ph.D. studies. That's impressive, to say the least! On top of that, he rapidly became one of the youngest department-head scientists at Merck before being actively recruited to a prestigious post at Harvard. The man must have an IQ in the stratosphere."

"I remember the curriculum vitae. But

that's not what's important now. Talk to me about Phil's take on the man's personality!"

"I remember Phil guessed he was self-centered and cocky because of the way he's so dismissive of his fellow scientists' work. I mean, most people, even if they feel that way, keep it to themselves. He's got to be brash."

"What else?"

They reached the door to the side room and hesitated. Farther down the hallway at the main entrance to the hearing room, a small crowd was milling about, and the babble of their voices drifted toward them.

Carol shrugged. "I can't remember much else, but I have the dossier with me that the staff put together, which certainly incorporates Phil's impressions. Do you want to take the time to read it over again before we begin the hearing?"

"I was hoping you'd talk to me about the man's fear of failure," Ashley said. "Is that something you remember?"

"Now that you mention it, yes, I believe that was one of Phil's points."

"Good!" Ashley said, with his eyes staring off into the distance. "And combining that with an apparent ego the size of a racehorse's paddock gives me an opportunity to exert some significant leverage, wouldn't you agree?"

"I suppose, but I'm not sure I'm following you. I do remember Dan thought that he had a fear of failure out of proportion to his accomplishments and his obvious intelligence. After all, he could probably be successful at anything he wanted to do, provided he put his mind to it. How does his fear of failure give you leverage, and leverage for what?"

"He might be able to do anything he sets his mind to, but apparently at this moment in time he wants to become a celebrity entrepreneur, a fact which he apparently shamelessly admitted in one of his interviews. And to do this, he's made a rather large gamble career-wise and financially. He wants his newly founded company based on his patented procedure to succeed for very personal, if not superficial, reasons."

"So what is it you want to do?" Carol asked. "Phil wants you on record favoring a ban on his procedure. It's that simple."

"Circumstances have made it a little more complicated than that. I want to make the good doctor do something he most assuredly wouldn't want to do."

Concern spread across Carol's broad face. "Does Phil know about this?"

Ashley shook his head. He made a motion for Carol to give him back the prepared opening statement and took it when she held it out.

"What is it you want the doctor to do?"

"You and he will know tonight," Ashley said, as his eyes began scanning the opening statement. "It would take too long to explain at the moment."

"This is scaring me," Carol admitted out loud. She looked up and down the hallway as Ashley read his speech. She shifted her weight uneasily. Carol's ultimate goal and the reason she'd sacrificed so much of her own life to her current position was that she wanted to run for Ashley's office when he retired, a situation that promised to occur sooner rather than later because of the Parkinson's disease diagnosis. She was more than qualified, having served as a state senator prior to coming to Washington to run Ashley's show, and at this late date with her goal in sight, she didn't want him pulling some sort of stunt to do what Bill Clinton did to Al Gore. Ever since that fateful evening visit to Dr. Whitman, Ashley had been preoccupied and unpredictable. She cleared her throat to get her boss's attention. "Exactly how are you planning on getting Dr. Lowell to do something he doesn't want to do?"

"By setting him up and then pulling the rug out from under him," Ashley said, with his eyes rising to meet Carol's. He grinned conspiratorially. "I'm in a battle here, and I want to win. To do that, I'm going to follow an age-old cue from *The Art of War*: Figure out the necessary points of engagement, then arrive there with overwhelming force! Let me see the financial report on his company!"

Carol juggled the file of papers she was carrying before producing the paper Ashley wanted. She handed it to him, and he rapidly scanned it. She watched his face for clues. She wondered if she should call Phil on her cell phone the second she had a chance and warn him to be ready for the unexpected.

"This is good," Ashley mumbled. "This is very good. It's a lucky thing I have those contacts over at the Bureau. We couldn't have gotten much of this on our own."

"Maybe you should go over with Phil whatever it is you are planning to do," Carol suggested.

"No time," Ashley responded. "In fact, what time is it now?"

Carol glanced at her watch. "It's after ten."

Ashley held out his left hand supported by his right in order to check for any tremor. There was a slight one, but it was hardly noticeable. "That's as good as can be expected. Let's go to work!"

Ashley entered the hearing room from the side door to the right of the horseshoe-shaped, raised dais. The room was filled with a meandering, jostling crowd of people from which emerged a buzz of incoherent conversation. Ashley had to worm his way between colleagues and staffers to reach his seat. The red-headed Rob appeared immediately with a second copy of Ashley's prepared opening statement. Ashley waved him off by flapping the copy he already had in his hand. Ashley took his seat and adjusted the goose-necked microphone.

After Ashley's eyes had made a rapid circuit around the comfortably familiar Greek revival décor of the hearing room, they came to rest on the two figures seated at the witness table below him. At first his attention was magnetically drawn to the attractive young woman with the shiny, minklike hair framing her face. Ashley had an affinity for beautiful women, and this female in front of him filled the bill. She was dressed in a demure, deep blue suit with a white collar that contrasted sharply with her tanned, olive complexion. Despite her modest attire, she exuded a healthy sensuality. Her dark eyes were riveted on Ashley, giving him the impression he was staring down two gun barrels. He had no idea who she was or why she was there, but he thought her presence promised to make the hearing a bit more enjoyable.

Reluctantly, Ashley switched his attention from the comely woman to Dr. Daniel Lowell. The doctor's eyes were paler than his companion's, yet they reflected an equal degree of brassiness with their unblinking stare. Ashley guessed the doctor was reasonably tall, despite the fact that he was slouching back in his chair. He was slight of build, with a thin, angular face capped by a shock of unruly salt-and-pepper hair. Even his dress suggested a degree of insolence comparable to that reflected in his eyes and posture. In contrast to his companion's appropriate business apparel, he was sporting a casual tweed jacket with leather elbow patches, an open shirt without a tie, and, his legs visible beneath the table, a pair of jeans and sneakers.

Ashley smiled inwardly as he picked up his gavel. He guessed that Daniel's apparent attitude and dressing down was a weak attempt to prove he wasn't threatened by being called to testify before a Senate subcommittee. Perhaps Daniel thought he could bring his Ivy League, academic persona as a form of intimidation against Ashley's small-town, Baptist college experience. But it wasn't going to work. Ashley knew he had Daniel in his arena with the usual home-court advantage.

"The Subcommittee on Health Policy of the Health, Education, Labor, and Pensions Committee will now come to order," Ashley announced with a pronounced Southern intonation as he banged his gavel. He waited for a few moments, as the previously disorderly group of attendees took their seats. Behind him, he could hear the various staffers do the same. He glanced down at Daniel Lowell, but the doctor had not moved. Ashley glanced to his right and left. Most of his subcommittee members were not present, although four were. Those present were either reading memoranda or talking in whispers with their aides. There wasn't a quorum, but it didn't matter. No vote had been scheduled, and Ashley was not going to call for one.

"This hearing will proceed on Senate Bill 1103," Ashley continued, as he placed his opening statement notes on the table in front of him, folded his arms, and cupped his elbows in his palms to forestall any potential tremor. He tilted his head back slightly to see the print better through his bifocals. "This bill is a companion bill to the bill already passed by the House to ban the cloning procedure called . . ."

Ashley hesitated and leaned forward, squinting at the sheet. "Bear with me for a moment," he said, obviously departing from his prepared text. "This procedure is not only scary, but it's a mouthful, and maybe the good doctor will help me if I stumble. It's called Homologous Transgenic Segmental Recombination, or HTSR. Wow! Did I get that right, Doctor?"

Daniel sat up and leaned forward to his microphone. "Yes," he said simply and leaned back. He too had his arms folded.

"Why don't you doctors speak English?"

Ashley questioned, while peering over the tops of his glasses at Daniel.

A few of the spectators tittered, to Ashley's delight. He loved to play to the crowd.

Daniel leaned forward to answer, but Ashley held up his hand. "That question is off the record, and there's no need to answer."

The clerk made the adjustment on her machine.

Ashley then looked to his left. "This is off the record too, but I was curious if the distinguished senator from Montana agrees with me that doctors purposefully have developed their own language just so that half the time we mere mortals have no idea under the sun what the dickens they are talking about."

There was more laughter from the spectators, as the senator from Montana looked up from his reading and nodded an enthusiastic yes.

"Now, where was I?" Ashley questioned, as he looked back at his prepared opening statement. "The need for this legislation lies in the problem that biotechnology in general and medical science in particular in this country have lost their moral and ethical underpinnings. We here on the Senate's Health

Policy Subcommittee feel it is our duty as concerned and moral Americans to reverse this trend by following the lead of our colleagues in the House. Ends do not justify means, particularly in the medical research arena, as was unequivocally stated as far back as the Nuremberg Trials. This HTSR is a case in point. This procedure once again threatens to create poor, defenseless embryos and then dismember them with the dubious justification that the cells derived from these nascent, tiny humans will be used to treat a wide variety of patients. But that's not all. As we will hear in testimony from its discoverer, whom we are honored to have here as a witness, this is no ordinary therapeutic cloning procedure, and I, as the bill's principal author, am shocked that this procedure is poised to become mainstream. Well, I say only over my dead body!"

A modest level of applause issued from a smattering of audience members. Ashley acknowledged it with a nod of his head and a short pause. Then he took a deep breath. "Now, I could go on about this new technique, but I'm not a doctor, and I respectfully defer to the expert, who has graciously come before this subcommittee. I would like to proceed with the witness, unless my eminent-ranking colleague from across the aisle would like to say a few words."

Ashley regarded the senator seated to his immediate right, who shook his head, covered his microphone with his palm, and leaned toward the chairman. "Ashley," he whispered. "I hope you are going to be expeditious about his. I've got to be out of here by ten-thirty."

"Have no fear," Ashley whispered back. "I'm going for the jugular here."

Ashley took a drink from the glass of water in front of him and peered down at Daniel. "Our first witness is the brilliant Dr. Daniel Lowell, who, as I've already mentioned, is the discoverer of HTSR. Dr. Lowell has impressive credentials, including M.D. and Ph.D. degrees from some of our country's most august institutions. Somehow he even found time to do a residency in internal medicine. He has received countless awards for his work and has held prestigious positions at Merck pharmaceuticals and Harvard University. Welcome, Dr. Lowell."

"Thank you, Senator," Daniel said. He moved forward in his chair. "I appreciate your kind remarks about my curriculum vitae, but, if I may, I'd like to take immediate issue with a particular point in your opening statement."

"By all means," Ashley responded.

"HTSR and therapeutic cloning do not, I repeat, do not involve the dismemberment of embryos." Daniel spoke slowly, emphasizing each word. "The therapeutic cells are taken before any embryo has started to form. They are taken from a structure called a blastocyst."

"Do you deny these blastocysts are incipient human life?"

"They are human life, but when disaggregated, their cells are similar to the cells you lose from your gums when you brush your teeth vigorously."

"I don't think I brush that vigorously," Ashley said with a short laugh. A few spectators joined in.

"We all shed live epithelial cells."

"Perhaps so, but these epithelial cells are not going to form embryos like a blastocyst."

"They could," Daniel said. "That is the point. If the epithelial cells are fused with an egg cell whose nucleus has been extracted, and then the combination is activated, they could form an embryo."

"Which is what is done in cloning."

"Precisely," Daniel said. "Blastocysts have a potential to form a viable embryo, but only if implanted in a uterus. In therapeutic cloning, they are never allowed to form embryos."

"I think we're getting bogged down in semantics here," Ashley said impatiently.

"It is semantics," Daniel agreed. "But it is important semantics. People have to understand that embryos are not involved in therapeutic cloning or HTSR."

"Your opinion regarding my opening statement has been duly recorded," Ashley said. "I'd like to move on to the procedure itself. Would you describe it for us here at the hearing and for the official transcript?"

"I'd be happy to," Daniel said. "Homologous Transgenic Segmental Recombination is the name we have given to a procedure that involves replacing the portion of an individual's DNA responsible for a particular illness with homologous disease-free DNA. This is done in the nucleus of one of the patient's cells, which is then used for therapeutic cloning."

"Hold it right there," Ashley interrupted. "I'm already confused, as I'm sure most of the audience is. Let me see if I have this straight. You're talking about taking a cell from a sick person and changing its DNA before doing the therapeutic cloning."

"That's correct," Daniel said. "Replacing the small portion of the cell's genetic material that's responsible for the individual's illness."

"And the therapeutic cloning is then done to make a bunch of these cells to cure the patient."

"Correct again! The cells are encouraged with various growth hormones to become the type of cells the patient needs. And thanks to HTSR, these cells will not have the genetic predisposition to reform the illness being treated. When these cells are put into the patient, not only will the patient be cured, he or she will not have the genetic tendency to come down with the same illness."

"Perhaps we could talk about a particular disease," Ashley suggested. "It might make it easier for us nonscientists to understand. I gather from some of the articles you've published that Parkinson's disease is one of the illnesses you believe will be amenable to this treatment."

"That's correct," Daniel said. "As well as many other maladies, from Alzheimer's and diabetes to certain forms of arthritis. It's an impressive list of illnesses, many of which have not been amenable to treatment, much less a cure."

"Let's concentrate on Parkinson's for a moment," Ashley said. "Why do you think HSTR will work with this ailment?"

"Because with Parkinson's, we are lucky enough to have a mouse model for testing," Daniel said. "These mice have Parkinson's disease, meaning their brains are missing nerve cells that produce a compound called dopamine that functions as a neurotransmitter, and their illness is a mirror image of the human form. We have taken these animals, carried out HTSR, and have cured them permanently."

"That's impressive," Ashley commented.

"It's even more impressive when you see it happen in front of your very eyes."

"The cells are injected."

"Yes."

"And there are no problems with that?"

"No, not at all," Daniel said. "There's already been considerable experience using this technique on humans for other therapies. The injection must be done carefully, under controlled conditions, but there's generally no problem whatsoever. In our experience, the mice have had no ill effects."

"Are the mice cured soon after the injection?"

"In our experience, the Parkinson's symptoms begin to subside immediately," Daniel said. "And it continues rapidly. With the mice we've treated, it's been truly remarkable. Within a week, the treated mice cannot be distinguished from the well controls."

"I suppose you are eager to try this on humans," Ashley suggested.

"Extremely so," Daniel admitted with a series of nods for emphasis. "After we complete our animal studies, which are moving ahead rapidly, we're hoping for a fast track with the FDA to begin human trials in a controlled setting."

Ashley saw Daniel glance at his companion and even grip her hand for a moment. Ashley smiled inwardly, sensing Daniel was thinking the hearing was going well. It was time to rectify that misconception. "Tell me, Doctor Lowell," Ashley began. "Have you ever heard the saying: *If something sounds too good to be true, it probably isn't*?"

"Of course."

"Well, I think HTSR is a prime example.

Putting aside for a moment the semantic argument about whether or not embryos are being dismembered, HTSR has another major ethical problem."

Ashley paused for effect. The audience was completely still.

"Doctor," Ashley said patronizingly. "Have you ever read that classic novel by Mary Shelley called *Frankenstein*?"

"HTSR has nothing to do with the Frankenstein myth," Daniel said indignantly, implying he knew full well where Ashley was headed. "To imply as much is an irresponsible attempt to take advantage of public fears and misconceptions."

"I beg to disagree," Ashley said. "In fact, I think Mary Shelley must have had an inkling that HTSR was coming down the pike, and that's why she wrote her novel."

The spectators again laughed. It was apparent they were hanging on to every word and enjoying themselves.

"Now I know I have not had the benefit of an Ivy League education, but I read *Frankenstein,* whose whole title includes *The Modern Prometheus,* and I think the parallels are remarkable. As I understand it, the word *transgenic,* which is part of the confusing name of your procedure, means taking bits and pieces of various people's genomes and mixing them together like you're making a cake. That sounds to this country boy pretty much the same thing Victor Frankenstein did when he made his monster, getting pieces from this corpse and parts from another and sewing them up together. He even used a bit of electricity, just like you people do with your cloning."

"With HTSR, we are adding relatively short lengths of DNA, not whole organs," Daniel retorted heatedly.

"Calm down, Doctor!" Ashley said. "This is a fact-finding hearing we're having here, not a fight. What I'm driving at is that, with your procedure, you're taking parts of one person and putting them in another. Isn't that true?"

"On a molecular level."

"I don't care what level it is," Ashley said. "I just want to establish the facts."

"Medical science has been transplanting organs for some time," Daniel snapped. "The general public does not see a moral problem with that, quite the contrary, and organ transplantation is certainly a better conceptual parallel with HTSR than Mary Shelley's nineteenth-century novel."

"In the example you gave concerning Parkinson's disease, you admitted you are planning on injecting these little molecular Frankensteins you are planning on mixing up so they end up in people's brains. I'm sorry, Doctor, but there haven't been too many brains transplanted in our current organ-transplant programs, so I don't think the parallel is any good at all. Injecting parts of another person and getting them into someone's brain is a step beyond the pale in my book, and I believe in the Good Lord's Book."

"The therapeutic cells we create are not molecular Frankensteins," Daniel said angrily.

"Your opinion has duly been recorded," Ashley said. "Let's move on."

"This is a farce!" Daniel commented. He threw up his arms for emphasis.

"Doctor, I must remind you that this is a congressional subcommittee hearing, and you are expected to abide by appropriate decorum. We're all reasonable people here, who are supposed to show respect for one another while trying to do our best to gather information."

"It's becoming progressively obvious this

hearing has been set up under false pretenses. You didn't come in here to gather information with an open mind about HTSR, as you so magnanimously suggest. You're just using this hearing to grandstand with preprepared emotive rhetoric."

"I'd like you to know," Ashley said condescendingly, "making that kind of inflammatory statement and accusation is specifically frowned upon in Congress. This is not *Crossfire* or some other media circus. Yet I refuse to take offense. Instead, I will once again assure you that your opinion has been duly recorded, and, as I said, I'd like to move on. As the discoverer of HTSR, you can't be expected to be entirely objective about the procedure's moral merits, but I'd like to question you about this issue. But first I would like to say that it has been difficult not to notice the disarmingly attractive woman who is sitting next to you at the witness table. Is she here to help you testify? If so, perhaps you should introduce her for the record."

"This is Dr. Stephanie D'Agostino," Daniel snapped. "She is my scientific collaborator."

"Another M.D., Ph.D.?" Ashley questioned.

"I am a Ph.D., not an M.D.," Stephanie said into her microphone. "And Mr. Chairman, I would like to echo Dr. Lowell's opinion about the biased way this hearing has been proceeding, but without his inflammatory words. I strongly believe that allusions to the Frankenstein myth in relation to HTSR are inappropriate, since they play to people's fundamental fears."

"I'm chagrined," Ashley said. "I always thought you Ivy League folks were addicted to alluding to various and sundry literary masterpieces, but here, the one time I give it a whirl, I'm told it's inappropriate. Now is that fair, especially since I distinctly remember being taught at my small, Baptist college that *Frankenstein* was, among other things, a warning about the moral consequences of unchecked scientific materialism? In my mind, that makes the book extremely apropos. But that's enough on this particular issue! This is a hearing, not a literary debate."

Before Ashley could continue, Rob came up behind him and tapped him on the shoulder. Ashley placed his hand over his microphone to prevent it from picking up any of his aide's comments.

"Senator," Rob whispered in Ashley's ear. "As soon as the request came through this morning for Dr. D'Agostino to join Dr. Lowell

at the witness table, we did a quick background check on her. She's a Harvard-
trained townie. She was brought up in the
North End of Boston."

"Is that supposed to be significant?"

Rob shrugged. "It could be a coincidence,
but I doubt it. The indicted investor in Dr.
Lowell's company whom the Bureau told us
about is also a D'Agostino who grew up in
the North End. They are probably related."

"My, my," Ashley commented. "That is curious." He took the sheet of paper from Rob
and put it next to the financial statement of
Daniel's company. He had trouble suppressing a smile after such a windfall.

"Dr. D'Agostino," Ashley said into his microphone after removing his hand. "Are
you by any chance related to Anthony
D'Agostino residing at Fourteen Acorn
Street in Medford, Massachusetts?"

"He is my brother."

"And this is the same Anthony D'Agostino
who has been indicted for racketeering?"

"Unfortunately, yes," Stephanie said. She
glanced at Daniel, who was looking at her
with an expression of disbelief.

"Dr. Lowell," Ashley continued. "Were you

aware that one of your initial and rather major investors had been so indicted?"

"No, I did not," Daniel said. "But he is far from a major investor."

"Hmmm," Ashley voiced. "Several hundred thousand dollars is a lot of money in my book. But we won't quibble. I don't suppose he serves as a director?"

"He does not."

"That's a relief. And I suppose we can assume the indicted racketeer Anthony D'Agostino does not serve on your ethics board, which I understand you have."

A suppressed titter sounded in the audience.

"He does not serve on our ethics board," Daniel rejoined.

"That's also a relief. Now let's talk for a moment about your company," Ashley said. "The name is CURE, which I understand is somewhat of an acronym."

"That's correct," Daniel said with a sigh, as if he were bored with the proceedings. "It was derived from Cellular Replacement Enterprises."

"I'm sorry if you are fatigued by the rigors of this hearing, Doctor," Ashley said. "We'll try to wrap things up as quickly as we can. But I understand your company is attempting to accomplish its second round of financing via venture capitalists, with HTSR as your major intellectual property. Is your ultimate intent to take your company public by having an initial public offering?"

"Yes," Daniel said simply. He leaned back in his chair.

"Now, this is off the record," Ashley said. He looked to his left. "I'd like to ask the distinguished senator from the great state of Montana if he thinks the SEC would find it interesting that one of the initial investors in a company planning on going public has been indicted for racketeering. I mean, there is a question of moral propriety here. Money derived from extortion and maybe even prostitution, for all we know, being laundered through a biotech startup."

"I'd think they'd be very interested," the senator from Montana said.

"That would be my thought as well," Ashley said. He looked back at his notes and then down at Daniel. "I understand your second round of financing has been held up by the S.1103 and the fact that the House has already passed its version. Is that correct?"

Daniel nodded.

"You have to speak for the transcript," Ashley said.

"Correct," Daniel said.

"And I understand your burn rate, meaning the money you're using to stay afloat currently, is very high and that if you don't get this second round of financing, you face bankruptcy."

"Correct."

"That's too bad," Ashley said, with all the appearances of sympathy. "However, for our purposes here at this hearing, I would have to assume that your objectivity in relation to the moral aspects of HTSR is in serious question. I mean, the very future of your company depends on S.1103 not being passed. Is that not true, Doctor?"

"My opinion has been and will continue to be that it is morally wrong not to continue to investigate and then use HTSR to cure countless suffering human beings."

"Your opinion has been recorded," Ashley said. "But for the record, I would like to point out that Dr. Daniel Lowell has chosen not to answer the posed question."

Ashley leaned back and looked to his right. "I have no further questions for this wit-

ness. Do any of my esteemed colleagues
have any questions?"

Ashley eyes moved around to the faces of
the senators seated at the dais.

"Very well," Ashley said. "The Subcommittee on Health Policy would like to thank doctors Lowell and D'Agostino for their kind
participation. And we'd like to call our next
witness: Mr. Harold Mendes of the Right to
Life organization."

three

11:05 A.M., Thursday, February 21, 2002

Stephanie could see the taxi in the middle of the oncoming pack of cars, and she put up her hand expectantly. She and Daniel had followed a suggestion they'd been given by a security officer in the Senate Office Building and had walked over to Constitution Avenue in hopes of catching a cab, but they hadn't had much luck. What had started out that morning as a reasonable day, weather-wise, had taken a turn for the worse. Dark, heavy clouds had blown in from the east, and with the temperature hovering in the lower thirties, there was a distinct possibility of snow. Apparently, under such conditions the demand for taxis far exceeded the supply.

"Here comes one," Daniel snapped, as if Stephanie had something to do with the lack of cabs. "Don't let it go by!"

"I see it," Stephanie responded in an equally clipped manner.

After leaving the Senate hearing, neither had spoken much other than the minimum necessary to decide to take the suggestion to walk over to Constitution Avenue. Similar to the gathering clouds, their moods had darkened as the morning's hearing had progressed.

"Damn!" Stephanie mumbled when the cab zipped by. It was as if the driver was wearing blinders. Stephanie had done everything save throwing herself in front of the speeding traffic.

"You let it go by," Daniel complained.

"Let it go by?" Stephanie shouted. "I waved. I whistled. I even jumped up and down. I didn't see you make any effort."

"What the hell are we going to do?" Daniel demanded. "It's colder than a witch's tit out here."

"Well, if you have any bright ideas, Einstein, let me know."

"What? Is it my fault there are no cabs?"

"It's not mine either," Stephanie retorted.

Both hugged themselves in a vain attempt to keep warm but made it a point to keep away from each other. Neither had brought a true winter coat on the trip. They had thought that they wouldn't need them, having flown four hundred miles south.

"Here comes another one," Daniel stated. "Your turn."

With his hand raised, Daniel ventured as far out into the street as he thought safe. Almost immediately, he had to retreat when he caught sight of a pickup truck bearing down on him in the outermost lane. Daniel waved and shouted, but the cab went by in the knot of vehicles without slowing.

"Well done," Stephanie commented.

"Shut up!"

Just when they were about to give up and begin walking west along Constitution Avenue, a cabbie beeped. He'd been waiting at the traffic light on First Street and Constitution, and had witnessed Daniel's antics. When the light changed, he turned left and pulled over to the curb.

Stephanie and Daniel piled in and buckled their seat belts.

"Where to?" the driver questioned while looking at them in the rearview mirror. He was wearing a turban and was as tan as if he'd just spent a week in the Sahara Desert.

"The Four Seasons," Stephanie said.

Stephanie and Daniel rode in silence while staring out their respective windows.

"I'd say that hearing was about as bad as it could have been," Daniel complained at length.

"It was worse," Stephanie responded.

"There's no doubt the bastard Butler will vote out his bill, and when that happens, I've been assured by the Biotechnology Industry Organization that it will pass the full committee and the Senate itself."

"So goodbye to CURE, Inc."

"It's a shame that in this country medical research is being held hostage by demagogic politics," Daniel snapped. "I shouldn't have even bothered coming down here to Washington."

"Well, maybe you shouldn't have. Maybe it would have been better if I'd come alone. You certainly didn't help things by telling Ashley he was grandstanding and didn't have an open mind."

Daniel turned and stared at the back of Stephanie's head. "Come again?" he sputtered.

"You shouldn't have lost control."

"I don't believe this," Daniel marveled. "Are you trying to imply that this crappy outcome is my fault?"

Stephanie turned to face Daniel. "Being sensitive about other people's feelings is not one of your strong points. And this hearing is a case in point. Who knows what would have happened if you hadn't lost your cool. Attacking him like you did was inappropriate because it stopped whatever dialogue you might have been able to maintain. That's all I'm saying."

Daniel's pale face turned crimson. "That hearing was a goddamn farce!"

"Maybe so, but that doesn't justify your saying as much to Butler's face, because it nipped in the bud any chance of success we might have had, however small. I think his goal was to get you mad so you'd look bad, and it worked. It was his way of discrediting you as a witness."

"You're pissing me off."

"Daniel, I'm as irritated about this outcome as you are."

"Yeah, but you're saying it's my fault."

"No, I'm saying that your behavior didn't help things. There's a difference."

"Well, your behavior didn't help things either. How come you never told me about your brother being indicted for racketeering? All you told me was that he was a qualified investor. Some qualifications! It was a fine time for me to learn about that little sordid tidbit."

"It was after he was an investor, and it was in the Boston papers. So it's not as if it was a secret, but it was something I felt I'd rather not talk about, at least at the time. I thought the reason you didn't bring it up was that you were being considerate. But I should have known better."

"You didn't feel like talking about it?" Daniel questioned with exaggerated astonishment. "You know I don't bother reading the stupid Boston rags. So how else would I have learned about it? And I would have had to know about it eventually because Butler was right. If we'd gone for an IPO, it would have had to be disclosed that we had a felon for an investor, and it would have held things up."

"He has been indicted," Stephanie said. "He's not been convicted. Remember, in our system of justice you're innocent until proven guilty."

"That's a rather lame excuse for not mentioning it to me," Daniel snapped. "Is he going to be convicted?"

"I don't know." Stephanie's voice had lost its edge as she coped with a tinge of guilt at not having been more forthright with Daniel about her brother. She'd thought about mentioning the indictment on occasion but had always put it off until a tomorrow that had never arrived.

"You have no idea whatsoever? That's a little hard for me to believe."

"I have had vague suspicions," Stephanie admitted. "I had the same suspicions about my father, and Tony has essentially taken over my father's businesses."

"What are the businesses we're talking about?"

"Real estate and a few restaurants, plus a restaurant and a café on Hanover Street."

"Is that all?"

"That's what I don't know. As I said, I had vague suspicions with such things as people coming and going from our house at all hours of the day and night, and the women and children being sent out of the room at the end of extended family meals so the men could talk. In many ways, in retrospect it seemed to me we were the cliché of an Italian-American Mob family. Certainly it wasn't on a scale like you'd see in gangster movies, but modestly similar. We females were expected to be consumed by the affairs of hearth and home and church without any interest or involvement in business whatsoever. To tell you the truth, it was an embarrassment for me, because we kids were treated differently in the neighborhood. I couldn't wait to get away, and I was smart enough to recognize that the best way was by being a good student."

"I can relate to that," Daniel said. The sharpness in his voice mellowed as well. "My father was also into all sorts of businesses, some of which were close to being scams. The problem was that they were all failures, meaning he and subsequently my siblings and I became the butt of jokes in the town of Revere, particularly at school, at least those of us who were not part of the 'in' crowd, which I surely wasn't. My father's nickname was 'Loser Lowell,' and unfortunately the epithet had a tendency to trickle down."

"For me, it was the opposite," Stephanie said. "We were treated to a kind of deference, which wasn't pleasant. You know how teenagers like to blend in. Well, it wasn't possible for me, and I didn't even know why. I hated it."

"How come you've never told me about any of this?"

"How come you've never told me about your family other than the fact that you have eight siblings, none of whom, I might add, I have met? I at least asked you about your family on several occasions."

"That's a good point," Daniel said vaguely. His eyes drifted outside, where a few lonely snowflakes could be seen dancing on the wind gusts. He knew the real answer to Stephanie's question was that he'd never cared about her family any more than he cared about his own. He cleared his throat and turned back to Stephanie. "Maybe we haven't talked about our families because we were both embarrassed about our childhoods. Or maybe it's been a combination of that and our preoccupation with science and founding the company."

"Perhaps," Stephanie said without a lot of conviction. She stared out through the front windshield. "It is true that academics have always been my escape. Of course my father never approved, but that only increased my resolve. Hell, he didn't think I should go college. He thought it was a waste of time and money, saying I was just going to get married and have kids like it was fifty years ago."

"My father was literally embarrassed that I was good at science. He told everyone that it had to have come from my mother's side, like it was a genetic disease."

"What about your brothers and sisters? Was it the same for them?"

"To some degree, because my father was a small enough person to blame his failings on us. You know, sapping the capital he needed to really get started in whatever was the current bright business idea. But my brothers, who were good at sports, fared a bit better, at least back when they were in school, because my father was a sports nut. But getting back to your brother, Tony. Whose idea was it that he invest in CURE, yours or his?" Daniel's voice regained some of its earlier brusqueness.

"Is this going to become an argument again?"

"Just answer the question!"

"What difference does it make?"

"It was a monumental error in judgment to allow a possible—or probable, as the case may be—mobster to invest in our company."

"It was a combination of both of us," Stephanie said. "In contrast with my father, he's been interested in what I've been doing lately, and I'd told him biotechnology was a good place to put some of his money from the restaurants."

"Wonderful!" Daniel exclaimed sarcastically. "I hope you realize that investors in general don't like losing money, despite having been adequately warned of the risks in start-up companies. My guess would be that such an attitude would be an understatement for a mobster. Have you ever heard of such inconveniences as smashed patellae?"

"He's my brother, for Christ's sake! There's not going to be any kneecap smashing."

"Yeah, but I'm not his brother."

"It's insulting to even suggest such a

thing," Stephanie snapped. She turned her head to look out her window. Generally she had a reservoir of patience to put up with Daniel's sarcasm, ego, and antisocial negativity, thanks to the awe she felt about his scientific brilliance, but at the moment and given the morning's events, it was wearing thin.

"Under the circumstances, I don't have a lot of interest in hanging around Washington for another night," Daniel said. "I think we should get our things together, check out, and get on the next shuttle back to Boston."

"Fine by me," Stephanie clipped.

Stephanie got out her side of the taxi as Daniel paid the fare. She headed directly into the hotel lobby, only vaguely aware that he was close behind her. She was upset enough to wonder what she'd do when they got back to Boston. In her current state of mind, the idea of returning to Daniel's Cambridge apartment where she'd been living was not appealing. Daniel's suggestion that her family was low enough to be capable of physical violence was galling. She wasn't sure if anyone in her family was involved in loan sharking or other questionable activities, but she was darn sure no one ever got hurt.

"Dr. D'Agostino, excuse me!" one of the concierges voiced loudly.

Unexpectedly hearing her name called out in the middle of the hotel lobby startled Stephanie enough that she stopped in her tracks. Daniel collided with her, causing him to drop the folder he was carrying.

"Good grief!" Daniel snapped, as he squatted down to retrieve the papers that had wafted out of the folder. A bellman lent a hand. The papers were professionally rendered schematics of HTSR. He'd brought them to the hearing in case it had been appropriate to hand them out to be sure people understood the procedure. Unfortunately, the opportunity hadn't presented itself.

By the time Daniel had righted himself, Stephanie had returned to his side from the concierge's desk.

"You could have let me know you were stopping," Daniel complained.

"Who is Carol Manning?" Stephanie questioned.

"I haven't the foggiest idea. Why do you ask?"

"You got an urgent message from her." Stephanie handed over the piece of paper.

Daniel read it rapidly. "I'm supposed to call her. It says it's an emergency. How can it be an emergency if I don't even know who it is?"

"What's the area code?" Stephanie questioned, as she looked over Daniel's shoulder.

"Two-oh-two!" Daniel said. "Where's that, do you know?"

"Of course I do! It's right here in D.C."

"Washington!" Daniel exclaimed. "Well, that settles it." He crumpled the note, stepped over to the concierge's desk, and asked one of them to file it in the circular file.

Stephanie was rooted to the spot where she'd handed Daniel the note. Her mind was churning as she watched Daniel start toward the elevators. Making a sudden decision, she dashed to the desk, took the note from the concierge who still had it clutched in his fist while speaking to another guest, and ran after Daniel.

"I think you should call," Stephanie said, slightly out of breath as she reached Daniel.

"Oh, really?" Daniel questioned superciliously. "I don't think so."

The elevator arrived, and Daniel boarded. Stephanie followed.

"No, I think you should call. I mean, what do you have to lose?"

"A little more of my self-esteem," Daniel said.

The elevator rose. Daniel's eyes were glued to the floor indicator. Stephanie's were glued to Daniel's. The doors opened. They started down the hall.

"I think I recognized the number's prefix from having called Senator Ashley Butler's office last week. I think the prefix was two-two-four, and if it was, then it is a Senate Office Building exchange."

"All the more reason not to call," Daniel said. He keyed open the door to their room and entered. Stephanie was right behind him.

While Daniel was removing his coat, Stephanie ducked into the sitting room. At the desk, she smoothed out the note. "It is two-two-four," she called out to Daniel. "The *emergency* is underlined. Maybe the old codger changed his mind!"

"That's about as likely as the moon dropping out of orbit," Daniel said, joining Stephanie. He looked down at the message. "It is weird. What the hell kind of emergency could it be? Originally I thought it was from the media, but not if it's a Senate Office

Building exchange. You know, I don't care.
Being cooperative with anyone who has anything to do with the U.S. Senate is not high
on my priority list at the moment."

"Call! You might be cutting off your nose to
spite your face. If you don't, I'll do it. I'll pretend I'm your secretary."

"You, a secretary? How entertaining! All
right, for God's sake, call!"

"I'll use the speakerphone so you can
hear."

"Wonderful," Daniel said sarcastically. He
sprawled out on the sofa with his head on
one of the furniture's arms and his feet on
the other.

Stephanie dialed. There was the sound of
only one electronic ring before the connection went through. A decidedly female voice
snapped a hello as if the person had been
eagerly waiting on the other end.

"I'm calling for Dr. Daniel Lowell,"
Stephanie said. She locked eyes with Daniel.
"Is this Carol Manning?"

"It is. Thank you for calling back. It is extremely important that I talk with the doctor
before he checks out of the hotel. Is he available?"

"Can I ask what this is in relation to?"

"I'm Senator Ashley Butler's chief of staff,"
Carol began. "You might have seen me this
morning. I was seated behind the senator."
Daniel quickly ran his index finger across
his throat to get Stephanie to hang up.
Stephanie ignored him.
"I need to talk with the doctor," Carol con-
tinued. "As I said, it is extremely important."
With the addition of an angry grimace,
Daniel again gestured with his finger as if he
were cutting his throat. He did it again when
Stephanie hesitated.
She motioned to him to stop his antics. It
was clear to her that he was not about to talk
with Carol Manning, but she was not about
to hang up.
"Is the doctor there?" Carol questioned.
"He's here, but momentarily indisposed."
Daniel rolled his eyes.
"May I ask with whom I am speaking?"
Carol questioned.
Stephanie hesitated again while she
thought of what to say, considering she'd told
Daniel she would pretend to be his secre-
tary. Thinking that was ridiculous now that
she was on the phone, she finally just gave
her name.
"Oh, good!" Carol responded. "From Dr.

Lowell's testimony, I understand you are a collaborator. Might I ask if your collaboration is close and perhaps even personal?"

A wry smile spread across Stephanie's face. She stared at the phone for a second as if it could tell her why Carol Manning would be willing to flaunt normal etiquette and ask such a question. Under more normal circumstances, it would have angered Stephanie. Now it merely magnified her intrigue.

"I don't mean to be inappropriate," Carol added, as if she sensed Stephanie's response. "This is a rather awkward situation, but I was told you were registered in the same suite. I hope you understand that my goal is not to invade your privacy but rather to be as discreet as possible. You see, the senator would like to arrange a secret meeting with Dr. Lowell, and in this town that is not easy, considering the senator's prominence and notoriety."

Stephanie's mouth had slowly dropped open as she'd listened to this surprising request. Even Daniel had brought his feet down from the arm of the sofa and had sat up.

"It had been my hope," Carol continued, "that I could have communicated this message directly to Dr. Lowell so that only the senator, the doctor, and myself would have known about the meeting. Obviously, that is no longer possible. I hope we can count on your discretion, Dr. D'Agostino."

"Dr. Lowell and I work very closely," Stephanie said. "You can most assuredly count on my discretion." She gestured frantically to see if Daniel wished to participate in the conversation now that it had taken such an unexpected twist. Daniel shook his head but motioned for her to continue.

"We are hoping the meeting could be arranged for this evening," Carol said.

"What can I tell Dr. Lowell this meeting is about?"

"I cannot tell you."

"Not telling me is going to cause a problem," Stephanie said. "I happen to know that Dr. Lowell was not pleased with what happened at this morning's hearing. I'm not sure he will be open to meeting with the senator unless he has some idea it would be to his advantage to do so." Stephanie looked at Daniel. He gestured he approved how she was handling the call by giving her a thumbs-up sign.

"This is also rather awkward," Carol said.

"Although I am the senator's chief of staff and I normally know everything that is going on in this office, I have absolutely no idea why the senator wants to meet with the doctor. The gist of what the senator said was that although Dr. Lowell might be irritated at today's events, he should hold off on coming to any conclusions about S.1103 until they meet."

"That's rather vague," Stephanie said.

"That's the best I can do with the information I have. Nonetheless, I strongly urge the doctor to meet with the senator. My sense is that it will indeed be to his advantage. I cannot imagine any other reason for this meeting. It is most out of the ordinary, and I should know. I have been working with the senator for sixteen years."

"Where would the meeting take place?"

"The safest place would be in a moving car."

"This is sounding overly melodramatic."

"The senator insisted on absolute secrecy, and as I said, that is not easy in this town."

"Who would be driving this car?"

"Myself."

"If the meeting were to take place, I'd have to insist on being present as well."

Daniel again rolled his eyes.

"Since I've already apprised you of the meeting, I will assume that would be acceptable, but to be one hundred percent certain, I'd have to run it by the senator."

"Can I assume you would come to the hotel and pick us up?"

"I'm afraid that would be inadvisable. The safest plan would be for you and Dr. Lowell to take a taxi to the Union Station. At exactly nine o'clock, I will come by in a black Chevrolet Suburban with tinted windows and District plates: GDF471. I will pull up to the curb directly in front of the station. In case there is any problem, I will give you my cell phone number."

Stephanie wrote the number down as Carol relayed it.

"Can the senator count on Dr. Lowell being there?"

"I'll convey this information to Dr. Lowell exactly as you have presented it to me."

"That's all I can ask," Carol said. "However, I'd like to reemphasize how extremely important this is for both the senator and for Dr. Lowell. The senator used those exact words."

Stephanie thanked the woman, said she'd call back in fifteen minutes, and disconnected. She stared at Daniel. "This has to be one of the more bizarre episodes I've ever been involved in," she said, breaking a short silence. "What's your take?"

"What the devil could this old geezer have in mind?"

"I'm afraid there's only one way to find out."

"Do you really think I should go?"

"Let's put it this way," Stephanie said. "I think you'd be a fool not to go. Since the meeting is secret, you don't even have to worry about losing any more self-esteem, unless you care what Ashley Butler thinks of you, and knowing what you think of him, I can't imagine that's the case."

"Did you buy this Carol Manning saying she didn't know what the meeting was about?"

"Yes, I did. I detected some hurt feelings when she said it. My sense is that the senator has something far from mainstream up his sleeve that he wasn't even willing to share with his chief aide."

"All right," Daniel said with a tinge of reluctance. "Call her back and say I'll be at the Union Station at nine."

"That's *we* will be at the Union Station,"

Stephanie said. "I meant what I said to Ms. Manning. I insist on going."

"Why not," Daniel said. "We might as well make it a party."

four

8:15 P.M., Thursday, February 21, 2002

It appeared to Carol that every light was blazing in the senator's modest Arlington, Virginia, home as she turned into the driveway and came to a stop. She glanced at her watch. With the vagaries of Washington traffic, it wasn't the easiest thing in the world to manage to arrive at Union Station at exactly nine o'clock. She hoped she'd timed it right, although things were not starting out auspiciously. It had taken ten minutes longer than she'd planned to get from her apartment in Foggy Bottom out to Ashley's house. Luckily, with her grand plan, she'd given herself an extra quarter-hour leeway.

Leaving the engine running and setting the emergency brake, Carol prepared to get out of her vehicle. But it turned out that exposing herself to the cold drizzle wasn't necessary. Ashley's front door opened, and the senator appeared. Behind him stood his portly wife of forty years, looking like the epitome of solid domesticity, dressed in a white, lace-fringed apron over a paisley housedress. Under the protection of the porch and following her apparent orders, he struggled to open his umbrella. What had started out that day as snow flurries had changed to steady rain.

With his face hidden beneath the inverted bowl of the black umbrella, Ashley began descending his front steps. He moved slowly and deliberately, giving Carol a moment to study the blocky, slightly stooped, heavyset man who in another life could have been a farmer or even a steel worker. For Carol, it wasn't a particularly cheerful sight watching her boss approach. There was something distinctly depressing and pathetic about the scene. The misty air and the sepia coloring contributed, as did the monotonous click-clack of the windshield wipers as they implacably traced their repeated arcs across the wet windshield. But for Carol, it was more what she knew than what she saw. Here was a man she had respected almost to the point of reverence, for whom she'd made count-less sacrifices for more than a decade, but who was now unpredictable and occasion-ally even mean. Despite her best efforts with the senator during the day, she still had no idea why he insisted on the upcoming clan-destine and politically risky meeting with Dr. Lowell, and due to his insistence on absolute secrecy, she'd not been able to ask anyone else. To make matters worse, she couldn't escape the feeling that Ashley had kept the reason for the meeting from her out of spite, purely because he instinctually knew how desperately she wanted to know. During the last year, thanks to a number of undeserved sarcastic comments, she sensed he envied her relative youth and good health.

Carol watched Ashley stop at the foot of the steps to make an adjustment on the flat ground. For a moment, he seemed frozen in place, a metaphor of his bullish stubborn-ness, a quality Carol had once admired when it involved his populist political beliefs but which now irritated her. In the past, he had fought for power to push his conservative agenda, but now it seemed he fought for power for power's sake as though he was addicted to it. She'd always thought of him as a great man who'd know when to step aside, but now she was no longer so confident.

Ashley began walking slowly, and with his black coat, rounded shoulders, and short shuffling steps, he reminded Carol of a large penguin. He gained speed as he moved. Carol expected him to come around to the passenger side, but instead he opened the back door directly behind her. She could feel the car shake gently as he climbed in. The door slammed shut. She heard the umbrella fall to the floor.

Carol twisted around. Ashley settled back into the seat. In the dim, brownish-gray light of the car's interior, his face appeared pallid, almost ghostlike, and his coarse features retreated back into his flesh as if dimpled into a loaf of unbaked bread. His thinning gray hair that typically knew its place was frazzled like a clump of steel wool. The lenses of his thick-framed glasses eerily reflected back the lights of his house.

"You're late," Ashley complained, without a trace of his Southern accent.

"I'm sorry," Carol responded by reflex. She was always apologizing. "But I think we'll be fine. Should we talk before we head back into town?"

"Drive!" Ashley commanded.

Carol felt a wave of anger wash over her. But she held her tongue, knowing full well what the consequences might be if she voiced her feelings. Ashley had the memory of an elephant for any perceived slights, and the maliciousness of his revenge was legendary. Carol put the hulking Suburban in gear and backed out of the driveway.

The route was simple with limited access roads most of the way. Carol worked her way over to the 395 highway with reassuring ease by catching all the traffic lights green. On the main artery, she was pleased to find less traffic than there had been fifteen minutes earlier, and she accelerated unimpeded to highway speed. Sensing her timing was going to be fine, she relaxed a degree, but as they neared the Potomac River, a commercial jetliner leaving Reagan National Airport thundered overhead. It sounded to Carol as if it were a mere fifty feet above them. As tense as she was, the sudden, reverberating noise startled her enough to cause the car to momentarily swerve.

"If I did not know better," Ashley said, reverting back to his signature Southern drawl and speaking up for the first time since his rude command, "I would have sworn on my mother's memory that jetliner's turbulence extended all the way down here to this highway. Are you fully in command of this vehicle, my dear?"

"Everything is fine," Carol said curtly. At the moment, she even found Ashley's theatrical accent aggravating, with the knowledge of how easily he could turn it on and off.

"I've been perusing the dossier you and the rest of the staff put together on the good doctor," Ashley said after a short pause. "In fact, I've darn near committed it to memory. I have to commend you and the others. You all did a fine job. I believe I know more about that boy than he does himself."

Carol nodded but didn't reply. Silence returned until they entered the tunnel running beneath the grassy expanse of the Washington Mall.

"I know you are displeased and cross with me," Ashley said suddenly. "And I know why."

Carol glanced back at the senator in her rearview mirror. Flashes of light from the tunnel's ceramic tiles reflected off his face in a flickering manner, making him appear more ghostlike than earlier.

"You're cross with me because I have not divulged my reasons for this imminent meeting."

Carol glanced at him again. She was taken aback. Such an admission was totally out of character. Never had he suggested he knew or cared what Carol was feeling. As such, it was more evidence of his current unpredictability, and she didn't quite know what to say.

"It reminds me of one time my mama was cross with me," Ashley said, now adding his anecdotal manner of speaking to his accent. Carol groaned inwardly. It was a mannerism she found equally trying. "This was back when I was knee-high to a grasshopper. I was in a mind to go fishing by myself in a river more than a mile from our home where there were reputed to be catfish the size of armadillos. I left before dawn, before anyone else had stirred, and I caused my mama a good deal of concern. When I returned home, she was fit to be tied and grabbed me by the scruff of the neck and demanded to know why I had not asked her permission to go on such a foolhardy journey at my tender age. I told her I did not ask her because I knew she would say no. Well, Carol, dear, that's the same situation with this impending meeting with the doctor. I know you well enough to know that you would be of a mind to try to change mine, and I am committed."

"I would only try to change your mind if it were in your best interest," Carol responded.

"There are times when your emulousness is transparently flagrant, my dear. Most people might not believe your true motivations, considering your apparent selfless devotion, but I know you better."

Carol swallowed out of nervousness. She did not know precisely what to make of Ashley's pompous comment, but she knew she did not want to go in the direction it implied, meaning he sensed her unspoken ambitions. Instead she asked, "Did you at least discuss the meeting with Phil to be certain of its potential political ramifications?"

"Heavens, no! I have not discussed the meeting with anyone, not even my wife, bless her soul. You, the doctors, and myself are the only people who even know it is about to take place."

Carol exited off the freeway and headed for Massachusetts Avenue. She was relieved they were closing in on Union Station to preclude the possibility of the conversation returning to the topic of her tacit goals. She looked at her watch. It was a quarter to nine.

"We are going to be a little bit early," she said.

"Then meander a bit," Ashley suggested. "I would prefer to be exactly on time. It will set a proper tone for the appointment."

Carol turned right on North Capital and then left on D. It was a familiar area because of its proximity to the Senate Office Building. By the time she was heading back to the Union Station, it was three minutes before nine. When she pulled directly in front of the station, it was nine on the dot.

"There they are," Ashley said, pointing over Carol's shoulder. Daniel and Stephanie were huddled beneath a Four Seasons umbrella. They stood out from the crowd because of their immobility. Everyone else in the area was hustling to gain shelter, either in the station or in one of the waiting taxis.

Carol flicked the high beams up and down to get the doctors' attention.

"There's no reason to cause a scene," Ashley growled. "They've spotted us."

Daniel could be seen checking his watch before sauntering toward the Suburban, Stephanie holding on to his left arm.

The doctors came to Carol's window. She lowered it.

"Ms. Manning?" Daniel asked offhandedly.

"I'm in the backseat, Doctor!" Ashley called out before Carol could respond. "How about you joining me back here and your ex-quisite collaborator joining Carol up front."

Daniel shrugged before he and Stephanie rounded the car. He held the umbrella for Stephanie to climb in, then he did the same himself.

"Welcome!" Ashley beamed, as he stuck out one of his broad, thick-fingered hands. "Thank you for coming out to meet with me on such a dreadfully wet evening."

Daniel eyed Ashley's hand but made no motion to take it in his own. "What's on your mind, Senator?"

"Now here's a true Northerner," Ashley said cheerfully, as he withdrew his hand and seemingly took no offense at Daniel's rebuff. "Always ready to cut to the quick without wasting time on the refinements of life. Well, so be it. There will be time for handshaking later. Meanwhile, my intention is for you and I to get to know each other. You see, I am very much interested in your Aesculapian talents."

"Where to, Senator?" Carol questioned, while peering at Ashley in her rearview mirror.

"Why don't we take the good doctors on a tour of our fair city," Ashley suggested. "Head down to the Tidal Basin so they can enjoy our city's most elegant memorial!"

Carol put the car in gear and headed south on First Street. Carol and Stephanie exchanged a quick, appraising glance at each other.

"Here's the Capitol itself on the right," Ashley said, pointing. "And on our left is the Supreme Court, which I just personally love architecturally, and the Library of Congress."

"Senator," Daniel said, "with all due respect, which I'm afraid isn't a lot, I'm not interested in your giving us a tour of the city, nor am I interested in getting to know you better, especially after the sham hearing you put us through this morning."

"My dear, dear friend . . ." Ashley began after a short of silence.

"How about cutting out the Southern bombast!" Daniel snapped scornfully. "And for the record, I'm not your dear friend. I'm not your friend at all."

"Doctor, with all due respect, which I mean sincerely, you do yourself a great disservice by indulging in such effrontery. If you allow me to offer a bit of advice: You hurt your own cause when you allow your emotions to overpower your considerable intellect as you did this morning. Despite your adequately expressed animosity toward me, I wish to negotiate with you on a man-to-man and preferably gentleman-to-gentleman basis on a most important but sensitive matter. We both have something the other desires, and in order to realize those desires, we each have to do something we would rather not do."

"You're talking in riddles," Daniel grumbled.

"Perhaps I am," Ashley admitted. "Do I have your interest? I shall not proceed unless I am convinced of your interest."

Ashley heard Daniel exhale impatiently, and he imagined the doctor had rolled his eyes by his body language, but he couldn't tell for certain because of the darkness in the car. Ashley waited while Daniel briefly stared out his window at the passing Smithsonian buildings.

"Merely admitting to your interest will neither obligate you or jeopardize you in any way," Ashley said. "No other persons than those in this vehicle know that we are chatting tonight, provided, of course, that you have not informed anyone."

"I would have been embarrassed to have told someone."

"I choose to be immune to your rudeness, Doctor, as I was immune this morning to your lack of courtesy by your attire, your disdainful body language, and your verbal attacks on me. As a gentleman, I could have been insulted, but I am not. So save your breath! What I want to know is whether you are interested in negotiating."

"What exactly would I be negotiating?"

"The viability of your start-up company, your current career, your chance of celebrity, and perhaps most important, an opportunity to avoid failure. I have reason to believe failure is a particular anathema to you."

Daniel stared at Ashley in the half-light. Ashley could feel the intensity of the doctor's

eyes, despite being unable to see their details. It made the senator confident that he
was indeed striking close to the man's inner
being.

"You believe I'm particularly adverse to
failure?" Daniel questioned, in a voice that
was less sardonic than earlier.

"Absolutely," Ashley returned. "You are a
powerfully competitive person, which, combined with your intellect, has been the driving force of your success. But powerfully
competitive people do not like to fail, especially when part of their motivation is to escape their past. You have done well and
come a long way from Revere, Massachusetts, yet your biggest nightmare involves a
downfall that would force you back to your
childhood roots. It is not a rational worry,
considering your credentials, but it haunts
you nonetheless."

Daniel gave a short, mirthless laugh. "How
did you come up with this ridiculously bizarre
theory?" he questioned.

"I know a lot about you, my friend. My
daddy always told me knowledge was
power. And since we would be negotiating, I
made it a point to take advantage of my considerable resources, including contacts at

the Bureau, to learn as much about you and your start-up company as possible. In fact, not only do I know about you, I know about your family back several generations."

"You've had me investigated by the FBI?" Daniel demanded. "I'm not sure I believe you."

"But you should! Let me give you some high points of what has turned out to be a most interesting story. First of all, you are directly related to the famous New England Lowell family named in the famous description of Boston society where the Lowells only talk to the Cabots and the Cabots only talk to God. Or is it the other way around? Carol, can you help me here?"

"You have it right, Senator," Carol said.

"I am relieved," Ashley said. "I do not want to damage my credibility so early in my discourse. Unfortunately, Doctor, being related to the famous Lowells has been no help to you. It seems that your alcoholic grandfather was disowned and, more important, disinherited after defying the family wishes first by dropping out of prep school to join the army as a doughboy during World War I, then by marrying a commoner from Medford after his discharge. It seems that he had had such a devastating experience in Europe during his service that he was psychologically unable to reintegrate into privileged society. This, of course, was in sharp contrast to his brothers and sisters, who had not been to the war and who were enjoying the excesses of the roaring twenties and who, even if they too might have risked becoming alcoholics, were at least finishing their schooling and marrying socially acceptable spouses."

"Senator, I'm not finding this amusing. Can we get to the point?"

"Patience, my friend," Ashley said. "Let me bring the history to the present. It seems that your alcoholic paternal grandfather was also not a particularly good father or role model for his ten children, one of whom was your daddy. *Like father like son* is certainly applicable to your father, who suffered through service in World War II. Although he avoided alcoholism for the most part, he was hardly a good father or role model to his nine children, as I am sure you would agree. Happily, with your competitiveness, intellect, and opportunity to avoid a war experience in Vietnam, you have broken this generational self-fulfilling downward spiral, but not without some scars."

"Senator, for the last time, unless you tell me what is on your mind in plain English, I will insist we be taken back to our hotel."

"But I have told you," Ashley stated. "When you first got into the car."

"You'd better run it by me again," Daniel sneered. "Apparently, it was so subtle I completely missed it."

"I told you I was interested in your Aesculapian talents."

"Evoking the Roman god of healing is still making this into a riddle that I have no patience for. Let's be specific, particularly since you were talking about this being a negotiation."

"Specifically, I want to barter your powers as a physician with my powers as a politician."

"I am a researcher, not a practicing physician."

"But you are a physician nonetheless, and the research you do is to cure people."

"Keep talking."

"What I am about to tell you is central to why we are here talking together. But I must have your absolute word as a gentleman that what I am about to tell you will remain confidential, irrespective of the outcome of this meeting."

"If it is truly personal, I have no problem keeping it a secret."

"Excellent! And Dr. D'Agostino! Do I have your word as well?"

"Of course," Stephanie stammered, surprised at being suddenly addressed. She was twisted in her seat, looking back at the men. She'd been in that position ever since the senator had started talking about Daniel's fear of failure.

Carol was struggling with her driving and had slowed considerably. Mesmerized by the conversation unfolding in the backseat, her eyes were more on Ashley's image in the rearview mirror than on the road. She was certain she knew what Ashley was about to say and now had an inkling of Ashley's plan. She was appalled.

Ashley cleared his throat. "Unfortunately, I have been diagnosed with Parkinson's disease. To make matters worse, my neurologist believes I have a rapidly progressive variant, which seems to be the case. On my last visit he even raised the specter the malady may soon begin to effect my cognitive abilities."

For a few moments there was absolute silence in the car.

"How long have you known about this?" Daniel questioned. "I've not noticed any tremor."

"About a year. The medication has helped, but as my neurologist predicted, it is rather quickly losing its effectiveness. Thus, my infirmity will soon become public knowledge unless something is done and done soon. I'm afraid my political career is at stake."

"I hope this whole charade is not leading up to what I think it is," Daniel stated.

"I imagine it is," Ashley admitted. "Doctor, I want to be your guinea pig or, more precisely, your surrogate mouse. You've been having such good luck with your mice, as you proudly reported this morning."

Daniel shook his head. "This is absurd! You want me to treat you like I have treated our mice!"

"Precisely, Doctor. Now, I knew you would not want to do it for a variety of reasons, and that is why this discussion is a negotiation."

"It would be against the law," Stephanie blurted. "The FDA would never allow it."

"I was not intending to inform the FDA," Ashley said calmly. "I know how meddlesome they can be on occasion."

"It would have to be done in a hospital," Stephanie said. "And without the FDA's approval, no hospital would allow it."

"No hospital in this country," Ashley added. "Actually, I was thinking of the Bahamas. It is a rather nice time of the year to go to the Bahamas. Besides, there is a clinic there that would serve our needs beautifully. Six months ago, my Health Policy Subcommittee had a series of hearings on the inappropriate lack of regulation of infertility clinics in this country. A clinic by the name of Wingate came up during the hearings as an example of how some of these clinics are ignoring even minimal standards to make enormous profit. The Wingate Clinic had recently moved to New Providence Island to avoid the few laws applicable to their operation, which included some very questionable undertakings. But what had caught my attention particularly was that they were in the process of building a brand-spanking-new, twenty-first-century research center and hospital."

"Senator, there are reasons medical research starts out with animals before moving on to humans. To do otherwise is unethical at best and foolish at worst. I cannot be part of such an undertaking."

"I knew you would not be excited about the idea at first," Ashley said. "Again, that is why this is a negotiation. You see, I am willing to promise you as a gentleman that my bill, S.1103, will never leave my subcommittee if you agree to treat me with your HTSR in total secrecy. That means that your second round of financing will come through and your company will go forward, and you will become the wealthy biotechnology celebrity entrepreneur that you aspire to be. As for myself, my political power is still ascendant and will remain so, provided this Parkinson's threat is removed. So . . . as a consequence of each of us doing something we would rather not do, we both win."

"What are you doing that you do not want to do?" Daniel questioned.

"I am accepting the risk of being a guinea pig," Ashley stated. "I am the first to admit I wish our roles were reversed, but such is life. I am also risking political consequences from my conservative constituents who ex-

pect S.1103 to be voted out of subcommittee."

Daniel shook his head in amazement.
"This is preposterous," he commented.

"But there is more," Ashley said. "Knowing
the degree of risk I am assuming in this new
therapy, I do not think our exchange of services is equal. To rectify that imbalance and to
help with the risk, I demand some divine intervention."

"I'm afraid to ask what you mean by *divine
intervention.*"

"As I understand it, if you were to treat me
with your HTSR, you would need a segment
of DNA from someone who does not have
Parkinson's disease."

"That's correct, but it doesn't matter who
the person is. There is no tissue matching involved, like with organ transplants."

"It matters to me who the person is," Ashley said. "I also understand you could get this
little segment of DNA from blood?"

"I couldn't get it from red blood cells, which
have no nuclei," Daniel said. "But I could get
it from white cells, which you can always find
in blood. So, yes, I could get it from blood."

"Thank the good Lord for white blood

cells," Ashley said. "Now, the source of the blood is what has captured my interest. My father was a Baptist minister, but my mother, rest her soul, was an Irish Catholic. She taught me a few things that have stayed with me all my life. Let me ask you a question: Are you acquainted with the Shroud of Turin?"

Daniel glanced at Stephanie. A wry smile of disbelief had appeared on his face.

"I was raised a Catholic," Stephanie offered. "I'm familiar with the Shroud of Turin."

"I know what it is as well," Daniel said. "It's a religious relic purported to be the burial shroud of Jesus Christ, which was proven a fake about five years ago."

"True," Stephanie said. "But it was more than ten years ago. It was carbon-dated to the mid-thirteenth century."

"I have no interest in the carbon-dating report," Ashley said. "Especially since it was debunked by several eminent scientists. Even if the report had not been challenged, my interest would be the same. The shroud held a special place in my mama's heart, and some of the devotion rubbed off on me when she took me and my two older brothers to Turin to be in its presence when I was no more than an impressionable moppet. Concerns about its authenticity aside, what is incontrovertible is that there are bloodstains on the cloth. Most everyone agrees about that. I want the little section of DNA needed for HTSR to come from the Shroud of Turin. That is my demand and my offer."

Daniel laughed derisively. "This is more than preposterous. It's crazy. Besides, how would I get a blood sample from the Shroud of Turin?"

"That is your responsibility, Doctor," Ashley said. "But I am willing and able to help. I am certain I can get details about access to the shroud from one of my archbishop acquaintances, who are always willing to exchange favors for special political consideration. I happen to know there are samples of the shroud containing blood stains that had been taken, given out, then recalled by the church. Perhaps one of those could be made available, but you would have to go and get it."

"I'm speechless," Daniel admitted, trying to suppress his amusement.

"That is entirely understandable," Ashley said. "I am certain this opportunity I have proposed has caught you unawares. I do not expect you to respond immediately. As a thoughtful man, I was confident you would like to mull it over. My suggestion is that you call me, and I will give you a special number to call. But I would like to say that if I do not hear from you by ten o'clock tomorrow morning, I will assume you have decided not to take advantage of my offer. At ten o'clock, I will order my staff to schedule a subcommittee vote on S.1103 as soon as possible so that it can be moved on to the full committee and on to the Senate. And I already know the BIO lobby has informed you that S.1103 will pass with ease."

five

10:05 P.M., Thursday, February 21, 2002

The taillights of Carol Manning's Suburban faded as the vehicle moved down Louisiana Avenue and then merged with the other traffic before disappearing into the general gloom of the night. Stephanie and Daniel had watched them until the point that they were no longer discernable, then looked into each other's faces. Their noses were mere inches apart, since their bodies were pressed together beneath their umbrella. They were once again standing motionless at the curb in front of Union Station, just as they had been an hour earlier when they were waiting to be picked up. Then they had been curious with anticipation. Now they were dumbfounded.

"Tomorrow morning, I'm going to swear this was all a delusion," Stephanie said, with a shake of her head.

"There's definitely a dreamlike unreality to it all," Daniel admitted.

"*Bizarre* is a better adjective."

Daniel lowered his eyes to the senator's business card he had clutched in his free hand. He turned it over. Scribbled in the senator's erratic handwriting was a cell phone number to be used to contact him directly in the next twelve hours. Daniel stared at the number as if committing it to memory.

A gust of wind erupted and changed the drizzle momentarily from vertical to horizontal. Stephanie shivered as the moisture peppered her face. "It's cold. Let's get back to the hotel! There's no sense standing here and getting soaked."

As if waking from a trance, Daniel apologized and glanced around the plaza in front of the station. A taxi stand was off to one side, with several cabs conveniently waiting. Angling the umbrella into the wind, he urged

Stephanie forward. Arriving at the first taxi in line, Daniel held the umbrella for Stephanie before climbing in himself.

"Four Seasons hotel," Daniel said to the driver, who was watching his rearview mirror.

"Tonight was ironic as well as bizarre," Stephanie said suddenly, as the cab pulled away. "The same day I hear a smidgen about your family from you, I hear the whole story from Senator Butler."

"I find that more irritating than ironic," Daniel said. "Hell, it's an out-and-out violation of my privacy that he had me investigated by the FBI. It's also appalling that the FBI would do it. I mean, I'm a private citizen under no suspicion of any crime. Such abuse smacks of the days of J. Edgar Hoover."

"So everything Butler said about you is true?"

"Essentially, I suppose," Daniel responded vaguely. "Listen, let's talk about the senator's offer."

"I can tell you my reaction to it right off the top. I think it stinks!"

"You don't see any positive aspects?"

"The only positive aspect I can see is that it has confirmed our impressions of the man as a quintessential demagogue. He's also a detestable hypocrite. He's against HTSR purely for political reasons, and he's willing to ban it and its research despite its potential to save lives and relieve suffering. At the same time, he wants it for himself. That's obscene and inexcusable, and we're certainly not going to be a party to it." Stephanie gave a short derisive laugh. "I'm sorry I gave my word to keep his illness a secret. This whole thing is a story the media would die for, and I'd love for them to have it."

"We certainly can't go to the media," Daniel stated categorically. "And I don't think we should be rash. I think Butler's offer deserves consideration."

A surprised Stephanie turned to look at Daniel. She tried to see his face in the dim light. "You're not serious, are you?"

"Let's list the knowns. We're well acquainted with growing dopaminergic neurons from stem cells, so it's not as if we'll be floundering around in the dark in that regard."

"We've done it with murine stem cells, not human cells."

"The process is the same. Colleagues have already done it with human stem cells using the same methodology. Making the cells is not going to be a problem. Once we have the cells, we can follow the exact protocol we used for the mice. There's no reason it wouldn't work for a human. After all, every last mouse we've treated has done remarkably well."

"Except for the ones that died."

"We know why the ones that didn't make it died. It was before we perfected the injection technique. All the mice that we injected properly have survived and have been cured. With a human volunteer, we would have available a stereotaxic device that doesn't exist for rodents. That will make the injection more exact, infinitely easier, and hence safer. Besides, we wouldn't do the injection ourselves. We'd find a neurosurgeon who'd be willing to lend a hand."

"I can't believe I'm hearing this," Stephanie said. "It sounds like you've already talked yourself into doing this crazy, unethical experiment, and that's what it would be: an uncontrolled, risky experiment on a single human subject. No matter what the outcome, it would be devoid of value, except possibly for Butler."

"I don't agree. By doing this procedure, we will save CURE and HTSR, meaning millions of people will ultimately benefit. It seems to me a minor compromise in ethics is a small up-front price to pay for an enormous back-end payoff."

"But we'll be doing exactly what Senator Butler accused the biotech industry of doing in his opening statement this morning: using ends to justify means. It would be unethical to experiment on Senator Butler, plain and simple."

"Yeah, well, perhaps to some degree, but who are we putting at risk? It's the villain! He's the one asking for it. Worse yet, he's conniving for it by extorting us with information he got by somehow coercing the FBI to do an illegal investigation."

"That all may be true, but two wrongs don't make a right, and it doesn't absolve us of our complicity."

"I think it would. We'll make Butler sign a release, and we'll put everything in the release, including the fact that we are fully aware that doing the procedure would be considered unethical by any research advisory board in this country, because it's being done without an appropriately approved protocol. The release will state unequivocally that it was Butler's idea to do the procedure and to do the procedure outside of the country. It will also state that he used extortion to get us to participate."

"Do you think he'd sign such a release?"

"We won't give him any choice. Either he signs it or he doesn't get the benefit of HTSR. I'm comfortable with the idea that we'll be doing the procedure in the Bahamas, so we won't be violating any FDA rules, and we'll have a rock-solid release in case we need it. The onus will be squarely on Butler's shoulders."

"Let me think about it for a few minutes."

"Take your time, but I really think the moral weight favors our doing it. It would be different if we were forcing him in any way, shape, or form. But we're not. It's the other way around."

"But it could be argued that he's uninformed. He's a politician, not a doctor. He doesn't truly know the risks. He could die."

"He's not going to die," Daniel said emphatically. "We'll err on the conservative side, meaning the worse-case scenario is that we won't give him enough cells to get his dopamine concentration high enough to get rid of all his symptoms. If that happens, he'll be begging us to do it again, which will be easy, since we'll maintain the treating cells in culture."

"Let me mull it over."

"Sure," Daniel said.

They rode the rest of the way in silence. It wasn't until they were going up in the hotel elevator that Stephanie spoke up: "Do you honestly think we would be able to find an appropriate place to do the procedure?"

"Butler spent a good deal of effort on all this," Daniel said. "He wasn't leaving anything to chance. Frankly, I'd be shocked if he didn't have the clinic he mentioned investigated for appropriateness at the same time he had me investigated."

"I suppose that's possible. Actually, I remember reading about the Wingate Clinic about a year ago. It was a popular, unaffiliated infertility clinic out in Bookford, Massachusetts, before it moved under pressure to the Bahamas. It was quite a scandal."

"I remember it too. It was run by a couple of maverick infertility guys. Their research department was doing unethical reproductive cloning experiments."

"Unconscionable is a better description, like trying to get human fetuses to gestate in pigs. I remember they were also implicated in the disappearance of a couple of Harvard coed egg donors. The principals had to flee the country and barely managed to avoid extradition back to the States. All in all, it sounds like the absolute opposite of the kind of place and people we should get involved with."

"We wouldn't be getting involved with them. We'd do the procedure, wash our hands, and leave."

The elevator doors opened. They started down the hall toward their suite.

"What about a neurosurgeon?" Stephanie asked. "Do you honestly think we'd be able to find someone to take part in this shenanigan? He or she will know there's something fishy about it."

"With the proper incentive, that shouldn't be a problem. Same with the clinic."

"You mean money."

"Of course! The universal motivator."

"What about Butler's demand for secrecy? How would we handle that?"

"Secrecy is more his issue than ours. We won't use his real name. Without those glasses and dark suit, I imagine he's a rather nondescript, nebbish sort of guy. With a splashy short-sleeved shirt and a pair of sunglasses, maybe no one will recognize him."

Stephanie used her keycard to open their door. They took off their jackets and went into the sitting room.

"What about something from the minibar?" Daniel suggested. "I'm in the mood to celebrate. A couple of hours ago, I thought we were stuck beneath a black cloud. Now there's a ray of sunshine."

"I could use some wine," Stephanie responded. She rubbed her hands together to warm them before curling up in the corner of the couch.

Daniel popped the cork on a half bottle of cabernet and poured a hefty portion into a balloon goblet. He handed it to Stephanie before getting himself a neat Scotch. He sat down in the opposite corner of the couch. They touched glasses and took sips from their respective drinks.

"So, you want to go ahead with this crazy plan?" Stephanie said.

"I do, unless you can come up with some compelling reason not to."

"What about this Shroud of Turin nonsense? I mean, *divine intervention!* What a preposterous and presumptuous idea!"

"I disagree. I think it is a stroke of genius."

"You have to be joking!"

"Absolutely not! It would be the ultimate placebo, and we know how powerful placebos can be. If he wants to believe he's getting some of Jesus Christ's DNA, it's fine by me. It would give him a powerful incentive to believe in his cure. I think it is a brilliant idea. I'm not suggesting we have to get DNA from the shroud. We could just tell him we have, and it would afford the same result. But we can look into it. If there is blood on the shroud like he contends and we can get access to it like he suggests, it would work."

"Even if the bloodstain is from the thirteenth century?"

"The age shouldn't make any difference. The DNA would be in fragments, but that wouldn't be a problem. We'd still use the same probe we'd use on a fresh DNA sample to form the segment we need, and then augment it by PCR. In a lot of ways, it would add a bit of challenge and excitement. The hardest part will be resisting the temptation to write the procedure up for *Nature* or *Science* after the fact. Can you imagine the title: 'HTSR and the Shroud of Turin Combine to

Produce the First Cure of Human Parkinson's Disease.'"

"We're not going to be able to publish this affair," Stephanie said.

"I know! It's just fun to think about it being a harbinger of things to come. The next step will be a controlled experiment, and we'll certainly be able to publish that. At that point, CURE will be in the limelight, and our funding miseries will be long gone."

"I wish I could share your enthusiasm."

"I think you will, once things start falling into place. Even though timing wasn't mentioned tonight, I'm going to assume the senator would be eager to do it sooner rather than later. That means we should start with the preliminaries tomorrow when we get back to Boston. I'll look into making the arrangements with the Wingate Clinic and lining up the neurosurgeon. How about you take on the Shroud of Turin portion."

"That should at least be interesting," Stephanie said, trying to generate some eagerness about the thought of treating Butler, despite what her intuition was telling her. "I'll be curious to find out why the church still considers it a relic after it was proved to be a fake."

"The senator obviously thinks it's real."

"As I recall, the carbon dating was confirmed by three independent labs. It would be hard for that to be debunked."

"Well, let's see what you find out," Daniel said. "In the meantime, we better start planning some serious travel."

"You mean Nassau?"

"Nassau and probably Turin, Italy, depending on what you find out."

"Where are we going to get the money for such travel?"

"From Ashley Butler."

Stephanie's eyebrows lifted. "Maybe this escapade isn't going to be so bad after all."

"So, are you with me on this?" Daniel questioned.

"Yeah, I suppose."

"That's not very positive."

"It's the best I can do at the moment. But I imagine I'll come around as things progress, like you suggested."

"I'll take what I can get," Daniel announced. He got up from the couch and gave Stephanie's shoulder a squeeze in the process. "I'm going to have another Scotch. Let me fill your glass."

Daniel poured the additional drinks, then

sat back down. After glancing at his watch, he put Butler's business card down in front of him and lifted the phone onto the coffee table. "Let's tell the senator the news. I'm sure he'll be irritatingly smug, but to borrow his phrase, *Such is life.*" Daniel used the speakerphone button to get a dial tone. The call went through and was picked up quickly. Ashley Butler's baritone Southern drawl inundated the room.

"Senator," Daniel called out, interrupting Ashley's verbose hello. "I don't mean to be rude, but it's late and I just wanted to let you know that I have decided to take you up on your offer."

"Well, glory be!" Ashley intoned. "And so soon! I was afraid you were going to let this simple decision spoil your slumber and that you would not be calling until the morning. Well, I am pleased as punch! Can I assume Dr. D'Agostino has agreed to participate as well?"

"I have agreed," Stephanie said, trying to sound positive.

"Excellent, excellent!" Ashley echoed. "Not that I am surprised, since this affair is to all our benefit. But I most sincerely do believe that being of the same mind and having unanimity of purpose is key to success, and we most certainly want success in this endeavor."

"We assume you would like to do this straightaway," Daniel said.

"Most assuredly, my dear friends. Most assuredly. I'm on borrowed time in terms of concealing my infirmity," Ashley explained. "There is no time to lose. Conveniently for our purposes, a Senate recess is coming up. It commences about a month from now on March twenty-second and runs through April eighth. Normally I head home to politick, but instead it is the period of time I have had my heart set upon for my treatment. Is a month an adequate amount of time for you scientists to formulate the appropriate curative cells?"

Daniel glanced at Stephanie and spoke to her softly, just above a whisper: "That's quicker than I thought he'd have in mind. What do you think? Could we do it?"

"It's a long shot," Stephanie whispered with a shrug. "First, we'd need a few days to culture his fibroblasts. Then, assuming a successful nuclear transfer creating a viable pre-embryo, we'd need five or six days for the blastocyst to form. After that, we'd need a couple of weeks of culturing on feeder cells after harvesting the stem cells."

"Is there a problem?" Ashley questioned. "I cannot for the life of me hear what you good folks are discussing."

"Just a second, Senator!" Daniel said into the speakerphone. "I'm talking with Dr. D'Agostino about timing. She would be doing most of the actual hands-on work."

"Then we'd have to get them to differentiate into the proper nerve cells," Stephanie added. "That will take another couple of weeks, or maybe a little less. The mouse cells were fine after only ten days."

"So what would you guess, if all goes well?" Daniel asked. "Would a month work?"

"It's theoretically possible," Stephanie said. "It could be done, but we'd have to start almost immediately with the cellular work, like tomorrow! The problem with that idea is that we'd have to have human oocytes available, and we don't."

"Oh, jeez!" Daniel mumbled. He bit his lower lip and furrowed his brow. "I'm so accustomed to working with a surfeit of cow eggs that I forgot about the supply problem with human eggs."

"It's a major stumbling block," Stephanie

admitted. "Even in the best of circumstances where we already had a egg donor waiting in the wings, we'd need a month or so to stimulate her and retrieve them."

"Well, perhaps our maverick infertility friends can help us in this regard as well. As a functioning infertility center, they'd surely have a few extra eggs available. Considering their unethical reputation, I bet with the right inducement we could talk them into providing us with what we will need."

"It's possible, I suppose, but then we'd be even more beholden to them. The more they do for us, the less easy it will be to wash our hands and leave like you so blithely suggested a moment ago."

"But we don't have a lot of choice. The alternative is giving up on CURE, HTSR, and all our blood, sweat, and tears."

"It has to be your call. But for the record, it makes me feel uncomfortable to be obligated to the Wingate people in any form, knowing their history."

Daniel nodded a few times as he mulled over the issues, sighed, and then turned back to the speakerphone. "Senator, there's a chance we can have some treatment cells in a month. But I have to warn you that it's going to require effort and a bit of luck, and we have to start immediately. You'll have to be cooperative."

"I will be as cooperative as a baby lamb. I've already started the process a month ago by making plans to arrive in Nassau on the twenty-third of March and to stay on the island for as much of the recess period as needed. I have even made a reservation for you. That's how confident I was about your participation. It is important to have done this early, because it is high season in the Bahamas at this time of the year. We'll be staying at the Atlantis resort, where I have had the pleasure of staying last year with this plan in mind. It is a hotel complex sizable enough to provide adequate anonymity of coming and going without raising suspicions. They also have a casino, and as you might imagine, I do enjoy gambling when I am fortunate enough to have a few extra dollars in my pocket."

Daniel exchanged glances with Stephanie. On the one hand, he was glad Ashley had made early reservations to help the project, but on the other hand, he was irritated at having been taken for granted.

"Will you be registered under your own name?" Stephanie questioned.

"Indeed I will," Ashley said. "But I will be using an assumed name for my trip to the Wingate Clinic."

"What about this clinic?" Daniel demanded. "I trust that you have looked into it as carefully as you have looked into my past."

"Your trust is well placed. I think you will find the clinic well suited for our purposes, although the personnel less so. The purported head of the clinic is Dr. Spencer Wingate, who is something of a blowhard, although apparently well qualified in the field of infertility. He seems more interested in being an island socialite and looks forward to flying off to the continent to drum up business in the courts of Europe. The man in secondary command is Dr. Paul Saunders, and he runs the show on a day-to-day basis. He is a more complicated individual who sees himself as a world-class researcher despite his lack of appropriate training beyond clinical infertility. I'm confident both individuals will be accommodating if you merely appeal to their individual vanities. For them to have the prospect of working with someone with your credentials and stature is a once-in-a-lifetime opportunity."

"You flatter me, Senator."

Stephanie smiled at Daniel's sarcasm.

"Only because it is well deserved," Ashley said. "Besides, one should have faith in one's doctor."

"It would be my guess that doctors Wingate and Saunders will be more interested in money than my resume," Daniel said.

"It is my thought that they will be interested in your resume to gain stature and to help them make money," Ashley commented. "But their venal nature and their lack of research training is not a concern of ours, other than to be aware of it and to take advantage of it. It is their facility and equipment we are interested in."

"I hope you realize that doing this procedure under these circumstances is not going to be cheap by any stretch of the imagination."

"Nor would I want it to be cheap," Ashley responded. "I want the expensive, high-quality, first-class version. Rest assured, I have access to more than sufficient funds to cover any expenses that impinge upon my political career. But I will expect your personal services to be pro bono. We are, after all, exchanging favors."

"Agreed," Daniel said. "But prior to rendering any services, Dr. D'Agostino and I will require you to sign a special release that we will draw up. This release will spell out the exact way that this affair originated as well as all the attendant risks involved, including the fact that we have never done the procedure on a human being."

"As long as I can be assured of the confidentiality of this release, I will have no qualms about signing it. I can understand you would want it for your protection. I am absolutely certain I would want the very same thing if I were in your position, so there should be no problem whatsoever, provided it does not include anything unreasonable or inappropriate."

"I can assure you it will be reasonable," Daniel said. "Next, I'd like to encourage you to use your resources as you suggested to find out about access to the Shroud of Turin so we can get a sample."

"I have already instructed Ms. Manning to initiate the appropriate meetings with the various prelates with whom I have had a working relationship. I will assume it will happen in the next few days. How big a sample would be required?"

"It can be extremely small," Daniel said. "Merely a few fibers would be adequate, but it would have to be fibers coming from a section of the shroud containing a bloodstain."

Ashley laughed. "Even an ignorant, non-scientist like myself would assume as much. The fact that you need only a small sample should help immeasurably. As I mentioned last night, I know there were such samples taken and then called back by the church."

"We'd need them as soon as possible," Daniel added.

"I understand completely the need for expeditiousness," Ashley responded. "Is there anything else you require of me?"

"Yes," Stephanie said. "We will need you to have a punch biopsy of your skin tomorrow morning. If there is a chance we can produce the curative cells in a month, we'll need to take your biopsy back with us tomorrow when we return to Boston. Your private physician can arrange having the biopsy with a dermatologist, who can have a courier bring it over to us at the hotel. It will serve as a source of fibroblasts that we will grow in tissue culture."

"I will see to it first thing in the morning."

"I believe that is all for now," Daniel said. He looked at Stephanie, and she nodded in agreement.

"I have a vitally important request of my own," Ashley said. "I think we should exchange special email addresses and use the Internet for all our communications, which should be generic and short. The next time we talk directly should be at the Wingate Clinic on New Providence Island. I am committed that this affair be a closely guarded secret, and the less direct contact we have, the better. Is that acceptable?"

"By all means," Daniel agreed.

"As for expense money," Ashley said, "I will advise you by email of a confidential account at an offshore bank in Nassau, set up by one of my political action committees, from which you will be able to withdraw funds. I will, of course, expect an accounting in the future. Is that acceptable?"

"As long as there's enough money," Daniel said. "One of the major expenses will be to obtain the necessary human egg cells."

"I reiterate," Ashley said, "there will be

more than adequate funds available. Rest assured!"

A few minutes later, after a final long-winded farewell from Ashley, Daniel leaned forward and disconnected the speaker-phone. He lifted the phone back onto the end table. Then he swung around to face Stephanie. "I had to laugh when he called the head of the Wingate Clinic a blowhard. Talk about the pot calling the kettle black."

"You were right about him putting a lot of thought into this affair. I was shocked when he said he'd made travel reservations a month ago. There's no doubt in my mind he had the Wingate Clinic investigated."

"Are you feeling better about being involved in curing him?"

"To a degree," Stephanie admitted. "Especially since he says he'll have no compunction signing a release that we write. At least I'll have the feeling he's considered the experimental nature of what we will be doing and the attendant risks. I wasn't at all sure of that before."

Daniel slid across the couch, put his arms around Stephanie, and hugged her against his body. He could feel her heart beating in her chest. Pushing himself back enough to look into her face, he stared into the dark depths of her eyes. "Now that we have seemingly gotten things under control in the political/business/research arena, how about starting out where we left off last night?"

Stephanie returned Daniel's stare. "Is that a proposition?"

"Indeed, it is."

"Is your autonomic nervous system going to cooperate?"

"A lot better than it did last night, I can assure you."

Daniel got to his feet and helped Stephanie to hers.

"We forgot the do-not-disturb sign," Stephanie said, as Daniel eagerly pulled her toward the bedroom.

"Let's live dangerously," he said, with a twinkle in his eye.

six

2:35 P.M., Friday, February 22, 2002

By the time Stephanie had awakened early that morning, she was caught up in the details of the Butler project. Her negative intuition about treating the senator's Parkinson's disease had not changed, but there was too much to do to obsess about such feelings. Even before she had showered, she used her laptop to fire off a series of emails to the senator about the handling of his biopsy.

First, she wanted the biopsy as soon as possible that morning. Second, she wanted to be absolutely certain it was a full-thickness skin, because she would need cells from deep in the dermis. And third, she wanted the sample merely to be placed in a flask of tissue culture fluid and not frozen or even iced. She was confident the tissue would be fine at room temperature until she got back to the laboratory in Cambridge, where she would deal with it appropriately. Her goal was to create a culture of the senator's fibroblasts, the nuclei of which she would ultimately be using to create the cells to treat him. She had always had better luck with fresh rather than frozen cells when she was doing HTSR followed by nuclear transfer, or therapeutic cloning, as some people insisted on calling the process.

To Stephanie's surprise and despite the early hour, the senator emailed her back almost immediately, indicating that not only was he an early riser but that he was as committed to the project as he had suggested the previous evening. In his message, he assured her he had already put in a call to his doctor and that when the doctor called back he would communicate her requests and insist they be followed.

Daniel was ebullient from the moment he'd thrown back the covers. He too was at his laptop, emailing before doing anything else. Dressed only in a hotel terry-cloth robe, he typed out a message to the West Coast venture capital group that had expressed interest in investing in CURE but had been reluctant to release any funds until there'd been a resolution of Senator Butler's bill. Daniel wanted to let them know that the bill was destined to languish permanently in the subcommittee and was no longer a threat. Daniel would have liked to explain how he knew this bit of news, but he knew he couldn't. Daniel had not expected a message back from the prospective investors for several hours, since it was only four in the morning on the West Coast when his message went out on the World Wide Web. Nonetheless, he was confident in their response.

As a splurge, they had ordered breakfast in the room. At Daniel's insistence, it included mimosas. Jokingly, he told Stephanie that she'd better get accustomed to such living, because it would become the order of the day once CURE went public. "I've had enough of academic poverty," he'd declared. "We are going to be on the A list, and we are going to act the part!"

At nine-fifteen, both had been surprised by a call from the concierge's desk saying that a courier had dropped off a package from a Dr. Claire Schneider labeled URGENT. They were asked if they wanted it sent directly to the room, and they had responded in the affirmative. As they assumed, the package contained Butler's skin biopsy, and they were duly impressed with Butler's efficiency. Its arrival was several hours earlier than they had hoped to see it.

With the biopsy in hand, they had been able to catch the ten-thirty shuttle flight to Boston, getting them into Logan Airport just after noon. Following an even more hair-raising taxi experience than those in Washington, as far as Daniel was concerned, with a driver from Pakistan in a rattletrap vehicle, they were dumped off at Daniel's condominium apartment on Appleton Street. A change of clothes and a quick lunch followed by a short ride in Daniel's Ford Focus brought them to CURE's current digs in East Cambridge on Athenaeum Street. They entered through the front door. The company occupied the ground-floor suite immediately to the right of the entrance.

When Daniel had first founded CURE, it

had occupied most of the first floor of the renovated, nineteenth-century brick office building. But as the money crunch deepened, space was first to go. Currently, it was one-tenth of its original size, with only a single laboratory, two small offices, and a reception area. Second to go were the nonessential personnel. The employees included Daniel and Stephanie, who'd not drawn salaries for four months, another senior scientist by the name of Peter Conway, operator-cum-receptionist/secretary Vicky McGowan, and three laboratory technicians soon to be reduced to two or maybe even one. Daniel had not yet decided. What Daniel had not changed was the board of directors, the scientific advisory board, and the ethics board, all of whom Daniel intended to leave in the dark about the Butler affair.

"It's only two-thirty-five," Stephanie announced, after closing the door behind them. "I'd say that's good timing, considering we woke up in Washington, D.C."

Daniel merely grunted. His attention was directed at Vicky, who was handing him a bundle of telephone messages, a few of which needed explanation. In particular, the venture capital people from the West Coast had called instead of returning Daniel's email. According to Vicky, they were hardly satisfied with the information they'd gotten and were demanding more.

Leaving Daniel to deal with business matters, Stephanie went into the laboratory. She called hello to Peter, who was seated before one of the dissecting microscopes. While Stephanie and Daniel had gone to Washington, he'd stayed behind to keep all the company's experiments going.

Stephanie unloaded her laptop onto the soapstone surface of the particular lab bench she used as her desk; her private office had been sacrificed in the initial downsizing. With Butler's skin biopsy in hand, she walked over to an operative area of the laboratory. She removed the piece of skin aseptically, minced it, and then placed the minced material in a fresh batch of culture medium, along with antibiotics. When it had been safely stored in an incubator in a T-flask, she returned to the area she used as her desk.

"How did things go in Washington?" Peter called out. He was a slightly built fellow who looked like a teenager, despite being older than Stephanie. His most distinguishing characteristics were ratty clothes and a shock of blond hair that he wore in a ponytail. Stephanie had always thought he could be a poster boy for the hippie-dominated sixties.

"Washington was okay," Stephanie answered vaguely. She and Daniel had decided not to tell the others about Senator Butler until after the fact.

"So, we're still in business?" Peter asked.

"It looks that way," Stephanie replied. She plugged in her laptop and turned it on. A short time later, she was connected to the Internet.

"Is the money coming from San Fran?" Peter persisted.

"You'll have to ask Daniel," Stephanie said. "I try to stay clear of the business side of things."

Peter got the implied message and went back to his work.

Stephanie had been eager to look into the issue of the Shroud of Turin from the moment Daniel had suggested she take it on as her initial contribution to the Butler project. She'd thought about beginning that morning after her shower and before Butler's skin biopsy had arrived but had decided against it because connecting to the Internet with a modem was agonizingly slow now that she was spoiled with CURE's broadband connection. Besides, she thought she'd no sooner get herself involved and have to break off. Now she had the rest of the afternoon.

Calling up the Google search engine, she entered SHROUD OF TURIN and clicked on the SEARCH button. She had no idea what to expect. Although she remembered sketchy references to the shroud when she was a child and still a practicing Catholic as well as something about its being declared a fake after carbon dating when she was in her first year of graduate school, she'd not thought of the relic in years and assumed other people felt similarly. After all, how excited could one get about a thirteenth-century forgery? But a blink of the eye later, when the Google search was completed, she knew she was wrong. Amazed, she found herself staring at the number of results: more than 28,300!

Stephanie clicked on the first result, called the Shroud of Turin website, and for the next hour found herself totally absorbed by the extent of information available. On the very first introductory page, she read that the shroud was "the single most studied artifact in human history"! With her relative lack of familiarity with the shroud, she found that a surprising statement, especially considering her general interest in history; her under-graduate major had been chemistry, but she'd had a minor in history. She also read that a number of experts felt strongly that the question of the shroud's authenticity as a first-century artifact had not been settled by the carbon dating results. As a woman of sci-ence, and knowing the precision of carbon dating, she could not understand how any-one could hold such an opinion and was ea-ger to find out. But before she did, she used the website to examine photographs of the shroud that were presented in both positive and negative format.

Stephanie learned that the first person to photograph the shroud in 1898 had been startled by the images being significantly more obvious in the negative, and it was the same for her. In the positive the image was faint, and looking at it and trying to see the figure reminded her of one of her youthful summer pastimes: attempting to see faces, people, or animals in the infinite variations of cumulus clouds. But in the negative, the im-age was striking! It was clearly that of a man who had been beaten, tortured, and crucified, which begged the question of how a medieval forger could have anticipated the development of photography. What had appeared on the positive as mere blotches were now agonizingly real rivulets of blood. Glancing back at the positive image, she was surprised that the blood had even retained its red color.

On the main menu of the Shroud of Turin website, Stephanie clicked on a button labeled FREQUENTLY ASKED QUESTIONS. One of the questions was whether DNA testing had ever been performed on the shroud. With excitement, Stephanie clicked on the question. In the answer provided, she learned that Texas researchers had found DNA in the bloodstains, although there were some questions about the provenance of the sample tested. There were also questions raised about how much DNA contamination could have been left by all the people who had touched the shroud over the centuries.

The Shroud of Turin website also included an extensive bibliography, and Stephanie turned to it eagerly. Once again, she was amazed at its extent. With her curiosity now piqued and as a lover of books, she went over a number of the titles. Leaving the shroud's website, she called up a book-seller's, which produced a hundred titles, many of which were the same as those in the shroud's website. After reading some of the reviews, she selected a few of the books that she wanted to have immediately. She was particularly drawn to those by Ian Wilson, an Oxford-educated scholar, who was cited as presenting both sides of the controversy concerning the shroud's authenticity even though he was convinced it was real, mean-ing not only was it a first-century artifact—it was the burial cloth of Jesus Christ!

Picking up the phone, Stephanie called the local bookstore. She was rewarded by learning that the store had one of the titles she was interested in. It was *The Turin Shroud: The Illustrated Evidence* by Ian Wil-son and Barrie Schwortz, a professional photographer who had been part of an American team that had extensively studied the shroud in 1978. Stephanie asked for the book to be put aside with her name on it.

Returning to the bookseller's website, she ordered a few more of the shroud books to be delivered overnight. With that accom-plished, she stood up and took her coat off the back of her chair. "I'm heading out to the bookstore," she called over to Peter.

"I'm going to pick up a book on the Shroud of Turin. Out of curiosity, what do you know about it?"

"Hmmm," Peter voiced, as he screwed up his face as if in deep thought. "I know the name of the city where it's kept."

"I'm serious," Stephanie complained.

"Well, let's put it this way," Peter said. "I've heard of it, but it's not that it comes up in conversation too often with me and my buddies. If I were pressed, I'd say it's one of those objects the medieval church used to fan the religious fires to keep the collection boxes full, like pieces of the true cross and saints' fingernails."

"Do you think it's real?"

"You mean Jesus' burial cloth?"

"Yeah."

"Hell, no! It was proved to be a fake ten years ago."

"What if I told you it was the most investigated artifact in human history?"

"I'd ask you what you'd been smoking lately."

Stephanie laughed. "Thank you, Peter."

"What are you thanking me for?" he asked, obviously confused.

"I was worried my lack of familiarity with the Shroud of Turin was somehow unique. It's reassuring to know it's not." Stephanie pulled on her coat and headed for the door.

"How come the sudden interest in the Shroud of Turin?" Peter called after her.

"You'll know soon enough," Stephanie yelled over her shoulder. She crossed the reception area diagonally and poked her head into Daniel's office. She was surprised to see him slouched over his desk with his head in his hands.

"Hey," Stephanie called. "Are you okay?"

Daniel looked up and blinked. His eyes were red, as if he'd been rubbing them, and his face was paler than usual. "Yeah, I'm okay," he said, as if exhausted. His earlier ebullience had fled.

"What's going on?"

Daniel shook his head as his eyes wandered around his littered desk. He sighed. "Running this organization is like keeping a leaky boat afloat with a thimble for bailing. The venture capital people are refusing to release the second round financing until I tell them why I'm so sure Butler's bill won't come out of the subcommittee. But I can't tell them, because if I do, it will invariably be leaked, and Butler would most likely renege about keeping his bill under wraps. Then all bets are off."

"What kind of money do we have left?"

"Almost nothing," Daniel moaned. "This time next month, we'll be dipping into our line of credit just to meet payroll."

"That gives us the month we need to treat Butler," Stephanie said.

"What a lucky break that is," Daniel snapped sarcastically. "It irritates me to death that we have to stop our research and deal with the likes of Butler and possibly those infertility clowns down in Nassau. It's a goddamn crime that medical research has become politicized in this country. Our founding fathers who insisted on separation of church and state are probably turning over in their graves with these relatively few politicians using their supposed religious beliefs to hold up what will undoubtedly be the biggest advance in medical treatment."

"Well, we all know what's really behind this current Luddite bioscience movement," Stephanie said.

"What are you talking about?"

"It's really abortion politics in disguise," Stephanie said. "The real issue is that these demagogues want a zygote to be declared a human being with full constitutional rights no matter how the zygote was formed and no matter what the zygote's future holds. It's a ridiculous stance, but nonetheless if it happened, *Roe versus Wade* would have to be thrown out."

"You're probably right," Daniel admitted. He exhaled like the sound of air coming out of a tire. "What an absurd situation. History is going to wonder what kind of people we were that allowed a personal issue like abortion to handicap a society for years on end. We took a lot of our ideas about individual rights, government, and certainly our common law from England. Why couldn't we have followed England's lead in how best to deal with the ethics of reproductive bioscience?"

"That's a good question, but it's not going to do us any good to worry over the answer at the moment. What happened to your enthusiasm about treating Butler? Let's get it done! Once he's treated, he's not going to renege on our deal even if there is a leak to the media, because we'll have his release. I mean, once he's been cured he can deal with the media by just denying any accusations as being politically motivated. What he wouldn't be able to deny is a signed release."

"You have a point," Daniel admitted.

"What about Butler's money?" Stephanie asked. "It seems to me that's the key question at the moment. Has there been any communication about that?"

"I haven't even thought to check." Daniel turned to his computer and, after a few strokes, looked at his special email inbox. "Here's a message that must be from Butler. It has an encrypted attachment, which is encouraging."

Daniel opened the attachment. Stephanie stepped around the desk to look over his shoulder.

"I'd say it looks very encouraging," Stephanie said. "He's given us an account number for a Bahamian bank, and it appears as if we both can draw from it."

"It's got a link to the bank's website," Daniel said. "Let's see if we can find out the balance in the account. That will tell us how serious Butler is about all this."

A few clicks later, Daniel tilted back in his chair. He looked up at Stephanie, and she returned his stare. Both were taken aback.

"I'd say he's very serious!" Stephanie remarked. "And eager!"

"I'm flabbergasted!" Daniel said. "I expected ten or twenty thousand, tops. I never expected a hundred. Where could he have gotten that kind of money so quickly?"

"I told you, he has a string of political action committees that are fund-raising workhorses. What I wonder is if any of the people who contributed this money could have ever imagined how the money was going to be spent. There's a hell of a lot of irony here if they are as conservative as I imagine they are."

"That's not our concern," Daniel said. "Besides, we'll never spend a hundred thousand dollars. At the same time, it's good to know it's there just in case. Let's get busy!"

"I already started the fibroblast culture with the skin biopsy."

"Excellent," Daniel said, as his exuberance of that morning began to return. Even his skin color improved. "I'll get cracking and find out what I can about the Wingate Clinic."

"Sounds good!" Stephanie said. She

started for the door. "I'll be back in about an hour."

"Where are you going?"

"The bookstore downtown," Stephanie called over her shoulder. She hesitated at the threshold. "They are holding a book for me. After I got the tissue culture started, I began looking into the Shroud of Turin issue. I have to say, I lucked out in our division of labor. The shroud is turning out to be much more interesting than I imagined."

"What did you find out?"

"Just enough to hook me, but I'll give you a full report in about twenty-four hours."

Daniel smiled, flashed Stephanie a thumbs-up, and turned back to his computer screen. He used a search engine to bring up a list of infertility clinics and found the Wingate Clinic's website. A few clicks later, he was connected.

He scrolled through the first few pages. As expected, it was composed of laudatory material to entice would-be clients. Under a section labeled MEET OUR STAFF, he made a brief side trip to read the professional resumes of the principals, which included the founder and CEO, Dr. Spencer Wingate; the head of Research and Laboratory Services, Dr. Paul

Saunders; and the head of Clinical Services, Dr. Sheila Donaldson. The resumes were as glowing as the descriptions of the clinic itself, although in Daniel's opinion, all three individuals had attended second-tier or even third-tier schools and training programs.

At the bottom of the page, he found what he wanted: a phone number. There was also an email address, but Daniel wanted to talk directly with one of the principals, either Wingate or Saunders. Picking up the phone, Daniel dialed the number. The call was answered quickly by a pleasant-sounding operator who launched into a short, rote eulogy of the clinic before asking with whom Daniel wished to be connected.

"Dr. Wingate," Daniel said. He decided he might as well start at the top.

There was another short pause before Daniel was connected to an equally pleasant-sounding woman. She politely asked for Daniel's name before committing whether Dr. Wingate was available. When Daniel mentioned his name, the response was immediate.

"Is this Dr. Daniel Lowell of Harvard University?"

Daniel paused momentarily, as he tried to

decide how to respond. "I have been at Harvard, although at the moment I am with my own firm."

"I'll get Dr. Wingate for you," the secretary said. "I know he's been waiting to talk with you."

After a sustained blink of disbelief, Daniel pulled the phone from his ear and stared at it momentarily, as if it could explain the secretary's unexpected response. How could Spencer Wingate be waiting to talk with him? Daniel shook his head.

"Good afternoon, Dr. Lowell!" a voice responded with a clipped New England accent a full octave higher than Daniel would have expected. "I'm Spencer Wingate, and I'm pleased to hear from you. We expected your call last week, but no matter. Would you mind waiting momentarily while I get Dr. Saunders on the line? It will take a minute, but we might as well make this a conference call, since I know Dr. Saunders is as eager to talk with you as I."

"Fine," Daniel said agreeably, although his bewilderment was deepening. He leaned back in his chair, lifted his feet onto his desk, and switched the phone to his left hand so he could use his right to drum a pencil on his desk. He'd been caught totally unawares by Spencer Wingate's response to his call and felt a twinge of anxiety. He kept hearing Stephanie's admonitions about getting involved with these infamous infertility mavericks.

A minute dragged on to five. Just when Daniel had recovered his equilibrium enough to question if he'd been inadvertently disconnected, Spencer popped back on the line. He was slightly out of breath. "Okay, I'm back! How about you, Paul? Are you on?"

"I'm here," Paul said, apparently using an extension in another room. In contrast to Spencer's voice, Paul's was rather deep, with a distinct Midwestern nasal twang. "I'm pleased to talk with you, Daniel, if I may call you that."

"If you wish," Daniel said. "Whatever suits you."

"Thank you. And please call me Paul. No need for formalities between friends and colleagues. Let me say right off how much I am looking forward to working with you."

"That's my sentiment as well," Spencer declared. "Heck! The whole clinic is eager. How soon can we expect you?"

"Well, that's one of the reasons I'm calling," Daniel said vaguely, struggling to be diplomatic, but intensely curious. "But first I'd like to ask how it is that you expected me to call?"

"From your scout or whatever his job title might be," Spencer answered. "What was his name again, Paul?"

"Marlowe," Paul said.

"Right! Bob Marlowe," Spencer said. "After he finished checking out our facility, he said you'd be contacting us the following week. Needless to say, we were disappointed when we didn't hear from you. But that's water under the bridge now that you have called."

"We're delighted you want to use our facility," Paul said. "It will be an honor to work with you. Now I hope you don't mind me speculating about what you have in mind, because Bob Marlowe was vague, but I'm assuming you want to try your ingenious HTSR on a patient. I mean, why else would you want to forsake your own lab and those great hospitals you have in Boston. Am I correct in this assumption?"

"How do you know about HTSR?" Daniel asked. He wasn't sure he wanted to admit to his motivations so early in the conversation.

"We read your outstanding paper in *Nature*," Paul said. "It was brilliant, simply brilliant. Its overall importance to bioscience reminded me of my own paper, *In Vitro Maturation of Human Oocytes.* Did you happen to read it?"

"Not yet," Daniel responded, forcing himself to continue to be tactful. "What journal was it in?"

"*The Journal of Twenty-first Century Reproductive Technology*," Spencer said.

"That's a journal I'm not familiar with," Daniel responded. "Who publishes it?"

"We do," Paul said proudly. "Right here at the Wingate Clinic. We're as committed to research as we are to clinical services."

Daniel rolled his eyes. Lacking peer review, scientific self-publishing was an oxymoron, and he was impressed with the accuracy of Butler's capsule description of these two men.

"HTSR has never been used on a human," Daniel said, still avoiding answering Paul's question.

"We understand that," Spencer interjected. "And that's one of many reasons why we would be thrilled to have it done here first. Being on the cutting edge is precisely the kind of reputation Wingate Clinic is striving to establish."

"The FDA would frown on performing an experimental procedure outside of an approved protocol," Daniel said. "They would never give approval."

"Of course they wouldn't approve," Spencer agreed. "And we should know." He laughed, and Paul chimed in as well. "But here in the Bahamas, there's no need for the FDA to know, since they have no jurisdiction."

"If I were to do HTSR on a human, it would have to be in absolute secrecy," Daniel said, finally indirectly acknowledging his plans. "It cannot be divulged and obviously could not be used for your promotional purposes."

"We are fully aware of that," Paul said. "Spencer was not implying we would use it right away."

"Heavens, no!" Spencer chirped. "I was thinking of using it only after it became mainstream."

"I would have to retain the right to determine when that might be," Daniel said. "I will not even be using the episode to promote HTSR."

"No?" Paul questioned. "Then why do you want to do it?"

"For purely personal reasons," Daniel said. "I'm confident HTSR will work just as well with humans as it has with mice. But I need to prove it to myself with a patient to give me the fortitude to deal with the backlash I'm facing from the political right. I don't know if you are aware, but I'm fighting a potential congressional ban on my procedure."

There was an awkward pause in the conversation. By demanding secrecy and taking away any potential advertising windfalls in the near future, Daniel was certain he'd negated one of the Wingate Clinic's reasons to be cooperative. Frantically, he tried to think of a way to cushion the disappointment, and just a moment before he spoke up and possibly made things worse, Spencer broke the silence: "I suppose we can respect your need for secrecy. But if we were to get no promotional value from your collaboration with us in the near term, what kind of compensation do you have in mind for using our facility and services?"

"We expect to pay," Daniel said.

There was another silence. Daniel felt a twinge of panic that the negotiations were not going well, raising the specter of losing the opportunity of using the Wingate Clinic for Butler's treatment. Considering the time constraints, such a loss could be the death knell for the project. Daniel sensed he had to offer more. Remembering Butler's assessment of Spencer and Paul's vanities, he gritted his teeth and said: "Then, down the road, after the FDA approves HTSR for general use, we could all coauthor a paper on the case."

Daniel winced. The idea of coauthoring a paper with such bozos was a painful thought, even though he rationalized he could delay it indefinitely. But despite the offer, the silence persisted, and Daniel's panic grew. Remembering his own response to Butler's demand to use blood from the Shroud of Turin for the HTSR, he threw in that tidbit as well, explaining the patient had insisted on it. Daniel even proposed the same title he'd jokingly suggested to Stephanie.

"Now that sounds like one hell of a paper!" Paul responded suddenly. "I love it! Where would we publish it?"

"Wherever," Daniel said vaguely. "*Science* or *Nature.* Wherever you'd like. I don't imagine it would be difficult to place."

"Would HTSR work with blood from the Shroud of Turin?" Spencer asked. "As I recall, that thing is about five hundred years old."

"How about around two thousand years old," Paul said.

"Wasn't it proved to be a medieval forgery?" Spencer questioned.

"We're not going to get involved in argument about its authenticity," Daniel said. "For our purposes, it doesn't matter. If the patient wants to believe it's real, it's fine with us."

"But would it work, as a practical matter?" Spencer asked again.

"The DNA would be fragmented, whether it's five hundred or two thousand years old," Daniel said. "But that shouldn't be a problem. We only need fragments, which our HTSR probes will seek out after PCR amplification. We'll enzymatically patch together what we need for whole genes. It will work fine."

"What about *The New England Journal of Medicine*?" Paul suggested. "That would be a coup for the clinic! I'd love to get something into that highfalutin publication."

"Sure," Daniel said, cringing at the idea. "Why not?"

"I'm beginning to like it too," Spencer said.

"That's the kind of article that would get picked up by the media like it was pure gold! It would be all over the newspapers. Hell, I can even see all the network anchors talking about it on the evening news."

"I'm sure you're right," Daniel said. "But remember, until the article comes out, there's got to be absolute secrecy about the whole affair."

"We understand," Spencer said.

"How are you going to get a sample from the Shroud of Turin?" Paul asked. "I understand the Catholic Church has it locked up in a kind of space-age vault over there in Italy."

"We're looking into that as we speak," Daniel said. "We have been promised high-level clerical assistance."

"I'd think you'd have to know the Pope!" Paul commented.

"Perhaps we should talk about costs," Daniel said, eager to change the subject now that the crisis had been averted. "We don't want any misunderstandings."

"What kind of services are we talking about?" Paul asked.

"The patient we'll be treating has Parkinson's disease," Daniel explained. "We will need a staffed OR and stereotaxic equipment for the implantation."

"We have the OR," Paul said. "But not stereotaxic equipment."

"That's not a problem," Spencer said. "We can borrow it from Princess Margaret Hospital. The Bahamian government and the medical community on the island have been very supportive of our relocation. I'm sure they will be happy to help. We just won't tell them what we're going to do with it."

"We'll need the services of a neurosurgeon," Daniel said. "One who is capable of being discreet."

"I don't think that will be a problem either," Spencer said. "There are several on the island who are, in my opinion, underutilized. I'm sure we could make arrangements with one of them. I don't know exactly how much he'd charge, but I can assure you, it will be a lot less than it would be in the States. My guess would be in the neighborhood of two or three hundred dollars."

"You don't think the confidentiality issue will be problematic?" Daniel asked.

"I don't," Spencer said. "They are all looking for work. With fewer tourists renting mopeds, head trauma has dropped off precipitously. I know, because two surgeons have come out to the clinic to leave their business cards."

"Sounds serendipitous," Daniel said. "Other than that, all we need is space in your lab. I assume you have a lab to do your reproductive work."

"You will be amazed at our lab," Paul said proudly. "It is state-of-the-art and a lot more than just an infertility lab! And in addition to myself, we have several talented technicians at your disposal who are experienced at nuclear transfer and who are eager to learn HTSR."

"We won't need the assistance of any lab personnel," Daniel said. "We'll do our own cellular work. What we do need are human oocytes. Is it possible for you to supply them?"

"Of course!" Paul said. "Oocytes are our specialty and soon to be our bread and butter. We're intending to supply them for all of North America in the future. What is your time frame?"

"As soon as possible," Daniel said. "This might sound overly optimistic, but we'd like to be ready to implant in a month. We're under a time constraint, with a short window of opportunity imposed by the patient volunteer."

"No problem on this end," Paul said. "We can supply you with oocytes tomorrow!"

"Really?" Daniel questioned. It seemed too good to be true.

"We can get you oocytes whenever you want," Paul said. Then he added with a laugh, "Even on holidays!"

"I'm impressed," Daniel said sincerely. "And relieved. I was worried that procuring oocytes might hold us up. But that brings us back to costs."

"Except for the oocytes, we have no experience what to charge," Spencer said. "To tell you the truth, we never anticipated someone using our clinic. Let's make it simple: How about twenty thousand for using the operating room, including its staff, and twenty thousand for the lab flat rate."

"Fine," Daniel said. "What about the oocytes?"

"Five hundred a pop," Paul said. "And we guarantee at least five divisions with each one or we replace it."

"That sounds fair," Daniel said. "But they have to be fresh!"

"They will be as fresh as a daisy," Paul said. "When can we expect you?"

"I'll get back to you either later today or

tonight," Daniel said. "Or, at the latest, by tomorrow. We really have to get moving on this."

"We'll be here," Spencer said.

Daniel slowly replaced the telephone receiver. When it was safely in its cradle, he let out a whoop. He had a strong feeling, despite the recent setbacks, that CURE, HTSR, and his own destiny were back on track!

Dr. Spencer Wingate had left his tanned hand on the telephone receiver after hanging up while his mind mulled over the conversation he'd just had with Dr. Daniel Lowell. It had not gone as he'd imagined or hoped, and he was disappointed. When the issue of the famous researcher wanting to use the Wingate Clinic had unexpectedly surfaced two weeks previously, he'd thought it providential since they'd just opened their doors after eight months of construction and confusion. In his mind, a professional association with a man who Paul said might win a Nobel Prize would have been a superb way to announce to the world that the Wingate was back in business after the regrettable fracas in Massachusetts the previous May.

But as things stood, there could be no announcement. Forty thousand dollars might be nice, but it was a mere pittance in comparison to the money they had just spent getting the clinic built and equipped.

Spencer's office door, which had been slightly ajar from when Spencer had recently rushed back in from locating his second-in-command, was pushed open to its full extent. Filling the doorway was Dr. Paul Saunders's short, square frame. A broad smile displayed his equally square, widely spaced teeth. He obviously did not share Spencer's disappointment.

"Can you imagine?" Paul blurted. "We're going to have a paper in the *New England Journal of Medicine*!" He threw himself into a chair facing Spencer's desk and punched the air with upraised fists like he'd just won a stage of the Tour de France. "And what a paper: 'The Wingate Clinic, the Shroud of Turin, and HTSR Combine for the First Cure of Parkinson's Disease.' It's going to be fantastic! People will be beating a path to our door!"

Spencer leaned back and put his hands with fingers intertwined behind his head. He regarded the head of research, a title Paul

had insisted upon, with a degree of conde-
scension. Paul was a hard worker with vi-
sion, but he could be overly enthusiastic,
and he lacked the practicality necessary to
run a business properly. In the clinic's previous incarnation in Massachusetts, he'd practically run it into the ground financially. Had
Spencer not mortgaged the clinic to the hilt
and socked away most of the clinic's assets
offshore, they wouldn't have survived.

"What makes you so sure there will be a
paper?" Spencer asked.

Paul's face clouded over. "What are you
talking about? We just discussed it on the
phone, title and all, with Daniel. He's the one
who suggested it."

"He suggested it, but how can we be sure
it will happen? I agree, it would be great if it
did, but he could just put it off indefinitely."

"Why the hell would he do that?"

"I don't know, but for some reason secrecy's high on his list, and a paper would
destroy that. He's not going to want to write
a paper, at least not soon enough for us,
and if we went ahead and did it without him,
he'd probably just deny any involvement in
the case. If that happened, no one would
publish it."

"You've got a point," Paul agreed.

The two men eyed each other across the expanse of Spencer's desk. A jet on its final approach to Nassau International Airport thundered overhead. The clinic was sited just west of the airport, on dry, scrubby land. It was the only place they could reasonably buy adequate acreage and fence it in appropriately.

"Do you think he was being straight about using the Shroud of Turin?" Paul asked.

"I don't know that either," Spencer said. "It sounds a bit fishy to me, if you know what I mean."

"On the contrary, the concept sounded intriguing to me."

"Don't get me wrong," Spencer said. "The idea is interesting and certainly would make a damn good scientific paper and international news story, but when you put it all together, including the secrecy issue, there's something decidedly dubious involved. I mean, did you buy his explanation when you asked him why he was going to all this trouble?"

"You mean about his wanting to prove HTSR to himself?"

"Precisely."

"Not completely, although it is true that the U.S. Congress is thinking of banning HTSR. And now that you've got me thinking, he did accept the fees you suggested a bit too quickly, as if the price didn't matter."

"I couldn't agree more," Spencer said. "I had no idea how much to ask to use our facilities, and I just pulled some figures out of the air and expected him to come back with a counteroffer. Hell, I should have asked for twice as much, as quickly as he agreed."

"So, what is your take?"

"I think the identity of the patient is the issue," Spencer said. "That's the only thing that comes to mind that makes sense."

"Like who?"

"I don't know," Spencer said. "But if I were forced to guess, my first thought would be a family member. My second guess would be someone wealthy, someone very wealthy and possibly famous and wealthy, which is where I'd put my money!"

"Wealthy!" Paul repeated. A slight smile appeared on his face. "A cure could be worth millions."

"Exactly, which is why I think we should

proceed with the rich-and-famous hypothesis. After all, why should Daniel Lowell potentially get millions while we get a paltry
forty thousand!"

"Which means we have to find out the
identity of this patient volunteer."

"I was hoping you'd see this affair from my
perspective. I was afraid you might feel it was
worth it just to work with this renowned researcher."

"Hell, no!" Paul snapped. "Not when we
can't get the promotional benefits we expected. He's even implied we're not going to
get hands-on instruction in HTSR when he
said he'd be doing his own cellular work.
Originally, I thought that was a given. I still
want to learn the procedure, though, so
when he calls back, mention that that has to
be part of the package."

"I'll be happy to tell him," Spencer said. "I'm
also going to tell him we want half of the
money up front."

"Tell him we also want special consideration in the future on licensing HTSR."

"That's a good idea," Spencer said. "I'll see
what I can do about essentially renegotiating
our deal without upping the cash. I don't

want to scare him off. Meanwhile, how about you taking responsibility for trying to find the identity of the patient? That's a kind of activity you are better at than I."

"I'll take that as a compliment."

"It was meant as a compliment."

Paul stood up. "I'll get Kurt Hermann, our security chief, right on it. He loves this kind of assignment."

"Tell the dishonorably discharged Green Beret, or whatever the hell he was, to kill as few people as possible. After all this investment and effort, let's not wear out our welcome on the island."

Paul laughed. "He's really very careful and conservative."

"That's not my take," Spencer said. He held up his hands to ward off an argument. "I don't think the whores on Okinawa he knocked off would call him conservative, and he was a bit heavy-handed up in Massachusetts in our employ, but we've been over this. I admit he's good at what he does, otherwise he wouldn't still be on the staff. Just humor me and tell him to be discreet! That's all I ask."

"I'll be happy to tell him." Paul stood up.

"But remember, since none of us, including Kurt, can go back to the States, he probably won't be able to accomplish much until Daniel, his team, and the patient get here."

"I don't expect miracles," Spencer said.

seven

4:45 P.M., Friday, February 22, 2002

The sawtooth spires of the Manhattan sky-
line were silhouetted against the darkening
midwinter sky as the Washington–New York
shuttle descended in its final approach to La-
Guardia Airport. The lights of the sprawling,
pulsating city sparkled like so many jewels in
the gathering gloom. Those of the many suspension bridges appeared like necklaces of
illuminated pearls slung between the soaring
stanchions. The undulating rows of headlights on the FDR Drive resembled strings of
diamonds, while the taillights suggested ru-

bies. A gaily bedecked cruise ship looked like a brooch, as it silently slid into a docking on the Hudson River.

Carol Manning turned from staring out the window at the inspiring scene to glance around the interior of the plane. There was no conversation. Oblivious to the majestic vista, the commuters were all absorbed by their newspapers, work documents, or laptops. Her eyes wandered to the senator seated in her row on the aisle one seat away. Like the other passengers, he was reading. His bulky hands gripped the stack of memoranda concerning the following day's agenda he'd snatched from Dawn Shackelton as he and Carol had bolted from the office in hopes of catching the three-thirty shuttle flight. They'd made it with seconds to spare.

At Ashley's insistence, Carol had phoned one of the cardinal's personal secretaries that morning to set up an impromptu meeting that afternoon. She was instructed to say it concerned an urgent matter but would only take fifteen minutes at most. Father Maloney had said he'd see what he could do since the cardinal's schedule was full, but he'd called back within the hour to say that the cardinal could see the senator sometime between five-thirty and six-thirty, following a formal reception for a visiting Italian cardinal and before a dinner with the mayor. Carol had said they'd be there.

Under the circumstances of having to run for the plane and worrying about the potential New York City traffic, Carol couldn't help but be impressed with Ashley's apparent equanimity. Of course, he had her to do his worrying for him, but had their roles been reversed and she had been facing what he was potentially facing, she would have been inordinately anxious, to the point of finding concentration difficult. But certainly not Ashley! Despite a slight tremor the individual pages of his memoranda were being rapidly scanned and flipped back in swift succession, suggesting his legendary reading speed had not suffered due to his illness or to the events of the previous twenty-four hours.

Carol cleared her throat. "Senator, the more I think about this current affair, the more surprised I am that you haven't asked my opinion. You ask my opinion about most everything else."

Ashley turned his head and gazed at Carol over the tops of his heavy-rimmed glasses that had slid down to perch on the very tip of his nose. His broad forehead was wrinkled condescendingly. "Carol, dearest," he began. "You do not have to tell me your opinion. As I indicated last evening, I am already well aware of it."

"Then I hope you are aware that I think you will be taking too big a risk with this supposed treatment."

"I appreciate your solicitousness, no matter what the motivation, but my mind is firm."

"You're allowing yourself to be experimented upon. You have no idea what the outcome will be."

"It may be true that I do not know the outcome for sure, but it is also true that if I were to do nothing in the face of my progressive, otherwise incurable neurological degenerative disease, I know exactly what the outcome would be. My daddy preached that the Good Lord helps those who help themselves. All my life I have been a fighter, and I am surely not going to stop now. I am not going out with a whimper. I will be kicking and screaming like a bagged polecat."

"What if the cardinal were to tell you what you are planning is inadvisable?"

"Such a response is hardly likely, since I

have no intention in the slightest of informing the cardinal of my intentions."

"Then why are we coming here?" Carol said in a tone that was close to anger. "I was hoping His Eminence could appeal to your better judgment during your discussions."

"We are not making this pilgrimage to the seat of North American Catholic continental power for counsel but rather merely to arrange for a piece of the Shroud of Turin as a hopeful hedge against the uncertainties of my therapy."

"But how do you intend to get access to the shroud without explaining why?"

Ashley held up one of his hands like an orator quieting an unruly crowd. "Enough, my dear Carol, lest your presence be more of a burden than assistance." He shifted his attention back to his papers as the plane headed for landing.

A flush of heat spread across Carol's face at being summarily dismissed. Such degrading treatment was becoming all too common, as was her associated irritation. Concerned her feelings would be apparent, she faced back out the window.

As the plane moved toward the gate, Carol kept her attention directed outside the air-

craft. Up close, New York was no longer jewellike, thanks to a smattering of litter and
scattered piles of dirty snow lining the taxi-
way. As befitted the dark, bleak scene, she
fretted about her conflicting emotions and
her guilt concerning Ashley's plan to deal
with his infirmity. On the one hand, she was
legitimately fearful of its experimental nature,
while on the other hand, she thought the
therapy might work. Although her initial reaction to Ashley's diagnosis had been appropriate sympathy, over the course of the year
she'd come to see it also as her opportunity.
Now the fear of a bad outcome competed
equally with the fear of a good one, even
though she had trouble admitting it to herself. In some sense, she felt like a Brutus to
Ashley's Caesar.

The transition from the plane to the limo,
which Carol had arranged, was effortless.
But forty-five minutes later, they were
bogged down in a sea of cars on the FDR
Drive, whose flow of traffic had come to a
halt since they'd passed overhead in the
plane.

Aggravated at the delay, Ashley tossed his
pages that he'd been studying aside and
switched off the reading light. The sedan's in-

terior reverted to darkness. "We are going to miss our window of opportunity," he growled in a voice devoid of accent.

"I'm sorry," Carol offered, as if it were her fault.

Miraculously, after five minutes at a dead stop and a number of expletives from Ashley, the traffic began to move once again. "Thank the Good Lord for small favors," Ashley intoned.

By exiting at Ninety-sixth Street, the driver skillfully used a back route to head downtown and was able to deposit the senator and his aide at the archbishop's residence on the corner of Madison and Fiftieth Street four minutes before the scheduled meeting interval. The driver was instructed to circle the block, as they planned to be on their way back to the airport within the hour.

Carol had never been to the residence. She eyed the nonimposing three-story, graystone, slate-shingled house that huddled in the shadow of the city's skyscrapers. It rose up from the sidewalk's edge without a strip of grass to soften its severity. A few prosaic window air conditioners blemished its façade, as did heavy iron bars on the ground floor. The bars gave the building the appearance of a small jail rather than a residence. A glimpse of Belgian lace behind one of the windows was the sole softening touch.

Ashley mounted the stone steps and gave the polished brass bell a pull. They didn't have to wait long. The heavy door was opened by a tall, gaunt priest with a strikingly Roman nose and red hair cropped short. He was dressed in a priestly black suit with a white clerical collar.

"Good afternoon, Senator."

"And to you as well, Father Maloney," Ashley said while entering. "I hope our timing is opportune."

"Most decidedly," Father Maloney answered. "I am to deposit you and your aide in His Eminence's private study. He will be joining you momentarily."

The study was a spartanly furnished room on the first floor. The decoration was a formal framed photo of Pope John Paul II and a small statue of the Holy Mother carved in pure white Carrara marble. The hardwood floor was without carpet, and Carol's shoes clicked loudly against the varnished surface. Father Maloney silently withdrew and closed the door behind him.

"Rather austere," Carol remarked. The

only furniture was a small, aged leather couch, a matching leather chair, a prie-dieu, and a small desk with a straight-backed wooden chair.

"The cardinal would like his visitors to believe he is not interested in the material world," Ashley said, as he lowered himself into the cracked leather chair. "But I know better."

Carol sat stiffly on the edge of the couch with her legs tucked to the side. Ashley sat back as if he were visiting a relative. He crossed his legs to reveal a black sock and a patch of pasty white calf.

A moment later, the door reopened and in walked the Most Reverend James Cardinal O'Rourke followed by Father Maloney, who closed the door behind them. The cardinal was dressed in full regalia. Over black pants and white neckband shirt, he wore a black cassock enhanced with cardinal red piping and buttons. Over the cassock was an open, scarlet cape. Cinched around his waist was a broad scarlet sash. On his head was a cardinal-red zucchetto skullcap. Around his neck hung a bejeweled silver cross.

Carol and Ashley rose to their feet. Carol was taken by the spectacle of the cardinal's

sumptuous attire, accentuated by the harsh-
ness of the room. But once standing, she realized the powerful prelate was shorter than
her own five-foot-six, and next to Ashley,
who was by no means tall, he appeared decidedly short and plump. Despite his regal
trappings, his benignly smiling face suggested a humble priest with soft, blemish-
free turgid skin, shiny red cheeks, and
rounded pleasant features. His sharp eyes,
however, told a different story and one more
consistent with what Carol knew of the powerful prelate. They reflected a formidable and
canny intelligence.

"Senator," the cardinal said, in a voice that
matched his projected gentle demeanor. He
extended his hand with a limp wrist.

"Your Eminence," Ashley said, marshaling
his most cordial Southern accent. He gave
the cardinal's hand more of a squeeze than a
shake, purposefully avoiding kissing the
prelate's ring. "Such a pleasure indeed.
Knowing full well the press of your engage-
ments, I am so very appreciative of your finding time to meet with this country boy on
such short notice."

"Oh, hush, Senator," the cardinal scoffed.

"It is a treat, as always, to see you. Please sit down."

Ashley reclaimed his seat and assumed his previous posture.

Carol flushed anew. Being ignored was as embarrassing as being dismissed. She'd fully expected to be introduced, especially when the cardinal's eyes darted across her face accompanied by a slight, questioning lift to his eyebrows. She sank back to a sitting position as the cardinal carried over the rough-hewn chair from the small desk. Father Maloney stood silently by the door.

"In deference to our schedules," Ashley began, "I do believe I should come right to the point."

Feeling strangely invisible, Carol eyed the two men seated beside her. All at once, she recognized their similarities of character, despite their differences in appearance and beyond their hardworking, demanding natures. Both found blurring the lines between church and state to be to their respective advantage; both were adept at flattery and cultivating personal relationships with whom they could trade favors in their respective arenas; both hid personalities that were tough, calculating, and iron-willed behind their outward personas (the humble priest for the cardinal and the cordial, ingenuous country boy for the senator); and both guarded their authority zealously and were infatuated with the exercise of power.

"It is always best to be direct," James said. He sat upright with his pudgy hands cupping his zucchetto, which he had removed from his mostly bald head.

Carol had the image of two fencing combatants warily circling.

"It has distressed me to no end to see the Catholic Church so beleaguered," Ashley continued. "This current sex scandal has taken a toll, particularly with division in her own ranks and an ailing, aged leader in Rome. I have lain awake at night wrestling with a way I might be of service."

Carol had to keep from rolling her eyes. She knew all too well the senator's real feelings about the Catholic Church. As a Congregationalist and fundamentalist, he had little regard for any hierarchical religion, and in his mind the Catholic Church was the most hierarchical.

"I appreciate your empathy," James said, "and I have had similar distress about the

U.S. Congress following the tragedy of September eleventh. I too have struggled with how best I could help."

"Your moral leadership is a constant aid," Ashley said.

"I would like to do more," James said.

"My concern for the church is that a relatively few priests with arrested psychosexual development have been able to put the entire philanthropic organization in financial jeopardy. What I would sincerely like to propose for a small favor in return is to introduce legislation to limit tort liability for recognized charities, of which the Catholic Church is a shining example."

For a few minutes, silence reigned in the room. For the first time, Carol became aware of the ticking of a small clock on the desk as well as the muted sounds of the traffic on Madison Avenue. She watched the cardinal's face. His expression did not change.

"Such legislation would be a great help in this current crisis," James said finally.

"As egregious as each individual episode of sexual abuse is for the victim, we should not victimize all those souls dependent on the church for their health, educational, and spiritual needs. As my mama used to say:

We should not throw out the baby with the dirty bathwater."

"What is the chance of such legislation passing?"

"With my full backing, which I certainly would give it, I would estimate it would have a better than even chance. As for the President, I think he would be happy to sign it into law. He is a man of great faith, with a strong belief in the need for religious charities."

"I'm sure the Holy Father would be grateful for your support."

"I am a servant of the people," Ashley said. "All races and all religions."

"You mentioned a small favor," James said. "Is this something I should know about now?"

"Oh, it is a small thing," Ashley said. "Something more for my mama's memory. My mama was Catholic. Did I ever mention that?"

"I don't think you have," James said.

Carol was again reminded of the image of two fencers parrying and riposting.

"Catholic as the day is long," Ashley said. "She was from the old country just outside Dublin and a very religious woman indeed."

"I assume from your syntax she has gone to her Maker."

"Unfortunately, yes," Ashley said. He hesitated for a moment, as if choked up. "Quite a few years ago, bless her soul, when I was just knee-high to a grasshopper."

This was a story Carol knew. One night after a lengthy session of the Senate, she'd gone out to a Capitol Hill bar with the senator. After a number of bourbons, the senator had become particularly loquacious and had told the sad story of his mother. She had died when Ashley was nine as the consequence of a septic backroom abortion that she'd had rather than a tenth child. The irony was that she feared she'd die during childbirth because of complications during the birth of her ninth child. Ashley's fire-and-brimstone father had been outraged and had told the family and his congregation that the woman had been damned to hell for all eternity.

"Would you want me to say a Mass for her soul?" James questioned.

"That would be very generous," Ashley said, "but it is not quite what I had in mind. To this day, I can remember sitting on her knee and listening to all the wonderful things she told me about the Catholic Church. And I particularly remember what she told me about the miraculous Shroud of Turin, which she held dear to her heart."

For the first time, the cardinal's expression changed. It was a subtle change, but Carol could tell it was definitely of surprise.

"The shroud is considered a most sacred relic," James said.

"I would not assume anything less," Ashley responded.

"The Holy Father himself has said off the record that he believes it to be the shroud of Jesus Christ."

"I am glad to hear my mother's beliefs being so confirmed," Ashley said. "In full recognition of my mother's pivotal role, I have been a minor student of the shroud all these years. I happen to know that a number of samples were taken from it, some used for testing and some not. I also happen to know that those samples not used were called back by the church after the results of the carbon dating. What I would like to have is a tiny"—Ashley pinched his thumb and forefinger together for emphasis—"tiny sample of blood-soaked fiber that had been called back."

The cardinal leaned back in his chair. He briefly exchanged glances with Father Maloney. "This is a very unusual request," he said. "However, the church has been very clear on this subject. There is to be no more scientific testing of the shroud, other than to insure its conservancy."

"I have no interest in testing the shroud," Ashley stated categorically.

"Then why do you want this tiny, tiny sample?"

"For my mama," Ashley said simply. "I would sincerely like to place it within the urn that holds her ashes the next time I am back home, so her remains could mingle with the Heavenly Host. Her urn stands next to my daddy's on the mantel in the old homestead."

Carol had to suppress a scornful laugh at how easily and convincingly the senator could lie. On the same night the senator had told her the story of his poor mother, he said that his father would not allow her to be buried in his church's cemetery, necessitating her burial in the town's potter's field.

"I believe," Ashley added, "that if she could

have one wish, this would be it, to help her immortal soul gain entrance into everlasting paradise."

James looked up at Father Maloney. "I don't know anything about these recalled samples. Do you?"

"No, Your Eminence," Father Maloney said. "But I could find out. Archbishop Manfredi, whom you know well, has been installed in Turin. And Monsignor Garibaldi, who I know well, is there also."

The cardinal looked back at Ashley. "You would be happy with just a few fibers?"

"That is all I ask," Ashley said. "Although I should add that I would like them just as soon as possible, since I will be planning a trip home in the very near future."

"If this tiny sample of fiber were to be made available, how would we get them to you?"

"I would immediately dispatch an agent to Turin," Ashley said. "It is not the type of thing I would trust to the mail or any commercial carrier."

"We'll see what we can do," James said, as he got to his feet. "And I assume you will introduce the suggested legislation soon."

Ashley got to his feet as well. "Monday

morning, Your Eminence, provided I hear from you by then."

Stairs were a distinct effort for the cardinal, and he took them slowly, pausing frequently to catch his breath. The main problem with wearing his formal regalia was that he felt restricted with so many layers and frequently became overheated, especially when climbing the stairs to his private quarters. Father Maloney was right behind him, and when the cardinal stopped, he stopped as well.

Holding on to the banister with one hand, the cardinal leaned his other arm on his raised knee. He exhaled through pale, puffed-up cheeks and ran a hand across his brow. There was an elevator, but he avoided it as a kind of penance.

"Is there something I can get for you, Your Eminence?" Father Maloney questioned. "I could bring it down to spare your climbing these steep steps. It has been a strenuous afternoon."

"Thank you, Michael," James said. "But I must freshen up if I am to last through the dinner with the mayor and our visiting cardinal."

"When do you want me to contact Turin?"

Father Maloney asked, to take advantage of the moment.

"Tonight after midnight," James said between breaths. "That will be six in the morning their time, and you should be able to catch them before Mass."

"It is a surprising request if I may say so, Your Eminence."

"Indeed! Surprising and curious! If the senator's information about the samples is correct, which I would be surprised if it weren't, knowing what I do of the man, it should be an easy request to fulfill since it obviates the need to touch the shroud itself. But in your conversations with Turin, be sure to emphasize that the affair is to be completely sub rosa. There should be strict confidentiality and absolutely no documentation whatsoever. Am I clear?"

"Perfectly clear," Michael said. "Are you questioning the senator's purported use of the samples, Your Eminence?"

"That is my only concern," James said, with a final deep breath. He recommended slowly mounting the stairs. "The senator is a master of bargaining. I am certain he would not want the sample to do any unauthorized testing, but he may be exchanging favors with someone who is interested in testing. The Holy Father has decreed ex cathedra that the shroud should not be subjected to any more scientific indignity, and I am in full agreement. But beyond that, I believe it is a noble cause to exchange a few of the sacred fibers for a chance to ensure the economic viability of the church. Do you agree, Father?"

"Most assuredly."

They reached the top of the stairs, and the cardinal paused again to catch his breath.

"Do you feel confident the senator will do what he proposes concerning the legislation, Your Eminence?"

"Absolutely," James said without hesitation. "The senator always fulfills his side of a bargain. As an example, he has been instrumental in the school voucher program that is going to save our parochial schools. In exchange, I saw that he got the Catholic vote in his last reelection. It was, as they say, a clear win-win situation. But this current exchange is not quite so clear. Consequently, if it is to be arranged, as added insurance, I want you to go to Turin to see who takes possession of the sample and then follow the sample to see to whom it is delivered. In that way, we will be able to anticipate any potentially negative fallout."

"Your Eminence! I cannot think of a more pleasant assignment."

"Father Maloney!" the cardinal snapped. "This is a serious commission and not one meant for your enjoyment. I expect absolute discretion and commitment."

"Of course, Your Eminence! I did not mean to imply anything less."

eight

7:25 P.M., Friday, February 22, 2002

"Oh, jeez!" Stephanie mumbled out loud after glancing at her watch. It was almost seven-thirty! It was amazing to her how time could fly when she was absorbed, and she'd been absorbed all afternoon. First, she'd been captivated at the bookstore with the books about the Shroud of Turin, and for the last hour, she'd been mesmerized by what she was learning sitting in front of the computer.

She had returned to the office just before six to find it empty. Assuming Daniel had gone home, she had sat down at her makeshift desk in the lab, and with the help of the Internet and a few newspapers' archives, she had involved herself in finding out what had happened to the Wingate Clinic a little less than a year previously. It had been engrossing if disturbing reading.

Stephanie slid her laptop into its soft case, grabbed the plastic bag from the bookstore, and pulled on her coat. At the lab door she killed the lights, which then required her blindly to make her way across the already darkened reception area. Once outside on the street, she turned toward Kendall Square. She walked with her head bent over against the biting wind. Typical of New England weather, there had been a marked change from earlier in the afternoon. With the wind now coming from the north instead of the west, the temperature had plummeted into the mid-twenties from the relatively balmy upper forties. Along with the north wind came snow flurries that had coated the city as if it had been dusted with confectioners' sugar.

At Kendall Square, Stephanie caught the Red Line subway out to Harvard Square, familiar territory from her university years. As usual and despite the weather, the square was alive with students and the rabble that gravitates to such an environment. Even a few street musicians had braved the harsh weather. With blue fingers, they serenaded the passersby. Stephanie felt sorry enough for them to leave a train of dollar bills in their upturned hats as she passed from Harvard Square through Eliot Square.

The lights and bustle of the honky-tonk quickly dropped behind as Stephanie trudged out Brattle Street. She passed through a section of Radcliff College as well as the celebrated Longfellow House. But she was unmoved by her surroundings. Instead, she mused about what she had learned over the previous three and a half hours and was eager to share it with Daniel. She was also interested to hear what he had found out.

It was after eight by the time she mounted the front steps of Daniel's condominium building. He occupied the top floor unit of a converted three-story late-Victorian house complete with all the trimmings, including elaborate bargeboard. He had bought the condo in 1985 when he had returned to academia at Harvard. It had been a big year for Daniel. Not only had he left his job at Merck pharmaceuticals; he had also left his wife of five years. He had explained to Stephanie that he had felt stifled by both. His wife had been a nurse whom he met while doing his combined medical residency and Ph.D., a feat Stephanie equated to running back-to-back marathons. He had told Stephanie that his ex-wife was a plodder and that being married to her had made him feel like Sisyphus, constantly rolling a rock up a hill. He had also said that she had been too nice and had expected him to be the same. Stephanie had not known what to make of either explanation, but she did not press the issue. She was thankful they had not had any children, which apparently the former wife had desperately wanted.

"I'm home!" Stephanie shouted, after pressing the apartment's door closed with her rear end. Balancing her laptop bag and book bag on the tiny foyer table, Stephanie got out of her coat and opened the closet door to hang it up.

"Is anybody here?" she yelled, although her voice was muffled from being directed into the closet. When she was finished with her coat, she turned around. She started to yell again, but Daniel's form filling the entrance to the hall startled her. He was no more than several feet away. The noise that issued from her lips was more of a peep than anything else.

"Where the hell have you been?" Daniel demanded. "Do you know what time it is?"

"It's around eight," Stephanie managed. She pressed a hand to her chest. "Don't sneak up on me like that!"

"Why didn't you phone? I was about to call the police."

"Oh, come on! You know me and bookstores. I went to more than one and got caught up. In both places, I ended up sprawled out in the aisle, reading and trying to decide what to buy. Then, when I got back to the office, I wanted to take advantage of the broadband."

"How come you didn't have your cell phone on? I've tried to call you a dozen times."

"Because I was in a bookstore and when I got to the office, it didn't cross my mind. Hey! I'm sorry if you were concerned about me, okay? But now I'm home, safe and sound. What did you make for dinner?"

"Very funny," Daniel growled.

"Ease up!" Stephanie said, giving Daniel's

sleeve a playful tug. "I appreciate your concern, really I do, but I'm starved and you must be too. How about we head back to the square for dinner. Why don't you call the Rialto while I jump in the shower. It's Friday night, but by the time we get there, we shouldn't have a problem."

"All right," Daniel said reluctantly, as if he were agreeing to some major undertaking.

It wasn't until nine-twenty before they walked into the Rialto restaurant, and just as Stephanie predicted, there was a table ready and waiting. Since they were both famished, they immediately studied the menu and quickly ordered. At their request, the waiter promptly brought out their wine and sparkling water to slake their thirst and bread to take the edge off their hunger.

"All right," Stephanie said, sitting back in her chair. "Who wants to talk first?"

"It might as well be me," Daniel said. "Because I don't have a lot to report, but what I do have is encouraging. I telephoned the Wingate Clinic, which sounds to me to be well equipped for our needs, and they will let us use their facilities. In fact, I've already agreed on the price: forty thousand."

"Whoa!" Stephanie remarked.

"Yeah, I know: It's a bit high, but I was reluctant to bargain. Initially, after I informed them they would not be able to take advantage of our use of their facilities for promotional purposes, I was afraid all bets were off. Luckily, they came back around."

"Well, it's not our money, and we certainly have enough. What about the oocyte issue?"

"That's the best part. I was told they can supply us with human oocytes without any problem whatsoever."

"When?"

"They claim whenever we want."

"My goodness," Stephanie said. "That certainly begs one's curiosity."

"Let's not look a gift horse in the mouth."

"What about a neurosurgeon?"

"No problem there either. There are several on the island beating the bushes for work. The local hospital even has stereotaxic equipment."

"That is encouraging."

"I thought so."

"My news is good and bad. What do you want to hear first?"

"How bad is bad?"

"Everything is relative. It's not bad enough

to preclude what we are planning, but it is bad enough for us to be wary."

"Let's hear the bad to get it over with."

"The principals at the Wingate Clinic are worse than I remembered. By the way, with whom did you speak when you called the clinic?"

"Two of the principals: Spencer Wingate himself and his majordomo, Paul Saunders. And I must tell you, they are a couple of clowns. Imagine this: They publish their own supposed scientific journal, and the process of writing and editing only involves themselves!"

"You mean there's no editorial review board?"

"That's my impression."

"That's laughable, unless someone subscribes to the journal and takes whatever's in the journal as gospel."

"My thoughts exactly."

"Well, they are a lot worse than clowns," Stephanie said. "And worse than just perpetrators of unethical reproductive cloning experiments. I used newspaper archives, particularly *The Boston Globe*'s, to read up on what happened last May when the clinic was suddenly moved offshore to the Bahamas. Remember I mentioned last night in Washington that they had been implicated in the disappearance of a couple of Harvard coeds? Well, it was a lot more than mere implication, according to a couple of extremely credible whistle-blowers who happen to have been Harvard Ph.D. candidates. They had managed to get jobs at the clinic to find out the fate of eggs they had donated. During their sleuthing, they found out a lot more than they had bargained for. At a grand jury hearing, they claimed to have seen the missing women's ovaries in what they called the clinic's 'egg recovery room.'"

"Good God!" Daniel said. "Why weren't Wingate people indicted, with that kind of testimony?"

"Lack of evidence and a high-priced legal defense team! Apparently, the principals had a preplanned evacuation protocol that included the immediate destruction of the clinic and its contents, particularly its research facilities. Everything went up in a maelstrom of flames while the principals left in a helicopter. So an indictment wasn't handed down. The final irony is that without an indictment, they were able to collect on their insurance for the fire."

"So what is your take on all this?"

"Simply that these people are definitely not nice, and we should limit our interaction with them. And after what I read, I'd like to know the origin of the eggs they will be supplying us with, just to be sure we're not supporting something unconscionable."

"I don't think that is a good idea. We've already decided that taking the ethical high road is a luxury we can't afford if we are going to save CURE and HTSR. Questioning them at this juncture might cause problems, and I don't want to jeopardize using their facilities. As I mentioned, they were not overly enthusiastic after I nixed any use of our involvement for promotional purposes."

Stephanie played with her napkin as she thought over what Daniel had said. She didn't like dealing with the Wingate Clinic at all, but it was true that she and Daniel didn't have a lot of choice with the time constraints they were under. It was also true that they were already violating ethics by agreeing to treat Butler.

"Well, what do you say?" Daniel asked. "Can you live with this?"

"I suppose," Stephanie said without enthusiasm. "We'll do the procedure and scram."

"That's the plan," Daniel said. "Now let's move on! What's your good stuff?"

"The good stuff involves the Shroud of Turin."

"I'm listening."

"This afternoon, before I went to the bookstore, I told you that the shroud's story was more interesting than I had imagined. Well, that was the understatement of the year."

"How so?"

"My current thinking is that Butler might not be so crazy after all, because the shroud might very well be real. This is a surprising turnaround, since you know how skeptical I am."

Daniel nodded. "Almost as much as I."

Stephanie eyed her lover after his last comment in hopes that there would be some evidence of humor like a wry smile, but there wasn't. She felt a twinge of irritation that Daniel had to be a little more, no matter what the issue. She took a sip of her wine to get her mind back to the subject at hand. "Anyway," she continued, "I started reading the material at the bookstore, and I had trouble stopping. I mean, I can't wait to get back to the book I bought. It was written by an Oxford scholar named Ian Wilson. Hopefully, tomorrow I'll be getting more books, thanks to the Internet."

Stephanie was interrupted by the arrival of their meal. She and Daniel impatiently watched as the waiter served them. Daniel held off speaking until the waiter had withdrawn. "Okay, you have piqued my curiosity. Let's hear the basis of this surprising epiphany."

"I started my reading with the comfortable knowledge the shroud had been carbon-dated by three independent labs to the thirteenth century, the same century in which it had suddenly appeared historically. Knowing the precision of carbon-dating technology, I did not expect my belief that it was a forgery to be challenged. But it was, and it was challenged almost immediately. The reason was simple. If the shroud had been made when the carbon dating suggested, the forger would have had to be shockingly ingenious several quanta above Leonardo da Vinci."

"You're going to have to explain," Daniel said between mouthfuls. Stephanie had paused to start her own dinner.

"Let's start with some subtle reasons the forger would have to have been superhuman for his time and then move on to more compelling ones. First off, the forger would have had to have knowledge of foreshortening in art, which had yet to be discovered. The image of the man on the shroud had his legs flexed and his head bent forward, probably in rigor mortis."

"I'll admit that's not terribly compelling," Daniel remarked.

"How about this one: The forger would have had to know the true method of crucifixion used by the Romans in ancient times. This was in contrast to all contemporary thirteenth-century depictions of the crucifixion, of which there were literally hundreds of thousands. In reality, the condemned individual's wrists were nailed to the crossbeam, not his palms, which would not have been able to hold his weight. Also, the crown of thorns was not a ringlet, but rather like a skullcap."

Daniel nodded a few times in thought.

"Try this one: The bloodstains block the image on the cloth, meaning this clever artist started with bloodstains and then did the image, which is backward from the way all artists would work. The image would be done first, or at least the outline. Then the details like blood would be added to be certain they would be in the correct locations."

"That's interesting, but I'd have to put that one in the category with the foreshortening."

"Then let's move on," Stephanie said. "In 1979, when the shroud was subjected to five days of scientific scrutiny by teams of scientists from the U.S., Italy, and Switzerland, it was unequivocally determined that the shroud's image was not painted. There were no brushstrokes, there was an infinite gradation of density, and the image was a surface phenomenon only with no imbibition, meaning no fluid of any kind was involved. The only explanation they came up with of the origin of the image was some kind of oxidative process of the surface of the linen fibers, as if they were exposed in the presence of oxygen to a sudden flash of intense light or other strong electromagnetic radiation. Obviously, this was vague and purely speculative."

"All right," Daniel said. "I must admit you are getting into the downright compelling arena."

"There's more," Stephanie said. "Some of the U.S. scientists examining the shroud in

1979 were from NASA, and they subjected the shroud to analysis by the most sophisticated technologies available, including a piece of equipment known as a VP-8 Image Analyzer. This was an analog device that had been developed to convert specially recorded digital images of the surface of the moon and Mars into three-dimensional pictures. To everyone's surprise, the image on the shroud contains this kind of information, meaning the density of the shroud's image at any given location is directly proportional to the distance it was from the crucified individual it had covered. All in all, it would have had to have been one hell of a forger if he anticipated all this back in the thirteenth century."

"My word!" Daniel voiced, as he shook his head in amazement.

"Let me add one other thing," Stephanie said. "Biologists specializing in pollen have determined that the shroud contains pollen that only comes from Israel and Turkey, meaning the supposed forger would have had to be resourceful as well as clever."

"How could the results of the carbon dating have been so wrong?"

"An interesting question," Stephanie said,

while taking another bite of her dinner. She chewed quickly. "No one knows for sure. There have been suggestions that ancient linen tends to support the continued growth of bacteria that leave behind a transparent, varnish-like biofilm that would distort the results. Apparently, there has been a similar problem with carbon-dating some linen on Egyptian mummies, whose antiquity is known rather precisely by other means.

"Another idea suggested by a Russian scientist is that the fire that scorched the shroud in the sixteenth century could have skewed the results, although it's hard for me to understand how it could have skewed it more than a thousand years."

"What about the historical aspect?" Daniel asked. "If the shroud is real, how come its history only goes back to the thirteenth century, when it appeared in France?"

"That's another good question," Stephanie said. "When I first started reading the shroud material, I gravitated to the scientific aspects, and I've just started with the historical. Ian Wilson has cleverly related the shroud to another known and highly revered Byzantine relic called the Edessa Cloth, which had been in Constantinople for over three hundred years. Interestingly enough, this cloth disappeared when the city was sacked by crusaders in 1204."

"Is there any documentary evidence that the shroud and the Edessa Cloth are one and the same?"

"That's right where I stopped reading," Stephanie said. "But it seems likely there is such evidence. Wilson cites a French eyewitness to the Byzantine relic prior to its disappearance, who described it in his memoirs as a burial shroud with a mystical, full, double-body image of Jesus, which certainly sounds like the Shroud of Turin. If the two relics are the same, then history takes it back at least to the ninth century."

"I can certainly understand why all this has captured your interest," Daniel said. "It's fascinating. And getting back to the science, if the image wasn't painted, what are the current theories as to its origin?"

"That question is probably the single most intriguing. There really aren't any theories."

"Has the shroud been studied scientifically since the episode you mentioned in 1979?"

"A lot," Stephanie said.

"And there are no current theories?"

"None that have stood up to further testing. Of course, there is still the vague idea of some kind of flash of strange radiation. . . . " Stephanie let her voice trail off as if to leave the idea hanging in the air.

"Wait a second!" Daniel said. "You're not about to spring some divine or supernatural nonsense on me, are you?"

Stephanie spread her hands palms-up, shrugged, and smiled all at the same time.

"Now I have the feeling you are toying with me," Daniel remarked with a chuckle.

"I'm giving you an opportunity to come up with a theory."

"Me?" Daniel questioned.

Stephanie nodded.

"I couldn't come up with a hypothesis without having actual access to all the data. I assume the examining scientists have used things like electron microscopy, spectroscopy, ultraviolet fluorescence, as well as appropriate chemical analysis."

"All of the above and more," Stephanie said. She sat back, with a provocative smile. "And still, there is no accepted theory about how the image was produced. It's a conundrum for sure. But come on! Be a sport! Can't you think of something with the details I've related?"

"You're the one who's done the reading," Daniel said. "I think you should come up with the suggestion."

"I have," Stephanie said.

"I'm wondering if I dare ask what it is."

"I find myself leaning in the direction of the divine. Here's my reasoning: If the shroud is the burial cloth of Jesus Christ, and if Jesus was resurrected, meaning he went from the material to the nonmaterial, presumably in an instant, then the shroud would have been subjected to the energy of dematerialization. It was the flash of energy that created the image."

"What the hell is the energy of dematerialization?" Daniel asked with exasperation.

"I'm not sure," Stephanie admitted with a smile. "But it stands there would be a release of energy with a dematerialization. Look at the energy released with rapid elemental decay. That creates an atom bomb."

"I suppose I don't have to remind you that you're employing very unscientific reasoning. You're using the shroud's image to posit dematerialization so you can use dematerialization to explain the shroud."

"It's unscientific, but it makes sense to me," Stephanie said with a laugh. "It also makes sense to Ian Wilson, who described the shroud's image as a snapshot of the Resurrection."

"Well, if nothing else, you've certainly convinced me to take a peek at the book you have."

"Not until I'm done!" Stephanie joked.

"What has this information about the shroud done to your reaction about using its bloodstains to treat Butler?"

"I've come around one hundred and eighty degrees," Stephanie admitted. "At this point, I'm all for it. I mean, why not enlist the potentially divine for all our sakes? And, as you said down in Washington, using the shroud's blood will add some challenge and excitement while creating the ultimate placebo."

Daniel lifted his hand, and he and Stephanie high-fived across the table.

"What about dessert?" Daniel questioned.

"Not for me. But if you have some, I'll have a decaf espresso."

Daniel shook his head. "I don't want dessert. Let's get home. I want to see if there are any emails from the venture capital people." Daniel motioned for the waiter to get the check.

"And I want to see if there are any messages from Butler. The other thing I learned about the shroud is that we're definitely going to need his help to get a sample. On our own, it would be impossible. The church has it sealed up under elaborate security within a space-age box in an atmosphere of argon. They also categorically stated there would be no more testing. After the carbon-dating fiasco, they are understandably gun-shy."

"Has there been any analysis of the blood?"

"Indeed there has," Stephanie said. "It was tested to be type AB, which was a lot more common in the ancient Near East than it is generally now."

"Any DNA work?"

"That too," Stephanie said. "Several specific gene fragments were isolated, including a beta globulin from chromosome eleven and even an amelogenin Y from chromosome Y."

"Well, there you go," Daniel said. "If we can get a sample, it will be a piece of cake pulling out the segments we need with our HTSR probes."

"Things better start happening quickly," Stephanie warned. "Otherwise, we're not going to have the cells in time for Butler's Senate recess."

"I'm well aware," Daniel said. He took his

credit card back from the waiter and signed the receipt. "If the shroud is going to be involved, we've got to go to Turin in the next few days. So Butler better get cracking! Once we have the sample, we can fly directly to Nassau from London on British Airways. I checked that out earlier this evening."

"We're not going to do the cellular work here at our lab?"

"Unfortunately, no. The eggs are down there, not up here, and I don't want to take the risk of shipping them, and I want them fresh. Hopefully, the Wingate lab is as well equipped as they claim, because we'll be doing everything there."

"That means we'll be leaving in a few days and be gone a month or more."

"You got it. Is that a problem?"

"I suppose not," Stephanie said. "It's not a bad time to spend a month in Nassau. Peter can keep things going in the lab. But I'll have to go home tomorrow or Sunday to see my mom. She's been under the weather, as you know."

"You'd better do it sooner rather than later," Daniel said. "If word comes through from Butler about the shroud sample, we're out of here."

nine

2:45 P.M., Saturday, February 23, 2002

Daniel sensed he was getting a vague idea of what it was like to have manic-depressive disorder as he hung up the phone from yet another disappointing conversation with the venture capital people in San Francisco. Just prior to the call, he felt on top of the world after outlining the schedule for the next month on a legal pad. With Stephanie now enthusiastically behind the plan to treat Butler, including using blood from the shroud, things were beginning to fall into place. That morning, between the two of them, they had

drawn up an encompassing release for Butler's signature and had emailed it to the senator. As per their instructions, it was to be
signed, witnessed by Carol Manning, and
faxed back.

When Stephanie had disappeared back
into the lab to check on Butler's fibroblast culture, Daniel had convinced himself that things
were going so smoothly that it was reasonable to call the moneymen in hopes of changing their minds about releasing the second
round of financing. But the call had not gone
well. The key person had ended the conversation by telling Daniel not to call back unless
he had proof in writing that HTSR would not
be banned. The banker had explained that in
light of recent events, word of mouth, particularly in the form of vague generalities, would
not be adequate. The banker had added that
unless such documentation was forthcoming
in the near future, the money allocated for
CURE would be transferred to another promising biotech firm whose intellectual property
was not in political jeopardy.

Daniel sagged in his chair with his hips
perched precariously on the edge, resting
his head on the chair's back. The idea of returning to stable-but-impecunious academia,

with its snail's-pace predictability, was sounding progressively appealing. He was beginning to loathe the precipitous ups and downs of trying to achieve the moneyed celebrity status he deserved. It was galling that movie stars only had to memorize a few lines and famous athletes only had to show mindless dexterity with a stick or a ball in order to command the lucre and attention showered on them. With his credentials and a brilliant discovery to his credit, it was ludicrous that he had to bear such travail and associated anxiety.

Stephanie's face poked around the corner. "Guess what?" she said brightly. "Things are going fantastic with Butler's fibroblast culture. Thanks to the atmosphere of five-percent CO_2 and air, a monolayer is already starting to form. The cells are going to be ready sooner than I anticipated."

"Wonderful," Daniel said in a depressed monotone.

"What's the problem now?" Stephanie asked. She came into the room and sat down. "You look like you're about to ooze off onto the floor. Why the long face?"

"Don't ask! It's the same old story about money, or at least the lack of it."

"I suppose that means you called the venture capitalists again."

"How very clairvoyant!" Daniel said sarcastically.

"Good grief! Why are you torturing yourself?"

"So now you think I'm doing this to myself."

"You are if you keep calling them. From what you said yesterday, their intentions were pretty clear."

"But the Butler plan is moving ahead. The situation is evolving."

Stephanie closed her eyes for a moment and took a breath. "Daniel," she began, trying to think how best to word what she was about to say without irritating him, "you can't expect other people to view the world as you do. You're a brilliant man, maybe too smart for your own good. Other people don't look at the world the way you do. I mean, they can't think the way you do."

"Are you being patronizing?" Daniel eyed his lover, scientific collaborator, and business partner. Lately, with the stress of recent events, it was more the latter than the former, and the business was not going well.

"Heavens, no!" Stephanie stated emphatically. Before Stephanie could continue, the phone rang. Its raucous sound in the otherwise silent office startled both of them.

Daniel reached for the phone but didn't pick it up. He glanced at Stephanie. "Are you expecting a call?"

Stephanie shook her head.

"Who could be calling here at the office on a Saturday?"

"Maybe it's for Peter," Stephanie suggested. "He's back in the lab."

Daniel lifted the receiver and used the long name of their business rather than the acronym. "Cellular Replacement Enterprises," he said officially.

"This is Dr. Spencer Wingate from the Wingate Clinic. I'm calling from Nassau for Dr. Daniel Lowell."

David motioned for Stephanie to go out in the reception area and pick up Vicky's extension. He then identified himself to Spencer.

"I certainly didn't expect to get you directly, Doctor," Spencer said.

"Our receptionist doesn't come in on Saturdays."

"My word!" Spencer remarked. He laughed. "I didn't realize it was the weekend. Since we've recently opened our new facility, we've all been working twenty-four-seven to iron out the wrinkles. Many pardons if I'm causing a disturbance."

"You are not disturbing us in the slightest," Daniel assured him. Daniel heard the faint click as Stephanie came on the line. "Is there some problem vis-à-vis our discussion yesterday?"

"Quite the contrary," Spencer said. "I was afraid there had been a change on your end. You said you would call last night or today at the latest."

"You're right, I did say that," Daniel responded. "I'm sorry. I've been waiting for word about the shroud to start the ball rolling. I apologize for not getting back to you."

"No apologies are necessary. Although I hadn't heard from you, I thought I'd call to let you know that I have already spoken with a neurosurgeon by the name of Dr. Rashid Nawaz who has an office in Nassau. He's a Pakistani surgeon trained in London who I've been assured is quite talented. He's even had some experience with fetal cell implants as a house officer, and he is eager to be of assistance. He's also agreed to arrange for the stereotaxic equipment to be brought from Princess Margaret Hospital."

"Did you mention the need for discretion?"

"Most certainly, and he is fine with it."

"Marvelous," Daniel responded. "Did you discuss his fee?"

"I did. It seems that his services will be somewhat more than I thought, perhaps due to the required discretion. He is asking for one thousand dollars."

Daniel momentarily debated with himself if he should make an effort to negotiate. A thousand dollars was significantly higher than the original estimate of two or three hundred. But it wasn't his money, and in the end he told Spencer to make the arrangements.

"Any further information about when we can expect you?" Spencer asked.

"Not at the moment," Daniel said. "I'll let you know as soon as I can."

"Perfect," Spencer said. "While I have you on the phone, there are a few details I'd like to discuss."

"By all means."

"First, we'd like to request half the agreed-upon fees up front," Spencer said. "I can fax you wiring instructions."

"You want the money immediately?"

"We'd like it as soon as we have a date for

your arrival. It will make it possible for us to begin scheduling appropriate staffing. Will that be a problem?"

"I suppose not," Daniel responded.

"Good," Spencer said. "Next, we'd like to arrange for instruction in HTSR for our staff, particularly for Dr. Paul Saunders, as well as the opportunity to discuss with you a future licensing agreement for HTSR and rates for the required probes and enzymes."

Daniel hesitated. His intuition was telling him he was being pushed for having agreed too quickly to the compensation the day before. He cleared his throat. "I will not have a problem with Dr. Saunders observing, but as for the licensing issue, I'm afraid I'm not at liberty to grant such requests. CURE is a corporation with a board of directors that would have to agree to any such arrangement, with full consideration of the stockholders. But as the current CEO, I can promise you we will visit the issue in the future, and your help in the current situation will be taken into consideration."

"Perhaps I was asking a bit much," Spencer admitted amiably. He chuckled. "But as the saying goes: There's no harm in trying."

Daniel rolled his eyes, lamenting the indignities he had to endure.

"One last thing," Spencer said. "We would like to know the name of the patient, so we can start the admission process and the patient record. We'd like to be prepared for his or her arrival."

"There is to be no record," Daniel said flatly. "Yesterday I made it clear this treatment is to be done under absolute secrecy."

"But we will have to identify the patient for lab tests and such," Spencer said.

"Call him Patient X or John Smith," Daniel said. "It doesn't make any difference. I anticipate his being in your facility for only twenty-four hours at most. We'll be with him the entire time, and we'll be doing all the lab tests."

"What if the Bahamian authorities question his admission?"

"Is that likely?"

"No, I suppose not. But if they do, I'm not sure what we would say."

"I'm trusting that with your experience dealing with the authorities during the clinic's construction, you can be creative. That's part of the reason we're paying you forty thousand dollars. Make sure they don't question."

"We'll need a bribe or two. Perhaps if you were to raise the price by five K, we could guarantee no problems with the authorities."

Daniel didn't respond immediately while he controlled his anger. He hated to be manipulated, especially by a clown of Wingate's caliber. "All right," he said at last, without camouflaging his irritation. "We'll be wiring twenty-two and a half thousand. However, I want your personal assurances that this operation will go smoothly from here on out, and there's to be no more demands."

"You have my assurance as the founder of the Wingate Clinic that we will make every effort to ensure your association with us meets your expectations and complete satisfaction."

"You'll be hearing from us shortly."

"We'll be here!"

The screaming jet engines made the walls of Spencer's office shudder as the Boeing intercontinental 767 passed over the Wingate Clinic at an altitude of less than five hundred feet in preparation for landing. With the building's heavy insulation, the vibration was more tactile than audible though strong enough to jiggle Spencer's array of framed diplomas. Spencer was already accustomed to the daily intermittent disturbance and paid no heed other than to absently right his diplomas on occasion.

"How did I do?" Spencer yelled through the open door.

Paul Saunders appeared in the doorway after having listened to Spencer's conversation with Daniel from his office next door. "Well, let's look on the bright side. You didn't find out the name of the patient, but you managed to eliminate close to half the world's rich and famous. We now know it is a man."

"Very funny," Spencer said. "We didn't expect him to give us the name on a silver platter. But I did get him to up the offer to forty-five thousand and agree to allow you to observe the cellular work. That's not bad."

"But you didn't press him on the favorable licensing issue. That could save us big bucks with our burgeoning stem cell therapy down the line."

"Yeah, well, he had a point. He's running a corporation."

"It might be a corporation, but it's a private company, and dollars to donuts, he's the major stockholder by a long shot."

"Well, we win some and lose some. Anyway, I didn't scare him off. Remember that was one of our worries—that if we pressed too hard, he'd go somewhere else."

"I've reconsidered that worry, provided he was telling us the truth about his tight time frame. We're probably the only place that can supply him overnight with a first-rate lab, a hospital setting, and human oocytes with no questions asked. But it doesn't matter. Our potential bonanza payoff is going to come from finding out the name of the patient. I'm convinced of it. And the sooner we find out, the better."

"I couldn't agree more, and to that end, I did find out Lowell was at his office for the day, which was the real purpose of the call."

"True! And I have to give you credit for that. As soon as you hung up, I called Kurt Hermann to let him know. He said he'd relay the information immediately to his compatriot who's positioned in Boston, waiting to break into Lowell's apartment."

"I hope this compatriot, as you've called him, is capable of finesse. If Lowell gets spooked—or, even worse, hurt—the whole thing might be off."

"I specifically relayed your fears about heavy-handedness to Kurt."

"And what did he say?"

"You know Kurt doesn't say much. But he understands."

"I hope you are right, because we could truly use a financial windfall. With what we've spent getting this place up and running, the well is just about dry, and besides our stem-cell work, there's very little infertility business on the immediate horizon."

Dr. Spencer Wingate sounds just like the sleaze I feared," Stephanie said. She'd come back into Daniel's office after listening in on the conversation. "He talks about bribery as if it were an everyday occurrence."

"Maybe it is in the Bahamas," Daniel said.

"I hope he's short, fat, and has a wart on his nose."

Daniel gave Stephanie a confused look.

"Maybe he's a chain-smoker and has bad breath."

"What on earth are you talking about?"

"If Spencer Wingate looks as bad as he sounds, maybe I won't lose complete faith in the medical profession. I know it is irrational, but I don't want him to look anything like my mental image of a physician. It scares me to think he's a practicing doctor. And that goes for his partners as well."

"Oh, come on, Stephanie! Don't be so naïve. The medical profession, like any profession, is far from perfect. There are good ones and bad ones, with the majority somewhere in between."

"I thought self-regulation was part of the definition of this profession. Anyway, the real issue is that I wish my intuition wasn't telling me that working with these people is a bad idea."

"For the last time," Daniel said with frustration, "we're not working with those clowns. God forbid! We're using their facilities and that's it. End of story."

"Let's hope it's that simple," Stephanie said.

Daniel returned Stephanie's gaze. They'd been together long enough for him to tell that she was not buying his simple assessment, and it irritated him that she wasn't being more supportive. The problem was, her misgivings called attention to his own, which he was actively trying to ignore. He wanted to believe the whole episode was going to go smoothly and soon be over, but Stephanie's negativity kept undermining his hopes.

The fax sprang to life out in the reception area.

"I'll see what it is," Stephanie said. She got up and went out of the room.

Daniel watched her go. It was a relief to escape her stare. People had a way of irritating him—even Stephanie, on occasion. He wondered if he'd be better off alone.

"It's the release from Butler already," Stephanie called out. "Signed and witnessed along with a note saying the hard copy is in the mail."

"Great!" Daniel yelled back. At least Butler's cooperation was encouraging.

"The cover sheet asks if we have checked our email this afternoon." Stephanie appeared at the door with a questioning expression. "I didn't check. Did you?"

Daniel shook his head and tilted forward, connecting to the Internet. At the new, special email account set up for Butler's treatment, there was a message from the senator. Stephanie came around Daniel's desk and looked over his shoulder as he opened it.

My dear doctors,
    I hope this note finds you busy with your preparations for my imminent treat-

ment. I too have been productively occupied, and I am happy to report that the custodians of the Shroud of Turin have been most helpful, thanks to the intercession by an influential colleague. You are to travel to Turin at your first opportunity. Upon arrival, you will call the Chancery of the Archdiocese of Turin to speak with Monsignor Mansoni. You will inform the monsignor that you are my representatives. At that point, my understanding is that the monsignor will arrange a meeting at an appropriate location to give you the sacred sample. Please understand that this is to be done with the utmost discretion and secrecy, so as not to jeopardize my esteemed colleague. Meanwhile, I remain your dear friend.

A.B.

Daniel took a moment to delete the message just as he and Stephanie had made a point of deleting the senator's other emails. It had been their collective decision that there was to be as little evidence as possible of the affair. When he was done, he looked up at her. "The senator is certainly doing his part."

Stephanie nodded. "I'm impressed. I'm also starting to get excited. The affair is definitely acquiring a touch of international intrigue."

"When can you be ready to leave? Alitalia has daily flights to Rome that depart in the evening with connections to Turin. Remember, you're going to have to pack for a month."

"Packing is not the problem," Stephanie said. "My two problems are my mom and Butler's tissue culture. I need to spend some time with my mom, as I mentioned. I also want to get Butler's tissue culture to a point where Peter can take over."

"How much time are you talking about with the culture?"

"Not long. As good as it looks this morning, probably by tomorrow morning I'll be satisfied. I just want to be sure a true monolayer is forming. Then Peter can maintain it, passage it, and cryopreserve it. My plan is for him to overnight an aliquot down to Nassau in a liquid-nitrogen container when we're ready for it. We'll keep the rest of the culture here in case we need it in the future."

"Let's not be pessimistic," Daniel said. "What about your mother?"

"Tomorrow I can see her for a few hours during the day. She's always in on Sundays, cooking."

"Then you could conceivably be ready to leave tomorrow night?"

"Sure, if I pack this evening."

"Then let's get back to the apartment ASAP. I'll make the necessary calls from there."

Stephanie walked back into the lab to get her laptop and her coat. After making sure Peter was planning to be in the lab the following morning so they could discuss Butler's culture, she returned to the reception area. She found Daniel impatiently holding the hallway door open for her.

"My, you are in a hurry!" Stephanie remarked. It was usual for Stephanie to have to wait for Daniel. Whenever they were going someplace, he always found one more thing to do.

"It's already almost four o'clock, and I don't want you to have an excuse for not being ready to leave tomorrow night. I remember how long it took you to pack to go to Washington for two nights, and this is for a month.

I'm sure it is going to take you longer than you think."

Stephanie smiled. It was true since, among other things, she needed to do some ironing. She also realized she'd want to hit the drugstore for some travel necessities. What she didn't expect was how fast Daniel drove once they were in the car. She hazarded a glance at the speedometer as they tore down Memorial Drive. They were going almost fifty in a thirty-mile-an-hour zone.

"Hey, slow down!" Stephanie managed. "You're driving like one of the taxi drivers you complain about."

"Sorry," Daniel said. He slowed down slightly.

"I promise I'll be ready, so there's no need to risk our lives." Stephanie glanced over at Daniel to see if he realized she was trying to be funny, but his determined expression didn't change.

"I'm eager to get this whole unfortunate affair over with now that I feel we're really starting," he said without taking his eyes from the road.

"I thought of something I should do," Stephanie said. "I'm going to set it up so that any future Butler emails also go to my cell phone inbox. That way, we'll know when a message comes in, and we'll be able to access it ASAP."

"Good idea," Daniel agreed.

They pulled up to the curb in front of Daniel's house. He turned off the engine and hopped out. He was halfway up the front walk by the time Stephanie got her laptop from the backseat. She shrugged. He could be such an absentminded professor when he became focused on a single thought. He could ignore her totally, as he was doing presently. But she wasn't about to take his behavior personally. She knew him too well.

Daniel took the stairs two at a time while deciding he'd first make the call to the airlines to book the flights and then get back in touch with the Wingate people. He thought that scheduling a single overnight stay in Turin would be appropriate. Then he reminded himself to get the money-wiring instructions from Spencer when he made the call to Nassau so he could get the money issue out of the way as well.

Daniel reached the third-floor landing and paused while he fiddled with his keys. It was at that moment that he noticed the apartment door was slightly ajar. For a split second, he tried to remember who had been the last one out that morning: he or Stephanie. Then he remembered it had been he, since he'd had to return for his wallet. He distinctly remembered locking the door, including the dead bolt.

The sound of the building's front door opening and closing drifted up the stairwell, along with Stephanie's footfalls on the creaky, aged stairs. Otherwise, the house was silent. The first-floor tenants were off to the Caribbean on vacation, while the second-floor tenant was never home during the day. He was a mathematician who haunted the MIT computer center and only came home to sleep.

Gingerly, Daniel pushed open the door to get a progressively larger view of his foyer. Now he could see down the hallway into the living room. With the sun nearing the distant southwestern horizon, the apartment was in deep shadow. All at once, he caught sight of a flashlight beam as it momentarily flickered across the living room wall. At the same time, he heard one of the drawers of his upright file click closed.

"Who the hell is in here?" Daniel shouted at the top of his lungs. He was outraged that

an intruder had gotten into his apartment,
but he was not foolhardy. Although the intruder had obviously entered through the
front door, Daniel was confident he'd cased
the apartment and knew of the back exit
from the study onto the fire escape. As
Daniel pulled out his cell phone to call 911,
he fully expected the burglar to flee by taking
this route.

   To Daniel's shock, the intruder immediately presented himself in Daniel's line of
sight and blinded him with his flashlight.
Daniel tried to block the beam with his hand.
He wasn't entirely successful, but it was
enough to see that the man was coming at
him with breathtaking speed. Before Daniel
could react, he was roughly shoved to the
side by a gloved hand hard enough to cause
him to literally bounce off the wall. His ears
rang from the concussion. Regaining his
equilibrium, Daniel caught sight of a large
man dressed in a tight-fitting black outfit, including a black ski mask, rapidly descend
the stairs on silent feet. After a shriek from
Stephanie, the front door to the building
burst open and banged shut.

   Daniel dashed to the banister and looked
down. On the landing below, Stephanie was

pressed up against the mathematician's locked door with her laptop clasped against her chest with both hands. Her face was white. "Are you okay?" he asked.

"Who the hell was that?" she demanded.

"A goddamn burglar," Daniel responded. He turned back to examine the door. Stephanie came up the final flight of stairs to look over his shoulder.

"At least he didn't break the door," Daniel said. "He must have had a key."

"Are you sure it was locked?"

"Absolutely! I specifically remember even locking the dead bolt."

"Who else has a key?"

"No one," Daniel said. "There's only two. That's all I had made when I bought the place and changed the locks."

"He must have picked the lock."

"If he did, then he was a professional. But why would a professional be breaking into my apartment? I don't own anything valuable."

"Oh, no!" Stephanie suddenly voiced. "I left all my jewelry on top of the bureau, including my grandmother's diamond watch." She pushed past Daniel and headed for the bedroom.

Daniel followed her down the hall. "That reminds me: I was stupid enough to leave all the cash I got from the ATM last night on the desk."

Daniel ducked into the study. To his surprise, the ATM money was exactly where he'd placed it in the center of the blotter. He picked it up, and as he did so he noticed that everything else on the desk had been moved. Daniel admitted he wasn't the neatest person in the world, but he was supremely well organized. There might be stacks of correspondence, bills, and scientific journals on his desk, but he knew their exact location, if not the order within each pile.

His eyes wandered over to his upright four-drawer file cabinet. Even the journal article reprints stacked on top and waiting to be filed had been moved. They hadn't been moved a lot, but their position had definitely been changed.

Stephanie appeared in the doorway. She sighed with relief. "We must have come home in the nick of time. Apparently, he hadn't yet had a chance to get into the bedroom. All my stuff was where I'd left it last night."

Daniel held up the stack of bills. "He didn't

even take the money, and he was in here for sure."

Stephanie laughed hollowly. "What kind of burglar was he?"

"I don't find this at all funny," Daniel said. He began opening individual drawers of both the desk and the file cabinet to check the appearance of their contents.

"I'm not suggesting I find it funny either," Stephanie said. "I'm trying to use humor to defuse my real feelings."

Daniel looked up. "What are you talking about?"

Stephanie shook her head and breathed out forcibly. She successfully fought back tears. She was trembling. "I'm upset. This kind of unexpected event really disturbs me. I feel violated that someone was in here, invading our privacy. It emphasizes the reality that we're always living on the edge, even when we don't know it."

"I'm disturbed too," Daniel said. "But not philosophically. I'm disturbed because there is something here I don't understand. It seems pretty clear to me that this intruder wasn't a run-of-the-mill burglar. He was looking for something specific, and I have no idea what it could be. That's troubling."

"You don't think we just came home before he had a chance to take anything?"

"He'd been here for a while, certainly long enough to take some valuables, if that was what he was after. He had time to go through the desk and maybe even the file cabinet."

"How can you tell?"

"I just know because of my own brand of compulsiveness. This man was a professional, and he was looking for something in particular."

"You mean like intellectual property perhaps associated with HTSR?"

"It's possible, but I doubt it. That's all covered with adequate patents. Besides, then the break-in would have been at the office, not here."

"Than what else?"

Daniel shrugged. "I don't know."

"Did you call the police?"

"I started to, but that was when he bolted out of here. Now I'm not sure we should."

"Why not?" Stephanie was surprised.

"What would they do? The man's obviously long gone. We don't seem to be missing anything, so there's no insurance issues, and besides, I'm not sure I want us to be asked a lot of questions about what we have been doing lately, if that were to come up. On top of that, we're leaving tomorrow night, and I don't want anything to mess that up."

"Wait a sec!" Stephanie said suddenly. "What if this episode has something to do with Butler?"

Daniel stared across his desk at Stephanie.

"How and why would it involve Butler?" Daniel asked.

Stephanie returned Daniel's gaze. The sound of the refrigerator compressor turning on in the kitchen broke the early evening silence. "I don't know," she said finally. "I was just thinking about his connections with the FBI, and the fact that he had had you investigated in some form or fashion. Maybe they haven't finished."

Daniel nodded as he considered Stephanie's idea, realizing it couldn't be dismissed out of hand, despite its outlandishness. After all, the clandestine nighttime meeting with Butler two nights previously had been equally outlandish.

"Let's try to forget this incident for the moment," Daniel said. "We've got a lot to do to get ready. Let's start!"

"Okay," Stephanie said, marshaling her

fortitude. "Maybe concentrating on packing will get me to relax. But first I think we should call Peter in the event this character is planning to break into the office as well."

"Good idea," Daniel said. "But we're not going to tell him about Butler. I mean, you haven't told him, have you?"

"No. I haven't told him a thing."

"Good!" Daniel said, as he picked up the phone.

ten

11:45 A.M., Sunday, February 24, 2002

As accustomed as Stephanie was to mercurial New England weather, she was still surprised at the balmy, beautiful day Sunday turned out to be. Although the winter sunlight was pale, the air was warm and the birds were loud and omnipresent as if spring were just around the corner. It was a far cry from her frigid Friday night walk home from Harvard Square with a dusting of snow on the ground.

Stephanie had parked Daniel's car in the city garage at Government Center and walked east into the North End, one of Boston's quaintest neighborhoods. It was a warren of narrow streets lined with three- or four-story brick row houses. Southern Italian immigrants had adopted the area in the nineteenth century and transformed it into an ersatz Little Italy, complete with the usual sights and smells. There were always people engaged in animated conversation on the street, and the aroma of simmering Bolognese sauce permeated the air. When school was out, there were children everywhere.

Everything seemed familiar to Stephanie as she descended Hanover Street, the commercial avenue that bisected the neighborhood. In general, the community had been a nice, social, and warmly nurturing environment for her to grow up. The only problems were the family issues she had recently admitted to Daniel. That conversation had reawakened feelings and thoughts she'd long since suppressed, the same way Anthony's indictment did.

Stephanie paused outside the open door of the Café Cosenza. It was one of her family's holdings and offered Italian pastries and gelato as well as the usual espresso and cappuccino. A babble of conversation mixed with laughter and accompanied by the hiss and clank of the espresso machine drifted out, as did the smell of freshly roasted coffee. She had spent many pleasant hours enjoying cannoli, ice cream, and the camaraderie of her friends in that room, with its kitschy wall painting of Mt. Vesuvius and the Bay of Naples, yet from her current perspective, it seemed like a hundred years ago.

Standing outside and looking in, Stephanie realized how separated she felt from her childhood and her family except, perhaps, her mother, whom she frequently phoned. Excluding her younger brother Carlo, who had gone into the priesthood, a calling she could not fathom, she was the only person in her family to have gone to college, much less get a Ph.D. And most all of her elementary school and high school girlfriends, even those who had gone on to school, were presently either living in the North End or in the Boston suburbs along with houses, husbands, SUVs, and children. Instead, she was cohabiting with a man sixteen years her senior, with whom she was struggling to keep a biotech start-up company afloat by secretly treating a U.S. senator with an unapproved, experimental, but hopefully promising therapy.

Continuing down Hanover Street, Stephanie pondered her disconnect with her previous life. She found it interesting that it did not bother her. In retrospect, it had been a natural reaction to her discomfort about her father's business deals and her family's role in the community. What she found herself wondering was whether her life story would have taken a completely different track had her father been more emotionally available. As a young child, she had tried to break through the barrier of his self-centered male chauvinism and his preoccupation with whatever it was he was doing, but it had never worked. The vain effort had eventually nurtured a strong independent streak that had carried her to where she was today.

Stephanie stopped when a curious thought occurred to her. Her father and Daniel had some things in common, despite their enormous and obvious differences. Both were equally self-centered, both could be brash on occasion to the point of being considered asocial, and both were fiercely competitive within their own worlds. On top of that, Daniel was equivalently chauvinistic; it just involved intellect rather than gender. Stephanie laughed inwardly. She questioned why the thought had never crossed her mind, since Daniel in his preoccupations could also be emotionally unavailable, especially lately, with the advent of CURE's financial difficulties. Although psychology was far from her forte, she vaguely wondered if the similarities between her father and Daniel could have had anything to do with the attraction she felt for Daniel in the first place.

Recommencing walking, Stephanie promised herself she'd revisit the issue when she had more time. Now she had too much to do with the Turin departure scheduled for that evening. She'd gotten up at the crack of dawn to finish packing. Then she had spent a good part of the morning at the lab with Peter, describing exactly what she wanted him to do with Butler's culture. Luckily, the cells were progressing commendably. She'd given the culture the name of John Smith, taking the hint from Daniel's conversation with Spencer Wingate. If Peter had any questions about what was going on regarding why they were going to Nassau, and why he was going to be sending down some of John

Smith's cryopreserved cells, he didn't mention them.

Stephanie turned left on Prince Street and quickened her pace. This area was even more familiar, especially when she passed her old school. Her childhood house where her parents still lived was half a block beyond the school on the right.

The North End was a safe community, thanks to an unofficial "neighborhood watch." There was always at least a half dozen people in sight who were socially addicted to knowing what everybody else was doing. The downside as a child was that you couldn't get away with anything, but at the moment Stephanie savored the sense of security. Although Daniel had seemingly recovered from the intruder the previous afternoon and had dismissed the episode as unimportant in the grand scheme, Stephanie hadn't gotten over it, at least not completely, and being back in her old surroundings was reassuring. What Stephanie continued to find unsettling was that without an explanation, the incident tended to exacerbate her unease about the Butler affair.

Stopping in front of her old house, Stephanie eyed the fake gray stone that covered the brick on the first floor, the red aluminum awning with white scalloped trim over the front door, and the gaudily painted, plaster statue of a saint that stood in its niche. She smiled at how long it had taken her to recognize how tacky these embellishments were. Prior to that revelation, she hadn't even noticed them.

Although she had a key, Stephanie knocked and waited. She'd telephoned from the office to say she'd be stopping by, so there was to be no surprise. A moment later, the door was pulled open by her mother, Thea, who welcomed her with open arms. Thea's grandfather had been Greek, and subsequently female given names had been favored on the family's maternal side down through the years, Stephanie's included.

"You must be hungry," Thea said, pulling back to eye her daughter. With her mother, food was always an issue.

"I could use a sandwich," Stephanie said, knowing that refusing would be impossible. She followed her mother's slight frame into the kitchen that was redolent with the aroma of simmering food. "Something smells good."

"I'm making osso buco, your father's favorite. Why don't you stay for dinner? We'll be eating around two."

"I can't, Mom."

"Say hello to your father."

Dutifully, Stephanie poked her head into the living room immediately adjacent to the kitchen. Its décor hadn't changed one iota from Stephanie's earliest memories. As per usual, prior to a Sunday dinner, her father was hidden behind the Sunday paper clutched in his beefy hands. A brimming beanbag ashtray was perched on one of the La-Z-Boy's arms.

"Hi, Dad," Stephanie said cheerfully.

Anthony D'Agostino Sr. lowered the top edge of his paper. He peered at Stephanie over his reading glasses with his mildly rheumy eyes. A halo of cigarette smoke hung around him like thick smog. Despite being athletic in his youth, he was now the picture of corpulent immobility. He had gained considerable weight over the last decade, despite dire warnings from his physicians, even after his heart attack three years ago. As much as her mother lost weight, he gained in an unhealthy inverse proportionality.

"I don't want you upsetting your mother,

you hear me? She's been feeling good the last few days."

"I'll try my best," Stephanie said.

He raised the paper back into position. *So much for conversation,* Stephanie thought, as she shrugged and rolled her eyes. She retreated back to the kitchen. Thea had gotten out cheese, bread, Parma ham, and fruit, and was arranging it on the table. Stephanie watched as Thea worked. Her mother had lost more weight since Stephanie had last seen her, which wasn't a good sign. The bones of her hands and face protruded, with minimal flesh. Two years before, Thea had been diagnosed with breast cancer. Following surgery and chemotherapy, she'd been fine until three months ago, when there had been a relapse. A tumor had been found in one of her lungs. The prognosis was not good.

Stephanie sat down and made herself a sandwich. Her mother got some tea and sat across from her.

"Why can't you stay for dinner?" Thea asked. "Your older brother is coming."

"With or without his wife and kids?"

"Without," Thea said. "He and your father have some business."

"That sounds familiar."

"Why don't you stay? We hardly ever get to see you."

"I'd like to, but I can't. I'm going away this evening for about a month, which is why I particularly wanted to come over today. I've got a lot to do to get ready."

"Are you going with that man?"

"His name is Daniel, and yes, we are going together."

"You shouldn't be living with him. It's not right. Besides, he's too old. You should be married to a nice, young man. You're not so young anymore."

"Mother, we've been over this."

"Listen to your mother," Anthony Sr. bellowed from the living room. "She knows what she is talking about."

Stephanie held her tongue.

"Where are you going?"

"Mostly to Nassau in the Bahamas. We're going someplace first, but only for a day or so."

"Is this a vacation?"

"No," Stephanie said. She told her mother the trip was work-related. She didn't give any specifics, nor did her mother ask, especially since Stephanie switched the conversation to her nieces and nephews. The grandchildren were Thea's favorite subject. An hour later, when Stephanie was about to make her exit, the door opened and in walked Anthony Jr.

"Will wonders never cease?" Tony said in mock surprise when he caught sight of Stephanie. He had a strong, cultivated blue-collar accent. "The high-and-mighty Harvard doctor has decided to pay us poor, working slobs a visit."

Stephanie looked up and smiled at her older brother. She held her tongue like she had earlier with her father. She had long ago learned not to be baited. Tony had always derided Stephanie's schooling, as did her father, but not entirely for the same reason. With Tony, Stephanie suspected it was more jealousy, since he'd barely made it through high school. Tony's problem wasn't a lack of intelligence, but a lack of motivation as a teenager. As an adult, he liked to pretend he didn't care that he hadn't gone to college, but Stephanie knew better.

"Mom says your boy is turning out to be quite the hockey player," Stephanie said, to turn the conversation away from the testy subject of schooling. Tony had a twelve-year-old son and a ten-year-old daughter.

"Yeah, a chip off the old block," Tony said. He shared Stephanie's coloring and approximate height, but he was built more squarely, with a thick neck and large hands like their father. And also like their father, Tony projected in Stephanie's mind an unflattering, chauvinistic male animus, which made her feel sorry for her sister-in-law and worry about her niece.

Tony kissed his mother on both cheeks before stepping into the living room.

Stephanie heard the rustle of the newspaper as it was thrown aside, a slapping of hands that she could picture as a handshake, and an exchange of "How's it going? Great! How's it going for you? Great." When the conversation switched to sports talk involving the various Boston professional teams, Stephanie tuned them out.

"I've got to be going, Mom," Stephanie said.

"Why don't you stay? I can have the dinner on the table in no time."

"I can't, Mom."

"Dad and Tony will miss you!"

"Oh, yeah, sure!" Stephanie said.

"They love you in their own way."

"I'm certain they do," Stephanie said with a smile. The irony was, she believed it. Stephanie reached across and squeezed Thea's wrist. It felt fragile, as though if she pressed too hard, the bones might break. Stephanie pushed back her chair and stood up. Thea did likewise, and they hugged.

"I'll call from the Bahamas as soon as I get situated and give you the details about where we're staying and the number," Stephanie said. She gave her mother a peck on her cheek before sticking her head back into the living room. The cigarette haze was denser with both men smoking. "Goodbye, you two. I'm on my way."

Tony looked up. "What's this? You're taking off already?"

"She's going on a trip for a month," Thea said over Stephanie's shoulder. "She has to get ready."

"No!" Tony said. "You can't go. Not yet! I got to talk with you. I was going to call you, but since you're here, face-to-face is better."

"Then you'd better come in here on the double," Stephanie said. "I really have to be on my way."

"You'll wait until we're finished," Anthony said. "Tony and I are talking business."

"It's okay, Pop," Tony said. He gave his father's knee a squeeze as he stood up. "What I have to say to Steph won't take long."

Anthony grumbled as he reached for his discarded newspaper.

Tony walked back into the kitchen. He sat down backward on one of the kitchen chairs and motioned for Stephanie to sit in one of the others. Stephanie hesitated for a moment. Tony had become increasingly peremptory since he'd assumed more of his father's roles, and it was irksome. To avoid making it an issue, Stephanie sat, but as a compromise with herself, she told her brother he'd better be quick. She also told him to put out his cigarette, which he did grudgingly.

"The reason I was going to call you," Tony began, "is because Mikey Gualario, my accountant, told me that CURE is about to tank. I said that's impossible, because my kid sister would have told me. But he says he read it in the *Globe*. What's the scoop?"

"We're having financial difficulties," Stephanie admitted. "It's a political problem that is holding up our second round of financing."

"So the *Globe* wasn't making this all up?"

"I didn't read the article, but as I said, we are in rather a bind."

Tony screwed up his face as if in thought. He nodded a few times. "Well, that's not such great news. I guess you can understand that I might be concerned about my two-hundred-thousand-dollar loan."

"Correction! It wasn't a loan. It was an investment."

"Wait a minute! You came to me crying that you needed money."

"Correction again! I said we needed to raise money, and I certainly wasn't crying."

"Yeah, well, you said it was a sure thing."

"I said I thought it was a good investment, because it was based on a brilliant and fully patented, newly discovered procedure that promises to be a boon to medicine. But I said it wasn't risk-free, and I gave you the prospectus. Did you read it?"

"No, I didn't read it. I don't understand that kind of crap. But if the investment was so good, what's the problem?"

"What's happened that no one anticipated

is the possibility of a congressional ban being enacted on the procedure. But I can assure you we're working on it, and we think we have it under control. The whole thing has been a bolt out of the blue for all of us, and proof of that is that both Daniel and I have invested every penny we have in the company, including mortgaging Daniel's condo. I'm sorry that at the moment the investment looks less than rock-solid. I might add, I'm sorry we took your money."

"You and me both!"

"What's going to happen about this indictment of yours?"

Tony batted the air as if shooing a fly. "Nothing. It's a bunch of nonsense. The DA is just trying to drum up publicity to get re-elected. But let's not change the subject. You said you think you have this political problem under control."

"We believe so."

"Does this have anything to do with this month-long trip your going on?"

"It does," Stephanie said. "But I can't give you the details."

"Oh, really?" Tony questioned sarcastically. "I got two hundred K involved here, and you can't give me the details. There's something wrong with this picture."

"If I were to divulge what we're doing, it would jeopardize its efficacy."

"Divulge, jeopardize, efficacy!" Tony mimicked derogatorily. "Give me a break! I hope you don't think I'm going to be satisfied with a handful of ten-dollar words. Not a chance! So where are you going, Washington?"

"She's going to Nassau," Thea said suddenly from where she was standing near the stove. "And don't you be nasty to your own sister. You hear me?"

Tony sat bolt upright with his hands dangling lifelessly at his sides. His lower jaw slowly dropped open in utter amazement. "Nassau!" he yelled. "This is getting crazier and crazier. If CURE's ready to tank because of a political bombshell, don't you think you should hang around and do something?"

"That's why we're going to Nassau," Stephanie said.

"Ha!" Tony shouted. "What it sounds like to me is this so-called boyfriend of yours has it in his mind to pull off a scam."

"That couldn't be further from the truth. Tony, I wish I could tell you more, but I can't.

Hopefully, in a month things will be back on track, and at that time we'll be happy to consider your money a loan, and we will pay it back with interest."

"I'll try to remember not to hold my breath." Tony sneered. "You say you can't tell me more, but I can tell you something. That two hundred grand wasn't all mine."

"No?" Stephanie questioned. She sensed the unpleasant conversation was about to get worse.

"You painted it as such a sweet deal, I felt I had to share it. Half the money came from the Castigliano brothers."

"You never told me that!"

"I'm telling you now."

"Who are the Castigliano brothers?"

"Business partners. And I can tell you something else. They are not going to like hearing about their investment loan going south. They are not accustomed to that. As your brother, I think I should tell you it's not a good idea to go to the Bahamas."

"But we have to."

"You said that, but you're not telling me why. It forces me to repeat myself: You and your Harvard boyfriend better stay put and mind the store, because it looks like you're planning on frolicking in the sun with our money while we stooges freeze our asses here in Boston."

"Tony," Stephanie said in the calmest, most reassuring tone she could muster. "We're going to Nassau, and we are going to deal with this unfortunate problem."

Tony threw his hands up into the air, palms up. "I tried! God knows I tried!"

Thanks to power steering, Tony only needed the index finger of his right hand to turn the steering wheel of his black Cadillac DeVille. With such a balmy evening, he had his window open with his left hand dangling outside, holding his cigarette. The distinctive crunching sound of the car tires on gravel drowned out his radio as he entered the parking area in front of the Castigliano Brothers Plumbing Supply building. It was a gray one-story, flat-roofed cinderblock structure that backed onto mudflats.

Tony came to a stop next to three vehicles similar to his own: All of them were Cadillacs, and all of them were black. He flicked his cigarette into a pile of rusting sinks and killed the engine. As he got out of the car, he was assaulted by the odor of the salt marsh. It wasn't pleasant. With night rapidly approaching, the wind had shifted to the east.

The building's façade was in need of paint. In addition to the firm's name in block letters, there was a smattering of graffiti on the walls. The door was unlocked, and Tony walked in without knocking, as was his custom. A counter stood in the middle of the room. Behind the counter were rows of floor-to-ceiling shelves filled with plumbing materials. No one was in sight. A radio on the counter was tuned to a station playing music from the fifties.

Tony skirted the counter and walked down the center aisle. At the rear, he opened a second door that led into an office. In contrast to the supply area, this area was relatively plush, with a leather sofa and two desks on a threadbare Oriental carpet. Small, paned windows looked out onto the mudflats that were ringed with cattails and dotted with discarded tires and other debris. There were three men sitting in the room, one at each desk and one on the sofa.

Along with terse greetings, Tony shook hands with the two men at the desks first and then with the man on the sofa before sitting down himself. The men at the desks were the Castigliano brothers. They were twins named Sal and Louie. Tony had known them from the third grade, but by name only and not as friends. In high school they'd been scrawny, pimply kids who'd been teased mercilessly, and as adults they were still gaunt, with cadaverous cheeks and deeply set eyes.

The man on the sofa next to Tony was Gaetano Baresse, who'd grown up in New York City. He was built like Tony, but larger and with heavier features. He normally manned the plumbing supply counter in the outer room. As a side job, he was the twin's muscle. Most people thought he was around to make up for all the teasing the twins had weathered as schoolkids, but Tony knew better. Gaetano's strong-arm contribution was an occasional requirement with the twins' other business activities: some legal, some less so. It was in these business activities that Tony and the twins had become acquainted.

"First off," Tony said, "I want to thank you all for coming out on a Sunday."

"No problem," Sal said. He was sitting to Tony's left. "I hope you don't mind that we invited Gaetano."

"When you called and said there was trouble, we thought he should be included," Louie added.

"No problem," Tony said. "I just wish we could have had this get-together a little earlier, which I'll explain."

"We did the best we could," Sal said.

"My cell phone battery was dead," Gaetano said. "I was at my sister-in-law's house, playing pool. I was hard to find."

Tony lit up a cigarette and offered them all around. Everyone took one. Soon they were all smoking.

After taking a few deep drags, Tony put his cigarette down. He needed his hands to gesture while he talked. Thus prepared, he told the Castigliano brothers word for word as he remembered it the conversation he'd had earlier that afternoon with Stephanie. He left nothing out, nor did he mince words. He said it was his opinion and that of his accountant that Stephanie's company was going belly-up.

While Tony spoke, the twins became progressively agitated. Sal, who had been fiddling with a paper clip by bending it back and forth, snapped it in two. Louie angrily stubbed out his half-smoked cigarette.

"I don't believe this!" Sal said when Tony concluded.

"Is your sister married to this twerp?" Louie demanded.

"No, they just live together."

"Well, I tell you, we're not going to sit around while this bastard enjoys himself in the sun," Sal said. "No way!"

"We have to let him know we're not pleased," Louie said. "He's either got to get his ass back up here and straighten things out, or else. You got that, Gaetano?"

"Yeah, sure. When?"

Louie looked at Sal. Sal looked at Tony.

"It's too late today," Tony said. "Which is why I would have liked to have seen you guys earlier. They're on their way someplace before they head to Nassau. But my sister will be calling my ma when she's settled in the Bahamas."

"You'll let us know?" Sal questioned.

"Yeah, sure. But the deal is, you leave my sister out of it."

"Our beef's not with her," Louie said. "At least, I don't think it is."

"It's not," Tony said. "Trust me! I don't want there to be bad blood between us."

"Our beef's with him," Sal said.

Louie looked at Gaetano. "I guess you'll be going to Nassau."

Gaetano cracked the knuckles of his right hand with his left. "Sounds good to me!"

eleven

7:00 A.M., Monday, February 25, 2002

"Stephanie!" Daniel called softly as he gently shook her shoulder. "They are about to serve breakfast. Do you want any, or should I let you sleep until we land?"

Stephanie forcibly opened her eyes, rubbed them, and yawned at the same time. Then she had to blink rapidly a few times before she was able to see. Her eyes were dry from the plane's parched atmosphere.

"Where are we?" she asked in a husky voice. Her throat was dry as well. She sat up and stretched. Then she leaned over and looked out the window. Although there was a hint of dawn along the horizon, the ground below was still dark. She could see the lights of cities and towns dotting the landscape.

"My guess would be we're over someplace in France," Daniel said.

Despite attempts at planning to avoid a last-minute rush, the night before had been an anxious scramble to get out of Daniel's apartment, get to Logan Airport, and get through security. They'd made the flight with less than ten minutes to spare. Thanks to Butler's money, they were flying Alitalia's Magnifica Class and were seated in the first two seats on the left side of the Boeing 767 aircraft.

Stephanie raised the back of her seat from its reclined position. "How come you're so wide awake? Did you sleep?"

"Not a wink," Daniel admitted. "I started reading these books of yours about the Shroud of Turin, particularly the one by Ian Wilson. I can see why you got hooked. It's fascinating stuff."

"You must be exhausted."

"I'm not," Daniel said. "Reading about the shroud has kind of energized me. I'm even more encouraged about treating Butler and using the shroud's DNA fragments. In fact, it occurred to me that maybe after we finish with Butler, we should go ahead and treat another celebrity someplace offshore with the same DNA source, somebody who doesn't mind publicity. Once the story of the cure hits the media, no politician would dare interfere, and better yet, the FDA would be forced to alter their protocol for approval of the treatment."

"Whoa!" Stephanie warned. "Let's not get ahead of ourselves. We need to concentrate on Butler for the time being. His cure is not a given by any stretch of the imagination."

"You don't think treating another celebrity is a good idea?"

"I need to give it some thought to respond intelligently," Stephanie said, trying to be diplomatic. "Right now my mind is a bit addled. I need to use the restroom, and then I want some breakfast. I'm starved. When my mind is firing on all cylinders, I want to hear what you have read about the shroud, particularly whether you have a hypothesis of how the image was formed."

Less than an hour later, they landed at Rome's Fiumicino Airport. Along with a crush of other people arriving at the same time from various international destinations, they got through passport control and then managed to find their way to the gate for their connecting flight to Turin. At a nearby coffee bar, Daniel indulged himself with an Italian espresso that he bolted down like the local patrons. There was no Magnifica Class on this leg, and once they boarded the plane, they found themselves in a tight cabin filled with businessmen. Stephanie was in the middle seat and Daniel on the aisle, halfway down the aircraft's cabin.

"This is cozy," Daniel commented. Thanks to his six-foot-one-inch frame, his knees were pressed up against the seat in front of him.

"How are you feeling now? Are you tired?"

"No, and especially not after that jolt of high-test coffee."

"Then talk to me about the shroud! I really want to hear." Thanks to the long line waiting to use the restroom on the flight from Boston to Rome, there hadn't been time for the subject to come up before they landed.

"Well, first off, I don't have any theory about how the image was formed. It's definitely an intriguing mystery, that much I'll agree, and I was particularly taken by the poetic way Ian Wilson described it as 'a photographic negative waiting dormant like a time capsule for the moment of photography's invention.' But the idea of the image being evidence of the Resurrection as both you and he suggested, I don't buy. It's faulty scientific reasoning. You can't posit an unknown and counterintuitive process of dematerialization to explain an unknown phenomenon."

"What about black holes?"

"What are you talking about?"

"Black holes have been posited to explain unknown phenomena, and black holes are certainly counterintuitive from our direct scientific experience."

There was a period of silence, save for the muffled roar of the jet engines mingling with the rustle of morning newspapers and the tapping of laptop keyboards.

"You have a point," Daniel admitted finally.

"Let's move on! What else caught your interest?"

"Quite a few things. One that comes to mind is the result of reflectance spectroscopy showing dirt on the images of the feet. It seemed to me to be such an ordinary discovery, until I learned that some of the granules were identified by optical crystallography to be travertine aragonite that had a spectral signature matching limestone samples taken from ancient Jerusalem tombs."

Stephanie laughed. "Leave it to you to be impressed by one of the more arcane scientific details. I don't even remember that tidbit."

"It strains one's credibility that a fourteenth-century French forger would have gone to such an extent as to obtain and sprinkle such detritus on his supposed creation."

"I couldn't agree more."

"Another fact that caught my attention was that when one looks at the intersection of the habitats of the three Middle-Eastern plants whose pollens are the most prevalent on the shroud, it narrows the shroud's apparent origin to the twenty miles between Hebron and Jerusalem."

"Curious, isn't it?"

"It's more than curious," Daniel said. "Whether the shroud is the burial cloth of Jesus Christ or not is certainly not proved—nor, I might add, can it ever be—but in my mind the artifact came from Jerusalem, and it wrapped a man who had been scourged in the ancient Roman fashion, whose nose had been broken, who had thorn wounds on his head, and who had been crucified and suffered a lance wound to his chest."

"What did you think of the historical aspect?"

"It was well presented and captivating," Daniel acknowledged. "After reading it, I'm willing to entertain the idea that the Shroud of Turin and the Edessa Cloth are one and the same. I was particularly taken by the way the shroud's crease marks have been used to explain how it could have been displayed in Constantinople as merely the head of Jesus, as the Edessa Cloth was generally described, or Jesus' entire body, front and back, as described by the crusader Robert de Clari. He was the individual who saw it just prior to its disappearance during the sacking of Constantinople in 1204."

"Which means the carbon-dating results are in error."

"As troublesome as that sounds to me as a scientist, it seems to be true."

Hardly had they gotten their orange juices before the seat-belt sign came back on, along with an announcement that the pilots were making their initial approach to Turin's Caselle Airport. Fifteen minutes later, they landed. As full as the plane was, it took them almost as long as the flight from Rome to get off the plane, walk the length of the concourse, and find the appropriate luggage carousel.

While Daniel waited for their bags to appear, Stephanie noticed a cell phone concession, and she went over to rent one. Before leaving Boston, she had learned that her stateside cell phone would not function in Europe, although it would in Nassau, and to be sure she did not miss any emails from Butler while in Turin, she needed a European cell phone number. As soon as she could, she planned to set it up so Butler's emails would go to both numbers.

Emerging from the terminal with their luggage in tow and their coats on, they joined a taxi line. While they waited, they got their first glimpse of the Piedmont. To the west and north they could see snow-capped mountains. To the south, a mauve haze hung over the industrial part of the city. The weather was cool and not too dissimilar to what they had left in Boston, which made sense, since the two cities were at approximately the same latitude.

"I hope I don't regret not renting a car,"

Daniel said, while watching the full taxis rocket away.

"The guidebook said parking in the city is impossible," Stephanie reminded him. "The positive side is that Italian drivers are supposed to be good, even if they are fast."

Once underway, Daniel held on with white-knuckle intensity as the driver lived up to Stephanie's description. The taxi was a postmodern Fiat with blocky styling that made it appear to be an amalgam of an SUV and a compact car. Unfortunately for Daniel, it was remarkably responsive to the accelerator.

Stephanie had been to Italy on several occasions and had specific expectations of what the city would look like. Initially, she was disappointed. Turin had none of the medieval or Renaissance charm she associated with places like Florence or Siena. Instead, it seemed to be an indeterminately modern city beset with suburban sprawl and, at the moment, caught in the clutches of morning rush hour. The traffic was heavy, and all the Italian drivers seemed equally aggressive, with lots of horn blowing, rapid accelerations, and equally rapid braking. The ride was nerve-racking, especially for

Daniel. Stephanie tried to start a conversation, but Daniel was too engrossed with watching for the next close call out the windshield.

Daniel had booked a single-night stay in what his guidebook described as the city's best hotel, the Grand Belvedere. It was in the center of the old city, and as they entered that quarter, Stephanie's impression of Turin began to change. She still wasn't seeing the kind of architecture she expected, but the city began to have its own unique charm, with wide boulevards, arcaded squares, and elegant Baroque buildings. By the time they pulled up in front of their hotel, Stephanie's disappointment had metamorphosed into a qualified appreciation.

The Grand Belvedere was the last word in late-nineteenth-century luxury. The lobby was embellished with more gilded putti and cherubs that Stephanie had ever seen in one place. Marble columns soared up to support archways, while fluted pilasters lined the walls. Liveried doormen rushed to carry in their luggage, which was a rather extensive collection, since they had packed for a month's stay in Nassau.

Their room had a high ceiling, a large Murano chandelier, and less ornamentation than the lobby, but it was just as glitzy. Gilded winged cherubs hovered in all four corners of the heavy cornice. The tall windows looked out onto the Piazza Carlo Alberto, on which the hotel was sited. Heavy, dark red brocade curtains with hundreds of tassels draped the windows. The furniture, including the bed, was all composed of massively carved dark wood. On the floor was a thick Oriental carpet.

After tipping the bellmen and the cutaway-attired receptionist who had accompanied them to their room, Daniel glanced around their digs with a satisfied expression on his face. "Not bad! Not bad at all," he remarked. He glanced in at the marbled bathroom before turning back to Stephanie. "I'm finally living the way I deserve."

"You're too much!" Stephanie scoffed. She opened her bag to get out her toiletries.

"Really!" Daniel laughed. "I don't know why I put up with being an academic pauper as long as I did."

"Let's get to work, King Midas! How are we going to figure out how to call the Chancery of the Archdiocese to get ahold of Monsignor Mansoni?" Stephanie went into the bathroom. More than anything else, she wanted to brush her teeth.

Daniel went to the desk and began pulling out drawers, looking for a city phone book. When that wasn't successful, he looked in the closets.

"I think we should go downstairs and have the concierge do it," Stephanie called out from the bathroom. "We can have them set up a dinner reservation for this evening as well."

"Good idea," Daniel said.

As Stephanie anticipated, the concierge was happy to help. Producing a phone book in a matter of seconds, he had Monsignor Mansoni on the line before Stephanie and Daniel had decided who should talk with him. After a moment of confusion, Daniel took the phone. As instructed in Butler's email, Daniel identified himself as a representative of Ashley Butler and that he was in Turin to pick up a sample. In an attempt to be discreet, he wasn't any more descriptive.

"I have been waiting for your call," Monsignor Mansoni answered with a heavy Italian accent. "I am prepared to meet with you this morning, if that is appropriate."

"The sooner the better, as far as we are concerned," Daniel replied.

"We?" the monsignor questioned.

"My partner and I are here together," Daniel explained. He thought the term *partner* was sufficiently vague. He felt uncharacteristically self-conscious talking to a Roman Catholic priest who might be offended at his and Stephanie's living style.

"Am I to assume your partner is a woman?"

"Very much so," Daniel answered. He looked at Stephanie to make sure she was comfortable with the term *partner.* He'd never before used it to describe their relationship, despite its appropriateness. Stephanie smiled at his discomfiture.

"Will she be coming to our meeting?"

"Absolutely," Daniel stated. "Where would be convenient for you?"

"Perhaps the Caffè Torino in Piazza San Carlo would be agreeable. Are you and your partner staying at a hotel within the city?"

"I believe we're right in the center."

"Excellent," the monsignor commented. "The café will be close to your hotel. The concierge could give you directions."

"Fine," Daniel said. "When should we be there?"

"Should we say in an hour?"

"We'll be there," Daniel said. "How will we recognize you?"

"There shouldn't be many priests present, but if there are, I will surely be the most portly. I'm afraid I have gained far too much weight with my present sedentary position."

Daniel glanced at Stephanie. He could tell she could hear the priest's side of the conversation. "We'll probably be easy to spot as well. I'm afraid we look rather American with our clothes. Also, my partner is a raven-haired beauty."

"In that case, I'm certain we will recognize each other. I will see you about eleven-fifteen."

"We look forward to it," Daniel said, before handing the phone back to the concierge.

"Raven-haired beauty?" Stephanie questioned in a forced whisper after they'd gotten their directions and were walking away from the concierge's desk. She was embarrassed. "You've never described me with such a cliché. Worse yet, it's patronizingly sexist."

"I'm sorry," Daniel said. "I was a bit nonplussed, making an assignation with a priest."

Luigi Mansoni opened one of the drawers of his desk. Reaching in, he picked up a slender silver box and pocketed it. He then gathered up his cassock to keep from stepping on the hem as he stood and hurried out of his office. At the end of the hall, he knocked on Monsignor Valerio Garibaldi's door. He was out of breath, which was embarrassing, since he'd walked less than a hundred feet. He checked his watch and wondered if he shouldn't have told Daniel an hour and a half. Valerio's voice bellowed for him to come in.

Switching to his native Italian, Luigi told his friend and superior about the phone conversation he'd just had.

"Oh, no," Valerio Garibaldi responded in Italian. "I'm certain this is sooner than Father Maloney expected. Let's hope he is in his room." Valerio picked up his phone. He was relieved when Father Maloney answered. He told the American what had transpired and that he and Monsignor Mansoni were waiting for him in his office.

"This is all very curious," Valerio said to Luigi while they waited.

"Indeed," Luigi responded. "It makes me wonder if we shouldn't alert one of the archbishop's secretaries so that if there is ultimately a problem, it will be his fault His Reverence was not notified. After all, His Reverence is the official custodian of the shroud."

"Your point is well taken," Valerio said. "I believe I will take your suggestion."

A knock preceded Father Maloney's arrival. Valerio gestured for him to take a seat. Although both Valerio and Luigi outranked Michael in the church's hierarchy, the fact that Michael was officially representing Cardinal O'Rourke, the most powerful Roman Catholic prelate of North America and a personal friend of their own archbishop, Cardinal Manfredi, they treated him with particular deference.

Michael sat down. In contrast to the monsignors, he was dressed in his usual simple black suit with a white clerical collar. Also in contrast to the others, who were both considerably corpulent, Michael was rail-thin, and with his hooked nose, his features were more stereotypically Italian than his hosts.

His red hair also set him apart, since the others were both gray.

Luigi related his conversation with Daniel once again, emphasizing that there were two people involved, and one of them was a woman.

"That's surprising," Michael commented. "And I'm not fond of surprises. But we'll just have to take it in stride. I assume the sample is ready."

"Absolutely," Luigi said. For Michael's benefit, he was speaking in English, even though Michael spoke passable Italian. Michael had gone to divinity school in Rome for graduate training, where learning Italian had been mandatory.

Luigi reached into the recesses of his cassock and produced the slender silver box reminiscent of a cigarette case from the mid-twentieth century. "Here it is," he said. "Professor Ballasari made the fiber selection himself to be sure it was representative. They definitely come from an area of bloodstain."

"May I?" Michael asked. He reached out with his hand.

"Of course," Luigi said. He handed the case to Michael.

Michael cupped the embossed case in both hands. It was an emotional experience for him. He had long ago been convinced of the authenticity of the shroud, and to hold a box that contained the real blood of his Savior rather than transubstantiated wine was overwhelming.

Luigi reached out and retrieved the case. It disappeared back beneath the voluminous folds of his cassock. "Are there any particular instructions?" he asked.

"There certainly are," Michael said. "I need you to find out as much as possible about these people to whom you deliver the sample: names, addresses, whatever. In fact, demand to see their passports and get the numbers. With that information and your contacts with the civil authorities, we should be able learn a good deal about their identities."

"What is it you are looking for?" Valerio asked.

"I'm not sure," Michael admitted. "His Eminence James Cardinal O'Rourke is exchanging this tiny sample in return for a major political benefit to the church. At the same time, he wants to be one hundred percent sure the Holy Father's dictums against scientific testing of the shroud are not violated."

Valerio nodded as if he understood, but he really didn't. Exchanging bits of a relic for political favors was beyond his experience, especially with the caveat of having no official documentation. It was worrisome. At the same time, he knew that the few fibers in the silver box had come from a sample of the shroud taken many years previously, and the shroud itself had not been recently disturbed. The Holy Father's main concern about the shroud was conservancy.

Luigi stood up. "If I am to make the appointment on time, I should be leaving."

Michael stood up as well. "We'll go together, if you don't mind. I'll watch the exchange from afar. After the sample is handed over, I intend to follow these people. I want to know where they are staying, in the event their identities are troublesome."

Valerio stood up with the others. His expression was one of confusion. "What will you do if, as you say, their identities are troublesome?"

"I will be forced to improvise," Michael said. "On that point, the cardinal's instructions were vague."

* * *

This city is rather attractive," Daniel said, as he and Stephanie walked west along streets lined with palatial ducal residences. "I wasn't impressed at first, but I am now."

"I had the same impression," Stephanie said.

Within a few blocks of walking, they reached Piazza San Carlo, and the vista opened up to a grand square the size of a football field lined with handsome, cream-colored baroque buildings. The façades were ornamented with a pleasing profusion of decorative forms. In the center of the square stood an imposing, bronze equestrian statue. The Caffe Torino was midway along the western side. Inside the café, they found themselves enveloped in an aroma redolent of freshly ground coffee. A number of large crystal chandeliers hanging from a frescoed ceiling washed the interior with a warm, incandescent glow.

They did not have to look long for Monsignor Mansoni. The priest stood up the moment they entered and waved them over to his table along the far wall. As they wended their way toward him, Stephanie glanced around at the other patrons. Monsignor Mansoni's odd comment that there shouldn't be many priests in the café was correct. Stephanie saw only one other. He was sitting by himself and, for a brief moment, Stephanie had the unsettling sensation that his eyes had locked onto hers.

"Welcome to Turin," Luigi said. He shook hands with both his guests and gestured for them to sit. His eyes lingered on Stephanie long enough to make her feel mildly uncomfortable, as she remembered Daniel's inappropriate description.

A waiter appeared in response to the monsignor's snapping of his fingers and took Stephanie and Daniel's order. Daniel had another espresso, while Stephanie was content with sparkling water.

Daniel eyed the prelate. His description of himself as being portly was no understatement. A large dewlap practically obscured the man's white clerical collar. As a medical doctor, he wondered what the priest's cholesterol level was.

"I suppose to begin we should introduce ourselves. I am Luigi Mansoni, formerly of Verona, Italy, but now I live here in Turin."

Daniel and Stephanie took turns introducing themselves by giving their names and

that they lived in Cambridge, Massachusetts. At that point, the coffee and water arrived.

Daniel took a sip and replaced the cup in
its tiny saucer. "Without meaning to be rude,
I'd like to get to business. I assume you have
brought the sample."

"Of course," Luigi replied.

"We must be sure the sample comes from
an area of the shroud with a bloodstain,"
Daniel continued.

"I can assure you that it does. It was selected by the professor entrusted with the
conservancy of the shroud by the Archbishop, Cardinal Manfredi, who is its current
custodian."

"Well?" Daniel questioned. "Can we have
it?"

"In a moment," Luigi said. He reached into
his cassock and produced a small pad and
pen. "Before I deliver the sample, I have
been instructed to get particulars as to your
identities. With the controversy and media
frenzy swirling about the shroud, the church
is insistent on knowing who has possession
of all samples."

"Senator Ashley Butler is to be the recipi-
ent," Daniel said.

"That is my understanding. However, until then we need to have proof of your identities. I'm sorry, but those are my instructions."

Daniel looked at Stephanie. Stephanie shrugged. "What kind of proof are you looking for?"

"Passports and current addresses would be adequate."

"I don't have a problem with that," Stephanie said. "And the address in the passport is my current address."

"I suppose I don't have a problem either," Daniel said.

The two Americans produced their documents and slid them across the table. Luigi opened each in turn and copied down the information. He then pushed them back. Pocketing his pad and pen, he produced the silver box. With obvious deference, he slid it toward Daniel.

"May I?" Daniel questioned.

"Of course," Luigi replied.

Daniel picked up the silver box. There was a small latch on its side, which he slid to the open position. Carefully, he lifted the lid. Stephanie leaned so she could see over his shoulder. Inside was a small, sealed, semi-transparent glassine envelope containing a

tiny but adequate mat of fibers of indeterminate color.

"Looks good," Daniel said. He closed the
lid and secured the latch. He handed the
case to Stephanie, who slipped it into her
shoulder bag along with their passports.

Fifteen minutes later, Daniel and
Stephanie reemerged into the pale midday
midwinter sunshine. They headed diagonally
across San Carlo Square en route back to
their hotel. Despite their jet lag, there was a
spring to their step. Both felt mildly euphoric.

"Now, that couldn't have been any easier,"
Daniel commented.

"I'd have to agree," Stephanie said.

"I would never remind you of your earlier
pessimism," Daniel teased. "I'd never do that."

"Wait a second," Stephanie chided. "We
got the shroud sample with ease, but we're
still a long way from treating Butler. My worries are about the whole affair."

"I think this little episode is just a harbinger
of things to come."

"I hope you are right."

"What do you think we should do with the
rest of the day?" Daniel asked. "Our flight to
London is not until five after seven in the
morning."

"I need a short nap," Stephanie said. "And you must need one as well. Why don't we go back to the hotel, have a bite of lunch followed by a half hour of shut-eye, and then head out? There are a few things I'd like to see while we're here, particularly the church where the shroud is housed."

"Sounds like a good plan to me," Daniel said agreeably.

Michael Maloney hung back as far as he dared without losing Daniel and Stephanie. He was surprised at how quickly they were moving, and he had to keep pace. When he'd emerged from the café, he'd been lucky to catch sight of them, as they had practically already cleared the square.

At the moment the two Americans had left the café, Michael had conferred briefly with Luigi to encourage him to run the identities through the civil authorities and let him know on his cell phone as soon as any information was available. Michael said he intended to keep the Americans in sight or at least know their location until he was satisfied with the information.

When the Americans disappeared around a corner, Michael broke into a run until they were back in sight. He was intent on not losing them. Taking a direct clue from his mentor and boss, James Cardinal O'Rourke, Michael was treating his current commission with great seriousness. He strongly aspired to rising in the church hierarchy, and to date, things had been going as planned. First, there had been the opportunity to study in Rome. Next had come the recognition of his talents by the then Bishop O'Rourke, the invitation to join his staff, and the elevation of the bishop to archbishop. At this point in his career, Michael knew his success depended solely on pleasing his powerful superior, and he intuitively knew this assignment concerning the shroud was a golden opportunity. Thanks to its importance to the cardinal, it was affording him a unique circumstance to demonstrate his unswerving loyalty, dedication, and even his ability to improvise, given the lack of specific guidelines.

Emerging into the Piazza Carlo Alberto, Michael surmised the couple was headed toward the Grand Belvedere. He quickened his pace to almost a jog in order to be right behind the Americans as they entered. Inside, he held back as they boarded an elevator, and then watched the indicator as it rose to the fourth floor. Satisfied, Michael retreated to the sitting area within the hotel's lobby. He sat down on a velvet couch, picked up a copy the *Corriere della Sera,* and began to read while keeping one eye on the bank of elevators. *So far, so good,* he thought.

He didn't have to wait long. The couple reemerged and then went into the dining room. Michael responded by moving from one couch to another, which afforded a better view of the dining room entrance. He was confident that no one had paid him the slightest heed. He knew that in Italy, wearing Roman Catholic priestly garb gave one both access and anonymity.

A half hour later, when the couple came out of the dining room, Michael had to smile. A half hour for lunch was so American. He knew that the Italians in the room were all settled in for at least two hours. The Americans went back to the elevator and once more rose up to the fourth floor.

Michael had considerably longer to wait on this occasion. Finishing the newspaper, he looked around for something else to read. Not finding anything and reluctant to risk going to the sundries shop, he began thinking about what he would do if the information he hoped to get from Luigi was not appropriate. He wasn't even sure what wasn't going to be appropriate. What he expected to learn was that at least one of the pair worked in some capacity for Senator Butler or possibly an organization that had ties to the senator. He remembered the senator specifically saying he would dispatch an agent to get the sample. Exactly what he meant by "agent" remained to be seen.

Michael stretched and looked at his watch. It was now going on three in the afternoon, and his stomach began to growl. He'd not eaten, save for the bit of pastry at the Caffè Torino. While his mind teased him with images of his favorite pastas, his cell phone buzzed in his pocket. He'd deliberately turned off its ringer. In a bit of a panic lest he miss the call, he got the phone out and answered. It was Luigi.

"The report just came in from my contacts with the immigration people," Luigi said. "I don't believe you are going to like what I have learned."

"Oh!" Michael commented. He tried to remain calm. Unfortunately, at that moment the Americans stepped from the elevator with coats on and guidebooks in hand, obviously ready to go on an outing. Fearing they might take a taxi, which would add an element of difficulty, Michael struggled to get into his own coat while keeping the phone pressed to his ear. The Americans moved quickly, as they had done earlier. "Hang on, Luigi!" Michael said, interrupting the monsignor. "I'm on the move here." With one arm in his coat, Michael had gotten the free sleeve caught in the revolving door. He had to back up to free himself.

"Prego!" the doorman said, as he lent a hand.

"Mi scusi," Michael responded. Freed from the door, he rushed outside and was rewarded to see the Americans passing the taxi stand and heading toward the northwest corner of the square. He slowed to a fast walk.

"Sorry, Luigi," Michael said into the phone. "The couple just decided to leave the hotel the moment you called. What were you saying?"

"I said they are both scientists," Luigi responded.

Michael felt his pulse quicken. "That's not good news!"

"I didn't think so either. Apparently, their

names came right up when the Italian authorities contacted their American counterparts asking for information. They are both Ph.D.s in the biomolecular arena, with Daniel Lowell more of a chemist and Stephanie D'Agostino more of a biologist. They are apparently well known in their fields, he more than she. Since they both have the same home address, they are apparently cohabitating."

"Good grief!" Michael commented.

"They certainly don't sound like normal couriers."

"This is a worst-case scenario."

"I agree. With their backgrounds, they must be planning on some sort of testing. What are you going to do?"

"I don't know yet," Michael said. "I've got to think."

"Let me know if I can help!"

"I'll be in touch," Michael said before terminating the call.

Although Michael had just told Luigi he didn't know what he was going to do, that wasn't quite true. He had already decided he was going to retrieve the shroud sample; he just didn't know how. What he did know is that he wanted to do it himself so that when he reported back to Cardinal O'Rourke, he could take full credit for saving his Savior's blood from further scientific indignity.

The Americans reached the expansive Piazza Castello but did not slow down. Michael's first thought was that they planned to visit the Palazzo Reale, the former residence of the House of Savoy, but he changed his mind when the Americans skirted the Piazzeta Reale to reach the Piazza Giovanni.

"Of course!" Michael said out loud. He knew the Duomo di San Giovanni stood on the square, and the church was the current home of the shroud following the 1997 fire in its chapel. Michael followed a little farther behind, to be certain of the Americans' destination. As soon as he saw them mount the front steps of the cathedral, he turned around and began retracing his steps. Assuming his charges would be suitably engaged away from their hotel for the time being, Michael thought he'd better take advantage of the opportunity. If he were to retrieve the shroud sample, this might be the best time, if not the only time, assuming they would be leaving in the morning.

Although Michael was already slightly out

of breath, he pushed himself to quicken his pace. He wanted to get back to the Grand Belvedere as quickly as possible. Despite his obvious inexperience with intrigue in general and with burglary in particular, he had to find out which room in the hotel Daniel and Stephanie occupied, manage to get into it, and find the silver case, all within a couple hours.

Is this the actual shroud we're looking at?" Daniel asked in a whisper. There were a number of other people in the cathedral, but they were either kneeling in prayer in the pews or lighting candles in front of religious statuary. The only sounds were the occasional echoes of heels against the marble floor as people moved about.

"No, it's not the shroud," Stephanie whispered back. "It's a full-sized photographic replica." She was holding the guidebook open to the proper page. She and Daniel were facing a glass-front alcove that encompassed the first floor of the north transept of the church. One story above the enclosure was the curtained box from which the former Dukes and Duchesses of Savoy witnessed the celebration of the Mass.

The photograph was displayed landscape-wise. The heads of the front and back image of the crucified man almost touched in the center, which was explained by the man having been placed supine on the cloth and then the cloth having been folded over on top of him. The frontal image was to the left. The photograph was positioned on what appeared to be a table fourteen feet long and four feet wide, draped to the floor with pleated blue fabric.

"The photograph is sitting on the new conservation case that houses the shroud," Stephanie explained. "It has a hydraulic system, so that when the shroud is to be displayed, the top can be rotated upward, and the relic can be viewed through bulletproof glass."

"I remember reading about it," Daniel commented. "It sounds like an impressive setup. For the first time in the shroud's long life, it rests completely horizontal in a controlled atmosphere."

"It's truly amazing that the image has lasted as long as it has, considering what it has been through."

"Looking at this full-size photo, I find the image more difficult to discern than I imagined. In fact, if this is what the shroud itself looks like, it's somewhat anticlimactic. It can be seen and appreciated better in the book you got."

"And better still in the negative," Stephanie added.

"Apparently, the image hasn't faded. What's happened is the background has yellowed, so the contrast is diminished."

"I hope the new conservation case keeps that from happening any more," Stephanie remarked. "Well, so much for where the shroud rests." She turned and glanced around the cathedral's interior. "I thought we might want to stroll around in here, but for an Italian Renaissance Church, this is rather plain."

"I was thinking the same thing," Daniel said. "Let's move on. How about taking a peek at the royal palace? The interior is supposed to be quintessentially rococo."

Stephanie looked at Daniel askance. "When have you become such an expert on architecture and interior design?"

Daniel laughed. "I just read it in the guidebook before we left."

"Well, I'd love to see the palace, except I have a problem."

"What kind of problem?"

Stephanie looked down at her feet. "I forgot to put on some decent walking shoes instead of these that I wore to lunch. I'm afraid my feet are going to be killing me if we traipse around all afternoon. I'm sorry, but would you mind terribly if we went back to the hotel briefly?"

"As far as I'm concerned, now that we got the shroud sample, we're just killing time. I don't care what we do."

"Thanks," Stephanie said, relieved. Daniel could be impatient with such lapses. "I really am sorry. I should have known better. And while we're there, I'm going to put on another sweater. It's colder out than I thought."

Except in conjunction with some harmless pranks as a college student, Father Michael Maloney had never knowingly broken a civil law, and the fact that he was now about to do so caused more anxiety than he had anticipated. Not only was he shaky and perspiring, but he also had enough epigastric distress to wish he had an antacid. Adding to his burden was the concern about time. He certainly did not want to be caught flagrante delicto by the Americans. Although he was confident they would be away for two or more hours on their sightseeing foray, he decided to limit himself to one hour just to be sure. The mere thought of being surprised made his knees feel weak.

As he had approached the Grand Belvedere, he had no idea how he was going to accomplish his goal, at least not until he had passed a flower shop in the same square with the hotel. Ducking into the shop, he had inquired if one of their prepared flower arrangements could be delivered immediately to the hotel. When he'd gotten a positive reply, he picked out an arrangement, addressed an envelope with the Americans' names, and signed the card: *Welcome to the Grand Belvedere, the management.*

And now, five minutes later, while Michael was sitting on the same sofa in the hotel lobby he'd occupied earlier, the flower arrangement came through the revolving door. Lifting his newspaper to cover his face, Michael watched surreptitiously as the same woman he'd dealt with in the flower shop delivered the flowers to the bell desk. One of the bellmen signed for them, and the woman left.

Unfortunately, for the next ten minutes

nothing happened. The flowers stood on the bell desk as the bellmen engaged in animated conversation with each other.

"Come on!" Michael voiced silently while gritting his teeth. He wanted to go over to the bell desk and complain, but he dared not. He didn't want to draw any attention to himself. His plan was to take full advantage of his priestly garb to appear harmless, if not relatively invisible.

Finally, one of the bellmen checked the envelope on the flowers and then went behind the bell desk. Michael could tell he was checking a computer screen by the reflection of light on the man's face. A moment later, he came from behind the desk, picked up the flowers, and headed for the elevator. Michael put his newspaper aside and stayed right behind him.

The bellman nodded a greeting to Michael as the doors closed. Michael smiled back. At the fourth floor, the bellman exited and Michael did the same. Keeping a little distance between himself and the bellman, Michael followed. When the bellman stopped outside room 408 and knocked, Michael passed by. The bellman nodded and smiled. Michael did the same.

Michael rounded a corner and stopped. Carefully, he looked back. He saw the bellman knock again before getting out a ring of keys on a chain. He opened the door and disappeared for a moment. When he reappeared sans flowers, he was whistling softly. He closed the door and walked back to the elevators.

When the bellman was gone, Michael walked back to room 408. He didn't expect the door to be unlocked, and it wasn't. Looking down the length of the corridor, he saw a cleaning cart. Taking a deep breath and blowing up his cheeks momentarily to bolster his courage, Michael headed toward the cart. It was positioned next to a door held open by a doorstop.

Michael knocked tentatively on the open door. *"Scusi!"* he called out. He heard a television playing in the background. Entering the room, he saw two middle-aged women in brown dress uniforms making the bed. *"Scusi!"* Michael called, considerably more loudly.

The women responded as if shocked. Both perceptively blanched. One recovered enough to run over and turn off the television.

Marshaling his best Italian, Michael asked the women if they could help him. He explained he'd left his key in room 408, and he needed to make an immediate telephone call. He wanted to know if they would be so kind as to open his door to keep him from having to go down to the front desk.

The women exchanged a confused glance. It took Michael a moment to realize that they spoke very little Italian. He explained his supposed predicament again, speaking slowly and distinctly. On this occasion, one of the women got the message, and to Michael's relief held up her passkeys. Michael nodded.

As if to make up for the communication difficulties, the woman pushed past Michael and practically ran down the hall. It was all Michael could do to keep up with her. She unlocked room 408 and held the door open. Michael thanked her as he stepped over the threshold. The door closed.

Michael exhaled. He didn't realize he'd been holding his breath. He backed up to lean against the door as he surveyed the room. The drapes were open, and there was plenty of light. There was more luggage than he expected, although all but two of the bags were still zippered or latched as if they had yet to be opened. Unfortunately, there was no silver box visible on the bureau, the desk, or the nightstands.

Michael could feel his pulse racing. He was also perspiring copiously. "I'm not good at this," he whispered. He desperately wanted to find the silver box and leave. It took all his willpower to stay in the room.

Pushing off from the door, he went first to the desk. Centered on the blotter between two laptop shoulder bags was a room key for 408. After a moment's hesitation, Michael picked it up and pocketed it. Rapidly, he searched the laptop bags: no silver case. It took only a moment for him to go through the desk drawers. Save for the hotel stationery, they were empty. Next was the bureau. It too was empty, except for laundry forms and plastic laundry bags. The small drawers of the nightstands were also empty. He checked the bathroom, but no silver box. Looking into the closet, he saw a safe and breathed a sigh of relief. The door was ajar and it was empty. He checked the pockets of a man's jacket hanging on the rod: nothing.

Turning back into the room, he eyed the unlatched suitcases. They were on luggage stands at the foot of the bed. Approaching each in turn, he raised their lids and ran his hand around their peripheries. He encountered various and sundry objects but no silver box. He then carefully lifted the clothing to search more thoroughly. Suddenly, he heard voices, and to his horror, it sounded like American English. He stood up, frozen in place. In the next instant, he heard the worst sound he could have imagined. It was the sound of a key being thrust into the door lock!

twelve

3:45 P.M., Monday, February 25, 2002

"What on Earth?" Stephanie questioned. She was standing in the doorway to their room. Daniel peered over her shoulder.

"What's the matter?" Daniel asked.

"There are flowers on the bureau," Stephanie said. "Who in God's name would be sending us flowers?"

"Butler?"

"He doesn't know we're here in Turin, unless you emailed him."

"I didn't email him," Daniel said, as if it were totally out of the realm of possibility.

"But with his intelligence connections, maybe he knows. After having me investigated, I wouldn't put it past him. Or maybe Monsignor Mansoni communicated that the sample had been delivered."

Stephanie walked over to the arrangement and opened the envelope. "Oh, for goodness sake. It's just the hotel management."

"That's nice," Daniel said indifferently. He went into the bathroom to use the toilet.

Stephanie moved over to her suitcase that was perched on the luggage stand. She had a pair of walking shoes tucked along the left side. Lifting up the unlatched top to the bag, she hesitated. A linen shirt she had painstakingly packed back in Boston was mildly amiss, with its edge folded over. With her finger, she righted the fold. As she feared, a crease remained, even after she tried to smooth it out with the palm of her hand. Mumbling one of her private vulgarities to herself, she started to reach for the walking shoes when her eye caught an article of lingerie, which was also slightly disarranged and which she had packed with equal care.

Stephanie righted herself and stared down at her open suitcase. "Daniel! Come in here!"

With the sound of the toilet flushing in the background, Daniel's face appeared in the bathroom doorway. He was holding a towel. "What's up?" he questioned with raised eyebrows. He could tell from the sound of her voice that she was mildly perturbed.

"Someone has been in our room!"

"We already knew that when we saw the flowers."

"Come over here!"

Daniel slung the towel over his shoulder as he walked over to stand next to Stephanie. He followed her pointing finger and looked down at her open suitcase.

"Someone has been in my bag," Stephanie said.

"How can you tell?"

Stephanie explained.

"Those are pretty subtle changes," Daniel said. He patted her patronizingly on her back. "You've been in your bag yourself before we went out. Are you sure you're not having a minor attack of paranoia, thanks to the Cambridge break-in?"

"Someone has been in my bag!" Stephanie repeated heatedly. She pushed his hand away. With her jet lag and being overtired, she felt instantly frustrated that

Daniel was being so dismissive. "Look in your suitcase!"

Rolling his eyes, Daniel opened his unlatched bag on the stand next to Stephanie's. "Okay, I'm looking in mine," he reported.

"Anything amiss?"

Daniel shrugged. He was far from the world's neatest packer, and he had rummaged in his bag earlier when retrieving clean underwear. All at once, he froze, then slowly raised his eyes to Stephanie's. "My God! There is something missing!"

"What?" Stephanie clutched Daniel's arm as she looked into his bag.

"Somebody took my vial of plutonium!"

Stephanie swatted Daniel's shoulder. He responded by protecting himself in an exaggerated fashion from further blows, which never came.

"I'm being serious," Stephanie complained stridently. Returning to her own bag, she picked up her hairbrush and brandished it. "Here's something else! When we left on our outing, this brush was directly on top of my clothes, not lying in the suitcase's gutter. I remember because I thought about taking it back into the bathroom. I'm telling you: Someone has been in my bag!"

"All right! All right!" Daniel soothed. "Take it easy!"

Stephanie reached into her bag's side pocket and pulled out a zippered velvet pouch. She opened it and peered inside. "At least my jewelry is okay, including the little bit of cash that I keep in here. It's a good thing I didn't bring anything truly valuable."

"Maybe housekeeping had to move the bags?" Daniel suggested.

"Give me a break!" Stephanie responded, as if Daniel's suggestion was preposterous. Her eyes wandered around the room until they came to rest on the desk. "My room key is gone! I left it on the blotter."

"Are you sure?"

"Don't you remember we talked about it before we left, whether we needed two keys?"

"Vaguely."

Stephanie strode into the bathroom. Daniel's eyes roamed the room. He couldn't decide if Stephanie's paranoia was worth indulging, since he was aware she was still upset about the intruder in Cambridge. He knew that hotel people such as housekeeping, minibar stockers, room-service personnel, and bellmen were in and out of rooms all the time. Maybe one of them had poked their hands into her bag. For some people, it might be a huge temptation.

"Someone has also been in my cosmetics bag," Stephanie called from the bathroom.

Daniel walked to the door and stood on the threshold. "Is anything missing?"

"No, nothing is missing!" Stephanie answered irritably.

"Hey, don't get mad at me!"

Stephanie straightened up, shut her eyes, and took a deep breath. She nodded a few times. "You're right. I'm sorry. I'm not mad at you, just frustrated you're not as upset about this as I."

"If we were missing something, it would be different."

Stephanie closed the cover of her makeup bag. She stepped over to Daniel and put her arms around him. He enveloped her similarly.

"It upsets me when people paw through my belongings, especially after what happened the day before we left."

"That's entirely understandable," Daniel said.

"It is curious nothing is missing, like the cash. That makes this episode exactly like the one in Cambridge, although having it happen here is more confusing. At least there we could postulate industrial espionage, even if it's unlikely. What could someone be looking for here if not valuables and cash?"

"The only thing I can think of is the shroud sample."

Stephanie leaned away from Daniel so she could see up into his face. "Why would someone be looking for that?"

"Beats me. It's just the only thing we have that's unique."

"But presumably the only person who knows we have it is the man who gave it to us." Stephanie's brows were knitted together as if she was troubled anew.

"Calm down! I don't think anyone was looking for the shroud sample. I was just thinking out loud. But as long as we are talking about it, where is it?"

"It's still in my shoulder bag," Stephanie said.

"Get it! Let's have another look!" Daniel thought it best to steer the subject away from a possible intruder.

They retreated back to the middle of the room. Stephanie picked up her bag from where she'd tossed it on the bed. She took out the silver case and opened it. Daniel gingerly lifted out the glassine envelope and held it up to the diffused light coming from the windows. Backlit, the mat of linen fibers was distinct, although its color was still indeterminate. "My gosh!" Daniel said with a shake of his head. "It is truly amazing to think that there is even the slightest chance this contains the blood of arguably the most famous person to have trod this Earth, and that's not even addressing the divine aspect."

Stephanie put the silver case down on the desk and took the envelope. Stepping over to the window, she too held it up to the light. Shielding the slanting rays of the sun from her eyes with her free hand, she used the pale but direct white light to examine the envelope. Now even the fibers' red ocher color could be appreciated. "It looks like blood," she said. "You know, it must be my Catholic background mysteriously reasserting itself, because I have a strong intuition it is the blood of Jesus Christ."

Although Father Michael Maloney could not see Stephanie D'Agostino, he was so close he could hear her breathe. He was terrified his own heartbeat pounding in his temples would give him away or, if not that, then the sound of drops of perspiration dripping from his face and falling to splatter against the floor. She was mere inches away.

In utter desperation when he'd heard the key thrust into the door, he'd dashed behind the drapes. It had been a reflex act. In retrospect, going behind the curtains was an embarrassment in and of itself, as if he were some common thief. He should have stood his ground, accepted his fate at being caught, and taken full responsibility for his actions. He understood the best defense was an offense, and in the present situation, to justify his actions he should have used his indignation about these people's true identities and the upcoming unauthorized testing of the shroud that they were obviously planning.

Unfortunately, his fight-or-flight reaction had been overwhelming, particularly on the flight side, such that when he'd come to his senses he was already hiding, and once hiding, it was too late to play the indignation card. Now all he could do was hope and pray he'd not be discovered.

At first he thought all was lost with Stephanie's exclamation the moment the door opened. He imagined that he'd either been seen or at the very least the curtain's movement had been apparent. It had been a relief beyond words when he realized it had been the flower arrangement that had caught her attention.

Then he had to endure Stephanie's discovery of his ineptness at searching her suitcase and the fact that he'd taken her key from the desk. That was when his pulse began to rise again after having slowed a degree from the initial shock. He feared she would start searching the room, which would mean he'd be immediately discovered. The embarrassment and consequences of such an event were too horrible to contemplate. What had begun as a way of ensuring his future career was now threatening to have the absolute opposite effect.

"What we think about the shroud is not important," Daniel said. "It's just what Butler thinks that matters."

"I'm not sure I agree with you entirely," Stephanie responded. "But that's a discussion for another day."

Michael stiffened as Stephanie brushed

against the drapes. Thankfully, they were heavy Italian brocade, and she apparently did not notice that she had also touched Michael's arm through the fabric. Another adrenaline rush coursed through Michael's body, resulting in more perspiration. To him, the sound of the intermittent drops of sweat splattering against the floor were as loud as pebbles dropping on a drum. He never imagined he could perspire so profusely, especially when he wasn't even all that hot.

"What should I do with the sample?" Stephanie asked, as she moved away.

"Give it to me," Daniel replied from someplace in the room.

Michael allowed himself to take a deep breath, and he relaxed a degree. He had himself pressed up against the wall as flat as he could be, to minimize the bulge his body made in the drape. He heard more sounds he could not identify, along with what he guessed was the silver casing snapping shut.

"You know, we could change rooms," Daniel said. "Or even hotels if you want."

"What do you think we should do?"

"I think we should just stay put. There are multiple keys for every room in every hotel.

Tonight when we sleep, we'll be sure to use the dead bolt."

Michael heard the heavy click of the security lock being activated on the door to the hall.

"That's a lock and a half," Daniel commented. "What do you say? I don't want you to feel nervous. There's no need."

Michael heard the door to the hall shake.

"I guess the lock's all right," Stephanie said. "It seems secure."

"With that dead bolt thrown, no one would be able to come through that door without us knowing it. They'd have to use a battering ram."

"Okay," Stephanie said. "Let's just stay here. It is only one night, and a short one at that, since you have us flying out to London at five after seven. What an ungodly hour. By the way: How come we're going through Paris?"

"There was no choice. British Airways apparently doesn't serve Turin. It was either Air France to Paris or Lufthansa to Frankfurt. I figured it was better not to backtrack."

"It seems ridiculous not to have a direct flight to London, of all places. I mean, Turin is one of the major industrial cities of Italy."

"What can I say?" Daniel questioned with a shrug. "But for now, how about you getting your walking shoes and whatever else you want so we can get back to our sightseeing."

"Oh, please do!" Michael pleaded silently.

"I've had a change of heart," Stephanie said, to Michael's immediate chagrin. "What about staying in until we go out to dinner? It's already after four, and it will be dark soon. As little as you slept last night, you must be exhausted."

"I am tired," Daniel admitted.

"Let's take off our clothes and get in bed. I'll even give you a little back rub, and we'll see what else happens, depending on how tired you are. What do you say?"

Daniel laughed. "I've never heard a better idea in my life. To be honest, I wasn't all that interested in the sightseeing. I was doing it more for your benefit."

"Well, that's no longer necessary, my dear!"

Michael cringed as he heard sounds of disrobing, giggles, and endearments. He feared one of them would come to close the drapes, but that didn't happen. He heard the sounds the bed made, as bodies settled into it. He heard the sound of lotion being squeezed from a bottle and even the sound of flesh against slippery flesh. There was the murmur of contentment from Daniel, as his massage progressed.

"All right," Daniel said finally. "Now it's your turn." The bed complained as bodies shifted.

Time dragged. Michael's muscles began to ache, particularly in his legs. Fearing he might get a cramp, which he knew would surely give him away, he shifted his weight, then held his breath in case his movement was noticed. Thankfully, it wasn't, but the pain came back within minutes. Yet worse than the physical discomfort was the torture of hearing the sounds of intimacy between a man and a woman leading to the rhythmic and unmistakable noise of actual lovemaking. Michael was being forced by circumstance to be an auditory voyeur, and despite his attempts at silently reciting by rote selections from his breviary, he found himself titillated to mock his vows of celibacy.

After a few moans of pleasure, the room fell silent for a few minutes. Then there were whispers Michael could not make out, followed by laughter and giggles. Finally, to Michael's relief, the couple went into the bathroom. He could tell by the muffled sounds of their voices over the sound of the shower.

Michael allowed himself to rotate his head, flex his stiff shoulders, raise his arms, and even walk briefly in place. After less than a minute, he returned to his frozen position, unsure when one of the couple would choose to return to the room proper. He didn't have long to wait and soon heard one of them at the suitcases.

Unfortunately for Michael, it took Stephanie and Daniel another three quarters of an hour to dress, don their coats, and find their remaining room key before they finally left for dinner. At first, the silence seemed deafening, as he strained to hear any noises that would suggest they were returning for some forgotten item. Five minutes crept by. Finally, Michael warily reached around the edge of the drape and slowly drew it aside, revealing progressively more of the now darkened room. The couple had left the light on in the bathroom, and it spilled out into the room to puddle alongside the bed.

Michael eyed the door to the hall and tried to estimate how quickly he could get to it, through it, and get it closed behind himself. It wouldn't take long, but it made him nervous he'd be completely exposed before putting some distance between himself and room 408. At this point, being caught would be significantly more problematic than when Stephanie and Daniel had first come home.

As Michael tried to build his courage to leave the relative safety of the drapes, his eyes roamed around the room. A glint off a shining object on the bureau next to the flower arrangement caught his eye. He blinked, not believing what he was looking at. "Praise be to God!" he whispered. It was the silver case.

Marveling at his luck after all, Michael took a deep breath and emerged from his hiding place. For another second he hesitated, listening before rushing to the bureau, snapping up the silver case, slipping it into his pocket, and dashing out the door. To his relief, the corridor was empty. He quickly moved away from room 408, afraid to look back and terrified someone would accost him. It wasn't until he reached the elevators that he allowed himself to glance back down the hallway. It was still empty.

A few minutes later, Michael passed through the hotel's revolving door and stepped out into the night. Never had the chill of a midwinter evening felt so good against his flushed face. He walked quickly away from the door, each step a bit more buoyant than the previous. With his right hand thrust into his jacket pocket, clutching the silver case as a reminder of what he'd been able to accomplish, an exhilaration spread through him not unlike the euphoria of absolution he'd occasionally felt after particularly difficult visits as a supplicant to the confessional. It was as if the stressful trials and tribulations of resaving his Savior's blood sample had made the experience that much more poignant.

Michael took a taxi from the hotel's cabstand and gave the address of the Chancery of the Archdiocese to the driver. He sat back and tried to relax. He looked at his watch. It was almost six-thirty. He'd been caught behind the couple's curtain for more than two hours! But it was a nightmare with a happy ending, as evidenced by the cold feel of the silver case in his pocket.

Michael closed his eyes and reveled in thinking about the best time to call James Cardinal O'Rourke to explain the unfortunate development concerning the identities of the so-called couriers, followed by the problem's ultimate resolution. Now that he was safe, he found himself smiling at what he'd had to endure. Hiding behind drapes in a hotel room while the couple made love was so preposterous as to defy belief. In some ways, he wished he could tell the cardinal, but he knew he couldn't. The only person he would ultimately tell would be his confessor, and even that was not going to be easy.

Knowing the cardinal's schedule, Michael thought it best to wait until ten-thirty P.M. Italian time to make the call. It was during the pre-dinner hour that the cardinal was the most accessible. During the call, what Michael was going to enjoy particularly was implying rather than directly telling the cardinal that it had been he who had by his own ingenuity single-handedly salvaged what could have been an embarrassment for the church in general and the cardinal in particular.

By the time the taxi pulled up in front of the chancery, Michael felt almost back to normal. Although his pulse was still rapid, he was no longer perspiring, and his breathing was entirely regular. The only problem was that his shirt and underclothes were damp from the ordeal, making him feel chilled.

Michael first went to see Valerio Garibaldi, whom he had befriended back when he'd attended the North American College in Rome, but he was informed that his friend had left the building on an official errand. Michael then walked down to Luigi Mansoni's office. He knocked on the open door, and the monsignor motioned for him to come in and sit down. The cleric was on the phone. He quickly terminated the call and directed his full attention to Michael. Switching from Italian to English, he asked how Michael had fared. From his unblinking stare, it was apparent he was intensely interested.

"Quite well, considering," Michael said obliquely.

"Considering what?"

"Considering what I had to go through." Triumphantly, he reached into his pocket and pulled out the embossed silver case. Carefully, he placed it on Luigi's desk before pushing it toward the monsignor. He sat back with a self-satisfied smile on his thin face.

Luigi's eyebrows arched. He reached out, carefully lifted the case, and held it between both his palms. "I'm surprised they were willing to give it up," he said. "They seemed like two very passionate people."

"Your assessment is more accurate than you know," Michael said. "But they are not yet aware that they have surrendered the sample back to the church. And to be honest, I did not so much as talk with them."

A slight smile dimpled Luigi's puffy face. "I'm thinking perhaps I shouldn't ask how you have managed to get it."

"You shouldn't," Michael advised.

"Well, then, that's how we will proceed. For my part, I will merely return the sample to Professor Ballasari, and that will be it." Luigi released the latch and lifted the case's cover. He then started while staring into its bare innards. After a few quick glances back and forth between Michael and the case, he said: "I'm confused. The sample is not in here!"

"No! Don't say that!" Michael sat bolt upright.

"I'm afraid I must," Luigi responded. He turned the empty case around and held it up so Michael could see.

"Oh, no!" Michael cried. He grabbed his head with both hands and slumped forward until his elbows rested on his knees. "I don't believe it!"

"They must have removed the sample."

"Obviously," Michael responded, as he exhaled. He sounded depressed.

"You are distraught."

"More than you would guess."

"Certainly all is not lost. Perhaps now you should approach the Americans directly and demand the sample's return."

Michael rubbed his face forcibly and then exhaled. He looked at Luigi. "I don't think that is an option, not after what I did to get the empty case. And even if I did, your assessment of their character is most likely correct. They would refuse. My sense is that they have a specific plan for the sample, to which they are committed."

"Do you know when they are leaving?"

"Tomorrow morning at five after seven on Air France. They are flying to London via Paris."

"Well, there is another option," Luigi said, tenting his fingers. "There is a sure way to get the sample back. I happen to be related on my mother's side of the family to a gentleman by the name of Carlo Ricciardi. He is a first cousin. He also happens to be the Soprintendente Archeologico del Piedmonte, meaning the regional director, of NPPA,

which stands for Nucleo Protezione Patrimo-
nio Artistico e Archeologico."

"I've never heard of it."

"It is not surprising, since their activities
are mostly carried out sub rosa, but they are
a special corps of the carabinieri responsible
for the safety of Italy's vast treasure of historical monuments and objects, which certainly
includes the Shroud of Turin, despite the
Holy See being its rightful owner. If I were to
call Carlo, he would have no trouble retrieving the sample."

"What would you say? I mean, you gave
the Americans the sample; it's not like they
stole it. In fact, since you gave it to them in a
public place, an enterprising Italian lawyer
could probably even produce a witness."

"I would not suggest the sample was
stolen. I would merely say that the sample
had been obtained under false pretenses,
which apparently is the case. But more importantly, I would state that no authorization
had been given for the sample to be taken
out of Italy. In fact, I would add that removal of
the sample from Italy had been strictly forbid-
den, and yet I had information the Americans
were planning to do so tomorrow morning."

"And these archeological police would have the authority to confiscate it."

"Most definitely! They are a very powerful and independent agency. To give you an example, a number of years ago your then President Reagan asked the then Italian president if the recently found ancient bronzes pulled from the sea off Reggio di Calabria could be brought to the Los Angeles Olympics as the game's icons. The Italian president agreed, but the regional Soprintendente Archeologico said no, and the statues stayed in Italy."

"Okay, I'm impressed," Michael said. "Does the agency have its own uniformed enforcement division?"

"They have their own plainclothes *ispettori,* or inspectors, but for general enforcement they use either uniformed carabinieri or Guardia di Finanza officers. At the airport, it would probably be the Guardia di Finanza, although if they are acting under Carlo's specific orders, the carabinieri most likely would participate as well."

"If you make the call, what will happen to the Americans?"

"Tomorrow morning, when they check in for their international flight, they will be arrested, jailed, and eventually tried. In Italy, charges of this nature are considered very serious. But they would not be tried right away. Such cases move slowly. But, the sample will be returned to us straightaway, and the problem will be solved."

"Make the call!" Michael said simply. He was disappointed, but all was not lost. Obviously, he would not be able to take credit for solving the problem with the shroud sample single-handedly. On the other hand, he could still make sure the cardinal knew he had been an indispensable participant.

A contented belch rumbled from the pit of Daniel's stomach to emerge between his puffed-up cheeks. His hand clasped his face in a halfhearted attempt to conceal his impish smile.

Stephanie cast him one of what she considered her most scornful looks. She never thought it was funny when he gave vent to his mischievously juvenile side.

Daniel laughed. "Hey, relax. We had a great dinner and a great bottle of Barolo. Let's not ruin it!"

"I'll relax after I check out our room," Stephanie said. "I think I have the right to be on edge after someone pawed through my belongings earlier."

Daniel keyed the door and pushed it open. Stephanie stepped over the threshold and let her eyes wander. Daniel started to go past her into the room. She held him back with her arm.

"I've got to use the bathroom," Daniel complained.

"We had visitors!"

"Oh! How can you tell?"

Stephanie pointed toward the bureau. "The silver case is gone."

"Gone it is," Daniel said. "I guess you were right all along."

"Of course I was right," Stephanie responded. She walked over and put her hand on the bureau where the silver case had been, as if she didn't believe it was gone. "But so were you. They must have been after the shroud sample."

"Well, I have to give you full credit for your idea of taking the sample out and leaving the case behind."

"Thank you," Stephanie said. "But first, let's make sure it wasn't just that they thought the case was something valuable." She went over to her suitcase and again checked her jewelry case. Everything was still in it, including the cash.

Daniel did the same. The jewelry, cash, and traveler's checks were all accounted for. He straightened up. "What do you want to do?" he asked.

"Get out of Italy. Never in a million years did I ever think I'd feel that way." Stephanie collapsed on the bed, coat and all, and stared up at the multicolored glass chandelier.

"I'm talking about tonight."

"You mean whether to change hotels or rooms?"

"Exactly."

"Let's just stay here and use the dead bolt."

"I was hoping you'd say that," Daniel said as he stepped out of his pants. Holding them by the cuffs, he arranged them to preserve the creases. "I cannot wait to climb into bed," he added, as he eyed Stephanie, sprawled out on her back. He then went to the closet and hung up his trousers. Holding onto the jamb, he stepped out of his loafers.

"It would be a humongous effort to move, and I'm bushed," Stephanie said. With great effort, she got back on her feet and shook off

her coat. "Besides, I'm not confident whoever has been plaguing us wouldn't be able
to find us wherever we went. Let's just not
leave this room until we're ready to leave the
hotel." She pushed past Daniel and hung up
her coat.

"Fine by me," Daniel said, as he unbuttoned his shirt. "In the morning, we can even
skip trying to have something to eat here at
the hotel. Instead, we can grab a bite of
breakfast at one of those coffee bars at the
airport. They all seem to have a selection of
pastries. The concierge said we should be
there around six, which means we are going
to have to get up pretty damn early, even if
we don't try to eat before leaving."

"Excellent idea," Stephanie said. "I can't
tell you how much I'm looking forward to getting to the airport, checking in, and getting
on that plane."

thirteen

4:45 A.M., Tuesday, February 26, 2002

Despite the hefty security lock on the door, Stephanie slept poorly. Every noise from inside the hotel or from outside had caused a minor panic reaction, and there had been a lot of noises. At one point just after midnight, when guests had keyed and entered a neighboring room, Stephanie had sat up, ready for battle, certain the people were coming into her room. She'd sat up so quickly that she'd pulled the covers from Daniel, whose response was to yank them back angrily.

After two A.M., Stephanie finally fell asleep. But it was far from a restful slumber, and it was a source of relief when Daniel shook her shoulder to wake her after what had seemed to her to be about fifteen minutes.

"What time is it?" she asked groggily. She pushed herself up on one elbow.

"It's five A.M. Rise and shine! We should be out in a taxi in a half hour."

"Rise and shine" had been a phrase her mother had used to wake her when Stephanie had been a teenager, and since Stephanie had been an Olympic-class sleeper who hated to wake up, the phrase had always bothered her. Daniel knew the story and used the expression deliberately to provoke her, which, of course, was an effective way to wake her up. "I'm awake," she said irritably when he shook her again. She eyed her tormentor, but he merely smiled before briefly mussing her hair with the palm of his hand. The gesture was something else Stephanie found irritating, even when her hair was in disarray, as it certainly was at that moment; it was demeaning, and she had told Daniel such on several occasions. It made her feel as if he considered her a child or, worse yet, a pet.

Stephanie watched Daniel go into the bathroom. She rolled over on her back and winced at the light. The multicolored glass chandelier was blazing above her. Outside, it was still as dark as pitch. She took a breath. It seemed as if the only thing she wanted to do in the whole world was to go back to sleep. But then the cobwebs in her mind began to clear, and she thought about how much she wanted to get on the plane with the shroud fibers and get out of Italy.

"Are you up?" Daniel shouted from the bathroom.

"I'm up!" Stephanie shouted back. She had no compunction about fibbing, not after how merciless he'd been in waking her up. She stretched, yawned, and then sat up. After shaking off a brief sensation akin to nausea, she got to her feet.

A shower worked wonders for both of them. Despite Daniel's acting to the contrary, he had been far from feeling chipper initially and had had almost as much trouble getting out of bed after the alarm went off as Stephanie. Yet by the time they had gotten out of the bathroom, they were both in high spirits in anticipation of getting to the airport. They dressed and packed with great efficiency. By quarter past five, Daniel called the front desk to arrange for a taxi and to get someone to come get their bags.

"It's hard to believe we'll be in Nassau by late this afternoon," Daniel said, as he closed and locked his suitcase. The day's itinerary was to fly to London on Air France via Paris, connect to British Airways, and then fly on directly to New Providence Island in the Bahamas.

"What I find difficult to comprehend is that we'll be going from winter to summer in a single day. It seems like ages since I've been in a pair of shorts and a summer top. I'm psyched."

The bellman arrived and took their luggage down to the lobby on a garment cart with instructions that it should be loaded into the taxi. While Stephanie dried her hair, Daniel stood in the bathroom doorway.

"I think we should tell the manager about our intruder," Stephanie said over the sound of the hotel's hair dryer.

"What would that accomplish?"

"Not much, I suppose, but I'd think they'd want to know."

Daniel looked at his watch. "I think it's a

moot point. We don't have time. It's almost five-thirty. We need to be on our way."

"Why don't you go down and check out," Stephanie suggested. "I'll be down in two minutes."

"Nassau, here we come," Daniel said as he left.

The phone's insistent jangle yanked Michael Maloney from the depths of sleep. He had the phone to his ear before he was totally awake. It was Father Peter Fleck, Cardinal O'Rourke's other personal secretary.

"Are you awake?" Peter asked. "Sorry to be calling you at such an hour."

"What time is it?" Michael asked. He fumbled for the bedside light, then tried to make out what time it was on his watch.

"It's twenty-five minutes before midnight here in New York. What time is it there in Italy?"

"It is five-thirty-five in the morning."

"Sorry, but you told me when you called this afternoon that it was imperative you speak with the cardinal as soon as possible, and His Eminence has just returned to the residence. Let me put him on the line."

Michael rubbed his face and patted his cheek to wake himself. A moment later, James Cardinal O'Rourke's gentle voice sounded in Michael's ear. He too apologized for calling at such an inconvenient hour and explained that he'd been forced to remain at an interminable function with the governor, which had started in the late afternoon.

"I'm sorry I must add to your burdens," Michael said, with some trepidation. He was not fooled by the powerful man's humble graciousness. Behind the apparent benevolence, Michael was well aware of how ruthless he could be, especially to a subordinate who was either foolish or unlucky enough to displease him. At the same time, to those who pleased him, he could be extraordinarily generous.

"Are you implying there has been a problem in Turin?" the cardinal questioned.

"Unfortunately, yes," Michael said. "The two people whom Senator Butler sent to receive the sample of the shroud are both biomolecular scientists."

"I see," James commented.

"Their names are Dr. Daniel Lowell and Dr. Stephanie D'Agostino."

"I see," James repeated.

"From your instructions," Michael continued, "I knew you would be distressed about this development because of its implications about unauthorized testing. The good news is that by working quickly with Monsignor Mansoni, I have managed to arrange that the sample will be returned forthwith."

"Oh," James said simply. There was an uncomfortable pause. As far as Michael was concerned, this was hardly the response he was expecting. By this point in the conversation, he counted on a definitively positive reaction from the cardinal.

"Obviously, the goal is to avoid any more scientific indignity for the shroud," Michael added quickly. A shiver ascended his spine. His intuition was telling him the conversation was about to take an unexpected turn.

"Have doctors Lowell and D'Agostino voluntarily agreed to give up the sample?"

"Not exactly," Michael admitted. "The sample will be confiscated by the Italian authorities when they check in for a flight to Paris this morning."

"And what will happen to the scientists?"

"I believe they will be detained."

"Was it true that the shroud itself did not

have to be touched to produce this sample, as Senator Butler suggested?"

"That is true. The sample was a tiny piece from a swatch that had been cut from the shroud a number of years ago."

"Was it turned over to the scientists in strict confidentiality, without official documentation?"

"To the best of my knowledge," Michael said. "I had communicated that that was your specific wish." Michael began to perspire, certainly not as copiously as he had while hiding in the hotel room the previous day, but from a similar stimulus: fear. He could feel a knot of anxiety building in his stomach and tensing his muscles. The tone of the cardinal's questions had a barely perceptible sharpness that most people would not have perceived but which Michael heard immediately and recognized. He knew His Eminence was becoming progressively angry.

"Father Maloney! For your information, the senator has already introduced his promised legislation limiting charitable tort liability, which he now believes with his backing has a better chance of passing than he did when he proposed the idea on Friday. I don't need to explain to you the value of this legislation for the church. As far as the shroud sample is concerned, with no official documentation, even if some ill-advised testing were to be done, the results could not be authenticated and could be simply repudiated."

"I'm sorry," Michael blurted lamely. "I thought Your Eminence would want the sample back."

"Father Maloney, your instructions were clear. You were not sent to Turin to think. You went there to find out who took possession of the sample and follow if necessary to see to whom it was ultimately delivered. You were not to arrange for the sample to be returned and thereby put in jeopardy an extremely important legislative process."

"I don't know what to say," Michael managed.

"Don't say anything. Instead, I strongly advise you to reverse what you have set in motion if it is not already a fait accompli; that is, of course, unless your immediate career goal is to be assigned a small parish someplace in the Catskill Mountains. I do not want the shroud sample confiscated, nor do I want the American scientists arrested, which is a more accurate term for what awaits them than the euphemism you employed. Most important, I do not want Senator Butler calling to say he has withdrawn his bill, which I believe will be his response if what you have described were to occur. Am I clear, Father?"

"Perfectly clear," Michael stammered. He found himself holding a dead line. The cardinal had abruptly disconnected.

Michael swallowed with some difficulty as he hung up the receiver. Being sent to a small parish in Upstate New York was the church's equivalent of being sent to Siberia.

All at once, Michael snapped the phone up out of its cradle. The American scientists' plane wasn't leaving until after seven. That meant there was still a chance to avert a career disaster. First, he phoned the Grand Belvedere, only to learn that the Americans had already checked out. Next, he tried to call Monsignor Mansoni, but the prelate had left his residence a half hour earlier on church business at the airport.

Galvanized by these revelations, Michael jumped into his clothes, which were conveniently draped over a bedside chair. Without shaving or showering or even using the toilet, he ran from his room. Unwilling to wait for the elevator, he took the stairs. Within minutes and out of breath, he fumbled with his rent-a-car keys before climbing into his rented Fiat. Once the engine turned over, he backed up and raced out of the parking lot.

Hazarding a glance at his watch, he estimated that he could get to the airport a little after six. The main problem was that he had no idea what he was going to do once he arrived.

Are you going to give him a big tip?" Stephanie questioned provocatively, as the taxi mounted the ramp leading to the departure-drop-off area of the Turin airport. Daniel's taxi phobia was beginning to get on her nerves, although to Daniel's credit, the driver had completely ignored Daniel's repeated requests for him to slow down. Every time Daniel had spoken, the man had merely shrugged his shoulders and said, "No English!" At the same time, he hadn't driven any faster than the other cars on the highway.

"He's going to be lucky if I even pay the fare!" Daniel snapped.

The taxi came to a stop in a sea of other taxis and cars discharging passengers. In contrast to the center city, the airport was already busy. Stephanie and Daniel climbed out, along with the driver. With the three of them working, they got all the luggage out of the small taxi and piled it on the curbside. Daniel grudgingly paid the man, and he left.

"How should we work this?" Stephanie asked. They had more bags than the two of them could reasonably carry. She glanced around the immediate area.

"I don't like the idea of leaving anything unattended," Daniel said.

"I agree. How about one of us going to get a cart while the other stands guard."

"Sounds good. What's your preference?"

"Since you have the tickets and passports, why don't you get them out and ready while I find the cart."

Stephanie worked her way through the crowd, keeping her eyes peeled for a cart, but all were in use. She had better luck inside the terminal especially after she had walked past the check-in counters to the security area. Travelers going through security to the departure gates had to leave their carts in the terminal proper. Stephanie took an abandoned one and retraced her steps. She found Daniel sitting on the largest of their suitcases, impatiently tapping his toe.

"It took you long enough," he complained.

"Sorry, but I did the best I could. This place

is hopping. There must be quite a few flights leaving around the same time."

Together they loaded all but their laptop cases on the cart to create a rather precarious pile. The laptops went over their shoulders. While Daniel pushed, Stephanie walked alongside to keep the stack of bags from toppling over.

"I noticed a lot of police wandering around," Stephanie said, as they entered the terminal. "More than I've ever seen. Of course, Italian carabinieri stand out with their snappy outfits."

They stopped about twenty feet inside the door. The crowds swirled about them like a river of people. Standing where they were, they created a minor cataract.

"Where do we go?" Daniel questioned. Several people jostled him. "I don't see any Air France display."

"The flights are listed on the LCD screens next to each check-in counter," Stephanie said. "Wait here! I'll find our flight."

It took Stephanie only a few minutes to find the right counter. When she got back to Daniel, she found that he had moved to the side to get out of the stream of people coming through the door. Stephanie pointed in the direction they had to go, and they set off.

"I see what you mean about the police," Daniel commented. "A half dozen walked by just while you were gone. What caught my attention were the machine guns."

"There's even a group behind the counter where we have to check in," Stephanie said.

They got to the rather sizable line waiting to check in for the Paris flight and joined the queue. Five minutes dragged by as the line inched forward.

"What the hell are they doing up there?" Daniel questioned. He stood on his tiptoes to try to see what was holding things up. "I can never imagine what takes so long. I wonder if the police are slowing up the process somehow."

"As long as we don't get bottled up going through security, I think we'll be fine." Stephanie glanced at her watch. It was twenty past six.

"Since this counter is just for this flight, we're all in the same boat." Daniel was still eyeing the front of the line.

"I hadn't thought of that, but you're right."

"My gosh!" Daniel said.

"What now?" Daniel's exclamation and his change of tone made Stephanie aware of how tense she still was. She tried to follow

Daniel's line of sight, but she couldn't see over the people in front of them.

"Monsignor Mansoni, the priest who gave us the shroud sample, is standing up there with the police behind the check-in counter."

"Are you sure?" Stephanie questioned. It seemed like too big a coincidence. She tried again to see but couldn't.

Daniel shrugged. He glanced back at the counter again before returning his attention to Stephanie. "It certainly looks like him, and I can't imagine there are too many priests quite as obese as he."

"Do you think this has anything to do with us?"

"I can't imagine, although combining his presence with the fact that someone tried to take our shroud sample from our hotel room makes me feel uneasy."

"I don't like this," Stephanie said. "I don't like this at all."

The line ahead of them moved forward. Daniel hesitated, unsure of what to do until the gentleman immediately behind impatiently nudged Daniel forward. Daniel pushed the towering cart forward but purposefully stayed shielded behind it. He and Stephanie were now four parties away from the front of the line. Stephanie moved a few steps laterally and surreptitiously glanced ahead. She returned immediately to stand with Daniel behind the cart.

"It's Monsignor Mansoni for sure," she said. She and Daniel stared at each other.

"What the hell are we going to do?" Daniel blurted out.

"I don't know. It's the police who bother me, not the priest."

"Obviously," Daniel retorted angrily.

"Where is the shroud sample?"

"I told you earlier. It's in my laptop case."

"Hey, don't yell at me."

The line moved ahead. With the man behind them breathing down Daniel's neck, he felt obligated to push the cart forward. Moving closer to the counter exacerbated both their anxieties.

"Maybe this is just a case of overactive imaginations," Stephanie suggested hopefully.

"It's too big a coincidence to explain away as mere paranoia," Daniel responded. "If it were just the priest or just the police it would be one thing, but with both at this particular counter, it's something else entirely. The problem is, we are going to have to make some sort of decision here. I mean, not doing anything is a decision of sorts, because in a couple of minutes, we'll be front and center, and whatever is going to happen will happen."

"At this point, what is there that we can do? We're hemmed in here by a crowd of people and burdened with a truckload of luggage. Worst case, we give them the sample if that's what they want."

"There wouldn't be this many uniformed policeman if they were merely planning to confiscate the sample."

"Excuse me," an out-of-breath, panicky voice called from behind them in irrefutable American English.

As tense as Stephanie and Daniel were, their heads shot around in unison to confront an obviously distressed cleric with wild, staring eyes. The man's chest was heaving, presumably from the exertion of running, while beads of perspiration dotted his forehead. Adding to his distraught appearance was an unshaven face and an uncombed shock of red hair, both of which were in sharp contrast to his reasonably pressed priestly attire. Apparently he'd reached Stephanie and Daniel by forcing his way between the check-in counter queues, judging from the expressions of irritation on nearby travelers' faces.

"Dr. Lowell and Dr. D'Agostino!" Father Michael Maloney panted. "It is imperative that I talk with you."

"Scusi!" the man behind Daniel said irritably. He gestured for Daniel to move ahead. The line had advanced, and while eyeing Michael, Daniel had yet to do so.

Daniel motioned for the man to go ahead of them, and he gladly did.

Michael cast a quick glance ahead over the top of Daniel and Stephanie's luggage cart. Catching sight of the monsignor and the police, he ducked down and squeezed in alongside Daniel. "We have only a few seconds," he blurted in a forced whisper. "You must not check in for your flight to Paris!"

"How do you know our names?" Daniel questioned.

"There's no time for me to explain."

"Who are you?" Stephanie asked. There was something about the man she recognized, but she couldn't place him.

"It doesn't matter who I am. What is important is that you are about to be arrested, and the shroud sample will be confiscated."

"I remember you," Stephanie said. "You

were in the café when we were given the sample yesterday."

"Please!" Michael begged. "You have to get away from here. I have a car. I will get you out of Italy."

"Drive?" Daniel questioned, as if the suggestion was ridiculous.

"It is the only way. Planes, trains, all mass transit will be watched, but particularly planes and particularly this flight to Paris. I'm serious; you are about to be arrested and jailed. Believe me!"

Daniel and Stephanie exchanged glances. Both were thinking the same thing: This distraught priest's sudden arrival and warning was unbelievably serendipitous, which lent powerful credence to what had been a mere fearful supposition seconds earlier. They were not going to check in for the flight to Paris.

Daniel started to turn the luggage cart around. Michael grabbed his arm. "There's no time for all the luggage."

"What are you talking about?" Daniel demanded.

Michael craned his neck to steal a brief glance at the counter a mere twenty feet away. Instantly, he pulled his head back down like a turtle, hunching his shoulders. "Damn! Now I've been seen, which means we're all seconds away from disaster here. Unless you are interested in spending time in jail, we have to run. You have to leave most of the baggage! You have to make a decision about what is more important: your freedom or your luggage."

"It's all my summer clothes," Stephanie said. She was aghast at the idea.

"Signore!" the man behind Daniel said, with obvious irritation, while gesturing for Daniel to move forward. *"Va! Va via!"* A number of people behind him chimed in as well. The queue had again moved forward, and by blocking the back of the line, Daniel and Stephanie were causing a scene.

"Where's the sample?" Michael demanded. "And your passports?"

"They're in my shoulder bag," Daniel responded.

"Good!" Michael snapped. "Keep your shoulder bags, but leave the rest! Later, I'll have the U.S. consulate try to deal with the remainder of your belongings and forward it to wherever you are going beyond London. Come on!" He tugged at Daniel's arm while pointing away from the counter.

Daniel looked over the top of the loaded cart just in time to see Monsignor Mansoni grab the arm of one of the uniformed policemen and point in their direction. With mounting urgency, Daniel switched his attention to Stephanie. "I think we better do as he says."

"Fine! We'll leave the bags." Stephanie responded with resignation by throwing up her arms.

"Follow me!" Michael barked. As rapidly as he could, he led the way away from the luggage cart. Travelers in the immediate area who were pressed together in their queues parted reluctantly and sluggishly. While repeating *"scusi"* over and over, Michael was forced to push people aside and trip over hand luggage resting on the floor. Daniel and Stephanie followed in his footsteps as if Michael were blazing a trail through a jungle of human beings. It was frustratingly hard going, and the effort reminded Stephanie of a nightmare she'd been having when Daniel awakened her an hour and a half earlier.

Cries of *"alt!"* coming from behind them spurred them on to greater efforts. Breaking free from the crowds surrounding the check-in counters, their progress was significantly easier, but Michael restrained them from running.

"It would be one thing if we were running into the terminal," Michael explained. "Running out will attract too much attention. Just walk quickly!"

All at once, directly ahead, two youthful-looking policemen appeared, hurrying toward them with their machine guns unslung from their shoulders.

"Oh, no!" Daniel moaned. He slowed.

"Keep going!" Michael said between clenched teeth. Behind them, there was now an audible commotion with unintelligible shouts.

Heading on a collision course, the two groups closed in on each other rapidly. Both Daniel and Stephanie were sure the policemen were coming to apprehend them, and it wasn't until the last minute that they realized they weren't. Both sighed with relief as the policeman swept by without a glance, presumably rushing toward the furor at the check-in area.

Other travelers began stopping to stare at the policemen, with varying degrees of fear registered on their faces. After 9/11, disturbances at an airport anyplace in the world, no matter what the cause, put people on edge.

"My car is at arrivals on the lower level," Michael explained, as he directed them toward the stairs. "There was no way I could leave it even for a moment on the departure level."

They descended the stairs as rapidly as they could. Below the terminal was relatively deserted, since incoming flights had yet to arrive. The only people in evidence were a handful of airport employees preparing for the onslaught of passengers and baggage, and rent-a-car agents readying their kiosks.

"It's even more important now not to rush," Michael said under his breath. A few people glanced in their direction, but only for a moment, before going back to their respective tasks. Michael led Daniel and Stephanie to the main doors, which opened automatically. They quickly exited, but then Michael halted. With his arms out to his sides, he stopped the others as well.

"This does not look good." Michael moaned. "Unfortunately, that's my rent-a-car up there."

About fifty feet ahead, a tan Fiat van with its blinkers flashing was parked by the curb. Immediately behind it was a blue-and-white police car with its blue light flashing. The heads of two officers were silhouetted in the front seat.

"What should we do?" Daniel asked urgently. "What about renting another?"

"I don't think the rent-a-car concessions are open yet," Michael retorted. "It would take too long."

"What about a taxi?" Stephanie offered. "We have to get away from this airport. We could rent a car in town."

"That's a thought," Michael said. He looked at the empty taxi line. "The problem is, there won't be taxis down here until the first flight arrives, and I don't know when that will be. For us to get a cab, we'd have to go back upstairs, which I hardly feel is a good idea. I think we have to risk taking my car. These are Vigli Urbani, or municipal traffic police. I doubt they are specifically looking for us, at least not yet. They're probably waiting for a tow truck."

"What will you say?"

"I'm not sure," Michael admitted. "There's no time to be particularly creative. I'll just try to take advantage of my status as a priest." He took a breath to fortify himself. "Come on! When we get to the car, just get in. I'll do the talking."

"I don't like this," Stephanie said.

"Nor do I," Michael admitted. He urged everyone forward. "But I think it is our best shot. In a few minutes, every security person here at the airport is going to be searching for all of us high and low. Monsignor Mansoni caught sight of me."

"You two know each other?" Stephanie asked.

"Let's say we are acquaintances," Michael responded.

There was no more talking as the group walked quickly and deliberately toward the Fiat Ulysse. Michael went around behind the police car to pass on the driver's side. When he got to the Fiat, he keyed it open and slid in behind the wheel as if he hadn't even noticed the police car. Stephanie and Daniel arrived at the passenger side and immediately climbed into the backseat.

"*Padre!*" one of the policeman yelled. He'd alighted from his car when he'd caught sight of Michael getting into the Fiat. The second policeman stayed in the car.

Michael had not yet closed the car door when the policeman called. He climbed back out of the car and stood up.

Daniel and Stephanie watched from inside. The policeman walked up to Michael. He was dressed in a two-tone blue uniform with a white belt and a white holster. He was a slightly built fellow who spoke in a rapid staccato fashion, as did Michael. The conversation was accompanied by lots of gesticulations culminating in the policeman pointing ahead and then making sweeping motions with his hand. At that point, Michael climbed back into the car and started the engine. A moment later, the Fiat emerged from beneath the departure ramp and headed for the airport exit.

"What happened?" Stephanie questioned nervously. She looked out the back window to make sure they were not being followed.

"Luckily, he was mildly cowed by my being a priest."

"What did you say?" Daniel asked.

"I just apologized and said it was an emergency. Then I asked where the nearest hospital was, which apparently he bought. From then on, all he was doing was giving me directions."

"You speak fluent Italian?" Stephanie asked.

"It's not too bad. I went to the seminary in Rome."

As soon as he could, Michael left the main thoroughfare to drive along a small country road. After driving a short distance, they were in a rural setting.

"Where are we going?" Daniel asked. He looked out the window with obvious concern.

"We are going to stay off the autostradas," Michael said. "It will be safer. To tell you the truth, I don't know the extent to which they will search for you people. But I just don't want to risk going through the tollbooths."

When an opportunity presented itself, Michael pulled off onto the shoulder and stopped the car. With the engine running, he got out of the car and disappeared for a few minutes into the darkness of the bushes. The sun had yet to come up, but it was light.

"What's going on?" Stephanie asked.

"I haven't the slightest idea," Daniel said. "But if I had to guess, I'd say he's relieving himself."

Michael reappeared and climbed back into the car. "Sorry," he said, without further explanation. He leaned across and got several maps out of the glove compartment.

"I'm going to need a copilot," he said. "Are either one of you good at reading a map?"

Daniel and Stephanie exchanged glances.

"She's probably better than I," Daniel admitted.

Michael unfolded one of the maps. He looked over his shoulder at Stephanie. "How about coming up here in the front seat. I really am going to need help until we get beyond Cuneo."

Stephanie shrugged, got out from the backseat, and came around to get in the front.

"This is where we are," Michael said, after turning on the interior light and pointing to a spot on the map northeast of Turin. "And this is where we are going." He moved his finger down to the base of the map and plunked it down on the coast of the Mediterranean.

"Nice, France?" Stephanie questioned.

"Yes. That's the closest major airport outside of Italy if we go south, which I recommend, since we can travel on minor roads. We could head north to Geneva, but that would require going on major roads, including a major border crossing. I think south is safer and therefore better. Do you both agree?"

Daniel and Stephanie shrugged. "I suppose," Daniel remarked.

"All right," Michael said. "Here's the route."

He again used his finger as he spoke. "We'll drive through Turin on our way to Cuneo. From there, we go over the Colle di Tenda. Once we cross the border, which is unmanned, we will stay in France, even though the main road south goes back into Italy. At Menton, on the coast, we can get on the toll road, which will take us in short order to Nice. That section will be the quickest part. As far as timing is concerned, I'd say the whole trip will take us five or six hours, but it's just a guess. Is this acceptable?"

Daniel and Stephanie again shrugged after glancing at each other. They were both so befuddled by the events that they hardly knew what to say. It was difficult even to think, much less talk.

Michael looked from one to the other. "I'll take the silence as a yes. I can understand your bewilderment; it's been an unexpected morning, to say the least. So first let's get through Turin. Hopefully, we can beat the worst of the traffic." He opened the second map, which was a plan of Turin and the immediate environs. He showed Stephanie where they were and where they wanted to go. She nodded.

"It shouldn't be difficult," Michael said.

"One thing the Italians are good at is sign-age. First we follow signs for Centro Citta, and then we follow signs for route S-twenty heading south. Okay?"

Stephanie nodded again.

"Let's do it!" Michael said. He settled back behind the steering wheel and put the car in gear.

At first the traffic was not bad, but as they got closer to the city, it got worse, and the worse it got, the more time the driving took, and the more time the driving took, the worse the traffic became, in a self-fulfilling prophecy. Just before they reached the city center, the day dawned clear and bright with a pale blue sky. They rode in silence, save for occasional directions from Stephanie, who attentively followed their progress on the map and pointed out appropriate signs. Daniel didn't say a word. He was at least pleased that Michael was a prudent and defensive driver.

It was almost nine A.M. by the time they broke free, heading south on S20 to leave the Turin rush-hour traffic behind. By then, Stephanie and Daniel had had time to relax a degree and collect their thoughts, which centered mostly on their driver and their abandoned luggage.

Stephanie carefully folded both maps and put them on the dashboard. From then on, the route was clear. She eyed Michael's hollow-cheeked, hawklike profile, the stubble on his face, and his mat of disarrayed red hair. "Perhaps this is a good time to ask who you are," she said.

"I'm just a simple priest at heart," Michael said. He smiled weakly. He knew the questions would come, and he wasn't sure how much he wanted to say.

"I think we deserve to know more," Stephanie said.

"My name is Michael Maloney. My present affiliation is with the Archbishop of New York, but I happen to be in Italy on church-related business."

"How did you know our names?" Daniel asked from the backseat.

"I'm sure both of you are intensely curious," Michael said. "And for good reason. But the fact of the matter is, I would rather not get into the details of my participation. It would be best for all concerned. Would it be possible for you to accept that I have been able to

save you from the major inconvenience of
being arrested without your questioning me?
I'm asking it as a favor. Perhaps you can just
attribute my help as a bit of divine intervention, for which I was merely the Good Lord's
servant."

Stephanie shot a glance back at Daniel
before refocusing on Michael. "It's interesting
you used the term *divine intervention.* It's a
coincidence, since we heard that specific
phrase in association with what brought us
to Italy, namely to get the sample of the
Shroud of Turin."

"Oh?" Michael questioned vaguely. He
tried to think of a way to turn the conversation away from sensitive areas, but nothing
came to mind.

"Why were we going to be arrested?"
Daniel asked. "That shouldn't have anything
to do with your participation."

"Because it was learned you are biomedical scientists. That was an unexpected and
unwelcome surprise. Presently, the church
does not want any more scientific testing
concerning the shroud's authenticity, and because of your backgrounds, there is the legitimate worry that that is what you intend to
do. At first, the church merely wanted the

sample of the shroud returned, but when that seemed not to be feasible, they wanted it confiscated."

"That explains a few things," Stephanie said. "Except why you decided to help us. Are you confident we are not going to test the sample?"

"I'd rather not get into that. Please!"

"How did you know we were going to London when we were checking in for a flight to Paris?" Daniel strained forward to hear. Michael's voice didn't carry well into the backseat.

"That is a question I'd be too embarrassed to answer." Michael's face reddened as he recalled hiding behind the curtain in the hotel room. "I beg of you. Can you just let it go? Accept what I have done as a favor: merely a friend helping a couple of fellow Americans in need."

They drove in silence for a few miles. Finally, Stephanie spoke up. "Well, thank you for helping us. And for whatever it's worth, we are not at all interested in testing the shroud's authenticity."

"I will convey that to the proper church authorities. I'm certain they will be relieved to hear it."

"What about our luggage?" Stephanie asked. "Is there a chance you can help us retrieve it?"

"I will be happy to do my best in that regard, and I am optimistic I will be successful, especially knowing for certain you have no intention of testing the shroud. If all goes well, I will have your belongings forwarded to your home in Massachusetts."

"We're not going to be home for a month," Daniel said.

"I will leave my card with you," Michael said. "As soon as you have an address, you can call me."

"We have an address already," Daniel said.

"I have a question," Stephanie said. "From now on, will we be personae non grata in Italy?"

"As with the luggage issue, I am confident that I will be able, as they say, to have your slates wiped clean. You won't have any trouble visiting Italy in the future, if that is your concern."

Stephanie turned and looked back at Daniel. "I suppose I can live without knowing the gory details. What about you?"

"I suppose so," Daniel said. "But I would

like to know who it was who managed to get into our hotel room."

"I certainly don't want to talk about that," Michael responded quickly, "which is not to suggest that I know anything in particular."

"Then just tell me this: Was he or she a member of the church or a professional hireling or part of the hotel staff?"

"I can't say," Michael added. "I'm sorry."

Once Daniel and Stephanie resigned themselves to the fact that Michael was not going to be forthcoming about the whys and wherefores of his helpful intervention, and once it was apparent to them that the Italian authorities had indeed been evaded by the Fiat's passing into France, they relaxed and enjoyed the drive. The scenery was spectacular as they rose up into the snow-covered Alps and passed through the ski village of Limone Piemonte.

On the French side of the pass, they descended the craggy Gorge de Saorge on a road literally cut out of the side of the canyon's sheer rock walls. At the French town of Sospel, they stopped for a bite of lunch. By the time they pulled into the Nice airport, it was after two in the afternoon.

Michael gave them his card and took the address of the Ocean Club in Nassau, where Daniel had made a reservation. He shook each of their hands, promised to look into the baggage issue the moment he got back to Turin, and then drove off.

Daniel and Stephanie watched the Fiat until it disappeared from sight before turning to each other.

Stephanie shook her head in amazement. "What a weird experience!"

Daniel nodded. "That's an understatement."

A quick, derisive laugh escaped from Stephanie's lips. "I don't mean to be cruel but I can't help but remember how you gloated yesterday morning how easy it had been to get the shroud sample and how you thought it was a harbinger of things to come in terms of treating Butler. Do you want to take that back?"

"Maybe I was a little premature." Daniel admitted. "Yet things turned out okay. We're certainly going to lose a day or maybe two, but otherwise it should all be smooth sailing from here."

"I can only hope," Stephanie said. She hoisted her bag onto her shoulder. "Let's get inside and see about connections to London. That's going to be the first test."

They walked into the terminal and looked up at the flight schedules displayed on a monster electronic board. Almost simultaneously, their eyes spotted a British Airways nonstop flight to London at three-fifty P.M.

"See what I mean," Daniel said happily. "Now that could hardly be more convenient."

fourteen

3:55 P.M., Thursday, February 28, 2002

"Holy crap!" Daniel shouted. "What the hell are you doing? You're going to have us killed!"

Daniel was straining against his seat belt with his hand on the back of the bench front seat of the taxi, which happened to be a vintage black Cadillac. Daniel and Stephanie had just arrived on New Providence Island in the Bahamas. Passport control and customs had been a mere formality since they had no luggage. What little clothing and toiletries Stephanie and Daniel had bought on their forced thirty-six-hour stay in London had been conveniently packed in a third carry-on bag. They had been the first of the people on their flight out of the terminal and had taken the first cab in the taxi line.

"My God!" Daniel moaned as the oncoming car swept past them on the right. His head swiveled around to watch the car recede into the distance.

Alarmed by the outburst, the taxi driver was eyeing his fares in his rearview mirror. "Hey, man! What's the matter?" he asked urgently.

Daniel swung back around to face forward, fearing more oncoming traffic. The color had drained from his face. The car that they passed had been the first they had encountered on the narrow two-lane road leading from the airport. As usual, Daniel had been nervously watching out the front window and had seen the car approach. Daniel had progressively stiffened as the driver, who had been carrying on a welcoming monologue as if he were a member of the island's chamber of commerce, began drifting to the left. Daniel had assumed the driver would notice his error and move over to the right. But he didn't. At the moment Daniel estimated it was too late for them to get over to the right to avoid an accident, he'd yelled in desperation.

"Daniel, calm down!" Stephanie soothed. She put a restraining hand on his tensed thigh. "Everything is okay. Obviously, they drive on the left here in Nassau."

"Why the hell didn't you tell me?" Daniel demanded.

"I didn't know, at least not until we passed the oncoming car. But it makes sense. It was a British colony for centuries."

"Then how come the steering wheel is on the left, like normal cars?"

Stephanie could tell Daniel was in no mood to be placated. Instead, she changed the subject. "I can't get over the color of the ocean from the plane when we flew over the Bahamas. It must be because it's shallow. I've never seen such bright aquamarine or such deep sapphire."

Daniel merely grunted. He was preoccupied with another car approaching. Stephanie switched her attention outside and rolled down the window, despite the car's air-conditioning. Coming from the dead of winter, the silky, tropical air and the lushness of the flora was startling, particularly the brilliant scarlet and luminous purple bougainvillea that seemed to be creeping over every wall. The tiny towns and buildings they were passing seemed reminiscent of New England, except for their vibrant tropical hues set off to full effect by the relentless Bahamian sun. The people they passed, whose skin color ranged from pale white to deep mahogany brown, appeared relaxed. Even from a distance, their smiles and laughter were apparent. Stephanie sensed it was a happy place, and she hoped it was an auspicious sign of what she and Daniel were there to accomplish.

As far as their accommodations were concerned, Stephanie had no idea of what to expect, since it had not been discussed. Daniel had made all the arrangements prior to leaving for Italy, while she had seen to Butler's fibroblast culture and had visited her family. On the twenty-second of March, exactly three weeks away, she knew where they would be staying. At that time, Ashley Butler would arrive, and she and Daniel would move with Butler to the enormous Atlantis hotel to take advantage of the reservations Butler had made. Stephanie imperceptibly shook her head at the thought of all they had to accomplish before the senator got there. She hoped his tissue culture was doing well back in Cambridge. If it wasn't, there was no way they would make the three-week dead-line to do the implant.

After a half hour of driving, they began to see some of the hotels off to their left on what the driver said was Cable Beach. Most of the structures were large high-rises and, as such, not particularly inviting to Stephanie. Next came the town of Nassau it-self, which was far more bustling than Stephanie had envisioned, with a profusion of cars, trucks, buses, scooters, mopeds, and pedestrians. Yet with all its hustle and bustle, imposingly elegant banks, and color-ful but official-appearing colonial buildings, there was the same sense of general happi-ness that Stephanie had noted earlier. Even being stuck in traffic was not only tolerated by the people she saw but seemingly en-joyed.

The taxi took them over a high, arched bridge to Paradise Island, which the driver said had been called Hog Island in colonial times. He said the original developer, Hunt-ington Hartford, had felt the name was not an attraction. Both Stephanie and Daniel agreed. On the island side of the bridge, the driver pointed out a modern shopping plaza to the right and the gigantic Atlantis resort to the left.

"Are there clothing stores in the shopping area?" Stephanie questioned. She turned to look back. The shops appeared to be unexpectedly upscale.

"Yes, ma'am. But they're expensive. If you're looking for islandwear, I recommend Bay Street in town."

After a short drive east, the taxi turned north onto what turned out to be a long, serpentine driveway lined with particularly lush, dense vegetation. At the entrance stood a sign proclaiming: PRIVATE, THE OCEAN CLUB, FOR GUESTS ONLY. What particularly impressed Stephanie was that the hotel itself could not be seen until the taxi made the final turn.

"This looks heavenly," she commented as the taxi pulled in under the porte cochere to be met by doormen in crisp white shirts and Bermuda shorts.

"It's supposed to be one of the best hotels," Daniel announced.

"You got that right, man," the driver commented.

The resort turned out to be even better than Stephanie could have hoped. It comprised low, two-story buildings scattered along a gorgeous concave stretch of beach and mostly hidden by flowering trees. Daniel had managed to reserve a ground-floor suite, from which the white-sand beach was a mere step away, across an expanse of manicured lawn. After they had put away their few clothes and arranged their toiletries in the marbled bath, Daniel turned to Stephanie. "It's five-thirty. What do you think we should do?"

"Not much," Stephanie responded. "It's almost midnight for us European time, and I'm bushed."

"Should we call the Wingate Clinic and let them know we're here?"

"I suppose it wouldn't hurt, although I'm not sure what it will accomplish, since we'll undoubtedly go over there in the morning. It would probably be more helpful if you went back to the lobby and arranged for a rent-a-car. What's more important is for me to call Peter and see if he's ready to overnight some of Butler's fibroblasts. There's really little we can do before we have them. Then after I call Peter, I need to call my mother. I promised her I'd get in touch with her to give her an address as soon as we got situated here in Nassau."

"We're going to need some more clothes," Daniel said. "How about this? I'll go get a rent-a-car, you make your calls, and then we'll head back to that shopping plaza near the bridge and see if there are any decent clothing shops."

"Why not just do the rent-a-car. I'm ready to take a shower, get something to eat, and hop into bed. There will be time for clothes shopping tomorrow."

"I suppose you're right," Daniel admitted. "My eagerness at having finally gotten here to Nassau has me fired up, whereas in actuality I'm bushed too."

As soon as Daniel left the room, Stephanie sat herself down at the desk. She was surprised and pleased to see she had a reasonable signal on her cell phone. As she'd suggested to Daniel, she made her first call to Peter, and as she suspected, he was still at the lab.

"John Smith's culture is doing fine," Peter said, in response to Stephanie's question.

"I've been prepared to overnight a cryopreserved aliquot for several days. I expected to hear from you on Tuesday."

"A minor problem held us up unexpectedly," Stephanie said vaguely. She smiled wryly at how much of an understatement that was, considering they had to flee out of Italy by car to avoid arrest and leave their luggage behind.

"Are you ready for me to ship it?"

"Absolutely," Stephanie said. "Pack it up with the usual HTSR reagents, plus the collection of dopaminergic gene probes and growth factors I put together. And I just thought of something else. Include the ecdysone construct with the tyrosine hydroxylase promoter we used with our recent mouse experiments."

"My gosh!" Peter intoned. "What on earth are you guys up to down there?"

"It's best if I don't explain," Stephanie said. "What are the chances you could ship the whole consignment out tonight?"

"I don't see why not. Worst case, I have to drive it out to Logan, but that's not a problem. Where do you want it sent?"

Stephanie thought for a moment. Her first thought was to have it come to the hotel, but then she thought it would be wise to limit its travel as well as get it into a liquid-nitrogen freezer, which she assumed the Wingate Clinic would have. Asking Peter to hold on, she used the house phone to contact the concierge's desk to get Wingate's island address. It was 1200 Windsor Field Road. She then passed it on to Peter along with the clinic's phone number.

"I'll get this in FedEx tonight," Peter promised. "When will you be back?"

"I'd say a month, maybe a little less."

"Good luck with whatever the hell you are doing!"

"Thanks. We'll need it."

Stephanie stared out at the pink-and-silver-tinted ocean with its gentle swells. A line of cumulus clouds was aligned along the horizon. Each was tipped with a dab of intense rose-purple from the setting sun off to her left. The sliding glass door was open, and a gentle breeze scented with some exotic flower caressed her face. The vista and ambience was luscious and calming after the frenetic days of travel and intrigue. She could feel herself begin to relax in such a serene environment, aided by the news about how well Butler's fibroblast culture had progressed. The nagging worry that it had gone sour had lurked in the back of her mind ever since she had left on the trip. All in all, she began to entertain the idea that perhaps Daniel's optimism about the Butler project might ultimately be reasonable, despite her intuition to the contrary and despite the trouble she and Daniel had experienced in Turin.

Once the sun set, night fell precipitously. Torches were lit along the edge of the beach to flicker in the breeze. Stephanie picked up her cell phone again and dialed her parents' number. She wanted her mother to have the name of the hotel, the room number, and the phone number, in case her mother took a turn for the worse. As the call went through, Stephanie found herself hoping her father wouldn't answer. It was always so awkward trying to have a conversation with him. She was pleased when she heard her mother's soft voice.

Although Tony had no reason to think that his headstrong sister wouldn't carry out her threat to languish in the Bahamas while her company tanked, he'd been entertaining the hope that she'd see the light after what he'd told her, cancel the trip, and do what she could to turn things around. But such was not to be the case, as her phone call to their mother had just proved. The bitch and her freaking boyfriend were in Nassau, staying at some posh ocean-front resort in a suite, no less, with a view of the beach. It was galling.

Tony shook his head at her nerve. Ever since she'd gotten into Harvard, she'd been thumbing her nose at him every time he turned around, which he'd tolerated since she was his kid sister. But now she'd gone too far, especially considering the academic nerd she was hooked up with. A hundred grand was a lot of money, no matter how you looked at it, and that wasn't even considering the Castiglianos' share. The whole situation wasn't right, that was for damn sure, yet she still was his kid sister, so things weren't as clear as they could have been.

The big Cadillac crunched over the gravel and came to a halt in front of the Castigliano Brothers Plumbing Supply store. Tony turned off his headlights and killed the engine. But he didn't get out of the car immediately. Instead, he sat for a moment to calm himself down. He could have just called and given the information to either Sal or Louie over the phone. But because it was his sister, he had to know what they had in mind. He knew they were just as pissed as he was, but without the restraint from having a family member involved. He didn't care what they did to the boyfriend. Hell, he wouldn't mind pushing him around himself. But his sister was another thing entirely. If she were to be pushed around, Tony wanted to be the perpetrator.

Tony opened the door and was assaulted by the putrid smell of the salt marsh. He couldn't understand how anyone could hang around a place where every time the wind changed direction, it smelled like rotten eggs. It was a moonless night, and Tony walked carefully. He didn't want to trip over a discarded sink or any other debris.

Since it was after hours, the store was closed, as evidenced by a sign in the door's window. But the door was unlocked. Gaetano was behind the cash register, totaling the day's receipts. He had a nub of a yellow wooden pencil tucked behind his surprisingly small ear, dwarfed by his large head.

"Sal and Louie?" Tony questioned.

Gaetano motioned toward the rear with his head without interrupting what he was doing. Tony found the twins at their respective desks. After a slapping handshake and the usual curt greeting with each, Tony sat down on the sofa. The twins eyed him expectantly. The only light in the room came from small, hooded desk lamps on each desk, emphasizing the twins' cadaverous faces. From Tony's perspective, their eye sockets were mere black holes.

"Well, they are in Nassau," Tony began. "I was hoping I could come here and tell you differently, but that's not the case. They just checked into a ritzy resort called the Ocean Club. They are in suite 108. I've even got the phone number."

Tony leaned over and put a small piece of paper on Louie's desk, which was closer to the sofa than Sal's.

The door opened, and Gaetano's head popped in. "You want me or what?"

"Yeah," Louie said, as he picked up the paper with the phone number and glanced at it.

Gaetano stepped into the room and closed the door.

"Any change in the company's prospects?" Sal asked.

"Not that I'm aware of," Tony said. "If there had been, my accountant would have told me."

"It's like this twerp's flipping us off," Louie said. He laughed mirthlessly. "Nassau! I still don't believe it. It's like he's asking us to beat the crap out of him."

"Is that what you are going to do?" Tony asked.

Louie looked over at his twin. "We want him to get his ass back here and save the company and our investment. Am I right, brother?"

"Damn straight," Sal said. "We've got to let him know who's involved here and emphasize we want our money back, come hell or high water. Not only does he have to get his ass back here, he's got to have a clear idea of what the consequences are if he ignores us or thinks he can hide behind a bankruptcy filing or some other legal shenanigan. He needs to be knocked around good!"

"What about my sister?" Tony asked. "She's not blameless in this mess, but if she's going to be knocked around, I want to be the person doing the knocking around."

"No problem," Louie said. He tossed the slip of paper with the phone number onto his desk. "Like I said Sunday: Our beef's not with her."

"Are you ready to go to Nassau, Gaetano?" Sal asked.

"I can leave first thing in the morning," Gaetano said. "But what should I do after I deliver the message? Should I hang around or what? I mean, what if he doesn't get the message?"

"You'd better be damn sure he gets the message," Sal said. "I don't want you to have the mistaken impression this some sort of paid vacation. Besides, we need you up here. After you give him the message, you get your ass back to Boston."

"Gaetano has a point," Tony said. "What will you do if this asshole ignores the message?"

Sal looked at his brother. There was an apparent immediate meeting of the minds as each nodded. Sal looked back at Tony. "If this twerp wasn't around, could your sister run the company?"

Tony shrugged. "How am I supposed to know?"

"She's your sister," Sal said. "Doesn't she have a Ph.D.?"

"She's got a Ph.D. from Harvard," Tony said. "Big deal! All it's done is make her impossible to get along with, thinking she's so high and mighty. And as far as I know, it only means she knows a ton of stuff about germs and genes and all that crap, not how to run a company."

"Well, the twerp's got a Ph.D. too," Louie said. "So it seems to me the company wouldn't be much worse off if your sister were running things. And if she were, you'd have a lot more influence about how things were going."

"So what are you saying?" Tony asked.

"Hey, am I not talking English here?" Louie questioned.

"Of course you're talking English," Sal added.

"Look," Louie said. "If the head of the company doesn't get the message, which I think we can count on Gaetano making very clear, then we whack him. Simple as that, and end of story for the professor. If nothing else, that should send a very specific message to your sister that she'd better mend her ways."

"You're right about that," Tony said.

"Are you okay with this, Gaetano?" Sal asked.

"Yeah, sure," Gaetano replied. "But I'm confused. Do you or don't you want me to stay down there until we're sure what his response will be to getting roughed up?"

"For the last time," Sal said threateningly. "You're to deliver the message and get back here. If it goes down easily and if the flight schedule is copasetic, maybe you can do it in one day. Otherwise, you'll stay over. But we want you back here ASAP, because there's a lot going on around here. If he's got to be whacked, you'll go back. Understood?"

Gaetano nodded, but he was disappointed. When the task was first suggested on Sunday, he'd hoped to get a week in the sun out of the deal.

"I've got a suggestion," Tony said. "Since we can't rule out Gaetano having to return, then I don't think he should do what he has to do at their hotel. If the professor turns out not to be cooperative, we don't want him on the run, which he might do if he thinks the hotel is not safe. In the Bahamas alone, there are literally hundreds of islands."

"You're right," Sal said. "We don't want him to disappear, not with our money on the line."

"So maybe I should stay down there and keep an eye on him," Gaetano suggested hopefully.

"What do I have to say to you, you moron,"

Sal spat while glaring at Gaetano. "For the last time, you're not heading south on a holiday. You're going to do your thing and get the hell back here. This problem with the professor isn't the only one we've got."

"Okay, okay!" Gaetano said, motioning as if surrendering. "I won't have my meeting with the guy at the hotel. I'll just use the hotel to spot him, which means I'll be needing some photos."

"I thought of that," Tony said. He reached into his jacket pocket and pulled out several snapshots. "These were taken of the lovebirds just this past Christmas." He handed them over to Gaetano, who was still standing at the door.

Gaetano glanced at the photographs.

"Are they okay?" Louie asked.

"They're not bad at all," Gaetano responded. Then, looking at Tony, he added, "I have to say, your sister's a looker."

"Yeah, well forget it," Tony said. "She's off-limits."

"Too bad," Gaetano said with a crooked smile.

"One other thing," Tony said. "With all this airport security nonsense, I don't think it's advisable even to pack a gun in a checked suitcase. If Gaetano needs one, it would be better to make arrangements to get one on the island through contacts in Miami. You do have contacts in Miami, don't you?"

"Sure," Sal said. "That's another good idea. Anything else?"

"I think that's about it," Tony said. He stubbed out his cigarette and stood up.

fifteen

9:15 A.M., Friday, March 1, 2002

It had been a long, delightful, and rejuvenating morning. With their circadian cycles awry, compliments of their brief European trip, both Stephanie and Daniel had awakened well before the sun had brightened the eastern horizon. Unable to fall back asleep, they'd gotten up, showered, and taken a protracted stroll around the hotel grounds and along the deserted Cabbage Beach, as a cloudless, tropical dawn broke. Back at the hotel, they'd been the first guests for breakfast and had lingered over their coffee while discussing the schedule for creating Butler's treatment cells. With only three weeks until his scheduled arrival, they knew they were up against a significant time constraint, and they were eager to get started, although they recognized they could do little until the package arrived from Peter. By eight o'clock, they'd called the Wingate Clinic to tell the receptionist they were in Nassau and would arrive at the clinic at about nine-fifteen. She said she'd let the doctors know.

"This western part of the island looks different than the eastern part," Daniel observed, as they drove west along Windsor Field Road. "It's much flatter."

"It's also less developed and a lot drier," Stephanie added. They were passing long, low stretches of semiarid pine forest infiltrated with palmettos. The sky was a deep azure, dotted with a few wispy white clouds.

Daniel had insisted on driving, which Stephanie didn't mind until he'd suggested she might have more trouble driving on the left than he. Her initial reaction was to challenge what seemed to her an unwarranted, chauvinistic assertion, but then she just let it go. The issue wasn't worth an argument. Instead, she climbed into the passenger seat and contented herself with getting out the map. As had been the case when they'd fled Italy, she'd be the navigator.

Daniel drove slowly, which was fine with Stephanie, considering the reflex to bear to the right at corners and while circling round-abouts. They'd driven along the northern coast of the island, noting once again the high-rise resorts lined up like soldiers at attention along Cable Beach. After passing a number of limestone caves sculpted by pre-historic seas, they'd turned inland. Bearing right at the next intersection on Windsor Field Road, they'd caught a glimpse of the airport in the distance.

Continuing west, they had no trouble finding the turnoff to the Wingate Clinic. It was on the left side of the road and marked by a huge sign.

Stephanie leaned forward to get a better view out the windshield as they approached. "My word! Do you see the sign?"

"It would be hard to miss. It's the size of a billboard."

Daniel made the turn onto the newly paved, tree-lined drive.

"They must have a lot of land," Stephanie said. She sat back. "I can't see the building."

After several turns through a dense copse of evergreens, the serpentine driveway was abruptly blocked by a gate. A formidable chain-link fence topped with razor wire disappeared into the pine forest in both directions. On Stephanie's side of the car stood a small booth. A uniformed guard, complete with a holstered sidearm, a visored, military-style hat, and aviator sunglasses, stepped out. He was holding a clipboard. Daniel pulled to a stop while Stephanie lowered her window.

The guard leaned over to look at Daniel across Stephanie's lap. "Can I help you, sir?" His voice was decidedly businesslike and devoid of emotion.

"It's Dr. D'Agostino and Dr. Lowell," Stephanie said. "We're here to meet with Dr. Wingate."

The guard checked his clipboard and then touched the brim of his hat before returning to the gatehouse. A moment later, the gate rolled open like a pocket door. Daniel accelerated forward.

It took another few minutes before the clinic came into view. Nestled among carefully landscaped shrubbery and flowering trees was a two-story, postmodern, U-shaped complex. It was composed of three separate buildings connected by arcaded covered walkways. Each building was clad in white limestone with white concrete tile roofs, the pediments of which were capped by fanciful, shell-themed acroteria reminiscent of an ancient Greek temple. Latticework was interspersed between multipaned windows along the sides of each structure. At the base of each lattice, young, brightly colored bougainvillea plants were beginning their climb skyward.

"Good grief," Stephanie exclaimed. "I wasn't prepared for this. It's beautiful. It looks more like a spa than an infertility clinic."

The driveway led to a parking area in front of a central building, the entrance of which was adorned by a columned portico. The columns were squat, with exaggerated entases and capped with simple Doric capitals.

"I hope they saved some money for their laboratory equipment," Daniel commented. He pulled their rented Mercury Marquis in between several new BMW convertibles. Several spaces away were two limousines, their liveried drivers smoking and chatting while leaning up against their vehicles' front fenders.

Daniel and Stephanie stepped out of the car and paused to gaze at the complex, which was dazzling in the bright Bahamian sun. "I'd heard that infertility was lucrative," Daniel commented, "but I didn't imagine it was this lucrative."

"Nor did I," Stephanie said. "But I wonder how much of this resulted from them being able to collect on their fire insurance following their flight from Massachusetts." She shook her head. "No matter where the money came from, with the cost of health-care, opulence and medicine are inappropriate bedfellows. There is something wrong with this picture, and my qualms about getting involved with these people are coming back big time."

"Let's not let our prejudices and self-righteousness run away with themselves," Daniel warned. "We're not here on a social crusade. We're here to treat Butler, and that's it."

The large bronzed front door opened and a tall, deeply tanned, silver-haired man appeared. He was dressed in a long white doctor's coat. He waved and called out "Welcome!" in a high, lilting voice.

"At least we're getting a personalized

greeting," Daniel said. "Let's go! And keep
your opinions to yourself."

Daniel and Stephanie met up at the front
of the car and began walking toward the entrance. "I hope that's not Spencer Wingate,"
Stephanie whispered.

"Why not?" Daniel whispered back.

"Because he's handsome enough to be a
soap-opera doctor."

"Oh, I forgot! You wanted him to be short,
fat, and have a wart on his nose."

"Precisely."

"Well, we can still hope he's a chain-
smoker and has bad breath."

"Oh, shut up!"

Daniel and Stephanie mounted the three
steps to the portico. As they approached,
Spencer extended his hand while keeping
the door open with his foot. He introduced
himself with a great flourish of smiles and
handshaking. He then grandly motioned for
them to precede him into the building.

In keeping with the exterior, the interior
had a simple classical ambience, with plain
pilasters, dentil moldings, and Doric columns. The floor was polished limestone,
softened with Oriental scatter rugs. The
walls were painted a very light lavender,

which at first glance appeared to be pale gray. Even the varnished hardwood furniture had a classical aura, with dark green leather upholstery. A faint smell of fresh paint permeated the air-conditioned air, as a reminder of the clinic's recent completion. For Daniel and Stephanie, the dry coolness was a welcome contrast to the moist tropical heat outdoors, which had been steadily climbing since sunrise.

"This is our main waiting room," Spencer said as he gestured around the voluminous room. Two moderately elderly, well-dressed couples were sitting on separate sofas. They were nervously flipping through magazines and briefly looked up. The only other occupant was a receptionist with bright pink fingernail polish who was manning a half-circle desk just inside the door.

"This building serves as the initial check-in location for new patients," Spencer explained. "It also houses our administration offices. We're very proud of the clinic, and we're eager to show you the entire complex, although we suspect you're mainly interested in our laboratory facilities."

"And the operating room," Daniel said.

"Yes, of course, the operating room. But

first, come up to my office for some coffee and meet the others."

Spencer led the way over to a spacious elevator, even though they were only going up one floor. During the brief ride, Spencer questioned like a concerned host whether their incoming flight had been pleasant. Stephanie assured him it had been fine. On the second level, they passed a secretary who interrupted her word processing to smile cheerfully.

Spencer's vast office was in the northeast corner of the building. The airport could be seen to the east and a blue line of the ocean to the north. "Help yourselves," Spencer said, motioning to a coffee service spread out on a low marble table in front of an L-shaped sofa. "I'll get the two department heads."

For a moment, Daniel and Stephanie were alone.

"This looks like an office of a CEO of a Fortune Five Hundred company," Stephanie said. "I have to say, I find all of this opulence obscene."

"Let's hold our value judgments until we see the lab."

"Do you think those two couples reading magazines downstairs are patients?"

"I haven't the slightest idea, nor do I care."

"They seemed a bit old for infertility treatment."

"It's not our concern."

"Do you think the Wingate Clinic is getting older women pregnant like that maverick infertility specialist in Italy?"

Daniel flashed Stephanie an exasperated, irritated look as Spencer reappeared. The clinic founder had a man and a woman in tow, both dressed like himself in white, highly starched, long doctor's coats. First, he introduced Paul Saunders, who was short and squat, and whose thick-necked silhouette reminded Stephanie of the columns supporting the building's entrance portico. In keeping with his body, everything about Paul's face was round with puffy, pasty, pale skin, all of which was in sharp contrast to Spencer's tall, slender frame, sharply angled features, and bronzed complexion. A mat of unruly dark hair with a striking white forelock completed Paul's eccentric image and accentuated his paleness.

As he vigorously shook hands with Daniel, Paul smiled broadly to reveal square, widely spaced, yellowed teeth. "Welcome to the Wingate, doctors," he said. "We're honored to have you here. I can't tell you how excited I am about our collaboration."

Stephanie smiled weakly as he moved to her and pumped her hand. She was mesmerized by the man's eyes. With his broadbased nose, his eyes appeared closer together than usual. Also, she'd never seen a person with different-colored irises.

"Paul is our head of research," Spencer announced, giving Paul a pat on the back. "He is looking forward to having you in his lab and eager to be of assistance and to learn a few things, I might add." Spencer then draped his arm over the shoulders of the woman, who was almost as tall as he. "And this is Dr. Sheila Donaldson, head of clinical services. She'll be making the arrangements for your use of one of our two operating rooms, as well as our inpatient facility, which we assume you'll be taking advantage of."

"I didn't know you had inpatient capabilities," Daniel said.

"We are a full-service, self-contained operation," Spencer said proudly. "Although for long-term inpatient care, which we don't expect, we will be referring patients to Doctors Hospital in town. Our inpatient facility is limited and more just for an occasional overnight, which should serve your needs admirably."

Stephanie pulled her attention away from Paul Saunders and looked at Sheila Donaldson. She had a narrow face framed by lank, chestnut hair. In comparison to the exuberant men, she seemed withdrawn, almost shy. Stephanie had the feeling the woman was reluctant to look her in the eye as they shook hands.

"No coffee for you folks?" Spencer questioned.

Both Stephanie and Daniel shook their heads. "I think we've both had our fill of coffee," Daniel explained. "We're still on European time, and we've been up since the crack of dawn."

"Europe?" Paul questioned enthusiastically. "Did your travel to Europe have anything to do with the Shroud of Turin?"

"Indeed it did," Daniel responded.

"I trust it was a successful trip," Paul said, with a conspiratorial wink.

"Withering, but successful," Daniel remarked. "We . . ." He paused, as if trying to decide what he wanted to say.

Stephanie held her breath. She was hoping Daniel wouldn't describe their Turin experience. She very much wanted to maintain a distance from these people. For Daniel to share their recent travail would be too personal and would cross a boundary she did not want to cross.

"We managed to get a bloodstained swatch from the shroud," Daniel said. "In fact, I have it with me at the moment. What I'd like to do is get it into a buffered saline solution to stabilize the DNA fragments, and I'd like to do it sooner rather than later."

"Sounds good to me," Paul said. "Let's head directly over to the laboratory."

"There's no reason the tour can't start there," Spencer said agreeably.

With a sense of relief that appropriate personal distance had been maintained, Stephanie let our her breath and relaxed a degree as the group trooped out of Spencer's office.

At the elevator, Sheila excused herself by saying there were patients scheduled, and she wanted to be certain things went smoothly. She then left the group to take the stairs.

The laboratory was off to the left side of the central building and was reached by traversing one of the gracefully curved, covered walkways. "We designed the clinic as separate buildings to force ourselves to get outside, even if we work all the time," Paul explained. "It's good for the soul."

"I get out a bit more than Paul," Spencer added, with a laugh. "As if you couldn't tell by my tan. I'm not quite the workaholic he is."

"Is this building all laboratory?" Daniel questioned, as he stepped through the door held open by Spencer.

"Not entirely," Paul explained, as he went ahead to stop by a periodical rack where he bent over to pick up a glossy-covered magazine from a stack. The group had entered a room that appeared to be a combination lounge and library. Bookshelves lined the walls. "This is our journal room, and I have here a copy for you of our latest issue of the *Journal of Twenty-first Century Reproductive Technology.*" He proudly handed the publication to Daniel. "There's a few articles you might find interesting."

"That's very kind of you," Daniel managed. He scanned the contents printed on the cover before handing it to Stephanie.

"This building has living accommodations in addition to the laboratory," Paul said. "That includes some guest apartments, which are nothing fancy but certainly adequate. We would like to offer for you to use them if you are inclined to be near your work. We even have a cafeteria, which serves three meals a day, in the clinic building across the garden, so you wouldn't have to leave the premises unless you wanted. You see, many of our employees live here in the complex, and their apartments are also in this building."

"Thank you for your offer," Stephanie responded quickly. "That's very hospitable of you, but we have very comfortable accommodations in town."

"Where are you staying, if I may ask?" Paul questioned.

"The Ocean Club," Stephanie said.

"A very good choice," Paul said. "Well, the offer holds if you decide to change your minds."

"I don't think so," Stephanie said.

"Let's get back to the tour," Spencer suggested.

"By all means," Paul said. He motioned for the group to move toward a pair of double doors leading into the depths of the building. "Besides the laboratory and living quarters, this building also houses some diagnostic equipment, like the PET scanner. We had it installed here because we felt we'd be using it more for research than clinical work."

"I didn't realize you had a PET scanner," Daniel said. He glanced at Stephanie with raised eyebrows to communicate his contented amazement as a counterpoint to her palpable negativity. He knew a PET scanner, which uses gamma rays to study physiological function, might be handy if a problem arose with Butler after the treatment.

"We've planned the Wingate to be a full-service research and clinical facility," Paul said proudly. "As long as we were putting in a CT scanner and an MRI, we thought we might as well add a PET."

"I'm impressed," Daniel admitted.

"I thought you'd be," Paul said. "And as the discoverer of HTSR, you'll surely be interested to know we plan to be a major player in stem-cell therapy as well as infertility."

"That's an interesting combination," Daniel said vaguely, unsure of his reaction to this unexpected news. As with so many things about the Wingate Clinic, the idea that they were thinking of doing stem-cell therapy was a surprise.

"We thought it a natural extension of our

work," Paul explained, "considering our access to human oocytes and our extensive experience with nuclear transfer. The irony is that we thought it was going to be a sideline, but since we've opened our doors, we've done more stem-cell treatment than infertility."

"That's true," Spencer said. "In fact, those patients you saw earlier in the main waiting area are here for stem-cell therapy. Word of mouth concerning our services seems to be spreading quickly. We haven't had to advertise at all."

Both Daniel and Stephanie's faces reflected their dismayed surprise.

"What kind of illnesses are you treating?" Daniel asked.

Paul laughed. "Just about anything and everything! A lot of people understand stem cells' promise for a host of ailments, from terminal cancer and degenerative diseases to the problems of aging. Since they can't get stem-cell treatments in the USA, they come to us."

"But that's absurd!" Stephanie exclaimed. She was aghast. "There are no established protocols for treating anything with stem cells."

"We're the first to admit we're breaking new ground," Spencer responded. "It's experimental, like what you folks are planning with your patient."

"Essentially, we're using public demand to fund the needed research," Paul explained. "Hell, it's only reasonable since the U.S. government is so chary about funding the work and making it so difficult for you researchers on the mainland."

"What kinds of cells are you using?" Daniel asked.

"Multipotent stem cells," Paul said.

"You're not differentiating the cells?" Daniel questioned, with mounting disbelief, since undifferentiated stem cells would not treat anything.

"No, not at all," Paul said. "Of course, we'll be trying that in the future, but for now we do the nuclear transfer, grow out the stem cells, and infuse them. We let the patient's body use them as it sees fit. We've had some interesting results, although not with everyone, but that is the nature of research."

"How can you call what you are doing research?" Stephanie questioned hotly. "And I beg to differ with you: There's no parallel between what we are planning to do and what you are doing."

Daniel gripped Stephanie's arm and eased her away from Paul. "Dr. D'Agostino's point is merely that we will be treating with differentiated cells."

Stephanie tried to pull her arm free from Daniel's grasp. "My point is a hell of a lot bigger than that," she rejoined. "What you people are talking about doing with stem cells is nothing but pure, unadulterated quackery!"

Daniel tightened his grip on Stephanie's arm. "Excuse us for just a moment," he said to Paul and Spencer, whose expressions had clouded. He forcibly pulled Stephanie to the side and spoke to her in an angry whisper. "What the hell are you doing, trying to sabotage our project and get us thrown out of here?"

"What do you mean, what am I doing?" Stephanie whispered back with equal vehemence. "How can you not be outraged? On top of everything else, these people are snake-oil charlatans."

"Shut up!" Daniel sputtered. He gave Stephanie a short shake. "Do I have to keep reminding you we're here for one thing and one thing only: to treat Butler! Can't you restrain yourself, for Christ's sake? The future of CURE and HTSR is on the line. These people are far from saints. We knew that from the start. That's why they are here in the Bahamas and not in Massachusetts. So let's not muck up everything with righteous indignation!"

For a moment, Daniel and Stephanie stared at each other with blazing eyes. Finally, Stephanie broke off and hung her head. "You're hurting my arm," she said.

"Sorry!" Daniel responded. He let go of her arm, which Stephanie immediately began to rub. Daniel took a deep breath to get his anger under control. He glanced back at Spencer and Paul, who were watching them with quizzical expressions. Returning his attention to Stephanie, he said, "Can we concentrate on the mission? Can we accept the fact that these people are unethical, venal morons and leave it at that?"

"I suppose the aphorism 'People in glass houses shouldn't throw stones' fits here, considering what we are planning. Maybe that's why this all bothers me so much."

"And maybe you're right," Daniel said. "But keep in mind we're being forced to push ethical boundaries. With that accepted, can I count on you to keep your reactions to the Wingate Clinic and its mission to yourself, at least until we get off by ourselves?"

"I'll try my best."

"Good," Daniel said. He took another deep breath for fortitude before walking back to join the others. Stephanie followed a few paces behind.

"I think we're suffering a bit of jet lag," Daniel explained to their hosts. "We've both been a tad emotional. Also, Dr. D'Agostino tends to exaggerate to make a point. Intellectually, she feels that differentiated cells would be a more efficacious way to take advantage of the promise of stem cells."

"We've been having some darn good results," Paul said. "Perhaps, Dr. D'Agostino, you'd like to review them before you make a blanket judgment."

"I'd find that very instructive," Stephanie managed.

"Let's move along," Spencer suggested. "We want you to see the rest of the clinic before lunch, and there is a lot to see."

In stunned silence, Daniel and Stephanie passed through the double doors into a vast laboratory. Once again, they were taken aback. The sheer size of the facility combined with its array of equipment, from DNA sequencers to mundane tissue culture-incubators, was much greater than either had envisioned or hoped. The only thing lacking was personnel. A single technician could be seen working in the distance at a dissecting stereomicroscope.

"We're understaffed at the moment," Spencer said, as if reading his guests' minds. "But that's soon to be rectified, as patient demand balloons."

"I'll get our lab supervisor," Paul said, before disappearing briefly into a nearby side office.

"We project to be up to full strength in about six months," Spencer said.

"How many technicians do you plan to have?" Stephanie asked.

"Around thirty," Spencer replied. "At least, that's what our current projections suggest. But if the stem-cell treatment demand continues to increase at its present rate, we'll have to adjust that figure upward."

Paul reappeared, holding the hand of a slight woman who appeared practically emaciated, with all her bony prominences poking through her skin, particularly her cheekbones. She had gray-streaked, mousy-colored hair and a narrow, knifelike nose that stood like an exclamation point above a small, tight-lipped mouth. She was wearing a short lab coat with the sleeves rolled up over a pantsuit. Paul brought her over to the group and introduced her. Her name was Megan Finnigan, as advertised by the laboratory supervisor nametag clipped to her jacket pocket.

"We're all ready for you," Megan said, after the introductions. She spoke softly, with a Boston accent. She pointed toward a nearby lab bench. "We've prepared this area with what we thought you would need. If there is anything else, all you have to do is ask. My office door is always open."

"Dr. Lowell needs a small flask of buffered saline," Paul said. "He has a fabric sample containing blood whose DNA he wants to preserve."

"That's no problem at all," Megan said. She called out for the single lab technician to get it. In the distance, the woman pushed back from her microscope and busied herself with the request.

"When would you like to start your work?" Megan asked, while Daniel and Stephanie inspected the area of the lab set aside for them.

"As soon as possible," Daniel said. "What about the human oocytes? Will they be available when we need them?"

"Absolutely," Paul said. "All we need is about twelve hours notice."

"That's amazing," Daniel said. "How is it possible?"

Paul smiled. "That's a trade secret. Perhaps after we have worked together, we can share such secrets. I'm equally interested in your HTSR."

"Does that mean you want to start today?" Megan asked.

"Unfortunately, we can't," Daniel said. "We have to wait for a FedEx package before we can start, other than getting the fabric sample into an appropriate salt solution." He turned to Spencer. "I don't suppose anything has come for us this morning."

"When was it sent?" Spencer asked.

"Last night from Boston," Stephanie said.

"How much did it weigh?" Spencer asked. "It makes a difference when it will arrive. Nassau is, after all, an international destination for a shipment from Boston. If it were an envelope or a very small package, it may get here overnight and be here sometime in the afternoon."

"It wasn't an envelope," Stephanie said. "It will be big enough to hold an insulated pack containing a cryopreserved tissue culture plus a stock of reagents."

"Then the earliest you can expect it is tomorrow," Spencer said. "It has to go through customs, which will take an extra day at least."

"It's important we get the tissue culture in the freezer before it thaws," Stephanie said.

"I can call customs and expedite it," Spencer said. "During our construction over the last year, we've been dealing with them almost on a daily basis."

The lab tech arrived with a stoppered flask of buffered saline. She was a light-skinned African-American in her early twenties who wore her hair in a tight bob. A sprinkling of freckles graced the bridge of her nose, and an impressive array of piercings with associated jewelry ringed the helices of her ears.

"This is Maureen Jefferson," Paul said, introducing her. "Her nickname's Mare. I don't mean to embarrass her, but she has the golden touch when it comes to micropipettes and nuclear transfer. So if you need any help, she'll be here. Am I right, Mare?"

Mare smiled demurely as she handed the saline container to Daniel.

"That's very generous," Stephanie said, "but I think we'll be fine in the cellular manipulation department."

While the others watched, Daniel took the sealed glassine envelope from his pocket. With a pair of scissors proffered by Megan, he cut off one end. By compressing the envelope from the edges, he got it to open. He then carefully dropped the small, pale-reddish swatch of aged linen into the solution without touching it. It floated on the surface of the fluid. He fitted the flask with its rubber stopper and pushed the stopper in tightly. With a grease pencil, also proffered by Megan, he marked the outside of the flask with the initials ST.

"Is there someplace safe to store this while the blood components elute?" Daniel questioned.

"The entire lab is safe," Paul said. "There's no need to worry. We have our own professional security department."

"Consider the clinic the Fort Knox of Nassau," Spencer said.

"I can lock it in my office," Megan suggested. "I can even put it in a small safe I have."

"I'd appreciate it," Daniel said. "It's irreplaceable."

"Have no fear," Paul said. "It will be safe. Believe me! Would you mind if I held it for a minute?"

"Of course not," Daniel said. He handed the flask to Paul.

Paul held the bottle up to backlight it with one of the overhead lights. "Can you imagine?" he questioned, squinting at the tiny bit of reddish fabric floating on the fluid's surface. "We have some of Christ's DNA! It gives me shivers just to think about it."

"Let's not be overly theatrical," Spencer said.

"How did you manage to get it?" Paul asked, ignoring Spencer's comment.

"We had high-level clerical assistance," Daniel said vaguely.

"And how did you arrange that?" Paul asked, as he continued gazing at the fluid-filled flask while slowly turning it.

"Actually, we didn't," Daniel said. "Our patient did."

"Oh, really," Paul said. He lowered the flask

and glanced at Spencer. "Is your patient associated with the Catholic Church?"

"Not to our knowledge," Daniel said.

"At the very least, he must have some serious pull," Spencer suggested.

"Perhaps," Daniel said. "We wouldn't know."

"Now that you've been over to Italy," Spencer said, "where do you come down on the issue of the Shroud of Turin's authenticity?"

"As I told you on the phone," Daniel said, with barely concealed exasperation, "we're not involving ourselves in the controversy about the shroud. We're only using it at our patient's insistence as a source of the DNA we need for HTSR." The last thing Daniel wanted to do was get into an intellectual discussion with these bozos.

"Well, I'm looking forward to meeting this patient of yours," Paul said. "He and I have something in common: We both believe the Shroud of Turin is the real thing." He handed the flask to Megan. "Let's be doubly careful now! I have a feeling this little tidbit is going to make history."

Megan took the flask and held it with both hands. She turned to Daniel. "What are your plans for this suspension?" she asked. "You don't expect the ancient linen to dissolve, do you?"

"Certainly not," Daniel said. "I just want to let the swatch sit in the saline to let the lymphocytic DNA present to leech into solution. In twenty-four hours or so, I'll run an aliquot through the PCR. Electrophoresis with some controls should give us an idea what we have. If we find we have enough DNA fragments, which I'm reasonably sure we will have, we'll amplify it and then see if our probes pick up what we need for HTSR. Of course, we may have to do the whole exercise a few times and sequence any gaps. Anyway, the swatch will stay in the saline until we have what we need."

"Very well," Megan said. "I'll put the flask in my safe as I suggested. Tomorrow, just let me know when you want it."

"Perfect," Daniel said.

"If we're finished here, why don't we head over to the clinic building," Spencer suggested. He checked his watch. "We want you to see our operating rooms as well as our inpatient facility. You can meet the personnel over there, and then we can show you our cafeteria. We've even planned a luncheon on your behalf, to which we have invited Dr. Rashid Nawaz, the neurosurgeon. We thought you'd like to meet him."

"We would indeed," Daniel remarked.

It seemed to have taken forever, but finally Gaetano was next in line at the rent-a-car concession at the Nassau International Airport. He wondered why it had taken the people ahead of him so long to rent a freakin' car, since all they had to do was sign the goddamn form. He looked at his watch. It was half past twelve in the afternoon. He had arrived only twenty minutes earlier, even though he'd left Logan Airport at six A.M., before it was even light. The problem had been the lack of nonstop or even direct flights, and he had had to change planes in Orlando.

Gaetano shifted his muscled weight nervously. Sal and Lou had made it crystal clear they wanted him to accomplish his mission in a single day and get his ass back to Boston. They specifically warned him they were not going to brook any lame excuses, even though in the same breath they admitted success depended on Gaetano connecting expeditiously with Dr. Daniel Lowell, which wasn't a given, since they graciously admitted there were a few variables. Gaetano had promised he'd do his best, yet there wasn't going to be any possibility whatsoever of getting the job done if he didn't get the hell over to the Ocean Club hotel ASAP.

The plan was simple. Gaetano was to go to the hotel, locate the mark, who Lou and Sal were absolutely sure would be lounging on the beach, considering the weather, lure him away from the hotel by some clever ruse, and do what he had to do, meaning deliver the bosses' message and beat the crap out of him so the message would be taken seriously. Then Gaetano was to race back to the airport and take one of the puddle jumpers back to Miami in time to catch the last flight to Boston. If that wasn't going to happen for some unknown reason, then Gaetano would carry out his mission that evening, providing the professor left the hotel, and then Gaetano would spend the night at some fleabag flophouse and return the following day. The only problem with the latter plan was that there was no way to guarantee that the mark would leave the hotel, which would mean pushing everything to the following day. If that happened, Lou and Sal would be mad, no matter what Gaetano said, so he felt he was caught between a rock and a hard place. The problem boiled down to the fact that Gaetano was needed in Boston. As his bosses had reminded him, there was a lot going these days, with the economy in a tailspin and people complaining that they did not have the cash to meet their loan and gambling obligations.

Gaetano wiped away the sweat that had beaded along the border of his dark, cropped hair and expansive forehead. He was dressed in what had been carefully pressed tan slacks, a flowered short-sleeve shirt, and a blue sports jacket. The idea was to look upscale so he wouldn't stand out like a sore thumb hanging around the Ocean Club. At the moment, he had the jacket slung over his shoulder, and his pants had some serious damp creases behind each knee. With his compact bulk, he was sensitive to the moist, tropical heat.

Fifteen minutes later, Gaetano was out in a parking lot that was as hot as Hades, looking for a white Jeep Cherokee. If he was hot before, he was boiling now, with triangles of sweat-soaked shirt under each arm. He was holding his carry-on overnight bag in his right hand while his left gripped his car rental papers and a map he'd gotten from the agent. The idea of driving on the left, as instructed by the rent-a-car agent, had initially given him pause, but now he thought he could handle it, provided he kept reminding himself. To him, it seemed the height of ridiculousness for the Bahamians to drive on the wrong side.

He found the car. Without delay, he climbed in and got it started. His first order of business was to get the air-conditioning on full blast and to redirect all the vents in his direction. After checking the map and spreading it out on the seat next to him, he started out of the lot.

There had been some talk of getting a gun, but the idea had been dropped. First of all, it would take time, and second of all, he didn't need it to deal with a pissant professor. He checked the map again. The route was pretty simple, since most of the roads led into the town of Nassau. From there, he'd take the bridge over to Paradise Island, where he assumed the Ocean Club would be easy to find.

Gaetano smiled at fate. A few years earlier, who would have guessed that he'd be driving along in the Bahamas, dressed to beat the band, feeling good, and anticipating some action? A quiver of excitement made the hairs on the back of his neck momentarily stand up. Gaetano liked violence in any form. It was an addiction of sorts that had gotten him into trouble in the past, starting in middle school but particularly in high school. He loved violent action movies and violent computer games, but mostly he loved the real thing. Thanks to his size, which he'd attained at a young age, and his athleticism, he managed to come out on top in most scuffles.

The biggest problem had occurred in the year 2000. He and his older brother had been employed as he was now, as enforcers or musclemen, but back then it had been in the big leagues in Queens, New York, for one of the major crime families. A job came up for which he and his brother, Vito, were both assigned. They were to teach a lesson to a cop who was on the take but not coming through with his side of the bargain. It was supposed to be straightforward, but it went awry. The cop pulled out a hidden gun and managed to seriously wound Vito before Gaetano disarmed him.

Unfortunately, Gaetano had seen red.

When it was over, not only had he killed the policeman, but he'd also killed the man's wife and the guy's teenage son, both of whom had stupidly tried to intervene, the woman with another gun and the kid with a baseball bat. Everyone was furious. None of it was supposed to have happened, and it caused a huge overreaction on the part of New York law enforcement, as if the cop had been some kind of hero. At first, Gaetano thought he was going to be sacrificed, either whacked himself or given over to the police on a silver platter. But then out of the blue came the opportunity to disappear by going to Boston to work for the Castigliano brothers, who were somehow distantly related to the family the Barreses had worked for.

Initially, Gaetano had hated the move. He hated Boston, which he considered a puny town compared to New York, and he hated being a clerk in the plumbing supply business, a position he felt was demeaning. But slowly he got used to it.

"Holy crap!" Gaetano voiced, as he caught his first view of the Bahamian ocean. He'd never seen such an intense blue and aquamarine. As traffic increased, Gaetano slowed down accordingly and enjoyed the scenery. He had adjusted more easily than he thought he would to driving on the left, which left his eyes free to wander, and there was a lot to see. He began to become optimistic about the afternoon until he got to Nassau itself. In town, he found himself bogged down completely and for a time stuck behind a bus at a complete standstill.

He looked at his watch. It was already after one in the afternoon. He shook his head as his optimism rapidly faded. He couldn't help but feel that the chances of being able to do what he needed to do and get back to the airport by four-thirty or so, which is what he'd have to do if he were to make the Miami-to-Boston flight, was getting smaller every minute that went by.

"Screw it!" Gaetano said vehemently. All at once, he decided he wasn't going to let the time factor ruin his day. He took a deep breath and looked out his side window. He even smiled at a handsome black woman who smiled back at him, making him feel that spending the night might be rather entertaining. He rolled his window down, but the woman had already disappeared. A moment later, the bus in front of him began to move forward.

Gaetano finally drove up and over the graceful span that connected New Providence Island with Paradise Island, and soon found himself in the Ocean Club's lot, which, by the look of the vehicles, was more for the employees than the guests.

Leaving his bag and jacket in the back of the Cherokee, Gaetano proceeded west on a tree- and flower-lined walkway before turning north between two of the hotel's buildings. That brought him to the lawn separating the hotel from the beach. Turning east, he wandered back toward the central buildings comprising the public spaces and restaurants. He was impressed with all he saw. It was a gorgeous setting.

An outdoor restaurant with a central bar and a thatched roof stood high above the steeply sloped beach's edge, affording a pleasant view up and down the strand. At one-thirty, the eatery was still filled to overflowing, including a line of people patiently waiting for tables or empty barstools. Gaetano stopped and took out his photos to review the images of the professor and Tony's sister. His eyes lingered on the sister, while he wished she were the mark. The thought of the various ways to give her a violent message brought a smile to his face.

Armed with a refreshed mental image of the people he was searching for, Gaetano took a slow walk around the bar/restaurant. The tables were arranged around the periphery, with the bar in the center. Every table and every seat at the bar were occupied, mostly with scantily clad people of all shapes, sizes, and ages in bathing suits and cover-ups.

Gaetano found himself back where he'd started, without seeing anyone who resembled either the guy or the girl. Leaving the restaurant, he took a flight of stairs that led down to a landing with several outdoor showers before descending another flight to the beach. To the right, at the foot of the stairs, was the hotel's beach concession, with towels, umbrellas, and lounge chairs for the guests. Gaetano took off his shoes and socks and rolled his pant bottoms before traipsing down to the water's edge, where gentle waves lapped at the shore. When he stuck his toes into the water, he found himself wishing he had on his bathing suit. The water was crystal clear, shallow, and delightfully warm.

Walking on the damp, densely packed sand, Gaetano first rambled to the east while scanning the faces of all the people on the beach. It wasn't particularly crowded, because most everybody was having lunch. When he ran out of people, he turned around and walked west. When he ran out of people in that direction, he decided the professor and the sister weren't on the beach. *So much for that idea,* he thought moodily.

Gaetano went back and retrieved his shoes. He helped himself to a towel and went up to the landing, where he rinsed his feet off. With his shoes back on, he climbed the remaining stairs and set off up the sidewalk that traversed the lush lawn in front of the hotel's plantation-style main building. Inside, he found himself in what looked like the living room of a large, luxurious house. A small bar in the corner with six stools reminded him it was, after all, a hotel. With no customers, the bartender was busy cleaning his glasses.

Using a house phone on a desk stocked with hotel stationery, Gaetano called the hotel operator. He asked how to dial one of the guest rooms and was told she would be happy to connect him. Gaetano said he wanted room 108.

While the phone rang, Gaetano helped himself to a bowl of fruit on the desk. He let it ring ten times before the operator came back on the line to ask if he'd like to leave a message. Gaetano said he'd try again later and hung up.

At that point, Gaetano wondered if the hotel had a pool. He hadn't seen one where he would have expected it, namely out in the middle of the expansive lawn, but since the hotel's grounds were obviously large, Gaetano figured there still could have been one. Accordingly, he walked across the living room—like lounge and entered the hotel's reception area. There he asked and was given directions.

It turned out the pool was to the east, set away from the ocean at the base of a formal garden that rose up in successive tiers to be capped by a medieval cloister. Gaetano was impressed with the setting but disappointed at having the same luck as he had on the beach. The professor and Tony's sister were neither at the pool nor in the snack bar next to the pool. They also weren't in a nearby health club or on one of the many tennis courts.

"Crap!" Gaetano mumbled. It was clear to him that his marks were currently not in the hotel. He looked at his watch. It was now after two. He shook his head. Instead of wondering if he would have to spend the night, he started thinking how many nights it might take at the rate he was going.

Retracing his steps back to the reception area, Gaetano found a comfortable couch that had another bowl of fruit as well as a stack of classy magazines and that was positioned so as to afford a clear view through an archway to the front entrance of the hotel. Resigned to waiting, Gaetano sat down and made himself comfortable.

sixteen

2:07 P.M., Friday, March 1, 2002

Leaving Spencer to go up to his expansive office, Paul took the stairs and descended into the basement of the central building after the two of them had said goodbye to their guests. Paul often wondered what Spencer did all day, rattling around in that huge room, which was four times the size of Paul's neighboring office and ten times more sumptuous. Yet Paul did not begrudge the situation. It had been Spencer's only demand during the building of the new clinic. Other than insisting on a ridiculously large personal space, Spencer had otherwise given Paul relatively free rein—most important, in regard to the laboratory and its equipment. Besides, Paul had a second office, albeit tiny, in the laboratory, which he used a hell of a lot more than the one in the admin building.

Paul was whistling as he opened the fire door on the basement level of the stairwell. He had reason to be in a good mood. Not only was he anticipating a serious enhancement of his legitimacy as a stem-cell researcher by collaborating with a potential Nobel laureate, but more important, he was looking at the prospect of a significant and needed financial windfall for the clinic. Like the mythological phoenix, Paul had again risen from the ashes, and this time there had been literal ashes. Less than a year before, he and the other principals at the clinic had to flee Massachusetts with barbarians in the form of Federal marshals at their former facility's gate. Luckily, Paul had anticipated problems because of what he had been spearheading in the research arena, although he envisioned the problems would come via the FDA, not directly from the Justice Department, and he had been making detailed plans to move the clinic out of harm's way offshore. For almost a year, he had been siphoning off funds behind Spencer's back, which had been easy, since Spencer had essentially retired to Florida. Paul had used the money to buy the land in the Bahamas, design a new clinic, and begin construction. The unexpected raid by law enforcement in the wake of a couple pesky whistle-blowers merely meant he and his cohorts' departure had to be precipitous and prior to the new clinic's completion. It also meant they had to activate a preplanned doomsday protocol, burning down their old facility to eliminate all the evidence.

The irony for Paul was that this recent rise from the ashes had been his second miraculous recovery. Only seven years before, his prospects had appeared dismal. He'd lost his hospital privileges and was poised to lose his medical license in the State of Illinois only two years after he'd finished his ob/gyn residency. It was over some stupid, diddly-squat Medicaid/Medicare billing scam he'd copied from some local colleagues and then refined. The problem had forced him to flee the state. Pure serendipity had taken him to Massachusetts, where he'd taken a fellowship in infertility in order to avoid the

Massachusetts Medical Board's finding out about his problems in Illinois. His luck continued when one of the fellowship instructors happened to be Spencer Wingate, who was contemplating retiring. The rest was history.

"If only my friends could see me now!" Paul mumbled happily, as he walked down the basement's central corridor. Such musings were a favorite pastime. Of course, he used the term *friends* loosely, since he didn't have many, having been forced to be a loner most of his life after being the butt of jokes throughout his formative years. He'd always been a hard worker, yet he was destined to continually come up short by society's usual criteria, save for getting a medical degree. But now, with a superbly equipped laboratory at his disposal and without even the threat of FDA oversight, he knew he was positioned to become the biomedical researcher of the year, maybe the decade . . . maybe even the century, considering the Wingate's potential to have a virtual monopoly with both reproductive and therapeutic cloning. Of course, for Paul, the idea he was to be a famous researcher was the biggest irony of all. He'd never planned on it, had no appropriate training for it, and even had the dubious honor of being the last in his class in medical school. Paul laughed silently, knowing that in reality he owed his present position not only to luck, but also to U.S. politicians' ongoing preoccupation with the abortion issue, which had effectively kept oversight from the infertility business as well as handicapped stem-cell research. If that hadn't been the case, researchers on the mainland would be where he was at the moment.

Paul rapped on Kurt Hermann's door. Kurt was the clinic's head of security and one of Paul's first hirelings. Soon after his arrival at the Wingate Clinic, Paul had sensed the enormous profit potential of infertility, particularly if one were willing to push the boundaries and take full advantage of the lack of oversight of the field. With that in mind, Paul had assumed security would be a big issue. Accordingly, he had wanted to find the right person for the job, someone without a lot of scruples, in case draconian methods became necessary, someone highly chauvinistic in the nonsexist sense of the term, and someone with some serious experience. Paul had found all of the above in Kurt Hermann. The fact that the man had been discharged from the U.S. Army's Special Forces under less-than-honorable circumstances following a series of prostitute murders on the island of Okinawa did not trouble Paul in the slightest. In fact, he had considered it a plus.

Hearing a "Come in," Paul opened the door. Kurt had designed his own basement office complex. The main room was a combination office with a couple desks and a couple chairs, plus a small gym with a half dozen exercise machines. There was also a mat for tae kwon do sparring. In addition, there was a video room with an entire wall of monitors showing feeds from cameras sprinkled all around the complex. Down a short interior corridor were a bedroom and a bathroom. Kurt had another, larger apartment over in the laboratory building, but on occasion he would stay right there in his office for several days on end. Across from the office's bedroom was a holding cell, complete with a sink, a head, and an iron cot.

The sharp metallic clank of weights caught Paul's attention and directed it toward the gym section of the room. Kurt Hermann sat up from a bench press. He was dressed as usual, in a tight-fitting black T-shirt, black pants, and black cross-trainer shoes, all of which contrasted sharply with his closely cropped, dirty blond hair. At one point, Paul had casually inquired why Kurt insisted on wearing black, considering the radiant power of the Bahamian sun. Kurt's response was only a slight shrug and an arching of his eyebrows. For the most part, he was a man of few words.

"We need to talk," Paul said.

Kurt didn't answer. He peeled off his Velcro wrist straps, ran a towel across his forehead, and sat down behind his desk. His bulging pectoral and triceps muscles strained the fabric of his T-shirt as he placed his forearms on the desktop. Once he was seated, he didn't move. Paul likened him to a cat ready to pounce.

Paul took hold of one of the side chairs, positioned it in front of the desk, and sat down himself.

"The doctor and his girlfriend have arrived on the island," Paul said.

"I know," Kurt responded in a clipped monotone. He turned around the monitor on his desk. The image was of Daniel and Stephanie, frozen in their approach to the front entrance of the administration building.

Both their faces were plainly visible, as they squinted in the morning sun.

"A good shot," Paul commented. "It certainly shows to good effect that the woman is downright attractive."

Kurt turned the monitor back around toward himself but didn't respond.

"Any information about the identity of the patient since the last time we talked?" Paul asked.

Kurt shook his head.

"So a repeat visit to their apartment back in Cambridge and one to their office didn't reveal anything?"

Kurt shook his head. "Nothing!"

"I hate to beat a dead horse," Paul said, "but we need to know who this person is as soon as possible. The longer we have to wait, the less chance we have of maximizing our compensation. And we do need the money."

"Things will be easier now that they are here in Nassau."

"What's your strategy?"

"When will they be starting their work here at the clinic?"

"Tomorrow, provided they get a FedEx package they are waiting for."

"I need possession of their laptops and their cell phones for a few minutes," Kurt said. "To do that, assistance from the lab people may be needed."

"Oh?" Paul questioned. It was rare for Kurt to ask for help from anyone. "Sure! I'll arrange for the assistance from Ms. Finnigan. What is it you'd want her to do?"

"Once they are working here, I need to know where they keep their computers, and hopefully phones, when they go over to the cafeteria."

"Well, that should be easy," Paul said. "Megan will surely provide them with some sort of lockable compartment for their personal effects. Why would you want their cell phones? I mean, I understand why you'd want the laptops, but why the phones?"

"To check their Caller IDs," Kurt said. "Not that I expect to learn anything, considering how careful they've been up to now. Nor do I expect anything from the computers. That would be too easy. These professor types are far from stupid. What I really want to do is insert a bug in each of their phones to monitor their calls. That is what is going to give us what we want. The downside is that the monitoring has to be close, within a hundred feet or so, because of power limitations. Once the bugs have been planted, Bruno or myself will have to stay within range."

"Now, that's going to be a chore!" Paul exclaimed. "I hope you remember that discretion is the key here. We can't have any type of scene over this; otherwise, Dr. Wingate will be apoplectic."

Kurt gave one of his signature inscrutable shrugs.

"We found out they are staying at the Ocean Club on Paradise Island."

Kurt nodded his head ever so slightly.

"We did learn something else today that might be helpful," Paul said. "This mystery patient might be someone high up in the Catholic Church, which could work nicely in our favor, considering the church's stand on stem cells. Maintaining the secrecy might be worth a lot of money."

Kurt didn't respond in the slightest.

"Well, that's it," Paul said. He slapped his knees before standing up. "Let me emphasize again, we need the name."

"I'll get it," Kurt said. "Trust me!"

What's going on?" Daniel questioned, with an edge to his voice. "Are you giving me the silent treatment or what? You haven't said boo since we left the clinic twenty-some minutes ago."

"You haven't said much yourself," Stephanie responded. She was staring broodingly out the front windshield and didn't bother to turn her head in Daniel's direction.

"I said it was a beautiful day when we got into the car."

"Oh, wow!" Stephanie remarked with unmistakable derision. "That's a stimulating conversation-starter, considering what we've experienced this morning."

Daniel cast Stephanie a quick, irritated glance before redirecting his attention to the road. They were driving along the north shore of the island, heading back to their hotel. "I don't think you are being fair. In front of our hosts, you carry on like a banshee, which I don't want you to do anymore, and now that we're alone, you're as quiet as a mouse. You're acting as if I did something wrong."

"Yeah, well, I can't understand why you're not outraged about what's going on at the Wingate Clinic."

"You mean about their supposed stem-cell therapy."

"Even calling it therapy is a gross misnomer. It is a pure, unadulterated medical scam. Not only is it bilking desperate people out of money and appropriate treatment, it will give stem cells a bad name, because it's not going to cure anything, except as an elaborate placebo."

"I am outraged," Daniel said. "Anybody would be, but I'm equally outraged about the politicians who are making it all possible and at the same time forcing us to deal with these people."

"And what about the Wingate's putative trade secret that enables them to supply human eggs on demand with only twelve hours notice?"

"That is equally as ethically worrisome, I have to admit."

"Worrisome!" Stephanie repeated scornfully. "It's a lot more than worrisome. Did you happen to see that there is an article about oocytes in the journal they gave us?" She unrolled the magazine, which she had clutched in her hand. She pointed. "Article number three's title is 'Our Extensive Experience with In Vitro Maturation of Human Fetal Oocytes.' What does that suggest?"

"Do you think they get their oocytes from aborted fetuses?"

"With what we know, that would not be an outlandish supposition. And did you notice all the pregnant young Bahamian women working in the cafeteria, none of whom, I might add, had any of the usual signs of being married? And what about Paul flaunting their experience with nuclear transfer? These people are probably offering reproductive cloning on top of everything else."

Stephanie exhaled forcibly while shaking her head. Instead of looking over at Daniel, she turned and looked out her passenger-side window. She had her arms tightly folded over her chest. "Just being there and talking with these people, much less working there, makes me feel like an accomplice."

They drove in silence for a few minutes. Daniel spoke up as they reached the outskirts of Nassau and had to slow because of traffic. "Everything you are saying is true. But it is also true that we had a pretty damn good idea of what these people were like before we got here. You're the one who checked them out on the Internet, and to quote you, you said, 'These people are definitely not nice, and we should limit our interaction with them.' Do you remember saying that?"

"Of course I do," Stephanie snapped. "It was at the Rialto restaurant in Cambridge, not even a week ago." She sighed. "My word! So much has happened in the last six days, it seems like a year has gone by."

"But you get my point," Daniel persisted.

"I suppose, but I also said I wanted to be sure that by working at their clinic, we wouldn't be supporting something unconscionable."

"At the expense of being ridiculously redundant, we're here to treat Butler, and nothing else. We agreed on it, and that's what we are going to do. We're not on a social crusade to expose the Wingate Clinic, not now and not even after we treat Butler, because if the FDA finds out what we've done, there could be trouble."

Stephanie turned around to face Daniel. "When I initially agreed to participate in treating Butler, I thought the only compromise we would be making was in regard to experimental ethics. Unfortunately, it seems as if we find ourselves on the proverbial slippery slope. I'm worried where this is going to take us, conscience-wise."

"You could always go home," Daniel said. "You're better at the cellular work, but I suppose I could muddle through it."

"Do you mean that?"

"I do. You have a far better technique with nuclear transfer than I."

"No, I'm asking if you would mind if I leave."

"If the ethical compromises we have to make are going to make you miserable, morose, and unpleasant to be with, then no, I don't mind if you leave."

"Would you miss me?"

"Is this a trick question? I already implied that I'd much prefer you to stay. Compared with you, I have two thumbs on each hand when I'm working with oocytes and blastocysts under a dissecting microscope."

"I mean miss me emotionally."

"Of course! That's a given."

"It's never a given, especially since you've never said as much. But don't get me wrong; I appreciate you saying it now, and I appreciate your willingness to let me leave. It means a lot to me." Stephanie sighed. "But as much as I'm conflicted about working with these morons, I don't think I could leave you here to carry on by yourself. But I'll think about it.

It makes me feel better to know it is an option, and such feelings are appreciated. After all, from day one, this whole affair has been against my intuition and better judgment, and this morning's experience hasn't helped."

"I'm aware of your misgivings," Daniel said. "And knowing them makes me even more appreciative of your support. But enough is enough! We know they are bad news, and what we've seen this morning just confirms it. Let's move on to another subject! What was your take on the Pakistani neurosurgeon?"

"What can I say? I liked his English accent, but he's kind of short. On the other hand, he's cute."

"I'm trying to be serious," Daniel said, with an edge returning to his voice.

"Well, I'm trying to be humorous. I mean, how can you evaluate a professional after meeting him for lunch? At least he's had good training at recognized academic centers in London, but whether he's a good surgeon, who's to say? At least he's personable." Stephanie shrugged. "What do you think?"

"I think he's terrific, and I think we're lucky

to have him on board. The fact that he had experience doing fetal cell implants for Parkinson's disease as a resident is an extraordinary plus. I mean, he's going to be doing the same procedure for us. Implanting our cloned dopaminergic neural cells will merely be a rerun, with the exception that it will work. I sensed a true frustration on his part that the results of the fetal cell study he was involved in were so poor."

"He is enthusiastic," Stephanie agreed. "I have to give him credit for that, but I wasn't totally convinced it wasn't because he needs the work. One thing that surprised me was that he thought it would only take him an hour or so."

"I'm not," Daniel said. "Setting the stereotaxic headgear in place is the only step that's time-consuming. The burr hole and the injection will be quick."

"I suppose we should be thankful to have found him so easily."

Daniel nodded.

"I know one other reason you were upset this morning," Daniel said suddenly, after a short break in their conversation.

"Oh?" Stephanie questioned, feeling herself tense up after finally relaxing to a degree. The last thing she wanted to hear was another upsetting detail.

"Your faith in the medical profession must now be at a new nadir."

"What are you talking about?"

"Spencer Wingate is hardly the short, fat, and warted individual you'd hoped, although, as I already said, he could still be a chain-smoker and have bad breath."

Stephanie gave Daniel several playful swats on the shoulder. "After all the things I've said lately, it's just like you to remember that."

In an equally playful fashion, Daniel pretended to be terrified and pressed himself up against his window to get out of her reach. At that moment, they were stopped at a traffic light just short of the bridge to Paradise Island.

"Now, Paul Saunders is another story," Daniel said, righting himself. "So maybe your faith hasn't suffered an irreversible blow, since his appearance certainly makes up for Spencer's matinee-idol good looks."

"Paul is not that bad-looking," Stephanie said. "He certainly has interesting hair, with such a striking white forelock."

"I know you have trouble saying anything

bad about someone's person," Daniel said. "Not that I understand it, particularly in this instance, considering how you feel about these people, but let's at least admit that the man is an odd-looking duck."

"People are born with their faces and their bodies; they don't choose them. I'll say Paul Saunders is unique. I've never seen anyone with two different-colored irises."

"He has an eponymous genetic syndrome," Daniel explained. "It's fairly rare, if I remember correctly, but I don't recall its name. It was one of those arcane diseases that would occasionally get tossed out during internal medicine rounds."

"A hereditary disease!" Stephanie remarked. "Well, that's exactly why I don't like to criticize people's basic appearances. Does this syndrome have any serious health consequences?"

"I can't remember," Daniel admitted.

The light changed, and they motored over the bridge. The view of the Nassau harbor was engaging, and neither spoke until they got to the other side.

"Hey!" Daniel blurted. He veered into a lane for making a right-hand turn across traffic and came to a stop. "What about heading over to this shopping plaza to get ourselves some more clothes? At the very least, we need bathing suits so we can visit the beach. After the FedEx package gets here, there's not going to be much opportunity to take advantage of Nassau's pleasures."

"Let's go back to the hotel first. It's time to give Father Maloney a call. By now, he should be back in New York, and maybe he has some information about our luggage. What clothes we buy will depend on whether we're going to get it or not."

"Good point!" Daniel said. He changed his turn signals and looked over his shoulder as he drove back into the line of traffic heading east.

A few minutes later, Daniel drove the car past the hotel's parking area and directly up to the front of the hotel. Liveried doormen came to both sides of the car and opened the doors simultaneously.

"You're not going to park it in the lot?" Stephanie questioned.

"Let's leave the car here with the doormen," Daniel said. "We'll give Father Maloney a try, but whether or not we get him, I want to go back and get us bathing suits."

"Fine by me," Stephanie said, as she slid out of the car. After the stress of the morning, a little shopping plus a relaxing visit to the beach sounded glorious.

As if he'd had a shot of speed, Gaetano felt his pulse quicken and the hairs rise up on the back of his neck. Finally, after lots of false alarms, the two people coming in through the front doors of the hotel looked like the pair he was searching for. He quickly withdrew the photo he had in the pocket of his flower-print shirt. While the couple was still in view, he compared their faces with those in the photograph. "Bingo," he said under his breath. He replaced the photo and glanced at his watch. It was a quarter to three. He shrugged. If the professor cooperated by either going for a long walk or, better yet, heading back into town, where the two of them must have been, Gaetano might make the evening flight to Boston after all.

The couple disappeared from view to Gaetano's right, apparently walking through the lobby, past the registration desks. Without causing a scene by hurrying, Gaetano replaced the magazine he'd been perusing, picked up his jacket, which he'd draped over the back of the sofa, smiled at the bartender, who'd been nice enough to engage him in chitchat, which had kept the hotel security from becoming suspicious, and headed after the couple. By the time he got outside, they were out of sight.

Gaetano headed along the serpentine walkway that wended its way among flowering trees and high bushes. He wasn't concerned that he couldn't see the couple, since he assumed they were headed to their room, and he knew exactly where room 108 was located. As he walked, he regretted his instructions not to confront the professor in the hotel. It would have been so much easier than having to wait for the man to leave the premises.

Gaetano caught sight of his quarry just as they were entering their building. He walked around to the ocean side, and found a strategically situated hammock stretched between two palm trees. After draping his jacket over one of the ropes, he gingerly climbed aboard. From that convenient vantage point, he would see them if they went to the beach, the pool, or any other of the hotel attractions. There wasn't much more he could do but wait and watch and hope their plans took them away from the hotel.

As the minutes passed, Gaetano's heart rate settled back to normal, although he was still titillated by the anticipation of imminent physical action. He was about as comfortable as he could imagine, with his head propped up on a little canvas pillow attached to the hammock and one foot out on the ground to gently sway himself. Only a smattering of sunlight sifted through the palm fronds overhead, which was a godsend. If he'd been in the direct sun, he would have broiled.

A woman in a skimpy bikini and a see-through cover-up walked by and smiled. Gaetano gave a wave in return, which nearly upended him. As far as he knew, he'd never been in a hammock before, and since it was stretched rather tightly between the trees, it wasn't as steady as he imagined. He felt better gripping both sides.

Gaetano was about to risk checking his watch when he saw the couple. Instead of going to the beach, they were on the walkway, heading back to the lobby. More important, they were dressed as they had been earlier. Gaetano didn't want to jinx himself, but attired as they were, they weren't going to the pool for damn sure, and just maybe they might be heading back out of the hotel.

In an attempt to get out of the hammock quickly, Gaetano caused it to flip completely over, resulting in his being ignominiously dumped face-first on the ground. He scrambled to his feet and was further embarrassed when he discovered that two toddlers and their mother had witnessed his fall.

He brushed off blades of grass adhering to the front of his slacks and picked up his sunglasses. It irritated him that both kids had smirks on their faces at his expense, and for a second, he thought about teaching them a lesson about respect. Luckily, the family moved on, although one of the brats looked back over his shoulder, with a mocking smile still plastered to his face. Gaetano gave him the finger. He then grabbed his jacket and took off after the couple.

This time, Gaetano ran, since it was now important to keep them in sight. He caught up with them before they reached the central building, and he slowed to a walk. He was breathing heavily. When they entered the lobby, Gaetano was right behind them. He was close enough to hear them talk. He was also close enough to appreciate that Stephanie was even more comely than her photograph suggested.

"Why don't you have them pull the car up," Stephanie was saying. "I'll be out in a second. I want to check with the concierge whether we need a reservation for dinner tonight in the courtyard."

"Fine," Daniel said agreeably.

Suppressing a smile to hide his delight, Gaetano reversed course and exited the lobby area through the door he'd just come in. Walking quickly, he beat it out to the parking lot and jumped into the Cherokee. After getting it started, he drove back toward the front of the hotel, positioning the car so he could see the roundabout and the porte cochere. Directly in front of the hotel entrance was a blue Mercury Marquis with its engine idling. Stephanie appeared from within and climbed into the front passenger seat.

"Score!" Gaetano happily said out loud. He looked at his watch. It was a quarter past three. Suddenly, things seemed to be falling into place.

The Mercury Marquis started forward and passed directly in front of Gaetano. Gaetano fell in behind, close enough at first to commit the license plate to memory. He then dropped back.

What did you think about my conversation with Father Maloney?" Stephanie asked.

"I'm just as confused about him as I was the day we left Turin."

"Me too," Stephanie agreed. "I was hoping he'd be a bit more forthcoming than he was back in Italy about divine intervention and his merely being the Good Lord's servant. But, hey, at least he's supposedly arranged for us to get our luggage. With us being fugitives and with what I know about lost luggage, that's got to be evidence of divine intervention."

"Maybe so, but without having any idea when it might arrive, it's not much help in the short run."

"Well, I'm going to think positively about it being soon, so my shopping is going to be restricted to a bathing suit and a few basics."

Daniel pulled into the strip mall's parking area and drove along the storefronts, pausing in front of a woman's clothing store immediately adjacent to a men's shop. Both window displays were tastefully done. The clothes looked European.

"Isn't this convenient," Daniel commented as he parked the car. He looked at his watch. "Let's meet back here at the car in half an hour."

"Sounds good to me," Stephanie said, as she stepped out of the vehicle.

With his heart rate back up to where it had been when he first saw the couple coming into the hotel, Gaetano nosed into a parking space that afforded a direct route back onto the street and hence directly over the bridge to Nassau. It was always important to provide a quick getaway in his line of work. He turned off the engine and looked back over his shoulder. He watched while the couple split up, with the professor going toward a men's haberdashery, while Tony's sister headed for an adjacent woman's shop.

Gaetano couldn't believe his luck. The question of how to deal with the woman while he took care of business with the professor had been a nagging concern, since by decree, she was supposed to be left out of the action. Now she wouldn't be a problem,

as long as the professor provided an appropriate opportunity while he was alone. Unsure how long he would be alone, Gaetano
leaped out of the Cherokee. As he quickened
his step to a jog, his anticipatory fervor
soared. For him, the necessary maneuvering
as he closed in on a mark was like foreplay in
a self-fulfilling cycle of excitement, while the
resulting violence was very nearly orgasmic.
In fact, for him, the entire experience was
similar to sex but better.

It was a relief for Daniel to be by himself,
even for only thirty minutes. Stephanie's
carping about her conscience was getting on
his nerves. Finding out Spencer Wingate et
al. were into questionable activities was
hardly a surprise, especially after what she
had reported learning during her Internet
search. He hoped that her current bother-
some self-righteousness wasn't going to
cause her to lose sight of the big picture and
get in the way. He could do without her, but
he'd been truthful when he admitted she was
better than he when it came to cellular manipulation.

Daniel did not like to shop, and as he entered the haberdashery, he intended to

make the visit quick so he could go back out to the car and just sit and relax. All he wanted to buy was a few pairs of under-pants, a bathing suit, and some appropriate clothes for work, such as khaki pants and short-sleeve shirts. In London, Stephanie had talked him into buying slacks, two dress shirts, and a tweed jacket, so he was fine in that arena.

The interior of the shop was surprisingly large, despite its modest storefront, since it was deep. Just inside the door was a sizable golf and smaller tennis section, while every-day apparel was farther back. The tempera-ture was pleasantly cool. The air was scented with cologne mixed with the odor of new fabric. Classical music issued from a multitude of wall speakers. The décor was decidedly clubby, with lots of dark red ma-hogany, horse prints, and dark green carpet-ing. There were a half dozen other shoppers, all of whom were in the golf area. Each was being helped by a salesperson.

No one came to greet Daniel, which he preferred. Officious haberdashers had al-ways put him off with their condescending manner, as if they were paragons of good taste. When it came to clothes Daniel was

Ivy League conservative. He essentially wore what he'd worn in college. Unaccosted and unaccompanied, he passed through the sports section and headed into the depths of the store.

Since he knew it would be easy, Daniel started with the bathing-suit quest. He found the appropriate section and then his size. After flipping through a few on the rack of dozens, he pulled out a solid, dark-blue, medium boxer. He thought that would do just fine. Immediately adjacent to the bathing suits was the underwear section. He was a classic brief man, and he found his size with ease.

With only a few of his thirty minutes of reprieve gone, Daniel went to the shirt section. He passed up the majority, which were flower prints in bright, tropical colors, and zeroed in on button-down oxfords with short sleeves. He found his size and took two in blue. With the bathing suit, underwear, and shirts in hand, he walked to the pants section. It was equally hard to find plain khakis, but he did, although with the pants, he wasn't sure of the size. Reluctantly, he took several of varying lengths and looked for the dressing rooms. He found them at the very back of the store beyond the deserted suits and sport jackets section.

There were four changing cubicles arranged along the back of a mahogany-paneled fitting room. The fitting room was reached by pushing through a pair of swinging doors. Three-way mirrors graced the end walls. Each cubicle had a paneled door that stood open. The first dressing room on the right was twice the size of the other three, and Daniel headed there.

Inside, he found a single upholstered chair, several clothes hooks, and a floor-to-ceiling mirror. Daniel closed and locked the door, put his intended purchases on the chair, and hung the pants on the hooks. After kicking off his shoes, he undid his belt and slipped out of his slacks. Taking the first pair of pants, he was about to pull them on when a reverberating thud preceded the changing-room door being rudely kicked open with such force to cause it to smash against the wall hard enough to drive the doorknob through the plasterboard. Daniel's heart leaped into his throat as a feeble moan escaped from his lips.

Literally caught with his pants down, Daniel merely stared at the hulking intruder, who closed the door despite the splintered casing. The man then stepped over to the startled Daniel, who looked up into a pair of dark, metallic eyes peering out of an over-sized head capped with black hair in a buzz cut. Before Daniel could respond, the pants he was holding were ripped from his grasp and tossed to the side.

At the exact moment Daniel found his voice to start to protest, a fist came out of nowhere and smashed into the side of his face, rupturing capillaries in his nose and crushing others in his lower right eyelid. Pro-pelled backward, Daniel slammed against the mirror before collapsing to a sitting posi-tion with his legs crumpled beneath him. The image of the attacker swam before him. Only partially aware of what was happening and offering no resistance, Daniel was yanked upright before he was sent sprawling into the upholstered chair on top of the clothes he'd intended to buy. He could feel blood trickle out of his nose, and he could barely see out of his right eye.

"Listen, asshole," Gaetano growled. He poked his head close to Daniel's face. "I'm going to make this short. My bosses, the Castigliano brothers, in the name of all stockholders in your freaking company, want you to get your ass back up north and put the company back on track. You hear me?"

Daniel tried to talk, but his vocal cords wouldn't respond. Instead, he nodded his head.

"It's not a complicated message," Gaetano continued. "They feel it's disrespectful for you to be frolicking down here in the sun while their hundred-grand investment is on the rocks."

"We're trying . . ." Daniel managed, but his voice was a high-pitched squeak.

"Yeah, sure you're trying," Gaetano scoffed. "You and your hot-ticket girlfriend. But it doesn't look that way to my bosses, who would much prefer you do your trying back in Beantown. And whether the company tanks or not, my bosses are going to expect their money back, no matter what kind of fancy lawyers you might employ. You understand?"

"Yes, but . . ."

"No buts," Gaetano interrupted. "I'm making this crystal clear. You gotta tell me you understand! Yes or no?"

"Yes," Daniel croaked.

"Good," Gaetano said. "But just to be sure,

I have something else I want you to think about."

Without warning, Gaetano hit Daniel again. This time, it was on the left side of Daniel's head, but in contrast to the first blow, Gaetano used an open hand. Nonetheless, it was a powerful whack that landed with enough force to propel Daniel out of the chair like a ragdoll and onto the floor.

The side of Daniel's face was stinging, and a high-pitched ringing sounded in his ear. He felt Gaetano nudge him with his foot before grabbing a handful of his hair and yanking his head off the carpet. Daniel opened his eyes. He squinted at the backlit image of his assailant hovering over him.

"Can I feel confident you have gotten the message?" Gaetano demanded. "Because I want you to know I could have hurt you bad. I hope you understand that. But at the moment, we don't want you hurt so bad that you can't get your company back on its feet. Of course, that might change if I have to fly the hell back down here from Boston. You catch my drift?"

"I get the message," Daniel squeaked.

Gaetano let Daniel's hair go, and his head

bounced down on the carpet. Daniel kept his eyes closed.

"That's all for now," Gaetano said. "I hope I don't have to come and visit you again."

A moment later, Daniel heard the door to the changing room creak open and then shut again. All was quiet.

seventeen

3:20 P.M., Friday, March 1, 2002

Daniel opened his eyes after lying perfectly still for a few minutes. He was alone in the changing cubicle, but he heard muffled voices beyond the door. It sounded as if a salesperson was directing a customer into one of the other cubicles. Daniel pushed himself up to a sitting position and looked at himself in the mirror. The left side of his face was beet red, and a trickle of blood went from his nose to the corner of his mouth before running down to the edge of his jaw. His right eye was beginning to swell shut and had a slightly bluish cast.

Gingerly, Daniel felt his nose and his right cheekbone with the tip of his index finger. Everything was tender, but there was neither pinpoint pain nor suspicious bony edges to suggest he had suffered a fracture. He got to his feet and, after a fleeting moment of dizziness, he felt reasonably well, except for a dull headache, wobbly legs, and a pervading sense of nervousness, as if he'd just drunk five cups of coffee. He held out his hand; he had a tremor to beat the band. The episode had terrified him; he'd never felt quite so vulnerable in his life.

Despite uncertain balance, Daniel managed to pull on his pants. He then wiped away the blood from his face with the back of his hand. In the process, he realized he'd suffered a gash inside his cheek. Carefully, he explored the area with his tongue. Luckily, it wasn't large enough for him to believe he needed any stitches. Then he smoothed out the thinning hair on top of his head by raking it with his fingers. He opened the door and stepped out into the fitting room.

"Good afternoon," a snappily dressed,

African-Bahamian salesman said with a strong English drawl. He was dressed in a pinstriped suit accented with a colorful silk pocket square that appeared to have exploded out of his breast pocket. He was leaning against the wall with his arms folded awaiting his client to emerge from his changing room. He gave Daniel a quizzical look with arched eyebrows but said nothing more.

Afraid of how his voice might sound, Daniel merely nodded in reply while managing a tentative smile. He started forward on unsteady legs, acutely aware of his tremor. He was afraid he might appear intoxicated. But the more he walked, the easier it became. He was relieved when the salesperson didn't confront him. Daniel wanted to avoid any conversation. He merely wanted to get out of the store.

By the time Daniel got to the door to the street, he was confident he was walking normally. He opened the door and stuck his head out into the sunny afternoon heat. A quick glance around the parking area convinced him that his muscular attacker had long since departed. He peeked through the window of the women's store and caught a glimpse of Stephanie happily shopping.

Confident she was okay, Daniel made a bee-line for the Mercury Marquis.

Once inside the car, Daniel rolled down the windows to allow the breeze to siphon off the ovenlike heat that had developed during the short time he'd been in the store. He sighed; it felt good to be sitting down within the familiar surroundings of his rent-a-car. Bending the rearview mirror in his direction, he examined himself more closely. He was particularly worried about his right eye, which was now practically shut. Still, he could tell the cornea was clear and there was no blood in the anterior chamber, although there were some petechial hemorrhages on the sclera. Having spent time in the emergency room as a medial resident, he knew something about facial trauma—in particular, a problem called a blowout fracture of the orbit. To make sure that hadn't happened, he checked to see if he saw double, especially when he looked up and down. Thankfully, he didn't. So he repositioned the rearview mirror and sat back to wait for Stephanie.

About a quarter of an hour later, Stephanie emerged from the women's clothing store with several shopping bags in tow.

Shielding her eyes from the sun, she looked in Daniel's direction. Daniel responded by sticking his hand out his open window and waving. She waved back and came running. He watched as she approached. Now that he'd had a few minutes to think about his assault and its probable origin, his mental state had changed from anxiety to anger, and a significant portion of it was directed at Stephanie and her screwed-up family. Although he'd not had his knees smashed, the modus operandi smelled suspiciously Mob-related, which immediately brought to mind Stephanie's indicted brother. Who the Castiglianos were he had no idea, but he was going to find out.

Stephanie came first to the passenger-side back door, opened it, and tossed her bundles onto the backseat. "How'd you make out?" she questioned happily. "I have to say, I did better than I expected." She slammed the back door and proceeded to get into the front while babbling about her purchases. She closed her door and grabbed her seat belt before she looked at Daniel. When she did, she stopped her ramblings in mid-sentence. "My God! What happened to your eye?" she blurted.

"It's good of you to notice," Daniel said scornfully. "Obviously, I got beat up. But before we get into the distasteful details, I have a question to ask. Who are the Castigliano brothers?"

Stephanie stared at Daniel, taking in not only the puffy eye, but also the red swelling on the side of his face and the crusted blood along the edges of his nostrils. She wanted to reach out and touch him empathically, but she held back. She could see the anger reflected in the one visible eye and heard it in his tone of voice. Besides, the Castigliano name and the significance it engendered momentarily paralyzed her. She looked down at her hands, limp in her lap.

"Is there some other little important tidbit you didn't feel like talking to me about?" Daniel continued, with equal sarcasm. "I mean, in addition to your brother being indicted for racketeering after becoming an investor. I repeat, who the hell are the Castiglianos?"

Stephanie's mind was racing. It was true that she'd not shared the news that her brother had farmed out half of his investment. She had no excuse for not being more forthcoming, especially since the news had disturbed her, and this second and related lapse made her feel like a thief caught twice in the same felonious act.

"I was hoping we could at least have a conversation," Daniel said, when Stephanie didn't respond.

"We can, and we will," Stephanie said suddenly. She looked at Daniel. She'd never felt quite so guilty in her life. He'd been hurt, and she had to accept that a significant amount of the responsibility was hers. "But first, tell me if you are okay."

"As well as can be expected, under the circumstances," Daniel started the car and backed out of the parking place.

"Should we go to a hospital or see a doctor?" Stephanie asked.

"No! There's no need. I'm going to live."

"What about the police?"

"An even more emphatic no! Going to the police, who might actually investigate, would risk derailing our plans to treat Butler." Daniel drove to the parking area exit.

"Maybe this is another omen about this whole affair. Are you sure you don't want to give up on this Faustian quest?"

Daniel flashed Stephanie an angry, scornful look. "I can't believe you'd even suggest such a thing. Absolutely not! I'm not about to roll over and give up everything we've worked for because a couple of lowlifes send down their Neanderthal henchman to give me a message."

"He talked with you?"

"In between blows."

"What exactly was the message?"

"To quote the muscleman, I'm supposed to get my ass back to Boston and get the company back on track." Daniel pulled out into the road and accelerated. "Some of our stockholders, having learned we're in Nassau, believe we're on vacation down here."

"Are we going back to the hotel?"

"Seeing as I've lost my enthusiasm for shopping, I want to get some ice on this eye of mine."

"Are you sure we shouldn't go to a doctor? Your eye looks pretty bad."

"It will probably come as a surprise if I remind you that I'm a doctor myself."

"I'm talking about a real, practicing doctor."

"Very funny, but excuse me if I don't laugh!"

They drove in silence the short distance back to the hotel. Daniel parked the car in the parking lot. They got out. Stephanie collected her parcels from the backseat. She didn't quite know what to say.

"The Castigliano brothers are acquaintances of my brother, Tony," Stephanie finally admitted, as they walked toward their building.

"How come I'm not surprised?"

"Other than that, I don't know them, nor have I ever met them."

They keyed open the door to their suite. Stephanie tossed her shopping bags to the side. As guilty as she felt, she didn't know how to handle Daniel's rightful anger. "Why don't you go in and sit down," she offered solicitously. "I'll get the ice."

Daniel stretched out on the couch in the sitting room but quickly sat upright again. Lying down made his head throb. Stephanie came in with a towel, which she wrapped around a handful of ice cubes she got from the ice bucket on the counter over the minibar. She handed a makeshift ice pack to Daniel, who gingerly placed it against his swollen eye.

"How about some ibuprofen?" Stephanie asked.

Daniel nodded, and Stephanie got several tablets, along with a glass of water.

While Daniel took the pain-reliever, Stephanie sat on the couch and tucked her feet underneath herself. She then told Daniel the details of her conversation with Tony the afternoon of the day they left for Turin. She concluded by abjectly apologizing for not having mentioned it. She explained that with everything else that was happening at the time, it seemed to be of minor importance. "I was going to tell you when we got back from Nassau and when the second-round financing came through, because I want to treat the two hundred thousand from my brother as a loan and return it with interest. I don't want him or any of his associates involved with CURE in the future."

"Well, at least we agree on something."

"Are you going to accept my apology?"

"I suppose," Daniel said, without a lot of enthusiasm. "So, your brother warned you about coming here?"

"He did," Stephanie admitted, "because I couldn't tell him why. But it was just a generic warning, and certainly without threats. I have to say, it's still hard for me to believe he's involved with your assault."

"Oh, really?" Daniel said sarcastically. "Start believing it, because he has to have been involved! I mean, other than your brother telling these Castiglianos, how would they know we are here in Nassau? It can't be a coincidence this thug appeared here the day after we arrived. Obviously, after you called your mom last evening, she called your brother, and he called his pals. And I don't suppose I have to remind you how mad you got when I brought up the issue of possible violence when dealing with people involved in racketeering?"

Stephanie blushed at the recollection. It was true; she'd been furious. With sudden determination, she reached for her cell phone, flipped it open, and began dialing. Daniel grabbed her arm. "Who are you calling?"

"My brother," Stephanie said hotly. She sat back with the phone against her ear. Her lips were pressed together in angered determination.

Daniel leaned toward Stephanie and took the phone. Despite Stephanie's flash of anger and apparent resolve, she didn't offer any resistance. Daniel closed the phone and tossed it onto the coffee table. "At the moment, calling your brother is the last thing we should do." He sat back upright, keeping the ice pack pressed against his eye.

"But I want to confront him. If he was truly involved, I'm not going to let him get away with it. I feel betrayed by my own family."

"You're angry?"

"Of course I'm angry," Stephanie retorted.

"So am I," Daniel snapped. "But I'm the one who got beat up, not you."

She lowered her eyes. "You're right. You're the one who deserves to be a lot more upset than I."

"I need to ask you a question," Daniel said. He adjusted his ice pack. "An hour or so ago, you said you'd be thinking about possibly going home to appease your conscience about working with the likes of Paul Saunders and Spencer Wingate. With this new development, I have to know now if you intend to or not."

Stephanie glanced back up at Daniel. She shook her head and gave a short, embarrassed laugh. "After what's happened, and as guilty as I feel about it, there's no way I could leave."

"Well, that's a relief," Daniel commented. "Maybe there's good in everything, even getting beaten to a pulp."

"I really am sorry you were hurt," Stephanie said. "I truly am. More than you know."

"All right, all right," Daniel repeated. He gave Stephanie's knee a reassuring squeeze. "Now that I know you are staying, here's what I think we should do. I think we should pretend this little episode of me being pummeled never happened, meaning no nasty calls to your brother or even your mother, for that matter. Future calls to your mother will emphasize that you and I are not vacationing here but rather hard at work on a job to save CURE. Tell her it's going to take three weeks and then we'll be home."

"What about this hooligan who attacked you? Don't we have to worry about him coming back?"

"That's a concern but apparently a risk we have to take. He's not from the Bahamas, and my educated guess is that he's already on his way home. He said that if he had to fly the hell back down here from Boston again, he'd, and I quote, hurt me bad, which leads me to believe that New England is his usual hangout. At the same time, he said he didn't want to hurt me so bad that I couldn't get the company back on its feet, meaning they have a vested interest in my well-being, despite how I feel at the moment. But most importantly, I'm hoping your phone conversations with your mother, which will undoubtedly get communicated to your brother, will convince the Castiglianos it's worth waiting three weeks."

"Should we change hotels, since I told my mother we're staying here?"

"I thought about that while I was sitting in the car, waiting for you to come out of the store. I even thought about taking Paul up on his offer to stay out at the Wingate Clinic."

"Oh, God! That would be like going from the frying pan into the fire."

"I wouldn't want to stay there either. It's going to be bad enough putting up with those charlatans during the day. So I think we should just stay here, unless it's going to drive you crazy. I don't want a repeat of our night in Turin. My feeling is that we should stay put but not leave the hotel, except to go to the Wingate Clinic, which, starting tomorrow, is where we are going to be most of the time anyway. Agreed?"

Stephanie nodded a few times as she absorbed everything Daniel had said.

"Do you agree or what?" Daniel asked. "You're not saying anything."

Stephanie suddenly threw up her hands in a burst of emotional frustration. "Gosh, I don't know what to think. You getting attacked just adds to my uneasiness about this whole Butler affair. From day one, we've been forced to make assumptions about people we know little or nothing about."

"Wait just a second!" Daniel growled. His face, already red, got redder still, and his voice, which had started out low, began to rise progressively. "We're not starting the debate again about whether or not we're going to treat Butler. That's been decided. Our current conversation is about logistics from this point on, period!"

"Okay, okay!" Stephanie said. She reached out and put a hand on his arm. "Calm down! Fine! We'll stay here and hope things work out for the best."

Daniel took a few deep breaths before saying, "I also think we should make it a point to stay together."

"What are you talking about?"

"I don't think it was an accident the muscleman assaulted me when I happened to be alone. Your brother obviously doesn't want you hurt; otherwise, we both would have been slapped around, or at a minimum, I still would have borne the brunt, but you would have had to witness it. I think the man waited until I was by myself; ergo, I believe our staying together at all times away from our room would provide a certain amount of safety."

"Maybe you're right," Stephanie mumbled equivocally. Her mind was a jumble. On the one hand, she was relieved that Daniel wasn't making a negative reference to their relationship when he mentioned staying together, while on the other hand, it was still hard for her to admit to herself that her brother could have had anything to do with the violence Daniel had experienced.

"Can you get me some more ice?" Daniel asked. "What I've got is just about melted."

"Of course," Stephanie said. She was relieved to have something to do. She took the soggy towel and exchanged it for a fresh one in the bathroom. Then she revisited the ice bucket on the bar. When she handed the fresh ice pack to Daniel, the phone on the side table suddenly sprang to life. For a few moments, its repetitive jangle inundated the otherwise silent room. Neither Daniel nor Stephanie moved. Both stared at the phone.

"Now, who the hell could that be?" Daniel questioned, after the fourth ring. He positioned the ice pack on his eye.

"Not very many people know we are here," Stephanie said. "Should I answer it?"

"I suppose," Daniel said. "If it is your mother or brother, remember what I said earlier."

"What if it's the person who attacked you?"

"That's highly unlikely. Answer it, but be nonchalant! If it is the thug, just hang up. Don't try to engage him in any conversation."

Stephanie went to the phone, picked it up, and tried to say hello normally while looking back at Daniel. Daniel watched her eyebrows raise slightly as she listened. After a few moments, Daniel mouthed, "Who is it?" Stephanie held up her hand and motioned for him to wait. Finally, she said, "Wonderful! And thank you." Then she listened again. Absently, she twirled the phone cord with her finger. After a pause, she said, "That's very nice of you, but it's not possible tonight. In fact, it's not possible any night." She then said goodbye in a clipped tone and replaced the receiver. She returned her eyes to Daniel's but for a moment didn't speak.

"Well? Who was it?" Daniel demanded. His curiosity was getting the best of him.

"It was Spencer Wingate." Stephanie shook her head in amazement.

"What did he want?"

"He wanted to let us know that he located our FedEx package, and he's arranged to have it delivered first thing in the morning."

"Hooray for small favors. That means we can start creating Butler's treatment cells. But that was a rather long conversation for such a short message. What else did he want?"

Stephanie gave a mirthless laugh. "He wanted to know if I would come to his house in Lyford Cay marina for dinner. Strangely enough, he made it clear that the invitation was just for me and not for us as a couple. I can't believe it. It was like he was trying to hustle me."

"Well, let's look on the bright side; at least he has good taste."

"I'm not amused," Stephanie countered.

"I can see that," Daniel said. "But let's keep the big picture in mind."

eighteen

11:30 A.M., Monday, March 11, 2002

Occasionally, Daniel had to give credit where credit was due. There was no doubt in his mind that Stephanie was far better at cellular manipulation than he, and that reality was underlined by what he was presently watching through the eyepieces of a double-headed dissecting stereomicroscope. He and Stephanie had placed the instrument on the corner of their lab bench at the Wingate Clinic to allow Daniel to watch while Stephanie worked. Stephanie was about to begin the process of nuclear transfer, otherwise known as therapeutic cloning, by extracting the nucleus of a mature oocyte whose DNA had been stained with a fluorescent dye. She already had the human egg cell fixated by suction with a blunt-tipped holding pipette.

"You make this look so easy," Daniel remarked.

"It is," Stephanie responded, as she guided a second pipette into the microscopic field with a micromanipulator. In contrast to the holding pipette, this pipette's hollow end was as sharp as the finest needle, and the pipette itself was only twenty-five-millionths of a meter in diameter.

"Maybe it's easy for you, but it's not for me."

"The trick is not to rush things. Everything has to be slow and even, and not jerky."

True to her word, the sharp pipette moved smoothly yet decisively toward the fixated oocyte to push against the cell's outer layer without penetrating it.

"This is the part I invariably screw up," Daniel said. "Half the time, I go clear through the cell and out the other side."

"Maybe because you are too eager, and therefore, a bit heavy-handed," Stephanie suggested. "Once the cell is adequately indented, it just takes a slight tap with the index finger on the top of the micro-manipulator."

"You don't use the micromanipulator itself to do the puncture?"

"Never."

Stephanie carried out the maneuver with her index finger, and within the microscopic field, the pipette was seen to enter cleanly the cytoplasm of the hapless egg cell.

"Well, you live and learn," Daniel said. "It proves I'm just a rank amateur in this arena."

Stephanie pulled away from her eyepieces to glance at Daniel. It wasn't like him to be self-deprecating. "Don't be so hard on your-self. This is busywork, which you've always had skilled technicians to do. I learned how to do it when I was a graduate-student grunt."

"I suppose," Daniel said without looking up.

Stephanie shrugged and directed her eyes back into the microscope. "Now I use the micromanipulator to approach the fluo-rescing DNA," she said. The tip of the pipette approached its target, and when Stephanie applied a tiny amount of suction, the DNA disappeared up into the pipette's lumen as if the pipette were a miniature vacuum cleaner.

"I'm not good at this part either," Daniel said. "I think I suck up too much cytoplasm."

"It's important to get just the DNA," Stephanie said.

"Every time I watch this technique, I'm even more amazed that it works," Daniel commented. "My mental image of the submicroscopic internal structure of a living cell is akin to a miniature glass house. How can it be that we can tear out the nucleus by its roots, essentially throw in another nucleus from an adult differentiated cell, and have the whole thing work? It boggles the imagination."

"Not only work, but cause the adult nucleus we toss in to become young again."

"That too," Daniel agreed. "I tell you, the process of nuclear transfer truly defies belief."

"I couldn't agree more," Stephanie said. "For me, the improbability of it working is evidence of God's involvement in the process, which rattles my agnosticism even more than what we learned about the Shroud of Turin." While she spoke, she guided a third pipette into the microscopic field. This pipette had within its lumen a single fibroblast cell from Ashley Butler's fibroblast culture: a cell whose ancestral nucleus Daniel had painstakingly manipulated, first with HTSR, to replace those genes responsible for the senator's Parkinson's disease with those derived from the shroud's blood, and second, with an added gene at Stephanie's suggestion for a special surface antigen. This fibroblast's nuclear DNA was going to replace the DNA Stephanie had removed from the egg cell.

As Daniel watched Stephanie's artful manipulations, he marveled at what he and she had been able to accomplish in the week and a half since his assault by the thug from Boston. Luckily, his physical injuries had healed and were for the most part a mere memory, save for some residual tenderness along his right cheekbone and the now yellow-and-green remainder of his resolving shiner. Unfortunately, Daniel still struggled with the psychological damage. Burned into the retina of his mind and appearing in recurrent nightmares was an image looming over him of the hulking attacker's huge head, small ears, and bulbous features. Most disturbing was the man's crooked smile and cruel, beady eyes. Even after eleven days, Daniel still suffered repetitive nightmares of that awful face and the feeling of utter defenseless vulnerability it engendered.

In the daytime, Daniel had fared considerably better than during sleep. As he and Stephanie had discussed immediately after the episode, they had made it a point to stay together practically like Siamese twins and not leave the hotel grounds, except to go to the Wingate Clinic. As it turned out, such a plan was hardly an imposition, since they had spent sunup to after sundown in the laboratory each and every day. There, Megan Finnigan was most helpful, providing them with a small office in addition to their own laboratory bench. Having room to spread out their paperwork and flow sheets was a godsend and a boon to their efficiency. Even Paul Saunders had helped by acting true to his word and producing ten fresh human oocytes twelve hours after they had been requested.

At first, there had been a convenient division of labor between Daniel and Stephanie. Her job initially was to work with the fibroblast culture sent by Peter. She got it thawed and growing with only minor glitches. Concurrently, Daniel attacked the buffered solution containing the shroud sample. After a single pass through the PCR machine to magnify the DNA present in the fluid, Daniel determined the contained DNA was primate and probably human, although decidedly fragmented, as he had expected.

Following a purification trick using microscopic glass beads, Daniel ran the isolated shroud DNA fragments through the PCR several more times before utilizing his dopaminergic gene probes. He was immediately successful, but with only parts of the required genes, a situation that required sequencing the gaps. After several sixteen-hour days, Daniel succeeded in attaching the appropriate fragments with nucleotide ligases to form the genes. At that point, he was ready for Ashley Butler's fibroblasts, which by then Stephanie conveniently had available.

HTSR was the next step, and it went practically without a hitch. Having developed the procedure, Daniel was intimately aware of its subtleties and pitfalls, but under his sure hand, the enzymes and viral vectors worked perfectly, and he soon had a number of the fibroblasts ready. The only problem had been Paul Saunders, who had insisted on shadowing Daniel's every move and frequently got in the way. Paul unabashedly admitted that he planned to add the technique to the Wingate's stem-cell therapy regimen, with the idea of charging the patients significantly more. Daniel doggedly tried to ignore him and bit his tongue to keep from ordering the quack out of his own laboratory, but it was difficult.

Once the HTSR had been completed, Daniel thought they were ready to do the nuclear transfer, but Stephanie had surprised him with the suggestion that they also transfect the HTSR-altered cell with an ecdysone construct, meaning several combined genes, capable of creating a unique nonhuman surface antigen on the ultimate treatment cells. Stephanie had argued that if there was ever a need or an interest to visualize the treatment cells within Butler's brain after the implant, it could be done with ease, since the treatment cells would have an antigen that none of Butler's other trillion cells had. Daniel had been impressed with the idea and had agreed to the additional step, especially after Stephanie told him she'd had the foresight to ask Peter to send the construct and its viral vector down from their Cambridge laboratory along with the Butler tissue culture. Daniel and Stephanie had used the same technique when they'd successfully treated the mice afflicted by Parkinson's, and it had been a valuable addition to the protocol.

"I always use the micromanipulator for this step," Stephanie said, pulling Daniel back from his musings. The pipette containing Butler's altered fibroblast pierced the oocyte's envelope without piercing the underlying cell membrane.

"I have trouble with this part too," Daniel admitted. He watched as Stephanie injected the relatively tiny fibroblast into the space between the egg's cell membrane and its comparatively thick outer covering. The pipette then disappeared from view.

"The trick is to approach the oocyte's envelope tangentially," Stephanie said. "Otherwise, you can inadvertently enter the cell."

"That makes sense."

"Well, I'd say that looks just dandy," Stephanie said, after viewing her handiwork. The appropriately granular enucleated egg cell and the comparatively tiny fibroblast were locked in an intimate embrace within the oocyte's envelope. "Time for the fusion process and then the activation."

Stephanie pulled away from the microscope's eyepieces and extracted the petri dish from beneath the microscope's objective. Slipping off her stool, she walked over to the fusion chamber, where she would subject the paired cells to a brief shock of electricity to fuse them.

Daniel watched her go. Along with the recurrent nightmares subsequent to his beating by the Castiglianos' henchman, Daniel struggled with other psychological sequelae from the experience. During the first few days, he had experienced continuous anxiety and fear that the man would reappear, despite what Daniel had reassuringly told Stephanie immediately after the event. It was also despite what the hotel did after Daniel had informed the administration of what had happened. To his credit, the hotel manager had voluntarily stationed a security person within Daniel and Stephanie's building for a week. Every night, the man had accompanied Daniel and Stephanie back to their room after they'd finished their dinner in the hotel's Courtyard Terrace restaurant, and the intimidatingly large individual had remained on guard in the hall until Daniel and Stephanie departed for the Wingate Clinic in the morning.

As Daniel's fear abated during the passing days, his anger at the event waxed, and a significant amount of the anger was redirected toward Stephanie. Although she had apologized and had been sincerely sympathetic initially, Daniel fumed at her lingering doubt about her family's role in the event. She hadn't said as much directly, but Daniel had gotten that sense from indirect comments. With such a screwed-up family and lack of judgment in dealing with them, Daniel couldn't help but question whether Stephanie would be too much of a liability over the long haul.

Stephanie's self-righteousness was also a problem. Even though she'd promised not to make waves with the Wingate people, she was constantly doing so with inappropriate comments about their supposed stem-cell therapy and even inappropriate questioning of the young, pregnant Bahamian women who worked at the clinic, which was an extremely sensitive issue with Paul Saunders. On top of that, she was embarrassingly dismissive of Spencer Wingate. Daniel recognized that the man was being progressively forward in expressing his social interest in Stephanie, a fact that might have been influenced by Daniel's passivity in the face of Spencer's comments, yet there were less rude ways for her to handle the situation than she was choosing. It irked Daniel to no end that Stephanie just couldn't seem to understand that her behavior was potentially jeopardizing everything. If she and Daniel got kicked out, all bets were off.

Daniel sighed as he watched Stephanie work. Although he felt conflicted over her long-term contribution, there was no question that she was needed in the short term. There were only eleven days left before Ashley Butler's arrival on the island, and in that time, they had to develop the dopamine-producing neurons from the senator's fibroblasts to treat the man. They were making progress with the HTSR and the nuclear transfer already done, but there was a long way to go. Stephanie's expertise with cellular manipulation was sorely needed, and there just wasn't time to replace her.

Stephanie could feel Daniel's eyes on her back. She recognized that her sense of guilt and her confusion about the implications of her family's role in his being attacked made her acutely sensitive, yet he was not acting like himself. She could only guess what it must have been like getting beaten up, but she had expected him to recover more quickly. Instead, he was still acting distant from her in many subtle ways, and although they continued to sleep in the same bed, there had been no intimacy whatsoever. Such behavior raised an old concern of hers that Daniel was either incapable or unmotivated to offer the kind of emotional support she felt she needed, particularly in periods of stress, no matter what the cause or whose fault it was.

Stephanie had followed Daniel's suggestions to the letter, so that couldn't be the explanation for his behavior. Despite an aching urge to call and confront her brother, she didn't. And on the relatively frequent conversations she had with her mother, she made it a point to stress that she and Daniel were in Nassau to work, and they were working very hard, which was certainly true. To back it up, she said they had not gone to the beach to swim even once, which was also true. In addition, on multiple occasions she had emphasized that they would be finished soon and would come home about March twenty-fifth to a financially stable company. She had studiously avoided bringing up the subject of her brother with her mother, although on a call the previous day, she had finally yielded to temptation. "Has Tony asked about me?" she had asked in as casual a voice as she could manage.

"Of course, dear," Thea had said. "Your brother worries about you and asks about you all the time."

"What exact words does he use?"

"I don't remember the exact words. He misses you. He just wants to know when you are coming home."

"And what do you say in return?"

"I tell him just what you tell me. Why? Should I say something different?"

"Of course not," Stephanie had remarked. "Assure him we'll be home in less than two weeks, and I can't wait to see him. And tell him our work is going extremely well."

In many respects, Stephanie was thankful about how busy she and Daniel were. It reduced her opportunity to anguish over emotional issues as well as lessened her chance to question the appropriateness of treating Butler. Her misgivings about the affair had increased, thanks to the assault on Daniel and her need to turn a blind eye to the depravity of the Wingate principals. Paul Saunders was by far the worst. She felt he was conscienceless, devoid of even rudimentary ethics, and dumb. The compiled results of the Wingate stem-cell therapy program, which he had touted, were a bad joke. They were merely a collection of descriptions of individual cases and their subjective outcomes. There was not one iota of scientific method involved, and the most disturbing part was that Paul didn't seem to realize it or care.

Spencer Wingate was another story, but he was more annoying than scary like the mad pretend scientist Paul. Still, Stephanie would not have liked to be caught unaccompanied in Spencer's house, as his persistent invitations proposed. The problem was that his lechery was bolstered by an ego that could not fathom his overtures being rejected. At first, Stephanie had tried to be reasonably polite with her regrets, but eventually she had to be blunt with her refusals, especially after it seemed Daniel was indifferent. Some of Spencer's more blatantly randy invitations had come in Daniel's company, with no response from him.

As if the personalities and behavior of these maverick infertility doctors wasn't enough to make Stephanie question the propriety of working at the clinic, there was the issue of the origin of the human oocytes. She tried to make discreet inquiries but was rebuffed by everyone except the lab technician, Mare. Even Mare was hardly forthcoming, but at least she said the gametes came from the egg room run by Cindy Drexler, located in the basement. When Stephanie asked for clarification about what the egg room was, Mare clammed up and told her to ask Megan Finnigan, the lab supervisor. Unfortunately Megan had already echoed Paul by saying the egg source was a trade secret. When Stephanie approached Cindy Drexler, she was politely told that all egg inquiries had to be directed to Dr. Saunders.

Switching tactics, Stephanie had tried talking to several of the young women who worked in the cafeteria. They were friendly and outgoing until Stephanie tried to turn the conversation around to their marital status, at which point they became shy and evasive.

When Stephanie then tried to talk about their pregnancies, they became withdrawn and reticent, which only fanned Stephanie's curiosity. As far as Stephanie was concerned, one didn't have to be a rocket scientist to guess what was going on, and despite Daniel's edict to the contrary, she intended to prove it to herself. Her idea was that, armed with such information, she would anonymously inform the Bahamian authorities after she, Daniel, and Butler had long since departed.

What Stephanie needed to do was get into the egg room. Unfortunately, she had not had an opportunity, as busy as she and Daniel had been, although over the next few hours, that was going to change. The current egg she was fusing with one of Butler's HTSR-altered fibroblasts had been a replacement for one of the original ten eggs that Paul Saunders had supplied. The replaced egg had failed to divide after nuclear transfer. Honoring their warranty, Paul had provided an eleventh egg. The other original nine eggs were dividing fine after receiving their new nuclei. Some were now at the five-day point and beginning to form blastocysts.

The plan that Stephanie and Daniel had

devised was to create ten separate stem-cell lines, each comprising cellular clones of Ashley Butler. All ten would contribute cells to be differentiated into dopamine-producing nerve cells. The tenfold redundancy was to serve as a safety net, since only one of the cell lines would ultimately be used to treat the senator.

Perhaps later that afternoon, or more likely in the morning, Stephanie would begin the process of harvesting the multipotential stem cells from the forming blastocysts, but until then she would have some free time. The only problem would be getting away from Daniel but staying within the safety of the Wingate Clinic, and thanks to his emotional detachment from her, she didn't think that would be an insurmountable problem, although outside the clinic, he refused to let her out of his sight.

"How did the fusion go?" Daniel called out from where he was sitting.

"Looks good," Stephanie said, peering at the construct under the lens of a microscope. The oocyte now had a new nucleus with a full complement of chromosomes. Following a process that no one yet understood, the egg would now begin mysteriously reprogramming the nucleus from its duties as the controller of an adult skin cell back to a primordial state. Within hours, the construct would mimic a recently fertilized egg. To initiate the conversion, Stephanie carefully transferred the artificially altered oocyte into the first of several activation mediums.

"Are you as hungry as I am?" Daniel called out.

"Probably," Stephanie responded. She glanced at her watch. It was no wonder. It was almost twelve. The last time she'd had anything to eat was at six that morning, and it was only a continental breakfast of toast and coffee. "We can head over to the cafeteria once I get this egg into an incubator. It's got only another four minutes in this medium."

"Sounds good," Daniel said. He slid off his stool and disappeared into their office to get out of his lab coat.

As Stephanie prepared the next activation medium for the reconstructed egg, she tried to think of some excuse to return by herself to the lab during their lunch. It would be a good time for a bit of sleuthing, since most everyone ate lunch between twelve and one, including the egg room technician, Cindy

Drexler. Lunch hour was a major socializa-
tion time for the clinic staff. Stephanie's first
thought was to blame her need to return on
the activation process of the eleventh egg,
but she quickly discarded the idea; Daniel
would be suspicious. He knew that once the
egg was in the second activation medium, it
was to sit undisturbed in the incubator for six
hours.

Stephanie needed some other excuse and
seemed to be coming up blank until she
thought of her cell phone. Particularly after
Daniel's beating, she'd been compulsive
about keeping it on her person, and Daniel
knew it. There were several reasons for her
compulsiveness, not least of which was that
she'd told her mother to use the cell number
rather than the hotel's. But having just talked
with her mother that morning and hence being assured of no imminent emergency with
her health status, Stephanie wasn't concerned about missing a call over the next
half hour. After glancing back toward their
tiny office to be certain Daniel wasn't watching, Stephanie pulled the tiny Motorola
phone from her pocket, switched it off, and
placed it on the reagent shelf over the lab
bench.

Satisfied with her plan, Stephanie returned her attention to the activation process. In another thirty seconds, it would be time to move the egg from the first medium to the next.

"What do you say?" Daniel questioned, as he reappeared without his lab coat. "Are you ready?"

"Give me another couple of minutes. I'm about to transfer the egg and put it into the incubator, and then we can be on our way."

"Sounds good," Daniel responded. While he waited, he stepped over to the incubator and looked in at the other containers, a few of which had been in there for five days. "Some of these might be ready to harvest stem cells this afternoon."

"I was just thinking the same thing," Stephanie responded. Gingerly, she carried the newly suspended reconstructed egg over to the incubator to join the others.

Kurt Hermann let his feet fall to the floor in an uncharacteristically sudden, uncontrolled movement. They had been perched on the countertop in the video room. At the same time, he sat bolt upright, causing the desk chair to roll backward a short distance. Regaining the serenity developed over many years of martial arts training, he scooted himself forward in a slow, deliberate fashion to get closer to the screen he'd been watching for the last hour. He couldn't believe his eyes. It had happened so quickly, but it appeared as if Stephanie D'Agostino had just taken the cell phone Kurt had been trying to get his hands on over the previous week and a half out of her pocket and had deliberately placed it behind some reagent bottles on the shelf over the laboratory bench. It was like she was hiding it.

With the button on top of the joystick that was currently connected to operate the minicam he was watching, Kurt zoomed in. Using the joystick itself, he kept the camera directed at what he hoped was the phone. It was! Its black, molded plastic tip was just visible as it protruded from behind a bottle of hydrochloric acid.

Confused at this unexpected but promising development, Kurt zoomed back out, only to realize that Stephanie had disappeared from the camera's angle. Using the joystick again, Kurt panned the room and quickly found both Stephanie and Daniel in front of one of the incubators. Increasing the gain on the volume control, he strained to listen in case she mentioned the phone, but she didn't. They were continuing their talk about going to lunch, and within minutes they left the laboratory.

Kurt's eyes rose to the screen just above the one he'd been watching. He saw the couple emerge from building number one and start across the central courtyard, toward building number three.

During the construction of the clinic, Paul Saunders had given his head of security carte blanche to make it secure, in hopes of avoiding a catastrophe similar to what had happened to the clinic in Massachusetts, when a couple whistle-blowers had penetrated the clinic's database. Because they managed to gain unauthorized access to the computer server room and avoid apprehension after their trespass, Kurt had made sure the entire new complex was bugged with audio and video. Both the cameras and the microphones were the latest stealth technology, integrated by computer and completely unobstrusive. Unbeknownst to Paul, Kurt had had them included in the restrooms, the guest apartments, and most of the staff living quarters, where they were concealed in various and sundry electrical fixtures. Everything could be viewed from the monitors in the video room off Kurt's office, and in the evenings, Kurt found watching some of them entertaining, even when security wasn't necessarily an issue. Of course, Kurt could make an argument to the contrary, for it was important in an organization like the Wingate Clinic to know who was sleeping with whom.

Kurt continued observing Daniel and Stephanie until they entered building number three, although his eyes were mostly on Stephanie. Over the last week and a half, he'd become addicted to watching her, despite the ambivalence she evoked. He was both attracted and repulsed by her innate sensuality. As with women in general, he appreciated her beauty yet at the same time he recognized her Eve-like qualities. Kurt had watched her make and receive calls in the laboratory, and although he could frequently hear her side of the conversation, he was unable to hear the caller. Consequently, he'd not been able to provide Paul Saunders with the name of the patient as Kurt had promised, and Kurt liked to keep his promises.

Kurt's attitude toward women had been

set in stone by his ultimate betrayer, his mother. She and he had had an intimate relationship fostered by long absences of his undemonstrative strict disciplinarian father who had demanded perfection from both wife and son but who only acknowledged failure. His father had preceded Kurt into the Army's Special Forces, and like Kurt, who had ultimately followed in his footsteps, he had been a trained covert-operations killer. But when Kurt was thirteen, his father had been killed in a classified operation in Cambodia during the final weeks of the Vietnam War. His mother's reaction was like a lovebird released from a cage. Ignoring Kurt's emotional confusion of grief and relief, she indulged a flurry of affairs, the intimacies of which Kurt had to endure audibly through the thin drywall of their army-base house. Within months, Kurt's mother consummated her frantic dating by marrying a prissy insurance salesman whom Kurt despised. Kurt felt that all women, particularly the attractive ones, were like the mythologized mother of his youth, plotting to lure him in by seduction, sap him of his strength, and then abandon him.

As soon as Daniel and Stephanie had disappeared inside building number three,

Kurt's eyes moved automatically to monitor twelve and waited for them to appear in the cafeteria. When they joined the line at the steam table, Kurt got to his feet and walked out into his office. From the back of his desk chair, he took his lightweight, black silk jacket and slipped it on over his black T-shirt. He wore the jacket to conceal the holstered pistol he always carried in the small of his back. He pushed the sleeves up above his elbows. From the corner of his desk, he picked up the box containing the tiny cell phone bug he'd been eager to implant in Stephanie's phone as well as its monitoring device. He also grabbed his jeweler's tool kit, which included a delicate soldering iron and a binocular watchmaker's loupe.

Moving catlike, he emerged from a basement door in building two with the equipment and tools in hand and headed for building one. Within minutes, he was at the lab bench assigned to Daniel and Stephanie. After a quick glance in all directions to be certain he was alone in the laboratory, he retrieved the phone, put on the loupe, and set to work.

In less than five minutes, the bug was in place and tested. Kurt was in the process of replacing the phone's plastic cover when he heard the distant door to the lab bang open. Expecting to see one of the lab personnel or possibly Paul Saunders, he bent over and looked beneath the reagent shelf back toward the entrance some eighty feet away. To his utter surprise, it was Stephanie who'd arrived and was approaching with a quick, determined step.

For a brief, panic-filled second, Kurt debated what to do. But his training prevailed, and he quickly regained his customary composure. He finished with the phone by snapping its cover into place, then slipped it back to its original position behind the hydrochloric acid bottle. Then he lent his attention to the jeweler's tools, the monitoring device, and the loupe. As silently as possible, he got them into a drawer and pushed it closed with his hip. Stephanie D'Agostino was now a mere twenty feet away and closing in rapidly. Backing away, Kurt intended to keep the lab bench and its overhead shelving between him and the researcher. It was not much cover, and she would surely see him, but there were no other options.

In truth, Tony was mostly pissed that he had to forsake a nice lunch, which was one of the high points of his day, while he made yet another visit to the freaking Castigliano brothers' crummy plumbing supply store. The rotten-egg smell of the salt marsh didn't help matters either, although with the temperature in the twenties, it was less of a problem than it had been on his last visit a week and a half earlier. At least it was easier visiting the stinkhole in the middle of the day rather than at night, since he didn't have to worry about tripping over any of the crap littered around the front of the place. The good part was that he had reason to believe this would be the last visit, at least concerning the problem with CURE.

Tony went through the entrance door and headed for the rear office. Gaetano looked up from dealing with a couple customers at the front counter and nodded a greeting. Tony ignored him. If Gaetano had done his job right, Tony would not be walking at that moment between dusty plumbing-supply shelves, with the smell of rotten eggs lingering in his nose. Instead, he'd be sitting at his favorite table at his Blue Grotto restaurant on Hanover Street, sipping a glass of '97 Chianti while trying to decide which pasta to have. When underlings screwed up, it irked him to death, since it never failed to mess up his life. As he'd grown older, he'd become a progressively firmer believer in the old saying, "If you want something done right, you have to do it yourself."

Tony opened the door to the rear office, stepped in, and pulled the door shut with a bang. Lou and Sal were at their respective desks, eating pizza. A fleeting shiver of nausea went down Tony's spine. He hated the smell of anchovies, especially combined with the residual aroma of rotten eggs.

"You people have a problem," Tony announced, pressing his lips together in a wry expression of disgust and bobbing his head like one of the dog figures some folks put in the rear windows of their cars. But to ensure that he wasn't implying any disrespect to the twins, he approached each of them for a quick, slapping handshake before retreating to the couch and plopping down. He unbuttoned his coat but left it on. He only intended to stay for a couple minutes. There was nothing complicated about what he had to say.

"What's wrong?" Lou asked through a mouthful of pizza.

"Gaetano screwed up. Whatever the hell

he did down in Nassau had no effect at all. Zero!"

"You're joking."

"Do I look like I'm joking?" Tony wrinkled his forehead and spread his hands widely.

"You're telling us that the professor and your sister didn't come back?"

"It's more than that," Tony said scornfully. "Not only didn't they come back, Gaetano's shenanigans, whatever they were, didn't even warrant a single word from my sister to my mother, and they talk almost every day."

"Wait a second!" Sal questioned. "You're saying that your sister didn't say they had a little problem or anything like her boyfriend got hurt? Anything at all?"

"Absolutely nothing! Zilch! All I hear is everything's going honky-dory in paradise."

"That doesn't jibe with what Gaetano said," Lou said, "which I find hard to believe, since he usually overdoes the physical stuff."

"Well, in this instance, he surely didn't overdo anything," Tony said. "The lovebirds are still down there, frolicking in the sun and insisting, according to my mother, that they are going to stay the three weeks or month or whatever they'd originally planned. Meanwhile, my accountant says nothing's changed with their company's downward spiral. He insists in a month they will be broke, so goodbye to our two hundred K."

Sal and Lou exchanged glances of disbelief, confusion, and escalating irritation.

"What did Gaetano say he did?" Tony asked. "Slap the professor's wrists and tell him he was being bad? Or did he not even go to Nassau and say he did?" Tony crossed his arms and legs and sat back.

"Something's screwy in all this!" Lou declared. "None of it adds up." He put his slice of anchovy-and-Italian-sausage pizza down, ran his tongue around the inside of his lips to loosen the debris on his teeth, swallowed, and leaned forward to press a button protruding on the surface of his desk. A muffled buzz sounded through the door connecting the office to the store proper.

"Gaetano went to Nassau!" Sal said. "We know that for damn sure."

Tony nodded, a grimace of disbelief on his face.

He knew he was pushing the twins' buttons, since they liked to believe they ran a tight ship. The idea was to inflame their passions, and it worked. By the time Gaetano poked his head through the door, the twins were ready to take it off.

"Get the hell in here and shut the door," Sal snapped.

"I got customers out at the counter," Gaetano complained. He motioned over his shoulder.

"I don't care if you have the President of the United States out there, you moron," Sal yelled. "Get your ass in here!" To make his point, Sal pulled out the center drawer of his desk, grabbed a snub-nosed thirty-eight revolver, and tossed it onto his blotter.

Gaetano's broad brow knotted as he did as he was told. He'd seen the gun on a number of occasions and wasn't worried because getting it out was one of Sal's quirks. At the same time, he knew Sal was pissed about something, and Lou didn't look much happier. Gaetano eyed the sofa but, with Tony occupying the middle, he decided to remain standing. "What's up?" he asked.

"We want to know exactly what the hell you did down in Nassau!" Sal barked.

"I told you," Gaetano said. "I did exactly what you asked me to do. I even managed to do it in one day, which was a ball-breaker, to be honest."

"Well, maybe you should have stayed an extra day," Sal said contemptuously. "Apparently, the professor didn't get the message we intended."

"What exactly did you tell the dirtbag?" Lou demanded with equal venom.

"To get his ass back here and fix his company," Gaetano said. "Hell, it wasn't complicated. It's not like I could have gotten it mixed up or something."

"Did you push him around?" Sal questioned.

"I did a lot more than push him around. I clocked him with a good one to start, which turned him into a rag doll such that I had to pick him up off the floor. I might have broken his nose, but I don't know for sure. I know I gave him a black eye. Then I walloped him the hell out of his chair at the end, after our little talk."

"What about a warning?" Sal questioned. "Did you tell him you'd be back if he didn't get his ass back here to Boston and get his company back on track?"

"Yeah! I said I'd hurt him bad if I had to

come back, and there's no doubt he got the message."

Both Sal and Lou looked at Tony. They shrugged in unison.

"Gaetano doesn't lie about this kind of thing," Sal said. Lou nodded in agreement.

"Well, then it's just another instance of this professor flipping us off," Tony said. "He certainly didn't take Gaetano seriously, and he obviously doesn't give a damn about our two hundred K."

For a few minutes, silence reigned in the room. The four men eyed one another. It was obvious everybody was thinking the same thing. Tony was waiting for someone else to bring it up, and Sal finally obliged: "It's like he's asking for it. I mean, we already decided if he didn't straighten up, we'd whack him and let Tony's sister take the reins."

"Gaetano," Lou said. "It looks like you're going back to the Bahamas."

"When?" Gaetano asked. "Don't forget, I'm supposed to push around that deadbeat eye doctor from Newton tomorrow night."

"I haven't forgotten," Lou said. He looked at his watch. "It's only twelve-thirty. You can go this afternoon via Miami, get rid of the professor, and be back tomorrow."

Gaetano rolled his eyes.

"What's the matter?" Lou demanded mockingly. "You got other things to do?"

"Sometimes it's not that easy to whack somebody," Gaetano said. "Hell, I got to find the guy first."

Lou looked at Tony. "Do you know where your sister and her boyfriend are staying these days?"

"Yeah, they're in the same hotel," Tony said, with a dismissive laugh. "That's how serious they took Gaetano's lame message."

"I'm telling you," Gaetano insisted. "It wasn't lame. I clocked the guy good several times."

"How do you know they're at the same hotel?" Lou asked.

"From my mother," Tony said. "She's been mostly calling my sister's cell phone, but she told me she'd also tried the hotel once when she couldn't get through on the cell. The lovebirds are not only at the same hotel, but they're still in the same room."

"Well, there you go," Lou said to Gaetano.

"Can I do the hit at the hotel?" Gaetano asked. "That will make it a hell of a lot easier."

Lou looked at Sal. Sal looked at Tony.

"No reason why not," Tony said with a shrug. "I mean, as long as my sister's not involved, and as long as it's done quietly, without a scene."

"That goes without saying," Gaetano remarked. He was warming to the idea. Heading all the way down to Nassau for an overnight might involve a lot of traveling, and it would be hardly a vacation in the sun, but it could be fun. "What about a gun? It's got to have a silencer."

"I'm sure our Colombian friends in Miami can arrange that," Lou said. "With as much of their junk as we push for them up here in New England, they owe us."

"How will I get it?" Gaetano asked.

"I imagine somebody will come to you when you land in Nassau," Lou said. "I'll work on it. As soon as you know the number of the flight you're going to take over to the island, let me know."

"What if there is a problem, and I don't get a gun?" Gaetano questioned. "If you want me back here for tomorrow night, everything has to go smoothly."

"If you arrive and no one approaches you, give me a call," Lou said.

"Okay," Gaetano said agreeably. "I'd better get my ass in gear."

nineteen

12:11 P.M., Monday, March 11, 2002

The sign's message was clear. It said: RE-
STRICTED ACCESS, AUTHORIZED PERSONNEL ONLY,
PROHIBITION STRICTLY ENFORCED. Stephanie
paused for a moment, gazing at the framed,
glazed sign. It was attached to a door next to
a freight elevator. It was from this door that
Cindy Drexler routinely emerged, most interestingly, when she'd brought the oocytes for
Stephanie and Daniel. Stephanie had seen
the sign obliquely from a distance but had
never gone over to read it. Now that she had,
it gave her pause. She wondered what it

meant for the prohibition to be strictly enforced, considering the Wingate principals'
tendency toward overkill in the security
arena. But she had come this far and wasn't
about to turn around and give up because of
a generic printed warning. She pushed
against the door. It opened. Beyond was a
stairway leading downward. The reassuring
thought went through her mind that if they
were so concerned about intruders in the
egg room, they would have locked the stairwell door.

With a final rapid glance over her shoulder
to make sure she was alone in the lab,
Stephanie stepped through the door. It
closed behind her. Immediately, she sensed
a contrast from the dry coolness of the air-
conditioned lab. Within the stairwell, the air
was considerably warmer and moister. She
started down the stairs, moving quickly,
aided by her flat shoes.

Stephanie was rushing as best she could
because she had planned to give herself a
mere fifteen minutes—twenty, tops—to be
away from Daniel. She checked her watch as
she descended; five minutes had already
been consumed just getting from the cafeteria to where she was at that moment. Her

only minor detour had been to grab her cell phone. She didn't want to forget and get back to the cafeteria without it, since it was her excuse for being away. Daniel had given her a strange look when she'd jumped up, saying she'd forgotten it, just after sitting down with her meal. She knew he'd be irritated if he knew what she was up to.

At the base of the stairs, Stephanie skidded to a stop. She found herself in a short, dimly lit corridor with access to the freight elevator along one wall and a shiny, stainless-steel door totally devoid of hardware at its end. There was no door handle or even lock. Stephanie approached the door and put her hand on it to push. It was warm to the touch but entirely immobile. She put her ear to it. She thought she could detect a slight whirring noise from beyond.

Stephanie leaned back and glanced around the blank door's periphery. It sealed against a metal jamb with a machinist's precision. Getting down on her hands and knees, she noted it was the same at the door's base. The care with which the door was fashioned fanned her already considerable curiosity. She got back on her feet, and with the side of her fist, she thumped quietly against the door. She was trying to gauge its thickness, which she surmised was considerable, since it was rock-solid.

"Well, so much for my mini-investigation," Stephanie whispered out loud. She shook her head in frustration while allowing her eyes to trace around the periphery once more. She was surprised there was no bell or intercom system, nor any obvious way to open the door or communicate with anyone within.

With a final sigh of exasperation accompanied by an expression of disgust, she turned back to the stairs, recognizing she'd have to conjure up another strategy if she intended to continue her clandestine sleuthing. But she only took a single step when her eye caught something she'd missed. Barely protruding from the wall opposite the freight elevator and quite inconspicuous in the dim light was a tiny, three-inch-long by three-quarters-of-an-inch-wide card swipe. Stephanie had not seen it earlier, because her attention had been overwhelmed by the gleaming door itself. Also, the swipe was the same neutral color as the wall and was more than six feet from the door.

Megan Finnigan had made sure Stephanie and Daniel had Wingate Clinic identification cards. Each had an ugly, mugshot-style Polaroid photo laminated on the face with magnetic strip on the back. Megan had said that the cards would be more important for security purposes when the clinic was up to strength personnel-wise, at which time they would be coded for the bearer's individual needs. In the meantime, Megan told them the cards were necessary to get into the lab's storeroom for basic supplies.

On the odd chance the ID card might work for the egg room at this early stage of the clinic's existence, Stephanie gave it a try. She was immediately rewarded by the stainless-steel door retracting to the side with a muffled *whoosh* of compressed air. At the same time, Stephanie noticed that she was enveloped by a weird glow emanating from the room beyond, which she guessed was a mixture of incandescent and ultraviolet light. There was also an accompanying waft of moist, warm air, and the whirring noise she'd thought she'd heard earlier with her ear to the door was now a definite presence.

Pleased at this sudden but welcome reversal of fortune, Stephanie quickly stepped over the threshold and found herself in what appeared to be a giant incubator. With the temperature in the vicinity of 98.6 degrees Fahrenheit, or body temperature, and the humidity close to one hundred percent, she felt perspiration break out all over her body. Although she was wearing a sleeveless blouse, she had a short, white laboratory coat over it. She now understood why Cindy wore a special lightweight cotton jumpsuit.

Racks similar to bookshelves but containing tissue culture dishes formed a gridlike floor plan similar to the stacks of a library. Each was about ten feet long, constructed of aluminum with adjustable shelves and extended from the tile floor to the rather low tile ceiling. All the tissue culture dishes in Stephanie's immediate view were empty. Ahead of her was a lengthy aisle, the shelving of which made it appear to be a study in perspective. It was so long that a dim, humid haze obscured its distant end. From the size of the facility, it was obvious the Wingate was preparing for significant production capacity.

Stephanie started forward at a rapid walk, glancing from side to side. Thirty paces into the room, she stopped when she found a rack that contained actively growing tissue cultures, as evidenced by fluid levels visible through the clear glass containers. She lifted one out. Written in grease pencil on its cover was OOGONIA CULTURE, accompanied by a recent date and an alphanumeric code.

Stephanie replaced the dish and checked others throughout the rack. They had different dates and different codes. Learning that the Wingate was seemingly successfully culturing primitive germ cells was both interesting and disturbing for a variety of reasons, but it was not her goal. What she was hoping to do was to ascertain the origin of the oogonia and the oocytes they were culturing and maturing. She thought she knew, but she wanted definitive proof that she could pass on to a Bahamian authority after Butler's treatment and after she, Daniel, and Butler had returned to the mainland. She glanced at her watch. Eight minutes had now gone by, which was about half her allotted time.

With mounting anxiety, Stephanie pressed ahead, quickening her pace while peering down the side corridors as well as cursorily glancing at each rack of shelves she passed. The problem was that she didn't know what she was looking for, and the room was enormous. To make matters worse, she began to notice a mild sensation of air hunger. It then dawned on her that the atmosphere in the egg room probably had an elevated level of carbon dioxide for the benefit of the tissue cultures.

After another twenty paces Stephanie stopped again. She'd come to a rack with unique and apparently customized tissue culture dishes. Stephanie had never seen anything like them. Not only were they larger and deeper than usual, but they also had a built-in internal matrix on which the cultured cells could grow. In addition, they were set on motorized bases to keep them in continuous, horizontal, circular motion, presumably to circulate the culture medium. Wasting no time Stephanie reached in and lifted out one of the dishes. On its cover was written MINCED FETAL OVARY, TWENTY-ONE WEEKS GESTATION; OOCYTES ARRESTED IN DIPLOTENE STAGE OF PROPHASE, followed again by a date and a code. Stephanie checked the other dishes in the rack. As with the oogonia cultures they all had different dates and different codes.

The next few racks were even more interesting. They housed tissue culture dishes, which were larger and deeper still, but there were fewer per shelf. Most of them were empty. Those that weren't contained a fluid growth medium that was being circulated by a complex of tubes to central machines, which appeared like a miniature kidney dialysis unit and which collectively made the background whirring noise that filled the room. Stephanie bent over and peered into one of the culture dishes. Submerged in the contained fluid was a small, ovoid, and ragged piece of tissue, approximately the size and shape of a manila clam. Vessels that protruded from the tiny organ were cannulated by minute plastic tubes leading to another, even smaller machine. The tiny organ was being internally perfused as well as being submerged in continuously circulated culture medium.

Stephanie stuck her head into the rack so she could look at the top of the container without disturbing it. Written in red grease pencil was FETAL OVARY, TWENTY WEEKS GESTATION along with a date and code. Despite the implications, she couldn't help but be impressed. It seemed that Saunders and his team were keeping intact fetal ovaries alive at least for a few days.

Stephanie straightened back up. Although

hardly definitive proof, what she was finding in the egg room was certainly consistent with her suspicions that Paul Saunders et al. were paying young Bahamian women to be impregnated and then aborted at about twenty weeks to harvest fetal ovaries. With her embryology training, she knew something most laypeople didn't know, namely that the diminutive ovary of a twenty-one-week-old fetus contains about seven million germ cells capable of becoming mature oocytes. Most of these eggs are destined to disappear inexplicably prior to birth and during childhood, such that when a young woman begins her reproductive years, her germ cell population has been reduced to approximately three hundred thousand. If obtaining human oocytes is the goal, the fetal ovary is the mother lode. Unfortunately, Paul Saunders seemed to know this as well.

With her fears at least partially substantiated, Stephanie shook her head in dismay at the utter immorality involved in aborting human fetuses for eggs. To her, it was worse than pushing ahead with reproductive cloning, which she also suspected was part of Paul Saunders's game plan. Stephanie

recognized it was maverick infertility organi-
zations like the Wingate Clinic that had the
power to cast a pall over biotechnology and
its promise by engaging in such unconscionable activities. It also passed through
her mind that Daniel's ability to turn a blind
eye to such a reality in this current instance
said something about him that she would
rather not have known, and that knowledge,
combined with the emotional distance he
was currently displaying, made her question
the future of their relationship more than
she'd ever done in the past. Impulsively, she
decided as a bare minimum that when they
got back to Cambridge she would move out
on her own.

But there was a lot to be done until then.
Stephanie checked her watch again. Eleven
minutes had elapsed. She was running out
of time, since she would have only four more
minutes, at most, on her current visit. She
needed to find a true smoking gun so Saunders couldn't claim the abortions were therapeutic. Although she could theoretically
return to the egg room another day, she intuitively knew it would be difficult, especially
coming up with another credible excuse to

be away from Daniel. He might not be emotionally supportive, but he was certainly staying close by physically.

Four minutes was not much time. Out of
desperation, Stephanie elected to race the
rest of the way down to the end of the room,
go laterally, and then return to the open door
along another of the numerous lengthwise
aisles. But after she'd gone only twenty feet,
she came to a sudden stop. On a glance to
her left down one of the side aisles, she saw
what appeared to be a laboratory or an office
separated from the main room by floor-to-
ceiling windows. It was about twenty feet
away from where she was standing. Bright
fluorescent light emanated from within and
inundated the immediate area. Stephanie
changed direction and hurried toward it.

As she approached, she saw that her initial impression had been correct. It was most
likely Cindy's office/lab positioned conveniently midway down the length of the egg
room and tucked against the building's foun-
dation. The room had a shallow, rectangular
shape no more than ten feet deep but some
twenty-five to thirty feet long. Running along
its back wall was a laminate counter top with
drawers below. In the center was a kneehole

to form a desk. At the extreme left was an in-counter sink with a typical laboratory faucet. Cabinets were above. The bright fluorescent light was coming from hidden, under-cabinet fixtures, which flooded the countertop with blue-white illumination.

The counter itself was cluttered with tissue-culture dishes, centrifuges, and all sorts of other laboratory paraphernalia, but none of it interested Stephanie. Her attention had been immediately drawn to what looked like a large, open ledger book positioned at the desk area. It was partially obscured by the high back of the office chair.

Knowing that time was slipping away relentlessly, Stephanie's eyes darted up and down the length of the windowed office, searching for a door. To her surprise, it was right in front of her, and except for its recessed handle, it looked like the other glass panels. Its hinges were on the inside.

With a keyhole suggesting the door could be locked, Stephanie prayed it wasn't. She lifted the door handle from its socket and gave it a twist. To her relief, it turned, and the door effortlessly opened inward. As she stepped into the long, narrow room, she could feel a breeze of the egg room air coming along with her, suggesting the egg room was slightly pressurized, probably to keep out airborne microbes. The interior of the narrow office was air-conditioned to a normal temperature and humidity. Letting go of the door and leaving it ajar, Stephanie moved over to the ledger and was immediately engrossed; she sensed that she had found what she was looking for.

She pushed the office chair aside to bend over for a closer look at the handwritten entries. It was indeed a ledger, but not for finance. Instead, it was a list of all the women who had been impregnated and aborted including the dates of both, along with other information. Flipping back a few pages, Stephanie could see that the program had begun well before the clinic had opened its doors. Paul Saunders had been planning his egg supply well in advance.

Stephanie picked out a few individual cases, and running her finger along individual entries, she learned that the women had been impregnated following in vitro fertilization. IVF made sense, since only female fetuses were wanted, and IVF would be the only way to guarantee such an outcome. She noticed the X chromosome sperm involved in the cases she was looking at were all from Paul Saunders, which testified to an abiding, conscienceless megalomania.

Stephanie was entirely captivated. Everything was duly recorded in a bold script. She could even tell what type of tissue culture was done from each case as well as the respective cultures' current status in the egg room. While some fetuses contributed whole ovary preparations, others had their ovaries minced and cultured, and others were reduced to providing disaggregated germ cell lines.

Returning to the original page displayed when she had come into the room, Stephanie began counting how many women were currently pregnant. She couldn't help but shake her head that Saunders and company not only had the temerity to carry out such a program but also the audacity to record all its sordid details in black and white. With such a discovery, all Stephanie would have to do was inform the Bahamian authorities of the ledger's existence and leave it up to them to confiscate it.

Suddenly, Stephanie froze as a thunderbolt of fear descended her spine. She hadn't quite finished counting the pregnant women when her heart leaped in her chest. With no sound or any warning whatsoever, a circle of cold steel had insinuated itself through her hair and pressed against the back of her perspiring neck. Instantly, she knew without a modicum of doubt that it was the barrel of a gun!

"Don't move, and put your palms on the desk," a disembodied voice threatened.

Stephanie felt her knees weaken. She was momentarily paralyzed. All the anxieties attendant to her snooping and aggravated by the press of time had coalesced in a maelstrom of sheer terror. She was bent at the waist over the ledger book, with one hand on the desk and the other poised in the air. She'd been using her index finger to help with the counting.

"Put your palms on the desk!" Kurt repeated with uncamouflaged anger. His voice quivered. He had to restrain himself from an urge to pistol-whip this shamefully provocative female who'd had the nerve to enter the egg room.

The gun barrel pressed in against Stephanie's neck just short of pain. Finding the strength to move, she did as she was told and put her right palm on the countertop.

Having both hands on the desk kept her from possibly collapsing. She was shaking from fright to the point that her leg muscles felt like jelly.

Thankfully, the barrel of the gun was withdrawn. Stephanie took a breath. Vaguely, she was aware of searching hands going into her jacket pockets. She felt her cell phone and the clutter of pencils and papers removed and then replaced. She was beginning to recover to a degree, when she felt hands come up under the lab coat and reach around to fondle her breasts.

"What the hell are you doing?" she managed to demand.

"Shut up!" Kurt snarled. His hands dropped down to pat along the sides of her thorax. Then they dropped further to her hips, where they momentarily stopped.

Stephanie held her breath. She was mortified and humiliated. The next thing she knew, the hands were cupping her buttocks. "This is an outrage!" she sputtered. Anger began to crowd out her fear. She started to straighten up, with the intention of confronting her tormentor.

"Shut up!" Kurt shouted again. A hand pressed into her back, hard enough to collapse her on top of the ledger with her arms splayed to the sides. The gun was again pressed against the nape of her neck, this time painfully. "Don't doubt for a second I wouldn't shoot you here and now."

"I'm Dr. D'Agostino," Stephanie managed, despite the crushing weight on her back. "I'm working here."

"I know who you are," Kurt snarled. "And I know you are not working here in the egg room. This is off-limits."

Stephanie could feel Kurt's hot breath. He was leaning over on top of her, pressing her down onto the desk. It was hard to breathe.

"If you move again, I'll shoot you."

"Okay," Stephanie squeaked. To her relief, the suffocating weight was released. She took a deep breath, only to feel a hand thrust between her legs to fondle her further. She gritted her teeth at the outrage. Then two hands patted down one leg and then the other, but not before her crotch was again groped. Next, the man's weight pressed back down on top of her, but not quite as forcibly as earlier. At the same time, she felt his hot breath on her neck as he rubbed himself lustfully against her and whispered in her ear: "Women like you deserve what they get."

Stephanie resisted the urge to try to fight back or even scream. The man on top of her had to be deranged, and her intuition silently shouted for her to be passive for the moment. After all, she was in a medical clinic and not in some isolated location. Cindy Drexler and perhaps others would be appearing shortly.

"You see, bitch," Kurt continued, "I had to make sure you were not carrying a camera or a weapon. Intruders tend to do that, and there's no telling where you could have hidden them on your person."

Stephanie stayed quiet and immobile. She felt the man straighten up again.

"Put your hands behind your back!"

Stephanie did as she was told. Then, before she knew what was happening, she felt herself being locked into handcuffs. It had happened so quickly that she didn't comprehend until she heard the second metallic click. A bad situation was deteriorating. She'd never been in handcuffs, and they bit into her wrists. Worse yet, she felt even more vulnerable than she had before.

Stephanie was then yanked upright by the scruff of her neck and spun around. She eyed her assailant, watching as the man's thin lips twisted back into a cruel, taunting smile, as if he were flaunting the fact that he was under marginal control.

Stephanie immediately recognized him. Although she'd never heard his voice until now, she'd seen him around the clinic grounds and in the cafeteria. She even knew his name and that he was the head of security. It had been in his office that she and Daniel had been photographed and had obtained their ID cards. He'd been at his desk at the time but had not said a word. Stephanie had purposefully avoided his silent, beady stare.

Kurt stepped out of the way and gestured toward the open door to the office. The gun had disappeared. Stephanie was only too happy to leave, but when she started walking back in the direction from which she'd originally come, Kurt grabbed her arm.

"Wrong way," he snapped. When she turned to look at him, he pointed in the opposite direction.

"I want to go back to the laboratory," Stephanie said. She tried to imbue her voice with authority, but it was difficult under the circumstances.

"I couldn't care less what you want. Move!"

Kurt gave her a forceful shove. Without her arms to help keep her balance, Stephanie nearly fell. Luckily, her feet stayed underneath her after the brush of a tissue-culture rack against her shoulder. Kurt gave her another push, and she stumbled ahead in the direction he'd indicated.

"I don't know why you're making such a big deal out of this," Stephanie said, after regaining her composure somewhat. "I was just looking around in here. I was merely curious about the origin of the oocytes Dr. Saunders had provided us with." Her mind was now churning in an internal debate whether she should follow Kurt's orders or just collapse and refuse to move. If they weren't going back to the lab, she wanted to stay in Cindy Drexler's office, where there was the comfort of knowing the woman would be returning. Having no idea where they were headed terrified her, but she didn't stop. What kept her moving was Kurt's threat to shoot her. As crazy and wired as he seemed, she took it seriously.

"Trespassing in the egg room is a big deal," Kurt responded scornfully, as if privy to her thoughts.

At the end of the room, they turned ninety

degrees and continued to a door similar to the one Stephanie had entered, but at the opposite end of the room. Kurt pressed a button on its jamb and the heavy, safelike door whooshed open. Kurt gave Stephanie a rude shove through it. Unaccustomed to her arms being secured behind her back, it was all Stephanie could do to keep her footing. Stumbling ahead, she found herself in a long, narrow, stuccoed corridor that curved off to the left. It was meagerly illuminated with infrequent fluorescent fixtures mounted on the outer wall. It was also a stuffy, un-air-conditioned space.

Stephanie stopped. She tried to turn around, but Kurt shoved her forward with such force that she fell. Unable to put her hands out to break her fall, she landed on her shoulder, scraping her cheek on the cement floor. A moment later, he lifted her like a rag doll by grabbing a handful of her lab coat and blouse in the middle of her back. Once she was upright, he propelled her forward. Stephanie reconciled herself to walking. She recognized resisting was going to invite immediate disaster.

"I demand to speak to Dr. Wingate and Dr. Saunders," Stephanie said, in a second attempt to be authoritative. Her fears were mounting as she wondered where this man was taking her. The damp warmth of the corridor suggested it was subterranean.

"In due course," Kurt said, with a lecherous laugh that gave Stephanie a shiver.

It didn't take Stephanie long before she guessed they were traveling in the same direction as the arcaded walkway that connected the laboratory building with the administration building. They just happened to be underground. Within a few minutes, they came to a regular, insulated fire door. When Kurt opened it, she saw that her assumption was correct. They were in the admin building basement. Stephanie remembered it from when she and Daniel got their IDs. With some relief, she now guessed they were heading to the security office, which also was soon confirmed.

"Down the hall!" Kurt commanded when they entered his office. He stayed behind her, out of her sight.

Stephanie passed a partially open door and caught a glimpse of a wall of television monitors. Kurt urged her on. At the end of the corridor, she stopped.

"You'll notice we have a jail cell to the left

and a bedroom to the right," Kurt said mockingly. "It's your choice."

Stephanie didn't answer. Instead, she stepped into the open cell. Kurt swung the barred door shut. It locked with a click that echoed off the concrete walls.

"What about the handcuffs?" Stephanie demanded.

"It's best they are left on," Kurt said. His cruel, thin-lipped smile had returned. "It's for safety's sake. The management doesn't look kindly on prisoners doing themselves in." Kurt laughed again. It was obvious he was enjoying himself. He started to turn back up the corridor but hesitated. Instead, he came back to stare in at Stephanie. "You've got a head in there, so feel free to use it. Don't let me bother you."

Stephanie turned to glance at the toilet. Not only was it completely exposed; it didn't even have a seat. She looked back at Kurt and glared. "I want to see Dr. Wingate and Dr. Saunders immediately."

"I'm afraid you are not in any position to give orders," Kurt said mockingly. He glared at Stephanie before breaking off and disappearing back up the corridor.

Stephanie let out her breath and relaxed a

degree with Kurt out of sight. She could only see a short distance up the hallway. Unable to look at her watch, she wondered what time it was. Daniel would have to start wondering where she was and start looking for her. In fact, maybe he was already. But then a new fear entered her mind: What if he was so angry at what she'd done that he didn't care if she'd been locked up?

Kurt Hermann sat down at his desk and put out his forearms. He was quivering from unconsummated desire. Stephanie D'Agostino had turned him on excruciatingly. Unfortunately, the pleasure of having his hands on her firm yet soft femaleness had been all too fleeting, and he wanted a repeat. She'd acted as if she hadn't enjoyed it, but he knew differently. Women were like that: one minute being provocative and the next minute pretending they didn't like the consequences. It was all an act, a put-on, a joke.

For a few minutes, Kurt tried to think of ways to put off calling Saunders. What he would have liked most to do was not to call him at all. Dr. D'Agostino could just disappear. Hell, it was what she deserved. But he knew it wouldn't work. Saunders would know, because Saunders understood that Kurt was aware of everyone who came in and out of the compound. If the woman doctor disappeared, Saunders would know Kurt was responsible or at least knew what had happened to her.

Calling on the discipline of his martial arts training, Kurt calmed himself. Within minutes, his muscles began to relax and his quivering stopped. Even his heart rate slowed to less than fifty beats per minute. He knew, because he frequently checked it. When he was fully in control, he got up and went into the video room.

The clock on the wall said it was twelve-forty-one. That meant that Spencer Wingate and Paul Saunders would be in the cafeteria. Kurt sat down and looked up at the bank of monitors. His eyes went to number twelve. Using the keyboard in front of him, he connected the joystick to minicam twelve and began to pan the room. Before finding his bosses, he found Daniel Lowell. Kurt zoomed in. The man was reading a scientific journal while feeding his face, completely oblivious to his surroundings. Across from him was Stephanie's untouched tray. A slight sneer played on Kurt's face. He had the man's girlfriend locked up in his private jail cell after feeling her up, and the man had no clue whatsoever. What a pompous jerk!

Kurt zoomed back out and continued looking for Spencer and Paul. He found them at their usual table and with the usual bevy of female employees. They were jerks as well, since Kurt knew for the most part whom they were screwing, although more for Paul than Spencer, since Paul lived in the compound. To Kurt, most of the men of the world were jerks, including most of his commanding officers when he'd been in the service. It was a burden he had to bear.

Kurt reached for the phone and put in a call to the cafeteria supervisor. When he got her on the phone, he told her to tell Spencer and Paul there was a security emergency that necessitated their immediate presence in his office. He told her to say specifically, "It's a major problem." Within seconds of his replacing the receiver, Kurt saw the woman appear on the monitor. She was frantic. She tapped Spencer and Paul on the shoulder in turn and whispered in their respective ears. Both leaped up and, with worried expressions, made a beeline for the exit. Spencer was slightly in the lead, since he was the first one the cafeteria supervisor had approached.

With a few clicks on the keyboard, Kurt brought up the image of the jail cell on the monitor directly in his line of sight and switched his attention to it. Stephanie was pacing back and forth like a caged cat. It was as if she were purposefully taunting him with her body.

Unable to watch another second, Kurt abruptly stood up. He retreated to his desk to rely again on his training to calm himself. By the time Spencer Wingate and Paul Saunders breathlessly arrived, Kurt was back to his stoic self. All he moved was his eyes, as the two fertility doctors rushed up to his desk.

"What's the major problem?" Spencer demanded. As the titular head of the clinic, Paul yielded to him. Spencer's complexion was slightly flushed, as was Paul's. The two men had run all the way from building three, which was more exercise than they were accustomed to. Both were panicked, because Kurt's message had been the same one he'd communicated back when Federal marshals had besieged the Wingate Clinic in its Massachusetts incarnation.

Kurt enjoyed their anxiety as payback for the scant recognition they gave him for all his efforts with getting the new clinic's security in line. He gestured for his bosses to be silent, then motioned for them to follow him as he led the way down to the video room. Once they were inside, he shut the door. He gestured for them to sit down in the two chairs present while he remained standing. He eyed them while basking in their anxious, undivided attention.

"What the hell is the emergency?" Spencer demanded, losing patience. "Out with it!"

"We had a break-in involving the egg room," Kurt said. "An obvious espionage situation that has compromised the egg-procurement program."

"No!" Paul exclaimed. He sat forward in his seat. The egg program was pivotal in his plans for the future of the clinic and his reputation.

Kurt nodded, enjoying drawing out the moment.

"Who?" Paul demanded. "Was it an inside job?"

"Yes and no," Kurt responded ambiguously without elaborating.

"Come on!" Spencer complained. "This isn't a goddamn guessing game."

"The perpetrator was caught perusing the Oocyte Register and apprehended."

"Good God!" Paul blurted. "This person was actually looking at the Register?"

Kurt pointed to the central monitor just above the counter. Stephanie had retreated back to sit on the iron cot. Unknowingly, she was looking almost directly into the minicam. It was clear she was distraught.

For a few minutes, silence reigned in the video room. All eyes stared at Stephanie.

"How come she's not moving?" Spencer asked. "She's all right, isn't she?"

"She's fine," Kurt assured him.

"Why is her cheek bleeding?"

"She fell en route to the cell."

"What did you do to her?" Spencer demanded.

"She wasn't being cooperative. She needed a bit of encouragement."

"Good Lord!" Spencer exclaimed. All in all, this was less of an emergency than he had feared, but it was still bad enough. "How come her arms are behind her back?" Spencer asked.

"She's handcuffed," Kurt said.

"Handcuffed?" Spencer questioned. "Isn't that a bit heavy-handed? Although, with your history, we should be thankful you didn't shoot her on the spot."

"Spencer," Paul said. "We should be thankful for Kurt's vigilance, not critical."

"It is standard operating procedure to cuff an individual when they are apprehended," Kurt snapped.

"Yeah, but she's in a jail cell, for Christ's sake," Spencer said. "You could have taken the handcuffs off."

"Forget the handcuffs for the moment," Paul suggested. "Let's worry about the implications of her behavior. I don't like the fact that she was in the egg room, much less having her looking at the register. She's been less than complimentary about our operation, particularly in regard to our stem-cell therapy."

"She is a bit high and mighty," Spencer admitted.

"I don't want her upsetting our oocyte program, not that there's a lot she can do here in the Bahamas," Paul said. "It's not like we're back in the States. But she could still make waves and get us some bad publicity, which might impinge on our uterine-rental recruitment efforts and then our bottom line. We've got to make sure that doesn't happen."

"Maybe that's why Lowell and she are here," Spencer suggested. "Maybe this treatment rigmarole they are doing is all an elaborate ruse. They could be industrial spies, intent on stealing our thunder."

"They're for real," Paul said.

"How can you be so sure?" Spencer said, looking away from Stephanie's image on the monitor and directing his attention to Paul. "You're rather gullible when it comes to dealing with real researchers."

"I beg your pardon!" Paul snapped.

"Oh, don't be so sensitive," Spencer responded. "You know what I mean. These people have real Ph.D.s."

"Which might account for their lack of creativity," Paul responded. "You don't need a Ph.D. to do groundbreaking science. But, be that as it may, I can assure you that these people are not faking what they are doing. I've seen with my own eyes that this HTSR is impressive."

"They could still be fooling you. That's my point. They are professional researchers, and you're not."

Paul glanced away for a moment to keep

from getting mad. Spencer was the last person in the world who should be suggesting he was an authority on who was and who wasn't a researcher. Spencer knew nothing about research. He was a mere businessman in doctor's clothing—and not even that good a businessman.

After a calming breath, Paul looked back at his titular boss and said, "I know they are doing real, honest-to-goodness, goal-directed cellular manipulations, because I took some of the cells into which they had patched some of Christ's DNA. The cells are amazing and extremely viable. I've used them myself to see if they work, and they do."

"Wait a second," Spencer said. "You're not going to sit there and say you've proved these cells have Christ's DNA."

"Of course not." Paul struggled to keep his composure. At times, discussing biomolecular science with Spencer was like talking with a five-year-old. "There's no test for 'Christness.' What I'm trying to tell you is that they brought with them a culture of fibroblasts from the person with Parkinson's disease whom they are planning on treating. Within these cells, they have swapped out the defective genes with genes they have been able to construct from DNA they've extracted from their sample of the Shroud of Turin. They've already done all this, and now they are on their way to make the actual treatment cells. It's true. There's absolutely no doubt in my mind this is what they are doing. I'm one hundred percent certain. Trust me!"

"All right, all right," Spencer repeated. "Since you have been in the lab with them, I suppose I have to take your word they're here for a legitimate therapeutic mission. But that accepted, it begs the issue of the patient's identity, about which I also took your word. You said you were going to find out who the patient is. Here we are a little more than a week away from our visitors' scheduled treatment D-day, and we're still in the dark."

"Well, that's another problem."

"Yeah, but it is associated. If we don't have a name soon, we're not going to have a financial windfall in this affair, that's for damn sure. What's the problem with finding out the identity? That's not asking that much."

Paul looked at Kurt. "Tell him!"

Kurt cleared his throat. "It's been a more difficult assignment than I had anticipated. We had their apartment and place of busi-

ness searched before they even got to Nassau. While they have been here, we've gotten ahold of their laptops and had our
computer nerd check their hard drives: nothing. On the positive side, just today I got a
bug in the woman's cell phone. I've been trying to get ahold of it from day one, but she
has been uncooperative. Never once did she
let it out of her sight."

"You planted the bug while she's been in
your custody?" Spencer asked. "Aren't you
worried she'd be suspicious?"

"No," Kurt said. "The bug went in before I
apprehended her. Today, for the first time,
she left her cell phone in the lab when she
went to the cafeteria. I'd just finished when
she returned unexpectedly to break into the
egg room. I was following her when she entered."

"Then why didn't you stop her before she
got in?" Spencer asked.

"I wanted to catch her flagrante delicto,"
Kurt said, as a lewd smile formed at the corners of his mouth.

"I suppose I wouldn't mind catching her
flagrante delicto myself," Spencer said, with
an equivalent smile.

"With the bug in the cell phone, we should

be in good shape," Paul said. "From the beginning, Kurt felt monitoring the cell phone was going to give us the patient's identity."

"Is that true?" Spencer asked.

"Yes," Kurt said simply. "But we have another option. With her in our custody, we could demand she tell us the name as a condition of her release."

The two Wingate Clinic principals eyed each other while they pondered Kurt's suggestion. It was Spencer who responded first with a shake of his head: "I don't like the idea."

"Why?" Paul asked.

"Mainly because I don't think they would tell us, and it would tip our hand about how much we want the name," Spencer said. "Obviously, keeping the patient's identity a secret is mighty important to them; otherwise, we'd know it already. At this point, with as much progress as you've said they've made in the lab, they could possibly pack up and go somewhere else for the final treatment. I don't want to jeopardize their second twenty-two-and-a-half-K payment. It's hardly a windfall, but it's something. Besides, they'll know we're bluffing. We can't keep her in jail unless we throw him in there as well, which we can't do, and he'll be yelling bloody murder as soon as he finds out where she is and how she's been treated."

"You've made good points," Paul responded. "I agree with you, and I'd prefer the condition of her release simply to be centered on a promise of confidentiality, which is reasonable under the circumstances. She can have her own opinions, but she should keep them to herself. My sense is that Dr. Lowell will back us on this. I've felt he's always trying to tone down her arrogance."

Spencer looked up at Kurt. "So, you're optimistic about finding out the patient's identity with the bug in the phone?"

Kurt nodded.

"I think we should stick to that," Spencer said. "And we'll press the confidentiality issue."

"Agreed," Paul said. "And speaking of Dr. Lowell, where is he?"

"He's in the cafeteria," Kurt said. His eyes rose up to monitor twelve. "At least, he was a few minutes ago."

"I think it is significant that Dr. D'Agostino was by herself when she went into the egg room," Paul said.

"How so?" Spencer asked.

"My guess would be that Dr. Lowell had no idea what she was doing."

"You might be right," Spencer said.

"Dr. Lowell is on his way to the lab," Kurt said. He pointed to the appropriate monitor, and all eyes went to it. Daniel was walking with a quick, determined gait from building three to building one, with a hand clasped against the collection of pens and pencils in his breast pocket. He reached building one and disappeared through the door.

"Where is the lab monitor?" Paul asked. Kurt pointed. They watched as Daniel appeared stage left. Spencer commented that he appeared to be searching for Stephanie. Kurt used the joystick to follow him. After checking the lab bench area that he and Stephanie used, Daniel looked into their assigned office. He even stuck his head into the ladies' room. He then made a beeline toward Megan Finnigan's office.

"I think he would have gone down to the egg room if he knew that's where she went," Paul said.

"A point well taken," Spencer said. "I bet you're right."

Paul picked up the phone on the counter and punched in Megan's extension. "I'll tell the lab supervisor where Dr. Lowell can find his collaborator."

"Or whatever the hell their relationship is," Spencer said scornfully. "I can't figure it out. By the way, Kurt, how was she able to get into the egg room?"

"She used her Wingate ID," Kurt said. "Access has yet to be restricted, even though it was on the security punch list I presented to the administration a month ago."

"That's my fault," Paul said, hanging up from his terse conversation with Megan Finnigan. "It slipped my mind getting the clinic up and running. Besides, we never planned on outsiders using the lab, and it didn't cross my mind when doctors Lowell and D'Agostino got here."

Spencer got up out of his chair. "Let's go down and have a chat with the alluring Dr. D'Agostino before Dr. Lowell gets here. It might help smooth the negotiation. Kurt, I want you to stay away for the moment."

The two doctors stepped out into the hall and started down toward the cell.

"This is a weird turn of events," Spencer whispered. "But it is certainly a lot better than I feared when we were running over here."

twenty

7:56 P.M., Monday, March 11, 2002

When push came to shove, Gaetano was a realist. As much as he was looking forward to arriving in Nassau on this second visit to complete what he'd started on his first, he was nervous. Mainly he was nervous about getting a gun, and it had to be a decent gun, because without a good gun, trouble was inevitable. There was no way he was going to club the guy to death or drown him in the bathtub or garrote him, like they occasionally did in the movies. Whacking a guy was not as easy as it was portrayed. It required planning. The method had to be decisive and fast, and the location moderately remote, to expedite a speedy get away and for quickness, there was nothing better than a gun. A good, quiet gun.

For Gaetano, the problem in the current situation was being dependent on people he didn't know and who didn't know him. Somebody was supposed to meet him when he landed on the island, but there was no guarantee it would happen. Since the trip had been patched together so quickly, there was no plan B or contacts to call, except Lou back in Boston, and Lou could be hard to get ahold of after-hours. Even if the mystery man showed up at the airport, there was always the chance he and Gaetano wouldn't hook up in the inevitable confusion, since neither knew what the other looked like. To make matters worse, Gaetano was supposed to be back in Boston the next day, so it wasn't like he had the benefit of a lot of time.

The other reason Gaetano was nervous was because he didn't like small planes. Big ones were okay, since he could talk himself out of believing he was up in the sky. Little ones were another story altogether, and the one he was on at the moment was the smallest he had experienced. To make matters worse, the plane was vibrating like an electric toothbrush and bouncing around like a billiard ball. Gaetano had nothing to hold on to, except the seatback in front of his nose. There wasn't much room in the cabin. With his bulk, he was literally wedged in against the window.

Gaetano had caught an American flight down to Miami, where he'd transferred to the plane he was currently on. The sun was setting when he took off on this second leg, and now it was pitch dark outside his window. He tried not to think about what was below the bobbing aircraft, although every time the engines sounded as if they were slowing down, the mental image of a vast, black ocean involuntarily popped into his mind's eye to add to his anxieties. Gaetano had a secret: He couldn't swim, and drowning was a recurrent nightmare.

Gaetano glanced around at the other passengers. There was no conversation, as if everyone were as terrified as he. Most were blankly staring ahead. A few were reading, with individual, narrow beams of light coming from over their heads to form isolated shafts of illumination in the general murkiness. The cabin attendant was seated facing her charges in response to a directive from the pilots about turbulence. Her bored expression provided a bit of reassurance, although it was partially trumped by her considerably more substantial seat belt with shoulder straps, as if she expected the worst.

A particularly solid thump followed by the plane quivering made Gaetano start. It was as if they had struck some airborne object. For a minute, he didn't even breathe, but nothing happened. He swallowed to relieve a suddenly dry throat. Resigning himself to his fate, he closed his eyes and leaned against the headrest. The moment he did so, the pilot's voice came over the intercom to announce that they would be landing shortly.

With a burst of optimism, Gaetano pressed his nose against the window and looked down. Instead of a black void, he now saw twinkling lights ahead. He exhaled with relief. It seemed that he was going to make it after all.

The plane landed with a welcome, distinctive thud. A moment later, the whine of the engines magnified, accompanied by a sensation of rapid braking. Gaetano supported himself against the seatback in front of him.

He felt so good about the plane being on the ground that he smiled at the passenger seated to his right. The man responded in kind. Redirecting his attention out the window, Gaetano was now able to concentrate on his worries about the gun.

With relatively few passengers on the plane, disembarking was rapid, and Gaetano was among the first on the tarmac. He sucked in the warm, tropical air while luxuriating in the sensation of being on terra firma. When everyone was out of the cabin, he and the rest of the passengers were herded into the terminal.

Clutching his small carry-on, Gaetano paused just inside the door. He didn't quite know what to do. He thought his size made him stand out, but no one approached him. He was wearing the same upscale clothes he had worn on the last visit, which included the short-sleeve Hawaiian print shirt, light tan slacks, and dark blue jacket. Pressure from people behind him made him move forward. It was like being carried along in a river flowing toward passport control. When it was his turn, Gaetano handed over his document. The agent was about to stamp it when he caught sight of the notations of Gaetano's recent visit. Not only was it a short time ago, it was only for a single day. He looked up at Gaetano questioningly.

"I was just checking the place out the first time," Gaetano explained. "I liked it, so now I'm back for vacation."

The man didn't respond. He stamped the passport, pushed it toward Gaetano, and reached for the next person's.

Gaetano pressed on, past the crowds at the baggage carousels and then approached customs. With his American passport in his hands and his carry-on, the agents waved him by. He walked out through a pair of double doors that were propped open. An attentive crowd of people stood behind a flimsy metal movable railing. They were all eagerly trying to see family and friends through the open doors. No one expressed any interest in Gaetano.

Unsure about what to do, Gaetano kept going. Initially, he had to move laterally to get beyond the railing before merging with the boisterous crowd. After walking a short distance, he stopped and scanned the terminal, hoping to make eye contact with someone. No one paid him the slightest heed. He scratched his head, wondering what to do.

For lack of a better plan, he made his way to the car-rental area and waited in line.

Fifteen minutes later, he had keys to another Cherokee, although this time it was supposed to be green. He wandered back to the international arrivals area and was about to try to call Lou when someone tapped him on the shoulder.

By reflex, Gaetano spun around, ready to do battle. He found himself staring into the dark eyes of the blackest, baldest man he had ever seen. There were enough gold chains around his neck to make bending over a resistance exercise, and there was enough light reflecting off his scalp to make Gaetano squint. The man responded to Gaetano's overreaction by stepping back and holding up both hands as if to parry a blow. One of the hands held a wrinkled brown paper bag.

"Easy, man!" the individual said. He spoke with the same colorful, Bahamian accent Gaetano remembered from his first visit. "I don't mean no harm."

Gaetano was embarrassed about his aggressiveness and tried to apologize.

"No problem, man." The voice had a definite lilt. "Are you Gaetano Baresse from Boston?"

"Speaking!" Gaetano said, with a smile of relief. For a second, he felt like hugging the stranger, as if he were a lost relative. "You have something for me?"

"If you're Gaetano Baresse, I do. The name is Robert. Let me show you what I have." With that, the man unrolled the top of his paper bag and reached in with the intention of lifting out the contents.

"Hey, don't whip that thing out here!" Gaetano forcibly whispered. He was horrified. "Are you crazy?" Gaetano's eyes made a nervous sweep around the terminal. There were several armed but bored policeman in the immediate area. Thankfully, they weren't paying any attention.

"You want to see it, don't you?" the man asked.

"Yeah, but not here in the middle of everything. Did you come in a car?"

"Sure, I came in a car."

"Let's go."

With a shrug, the man led the way out of the terminal. A few minutes later, they climbed into a pastel, vintage Cadillac with huge tail fins. The man switched on the overhead light and handed Gaetano the bag. Gaetano was expecting some sort of Saturday night special, but what he pulled out surprised him considerably. It was a nine-millimeter SW99 equipped with a LaserMax and a Bowers CAC9 suppressor.

"Okay?" Robert asked. "You happy?"

"More than happy," Gaetano said. He admired the unmarred, black melonite finish, which suggested the gun was brand-new. It was an imposing weapon. Although it had only a four-inch barrel, the attached silencer made it more like ten inches.

After making sure no one was in the immediate area, Gaetano aimed the handgun out the windshield at a nearby car and briefly activated the laser. Fifty feet away, he saw the red dot flash on a car's back bumper. He was thrilled with the weapon until he noticed the magazine was missing in the butt.

"Where's the magazine?" Gaetano questioned. Without a magazine and ammunition, the gun was worthless.

Robert smiled in the car's semidarkness. Against his burnished ebony skin, his teeth were truly pearly whites. He patted his left pants pocket. "I got it safely right here, man, all loaded up and ready to go. There's even an extra one for good measure."

"Good," Gaetano said. He stuck out his hand. He was relieved.

"Not so fast," Robert said. "It seems to me this is worth something to me personally. I mean, I did come all the way out here instead of sitting home with a cold one. You catch my drift?"

For a moment, Gaetano just stared into the man's eyes, which in the darkness looked surprisingly like two bulletholes in a dirty white blanket. He knew it was a shakedown of sorts, and probably the man's idea. Gaetano's first thought was to grab the guy's head and bounce it off the steering wheel to let him know exactly with whom he was dealing, but clearer thoughts prevailed. The guy could have another gun, which could make things dicey and was certainly not the way this current trip should start. More important, Gaetano had no idea of this guy's relation to the Miami Colombians who Lou had contacted to set everything up. The last thing Gaetano needed or wanted while he was in Nassau on business was to have a group of guys after his own ass, especially the Colombians.

Gaetano cleared his throat. He was carrying a significant amount of cash, since on such a foray, everything he did was for cash. "Robert, I suppose you deserve a small token of appreciation. What do you have in mind?"

"A c-note would be nice," Robert said.

Without another word, Gaetano leaned forward to get his free hand into his right pants pocket. While he did so, he didn't take his eyes off Robert. He peeled off a bill from a roll, pulled it out, and handed it over. Robert then produced the magazines. Gaetano slipped one into the butt of the handgun. It clicked home. Discarding a fleeting fantasy of trying out the gun on Robert, Gaetano stepped from the car. He put the second magazine into the side pocket of his jacket.

"Hey, man!" Robert called. "You need a ride into town?"

Gaetano leaned back inside the vehicle. "Thanks, but I have my own wheels." Standing back up, he slipped the gun into his left pants pocket, which had a customized, hemmed opening at the bottom to accommodate the automatic's silencer. Having the hole was a trick he'd learned from a mentor when he'd first started working for the New York family. The permanent hole's only drawback was having to learn never to put anything else in the pocket, like coins or keys, which would tumble down his pant leg. As Gaetano walked toward the rent-a-car's lot, he could feel the cold steel of the silencer moving against his bare thigh. For him, it was like a caress.

Twenty minutes later, Gaetano directed his rented Cherokee into the Ocean Club's hotel parking lot. The drive had given him time to calm down after Robert's mini-extortion episode. The crunching sound of the tires on the gravel was particularly loud with all the vehicle's windows down. Enjoying the summerlike, evening air, Gaetano had opted to leave the air-conditioning off. Once in the lot, he took a full loop around. He wanted a spot that was not only close to the hotel but also afforded a direct shot out to the driveway. After whacking the professor, he wanted to be able to leave with dispatch.

Before getting out of the car, Gaetano flicked on the interior light and checked himself in the rearview mirror. He wanted to be sure he was presentable in the posh hotel. He smoothed his rather bushy eyebrows and adjusted the lapels of his jacket. When he thought he looked the best he could, he got out of the car. The car keys went into his right pants pocket, and he patted them through the fabric for good measure. The last thing he wanted when he was leaving was to have to search for the keys. Thus prepared, he started off.

Following the same approach he'd used on his first visit to the hotel, Gaetano headed for the building that housed suite 108. It was eight-thirty at night, so he expected the professor and his girlfriend to be at dinner, but he still wanted to check the room first. He walked at a leisurely pace and passed several smartly dressed guests going in the opposite direction.

At the appropriate location, Gaetano cut between two buildings to reach the lawn on the ocean side. He continued, almost to the tangle of sea grapes that covered the steep slope down to the beach. There, he turned to stroll parallel to the front of the appropriate building. He was close enough to the water to hear the gentle lapping of the waves on the beach to his right. The weather was glorious, with fast scudding clouds racing across a canopy of stars partially obscured by a bright gibbous moon. Soft ocean breezes rustled the palm trees. It was not hard for Gaetano to understand why people liked the Ocean Club.

As Gaetano came abreast of suite 108, affording a view into its interior, a shiver of excitement raised the hairs on the back of his neck and sent a chill up his spine. Not only were the lights blazing and the curtains wide open, but the professor and his girlfriend were there in plain sight! He couldn't believe his luck that his mission was to climax so easily and so quickly, and for a moment, he merely watched while his pulse quickened in anticipation of the imminent violence. But then his arousal plateaued as he questioned what he was seeing. He blinked a few times to make sure nothing was wrong with his eyes. Something weird was going on with the professor and Tony's sister, scurrying around like a couple of chickens and then flapping a blanket in the air. In the background, the door from the room to the hall was wide open, and a TV was turned on.

Irresistibly drawn toward the confusing spectacle, Gaetano advanced across the dark lawn. His hand had instinctively slipped into his left pocket to grip the handgun. Sud-

denly, he stopped, with a disappointing real-
ization. The people he was watching were
not his quarry but rather maids doing a turndown service. "Crap!" He groaned. Then he
sighed and shook his head dejectedly.

For a few minutes, Gaetano stood in the
darkness and rationalized that it was better
this way. If he'd been able to walk up to the
lanai, pull off a quick shot to nail the professor, and then skedaddle, it would have been
less than satisfying. It would have been too
easy and too quick. Far better was a more
protracted stalking, involving a bit of danger
that called upon his experience and expertise. That was when the process was truly
satisfying.

Gaetano let go of the gun, wiggled his leg
so the silencer dangled properly within his
pant leg, and straightened his jacket. Then
he turned around and headed for the hotel's
common areas: If the professor and the girl
had not left the hotel for dinner, that's where
they would be.

The first restaurant was sited considerably
closer to the beach than the buildings hous-
ing the hotel's rooms, requiring Gaetano to
walk along the edge of the sea grapes with

the beach now to his left. The dining room's French doors opened directly toward the ocean, and Gaetano was close enough to hear conversation. He picked up his pace to move quickly beyond the diners' line of sight. His worry was the possibility that the professor would recognize him. That was where the danger lay, because if the professor saw him, security would be alerted, and probably the police.

Once beyond the French doors, Gaetano entered the restaurant by its front entrance, all the while keeping a sharp lookout for the professor. He walked past the hostess's desk, where several couples were waiting to be seated, and paused at the entrance to the dining room, quickly and methodically scanning the room. When he was certain the professor wasn't there, he left as quickly as he had arrived.

Next was the more casual restaurant with a bar at its center that Gaetano had strolled through on his first visit. It was built right at the edge of the beach, with a thatched roof like an enormous tiki hut. It was packed with guests, particularly the bar. Once again, being extremely careful, Gaetano made a loop around, walking between the center bar and the periphery tables. The professor was not there.

Resigning himself that his mark had probably left the hotel for dinner, Gaetano followed the walkway that traversed the lawn to the main building. His intent was to reoccupy the same couch he'd used on his previous visit, which afforded a view of the hotel's entrance. He hoped the bowls of fruit would still be there. After walking through the two restaurants and smelling the savory aromas, Gaetano's stomach was grumbling.

There were a few people in the main lounge. Unfortunately, Gaetano's sofa was occupied by a couple carrying on a conversation with two others in facing chairs. Gaetano wandered over to the small bar and its bowl of peanuts. By coincidence, it was manned by the same gentleman Gaetano had chatted with on his previous visit. Gaetano could still see the hotel's entrance, although not quite as well as from the couch, yet it was good enough.

"Hey!" the bartender said. He extended a hand. "Long time no see!"

Gaetano was mildly disturbed that the

man recognized him, with as many people as the man undoubtedly saw on a daily basis. Gaetano smiled weakly, shook the man's hand, and took a handful of peanuts. The bartender was a transplanted New Yorker, which had been the topic of conversation a week and a half earlier.

"Can I get you something?" the bartender asked.

Gaetano saw one of the hotel's beefy security men appear at the archway into the reception area. With his arms akimbo, he casually scanned the room. He was dressed in a nondescript dark suit. It was obvious he was security, because he wore an earpiece in his left ear, with the wire snaking under his jacket.

"A Coke would be nice," Gaetano said. It was best to look relaxed and engaged so as not to appear as if he didn't belong. He half sat on one of the barstools with his left leg straight, so as not to disturb the hidden gun with its silencer. "Ice with a twist of lemon would make it perfect."

"You got it, pal," the bartender said. He set to work opening the Coke and filling a glass with ice. He twisted the lemon peel, ran it around the glass's rim, and put the drink in front of Gaetano. "Are your friends still staying here at the hotel?"

Gaetano nodded. "I was supposed to run into them here at the hotel tonight, but they're not in their room or at either of the restaurants."

"Did you try the Courtyard?"

"What's that?" Gaetano asked. Out of the corner of his eye, he saw the security person disappear back into the reception area.

"That's actually our best restaurant," the bartender explained. "It's only open for dinner."

"Where is it?"

"Just go up into reception and turn left. Go through the doors, and you're there. It's literally in the courtyard of the oldest part of the hotel."

"I'll give it a try," Gaetano said. He tossed back the Coke and grimaced at its effervescence. He put a sawbuck on the bar and patted it. "Thanks, buddy!"

"No problem," the bartender said, pocketing the bill.

Gaetano walked up the two steps into reception, keeping an eye out for the security man. He saw him immediately engrossed in a conversation with the head doorman. Following the bartender's directions, Gaetano turned left, went through a door separating the air-conditioned space from the non-, and found himself in a courtyard-cum-restaurant. It was a long, rectangular space filled with palm trees, exotic flowers, and even a central fountain beside the tables and chairs. Encircling the area was a two-story hotel building. A balcony ran around the second story with a wrought-iron railing. Live music floated out over the scene from an ensemble above and out of Gaetano's sight.

"Can I help you?" a dark-haired woman asked from behind the hostess podium. She was dressed in a tight, tropical-print, ankle-length spaghetti-strap dress that made Gaetano wonder if she could walk without pulling it up to her waist.

"I'm just looking," Gaetano said. He smiled. "It's a beautiful setting." Although there was some dim light coming from the hotel's open hallways, most of the illumination in the dining area came from a combination of tall candles on each table and the moon overhead.

"You'll need a reservation if you want to join us one evening," the hostess said. "We're completely booked this evening."

"I'll keep that in mind. Is it all right if I just look around a bit?"

"Certainly," the hostess said, gesturing for Gaetano to proceed.

Gaetano saw a stairway to the second floor, and believing he would have a better view from there, he climbed it. Reaching the second floor, he saw the musicians. They were set up in a small sitting area directly above the hostess stand. To make room, they had pushed the hotel's furniture aside.

Gaetano walked down the open hallway on the right, running his hand along the railing as he progressed. He had a good view of the diners below, at least at those tables not obscured by the vegetation. The candles conveniently illuminated the people's faces. Intending to make a full circuit, Gaetano was confident he would be able to see everyone unobtrusively.

All at once, he stopped, and the same hairs that had arisen earlier stood bolt upright once again. Not more than fifty feet away, sitting at a table beyond a flowering oleander bush, was the professor, engaged in what looked like an animated conversation. His head was bobbing as he talked, and he was even jabbing an index finger in the air as if to make a point. Gaetano couldn't see Stephanie's face, as she was facing in the opposite direction. Quickly, Gaetano backed up to put the oleander back between himself and the professor. Now came the fun part. If he had a rifle with a scope, he could pop the professor from where he was standing, but he didn't have a rifle, and besides, such a hit would hardly be sporting. He knew all too well that with a handgun, even with a laser sight, you had to be practically on top of the mark to be sure it was a kill. With that in mind, he knew he'd have to bide his time.

Gaetano looked around. Now that he found the lovebirds, he wondered where he could wait for them to finish their romantic dinner. As soon as they did, they undoubtedly would head back to their room on one of the many dark, isolated walkways, which would be a perfect location for the hit. Worst case, they'd take a walk on the beach, which would be equally fine as far as Gaetano was concerned. With his excitement growing, Gaetano smiled contentedly. Finally, everything was falling into place.

Ahead, there wasn't much except a stairway. It led to a spa, at least according to a sign Gaetano could read from where he was standing. Gaetano glanced back at the sitting area where the musicians were playing and decided it would be a perfect place to wait. Although he probably wouldn't be able to see the professor or Tony's sister, due to the intervening oleander bush by their table, he'd see when they got up to leave, which was the important thing. Equally important was that while he waited, it would look like he was sitting there listening to the ensemble if one of the security people happened by.

Daniel rubbed his eyes to give himself patience. He blinked a few times before looking back at Stephanie, whose expression was one of exasperated anger that perfectly mirrored his own. "All I'm saying is that the security man, whatever his name is, said he searched you when he found you trespassing, which isn't so unexpected."

"His name is Kurt Hermann!" Stephanie spat. "And I'm telling you, he groped me disgustingly. I was humiliated and terrified, and I'm not sure which was worse."

"Okay, so he groped you as well as searched you. I'm not sure where one stops and the other begins. But be that as it may, you shouldn't have been the hell in the egg room in the first place. It's like you were asking for it!"

Stephanie's mouth slowly dropped open. She was appalled that Daniel could say such a thing. It was the most insensitive thing he'd ever said, and he'd said some pretty insensitive things during their relationship. Abruptly, Stephanie pushed back her wrought-iron chair, which made a considerable grating noise against the concrete pavement, and stood up. Daniel reacted almost as quickly by leaning forward and grabbing her forearm.

"Where do you think you're going?" he demanded.

"I'm not sure," Stephanie snapped. "At the moment, I just want to leave."

For a few beats, they eyed each other across the table. Daniel did not let go, but Stephanie did not try to struggle either. They had become aware that the people sitting at the nearby tables had gone silent. When both Daniel and Stephanie glanced around, they saw that all eyes were on them. Even several waiters had stopped in mid-stride to stare.

Despite how she felt, Stephanie sat back down. Daniel continued to hold her arm, although his grip significantly loosened.

"I didn't mean that last statement," Daniel said. "I'm angry and upset, and it slipped out. I know you weren't looking to be molested."

Stephanie's eyes were blazing. "You sound like one of those people who think rape victims purposefully put themselves at risk by what they wear or how they act."

"Absolutely not," Daniel said. "It was a slip of the tongue. I'm just really angry you went into that egg room and caused this major flap. You promised you weren't going to make waves."

"I didn't promise," Stephanie retorted. Her voice had lost a bit of its edge. "I said I would try my best. But my conscience is hounding me. I went into that egg room to try to prove what I feared, and I did. Among the other things we already knew about, they are definitely impregnating women and then aborting them for fetal ovaries."

"How can you be so sure?"

"I saw definite proof."

"Okay, can we talk about this without yelling at each other?" Daniel eyes darted around at the nearby tables. People had gone back to their own conversations, and the waiters had resumed their duties.

"Not unless you avoid saying things like you just did a second ago."

"I'll try my best."

Stephanie eyed Daniel, trying to decide if his last statement was deliberately passive-aggressive or if he was making fun of her by echoing her. From her perspective, it had to be one or the other, and along with everything else, it wasn't a good sign.

"Come on!" Daniel said. "Tell me this definitive proof!"

Stephanie continued to stare at Daniel. Now she was trying to decide if he had changed during the last six months or if he'd always been so dispassionate about everything but his work. She looked away for a moment to reprogram her emotions and get herself under a semblance of control. It wasn't going to solve anything if she stalked off or they sat there and bickered. Turning back to Daniel, she took a deep breath and described everything she had seen, particularly the details about the ledger book that had laid it all out in black and white. When she finished, they stared at each other across their unfinished dinners. It was Daniel who finally broke the silence.

"Well, you were right. Does being right at least give you some satisfaction?"

"Hardly!" Stephanie said, with a sarcastic laugh. "The question is: Can we proceed at this point, knowing what we do?"

Daniel looked down at the table and fiddled absently with his silverware. "The way I see it is that we accepted the oocytes before we knew the details of their origin."

"Ha!" Stephanie scoffed. "That's a mighty convenient excuse and a world-class example of fair-weather ethics."

Daniel raised his eyes to meet Stephanie's. "We are so close," he said, solemnly enunciating each word. "Tomorrow, we'll start differentiating the cells. I'm not stopping now because of what is going on at the Wingate Clinic. I'm sorry you were manhandled, mistreated, and molested. I'm also sorry I got beat up. This has not been a picnic, but we knew treating Butler was not going to be easy. We were well aware from the outset that the Wingate principals were unethical, venal idiots, yet we decided to proceed in spite of it. The question is: Are you still with me or not?"

"Let me ask you a question," Stephanie said, leaning closer to Daniel and lowering her voice. "After Butler has been treated, and we go home, and CURE has been saved, and everything is hunky-dory, can we somehow anonymously alert the Bahamian authorities to what is going on at the Wingate?"

"That would be problematic," Daniel responded. "To get you out of Kurt Hermann's private jail cell immediately, which I thought was of prime importance for all concerned, I signed a confidentiality agreement that precluded doing what you just suggested. These people we are dealing with might be crazy, but they are not stupid. The agreement also spelled out what we are doing at the Wingate, meaning that if their secret is revealed, they will reveal ours, which could undo everything we've tried to accomplish by treating Butler."

Stephanie absently twirled her wineglass, which she had otherwise not touched. "What about this idea?" Stephanie said suddenly. "Maybe once Butler is cured, he won't be so emphatic about secrecy."

"I suppose that's a possibility," Daniel offered.

"Can we then say we will at least leave the issue open for discussion down the road?"

"I suppose," Daniel repeated. "I mean, who knows? Things might happen that we have not anticipated."

"That seems like a fair description of the whole affair to date."

"Very funny!"

"Well, nothing has happened exactly as we've planned!"

"That's not quite true. Thanks to you, the cellular work has progressed exactly as we planned. By the time Butler gets here, we could have ten cell lines available, any one of which could cure him. What I need to know is whether you are with me, so we can complete what we need to do and get out of Nassau."

"I do have one more demand," Stephanie said.

"Oh?"

"I want you to make it clear to Spencer Wingate that you're not happy he is making inappropriate overtures toward me. And while we're on the subject, why have you been so passive about it? It's humiliating. You've never even brought it up between us."

"I'm just trying not to make waves."

"That's making waves! I don't understand! If Sheila Donaldson was making equivalent overtures to you, I would certainly support you however you wanted me to."

"Spencer Wingate is a self-centered blowhard egotist who thinks he's a gift to womankind. I was confident you could handle him without turning the situation into a bad scene."

"It's already been a bad scene. He's become progressively and offensively insistent, even to the point of touching me, although after today's flap, maybe he'll be less so. Anyway, I want some support from you about this. Okay?"

"All right! Okay!" Daniel said. "Is that it? Can we just move on and finish this whole Butler affair?"

Stephanie nodded. "I suppose," she said without a lot of enthusiasm.

Daniel ran his fingers through his hair several times, puffed up his cheeks, and then let his breath out like a balloon deflating. He smiled weakly. "I'm sorry again for what I said a little while ago. I've just been beside myself since hearing you were locked up in that jail cell. I thought for sure we were going to be kicked out of the Wingate because of your nosing around, just when we were in sight of success."

Stephanie silently wondered if Daniel had any inkling of how self-centered he was himself. "I hope you are not leading up to saying I shouldn't have gone into the egg room."

"No, not at all," Daniel admitted. "I understand that you did what you felt you had to do. I'm just glad that ultimately our project hasn't been derailed. But this episode has made me realize something else. We've been so busy and preoccupied that we haven't taken a moment to ourselves other than to eat." Daniel put his head back and looked up through the palm fronds at the star-speckled sky. "I mean, here we are in the Bahamas in the middle of the winter, and we haven't taken advantage of it in any way or form."

"Are you suggesting something in particular?" Stephanie asked. Occasionally, Daniel surprised her.

"I am," he answered. He took his napkin off his lap and plopped it onto his dinner plate. "Neither of us seems particularly hungry, and we're both stressed. Why don't we take a moonlit stroll up through the hotel's formal garden and visit that medieval cloister we saw from a distance on our walk our first morning here. We were both curious about it, and it would be awfully appropriate. In the middle ages, cloisters were shelters from the turmoil of the real world."

Stephanie lifted her own napkin and put it on the table. Despite her current aggravation with Daniel and the further questions it raised about her future relationship with him, she couldn't help but smile at his cleverness and razor-sharp intellect, traits that had had a lot to do with her initial attraction to him. She stood up. "That might be the best suggestion you've made in six months."

This looks promising! Gaetano said to himself as he saw Stephanie's head and then Daniel's appear over the top of the oleander that blocked his view of their table. He'd seen Stephanie's for a moment earlier, but she had apparently sat back down. Gaetano hunkered down in his chair, lest Daniel chance to look up at the ensemble on the balcony. Gaetano fully expected the couple to make their way in his direction and pass the hostess desk directly below on their way back to their suite. But they fooled him. They started off in the opposite direction and never looked back.

"Crap!" Gaetano mumbled. Every time he

thought he had everything under control, something unexpected happened. He glanced over at the lead musician, with whom he'd made eye contact during the time he'd been waiting. The man had been demonstrably appreciative of Gaetano's attention. Gaetano smiled and gave a little wave as he got to his feet.

At first Gaetano walked at a normal pace along the balcony to avoid giving the impression that he was hurrying. But once he was far enough away from the musicians, he upped his pace while keeping a hand on the gun in his pants pocket to keep it from banging against his leg. In the courtyard below, the professor and the girl had already disappeared into the spa that occupied the first floor of the eastern end of the building.

At the opposite end of the balcony, Gaetano skidded to a stop at the head of the stairs. He descended rapidly, still clutching the gun through the fabric of his slacks. When he arrived at the spa door, he stopped, briefly composed himself, made sure he wasn't being observed by anyone in the restaurant, and then slowly opened it. He had no idea what to expect. If the professor and the girl were in sight, signing up for a treatment, he'd just back out and rethink what he should do. But the spa was shut for the night, as evidenced by a sign on the empty reception desk illuminated by a single votive candle. All at once, Gaetano remembered having passed through the same area on his first visit when he had been searching for the hotel's pool. Guessing the pool was the professor and his girlfriend's destination, he hurried across the empty room and out the other side.

Gaetano was now in the section of the hotel grounds composed of individual villas. Splotches of dim light defined each entrance, but the area was otherwise dark beneath a canopy of palms. Gaetano walked briskly, remembering the route. He was pleased. Guessing the pool and its snack bar would also be closed and deserted, he'd have his choice of appropriate locations to do what he needed to do.

As he rounded a sharp right-hand turn in the walkway, Gaetano caught a glimpse of the professor and Tony's sister before they disappeared down a short run of stairs beyond a baroque limestone balustrade. Gaetano picked up his pace again. Reaching the balustrade, he looked out over the pool area.

As he had expected, it was closed for the night, and the surrounding buildings were dark. The pool itself was illuminated with underwater lights and appeared like a huge, flat emerald.

"I don't believe this!" Gaetano whispered to himself. "It's so perfect!" His excitement was palpable. Daniel and Stephanie had walked around the edge of the pool and were now starting off into the extensive, dark, and deserted formal gardens. In the darkness, Gaetano couldn't see many of the details beyond some isolated suggestions of statuary and hedges. But what he could see clearly was the lighted medieval cloister. It stood gleaming in the distant moonlight like a crown capping a series of rising, shadowy garden terraces.

Gaetano's hand slipped into his left pants pocket and wrapped itself around the handle of the silenced automatic. He shivered from the sensation the cold steel caused, and in his mind's eye, Gaetano could see the red laser dot on the professor's forehead, which would precede his pulling the trigger.

twenty-one

9:37 P.M., Monday, March 11, 2002

"I recognize this statue from somewhere," Daniel said. "Do you know if it's famous?"

Daniel and Stephanie were standing on a manicured patch of grass, gazing at a white marble reclining nude that appeared to glow in the humid, misty semidarkness of the Ocean Club's Versailles-inspired garden. A silvery blue illumination washed over the formal landscape and contrasted sharply with the deep purple shadows.

"I think it's a copy of a Canova," Stephanie replied. "So, yes, it's reasonably famous. If it is the one I'm thinking of, the original is in the Borghese Museum in Rome."

Daniel shot an awed glance in her direction, which she missed. She was absorbed in lightly touching the woman's thigh. "It's amazing how much like skin the marble appears in the moonlight."

"How on earth did you know it is a copy of a Canova, whatever the hell that is?"

"Antonio Canova was a renowned eighteenth-century neoclassical Italian sculptor."

"I'm impressed," Daniel said, with continued awed disbelief. "How do you happen to have such arcane facts at your fingertips? Or are you pulling my leg from having read about this garden in the brochure in the room?"

"I didn't read the brochure, but I saw you reading it. Maybe you should be giving us a tour."

"Not a chance! The only part I read carefully was about the cloister up on the hill. Seriously, how did you know about Canova?"

"I was a history minor in college," Stephanie said. "That included a survey course in art history, which I remember more about than most of my other classes."

"You amaze me sometimes," Daniel commented. Following Stephanie's example, he reached out and touched the marble cushion on which the woman reclined. "It is uncanny how these guys were able to make marble appear so soft. Look at the way her body indents the fabric."

"Daniel!" Stephanie said with sudden insistence.

Daniel straightened up and tried to read Stephanie's expression in the darkness. She was staring back toward the pool area. He followed her line of sight but saw nothing out of the ordinary in the shadowy moonlit landscape. "What's the matter? Did you see something?"

"I did," Stephanie said. "I saw movement out of the corner of my eye. I think there is someone over there behind that balustrade."

"So what! There's bound to be people wandering around out here, as beautiful as this place is. It's not as if we can expect to have this huge garden to ourselves."

"True," Stephanie agreed. "But it just seemed as if whoever I saw ducked away as soon as I turned my head. It was like they didn't want to be seen."

"What are you trying to suggest?" Daniel

questioned, with one of his scornful laughs. "Someone is spying on us?"

"Well, yeah, something like that."

"Oh, come on, Stephanie! I wasn't serious when I suggested it."

"Well, I'm serious. I really think I saw someone." She raised herself up on her tip-toes and strained to see in the darkness. "And there's someone else!" she said excitedly.

"Where? I don't see anybody."

"Back by the pool. Someone just disappeared from the light into the shadows of the snack bar."

Daniel reached out and gripped Stephanie by both shoulders, making her turn to look at him. She resisted initially. "Hey! Come on! We're out here to relax. We've both had a hell of a day, and you in particular."

"Maybe we should go back and take a walk on the beach, where there are always people. This garden seems too big, too dark, and too isolated for my current taste."

"We're going up to that cloister," Daniel said authoritatively, pointing up the hill. "We've both been intrigued by it, and as I said earlier, our visiting it is metaphysically apropos. We need some shielding from our current turmoil. And nighttime is the best time to visit ruins. So pull yourself together and let's go!"

"What if I really did see someone duck behind that balustrade?" Stephanie went back to craning her neck to see over the bougainvilleae.

"Do you want me to run back there and check? If you do, I'll be glad to go to put your mind at ease. You're being understandably paranoid, although paranoid nonetheless. We're on the hotel's grounds, for Christ's sake. They have security all over this place, remember?"

"I suppose," Stephanie reluctantly agreed. A fleeting image of Kurt Hermann leering at her passed through her mind. She had a lot of reasons to be on edge.

"What do you say; do you want me to run back there?"

"No, I want you to stay here."

"Well, come on then! Let's go up to the cloister." Daniel took her hand and guided her back to the central promenade that led through a number of terraces and up widely spaced flights of steps to the crest of the hill where the cloister was sited. In contrast to the dark garden, the cloister was illuminated with hidden ground-level lights to highlight its gothic arches and give it a jewellike quality in the distance.

As they gained each terrace and skirted a central fountain or statue, they noticed additional statuary to either side within shadowed arbors. Some of these side statues were marble, while others were stone or cast bronze. Although tempted to take a look at them, they avoided any more detours.

"I had no idea there was so much art out here," Stephanie commented.

"It was a private estate before it was a hotel," Daniel said. "At least according to the brochure."

"What did it say about the cloister?"

"All I remember is that it's French and was built in the twelfth century."

Stephanie whistled in wonderment. "Very few cloisters have ever left France. In fact, I only know of one other, and it's not that old."

They climbed the last flight of steps, and when they reached the top, they found a paved public road cutting across their path and isolating the cloister from its formal gardens. When they had viewed the cloister from below, there was no way to see the road unless a vehicle had gone by, and none had.

"This is a surprise," Daniel said, looking up and down the road. It ran east to west along the spine of Paradise Island.

"I guess it's the price of progress," Stephanie said. "I bet it goes out to the golf course."

They crossed the road, the blacktop of which was still radiating the heat of the day, and climbed a few more steps to gain the crown of the hill dominated by the cloister. The ancient structure was merely a square, roofless, double row of gothic-columned arches. The inner row had a bit of tracery in the form of a single foil within each arch.

Daniel and Stephanie approached the edifice. They had to watch their footing, because in contrast to the lower garden, the ground near the cloister was uneven and littered with chunks of stone and crushed seashells.

"I have a feeling this is going to be one of those things that looks better from a distance than close-up," Stephanie said.

"That's part of the reason ruins are better viewed at night."

They reached the structure and carefully made their way into the aisle that ran between the two rows of columns. Their eyes, adapted to the dark, had to squint against the glare of the outside illumination.

"This portion was roofed in its former life," Stephanie said.

Daniel looked up and nodded.

Avoiding the debris underfoot, they stepped over to the inner balustrade. Both leaned on the ancient limestone handrail and peered into the central courtyard. It was about fifty feet square and filled with flat mounds of stone and shell fragments, plus a complicated interplay of shadows from the display lights and the intervening arches.

"It's sad," Stephanie commented. She shook her head. "Back when this was the center of a functioning cloister, this courtyard would have had a well and maybe even a fountain, plus a garden."

Daniel's eyes roamed around the enclosure. "What I find sad is that after lasting almost a thousand years in France, it's not going to last very long here, exposed to the tropical sun and sea air."

They straightened up and looked at each other. "This is a bit anticlimactic," Daniel said. "Let's go take that stroll you suggested on the beach!"

"Good idea," Stephanie said. "But first, let's

give this structure the benefit of the doubt and a bit of respect. Let's at least take one walk around the ambulatory."

Hand in hand, they helped each other avoid the obstacles on the ground. With the glare of the outside lights, it was hard to see details. On the side opposite their hotel, they paused briefly to admire the view out over Nassau's harbor. The illuminating lights made that difficult as well, and soon they were back on their way.

Gaetano was ecstatic. There was no way he could have planned things any better. The professor and Tony's sister were now standing in a square of light that kept Gaetano all but invisible as he approached within striking distance. He could have approached back in the darkness of the garden, but he'd correctly guessed their destination, and he knew it would be perfect.

Gaetano had decided it was best for Tony's sister to know without an ounce of doubt where the hit was coming from, so as not to think the professor was a victim of a random act of violence. Gaetano considered this significant, since she was going to be taking over the company. He thought it was important that she knew exactly how the Castigliano brothers felt about their loan and about how the company was being managed.

At that moment, the couple was on the far side of the ruins, making a slow circuit of the edifice. Gaetano had positioned himself just outside the pool of light along the western side. His intention was to wait until they were no more than twenty feet away before vaulting into the aisle to confront them.

Gaetano's pulse began to race as he watched Daniel and Stephanie round the final corner and start toward him. With growing excitement, he extracted the gun from its makeshift holster and made sure a bullet was in the chamber. Holding it up alongside his head, he prepared himself for what he loved best: action!

I don't think we should be reopening this subject," Stephanie said. "Not now, and maybe not ever."

"I apologized for what I said back at the restaurant. All I'm saying now is that I would rather be groped than beaten up. I'm not saying that being groped isn't unpleasant; it's just easier to take than being beaten and physically injured."

"What is this, a contest?" Stephanie questioned derisively. "Don't answer that! I don't want to talk about it anymore."

Daniel was about to respond when he gasped, stopped in his tracks, and tightened his grip on Stephanie's hand. Stephanie had been looking down at the ground so she could navigate over a large hunk of stone when Daniel's response shocked her into raising her eyes. When she did, she gasped as well.

A hulking figure had leaped into their path, holding a huge handgun and pointing it at them with an outstretched arm. Daniel, more than Stephanie, was aware of a red dot just beneath the gun's barrel.

Neither Daniel nor Stephanie could move, as the man slowly approached. He had a sneering expression on his broad, flat-featured face, which Daniel recognized with a shudder. Gaetano came within six feet of the stunned and immobile couple. At that point, it was abundantly clear that the gun was aimed directly at Daniel's forehead.

"You made me come back, asshole," Gaetano growled. "A bad decision! The Castigliano brothers are very disappointed you did not return to Boston to safeguard their loan. I thought you had gotten my message, but apparently not, and you made me look bad. So goodbye."

The sound of the shot was loud in the humid stillness of the night. Gaetano's arm holding the gun fell to his side while Daniel staggered backward, dragging Stephanie with him. Stephanie screamed as the body fell heavily, facedown, arms out to the sides. There were a few muscular twitches, but then all was still. A large exit wound on the back of his head oozed blood and gray matter.

twenty-two

9:48 P.M., Monday, March 11, 2002

For the duration of several heartbeats, Daniel and Stephanie did not budge. When they did move, it was only to allow their eyes to engage each other after having been transfixed on the prone body sprawled at their feet. In their befuddlement, they did not even breathe, each vainly hoping the other would explain what they had just witnessed. With their mouths agape, their faces reflected a mixture of fear, horror, and confusion, but fear quickly won out. Without saying a word and unsure of who was leading whom, they fled by scrambling over the low wall to their left and ran headlong back the way they had come in the direction of the hotel.

At first, their flight was relatively controlled, thanks to the illumination provided by the ground-level display lights directed at the cloister. But as soon as they passed into the darkness, they encountered trouble. With their eyes now accustomed to the cloister's lights, they were like blind people rushing across an uneven, obstacle-filled landscape. Daniel was the first to trip over a low bush and fall. Stephanie helped him up but then fell herself. Both suffered minor abrasions, which they didn't even feel.

Marshaling their willpower, they forced themselves in their blindness to walk to avoid further falls, even though their terrified brains were screaming at them to run. Within minutes, they reached steps leading down to the road. By then, their eyes were beginning to discern details in the moonlight, and by seeing the terrain, they could up their pace.

"Which way?" Stephanie demanded in a breathless whisper when they gained the pavement of the road.

"Let's stick to the route we know," Daniel hurriedly whispered back.

Hand in hand, they fled across the road and descended the first of the garden's many flights of hand-laid stone steps as rapidly as their slip-on dress shoes would allow. The steps' unevenness contributed to their difficulties, although on the intervening patches of grass, they sprinted full-tilt. The farther away from the cloister they got, the darker it became, but their eyes progressively adapted, and the moonlight was more than enough to help them avoid careening into any of the statuary.

After the third flight of stairs, their exhaustion slowed them to a jog. Daniel was more out of breath than Stephanie, and when they finally entered the sphere of illumination coming from the pool and what they felt was relative safety, he had to stop. Stooped over, he put his hands on his knees and panted. For a moment, he couldn't even talk.

With her own chest heaving, Stephanie reluctantly glanced back the way they had come. After the shock of what had happened, her imagination had them pursued by all manner of demons, but the moonlit view of the garden was as idyllic and peaceful as it had been earlier. Somewhat relieved, she turned her attention back to Daniel. "Are you okay?" she managed between breaths.

Daniel nodded. He still couldn't speak.

"Let's get into the hotel," she added.

Daniel nodded again. He straightened up, and after a brief glance of his own back the way they had come, he took Stephanie's outstretched hand.

Permitting themselves to walk, albeit quickly, they skirted the pool and started up the flight of limestone stairs that led up to the Baroque balustrade.

"Was that the same man who assaulted you in the clothing store?" Stephanie asked. She was still breathing heavily.

"Yes!" Daniel was able to answer.

They passed the villas and entered the candlelit, deserted reception area of the spa, which also functioned as a pass-through into the hotel from the pool complex. After the shocking carnage they'd witnessed up in the ruined cloister, and the subsequent terror it had engendered, the spa's simple Asian aura, cleanliness, and utter serenity seemed otherworldly to the point of being schizophrenic. By the time they entered the Courtyard Terrace restaurant filled with smartly dressed diners, live music, and tuxedo-clad waiters, they felt even more discombobulated. Without speaking to anyone or each other, they passed into the hotel proper.

In the high-arched reception area, Stephanie pulled Daniel to a stop. To their right was the living room, with guests carrying on quiet conversations punctuated with muted laughter. To their left was the open entrance of the hotel, leading out to the porte cochere. Liveried doormen stood at the ready. Ahead were the individual reception desks, only one of which was occupied. Above, tropical fans turned lazily.

"Whom should we talk to?" Stephanie questioned.

"I don't know. Let me think!"

"What about the night manager?"

Before Daniel could respond, one of the doormen approached. "Excuse me," he said to Stephanie. "Are you all right?"

"I think so," Stephanie responded.

The doorman pointed. "Do you know your left leg is bleeding?"

Stephanie glanced down and for the first time realized how bedraggled she looked. The fall she had taken in the darkness had soiled her dress and torn its hem. Her thigh-high hose were in worse shape, particularly below her left knee, where they were shredded. Runs extended all the way down to her ankle, along with a rivulet of blood descending from her knee. She then noticed that her right palm was also abraded, with tiny pieces of broken shell still clinging.

Daniel had not fared much better. There was a tear in his trousers just below the right knee, with an associated bloodstain, and his jacket was peppered with broken shell fragments and had all but lost its right side pocket.

"It's nothing," Stephanie assured the doorman. "I wasn't even aware I'd hurt myself. We tripped out by the pool."

"We have a golf cart right outside," the doorman said. "Can I give you a ride to your room?"

"I think we'll be fine," Daniel said. "But thank you for your concern." He took Stephanie's arm and urged her ahead, toward the door that would take them back to their room.

At first, Stephanie allowed herself to be led forward, but just before they got to the door, she pulled her arm free. "Wait a second! Aren't we going to talk to someone?"

"Lower your voice! Come on! Let's get to the room and get cleaned up. We can talk more there."

Confused at Daniel's behavior, Stephanie let herself be guided outside onto the walkway, but after a few steps, she stopped. She again took her arm out of Daniel's grasp and shook her head. "I don't understand. We saw a man get shot, and he's seriously injured. An ambulance and the police have to be called."

"Keep your voice down!" Daniel urged. He glanced around, thankful no one was in earshot. "That thug is dead. You saw the back of his head. People don't recover from that kind of injury."

"All the more reason to call the police. We witnessed a murder, for God's sake, right in front of our faces."

"True, but we sure as hell didn't see who did it, nor do we have the slightest clue who could've done it. There was a shot, and the guy fell down. We saw nothing except the victim fall: no people and no vehicles! We were eyewitnesses only to the fact that the man was shot, which certainly will be clear to the police without our help."

"But we still witnessed a murder."

"But we would not be able to add anything from having seen it. That's the point. Think about it!"

"Hold on here!" Stephanie said, trying to organize her chaotic thoughts. "What you are saying may be true, but as I understand it, it's a crime not to report witnessing a crime, and we definitely saw a crime."

"I have no idea whether keeping quiet is a crime or not here in the Bahamas. But even if it is, I think we should take the risk of committing it, because at this moment in time, I don't want us to be involved with the police. On top of that, I have zero sympathy for the victim, which I suspect is your feeling as well. Not only was he the one who beat me up, he was threatening to kill me, for Christ's sake, and maybe you too. My worry is that if we go to the police and get drawn into a murder investigation, which we will not be able to aid in any way, we'll risk putting the Butler project in jeopardy, and we are so close to finishing. The long and short of it is that we'd be risking everything for nothing. It's as simple as that."

Stephanie nodded a few times and ran a nervous hand through her hair. "I suppose I see your point," she said reluctantly. "But let me ask you this: You thought my brother was involved when you were beat up. Do you think he was involved this time?"

"Your brother had to be implicated in the first instance. But this time, I have my doubts, since the thug didn't keep you out of it like he obviously did on the previous occasion. Yet who's to know for sure?"

Stephanie stared off into the distance. Her mind and emotions were a jumble. Once again, she felt conflicted concerning what she should do, thanks to a strong sense of guilt. Ultimately, she felt responsible for involving her brother, who had involved the Castiglianos, who certainly had now proved themselves to be mobsters.

"Come on!" Daniel urged. "Let's go to the room and clean up. We can talk some more if you'd like, but I have to tell you, my mind is made up."

Stephanie allowed herself to be guided along the pathway toward their suite. She felt almost numb. Although she was hardly saintly, she'd never knowingly broken the law. It was a strange sensation to think of herself as some sort of miscreant because she failed to report a felony. Equally strange was the thought that her brother was involved with people capable of murder, especially since such an association gave a whole new meaning to his racketeering indictment. Adding to her agitation were the residual physiological effects of having witnessed violence. She could feel herself trembling, and her stomach was doing flip-flops. She had never seen a dead person, much less one killed in front of her in such a graphic manner.

Stephanie shook off a wave of nausea at the horrid image now etched for life into her memory. She wished she was anyplace but where she was. From the moment Daniel had suggested surreptitiously treating Butler, she had thought it was a bad idea, but never in her wildest imagination did she think it could have gotten as bad as it was. Yet she was caught in the affair as if it were a bog of quicksand, sinking in deeper and deeper, unable to get out.

Daniel was feeling progressively more confident about his decision. At first he'd not been so sure, but that had changed when his memory of Professor Heinrich Wortheim's prophecy of disaster came back to haunt him. Daniel had vowed from the outset that he was not going to fail, and to avoid failure, Butler had to be treated, meaning entanglement with the police had to be avoided. Since he and Stephanie would be the only leads associated with the murder, if not outright suspects, even a slipshod investigation would invariably involve what they were doing in Nassau. At that point, Butler would have to be apprised of the situation, because after his arrival, his involvement would most likely be discovered in the course of the inquiry, which would ignite a media firestorm. With the threat of such a scenario, Daniel doubted Butler would come at all.

When they got to their suite, Daniel keyed open the door. Stephanie went in first and turned on the lights. The turndown service had come and gone, and the room was the picture of tranquility. The drapes were closed, classical music issued softly from the bedside radio, and the beds were prepared, with candies on the pillows. Daniel secured the door using all the locks.

Stephanie lifted her dress to look at her knee. She was relieved that her injury wasn't as bad as suggested by the amount of blood, which by now had run all the way down into her shoe. Daniel checked his own knee by dropping his pants. Similar to Stephanie's wound, he had an abrasion the diameter of a golf ball. Both injuries had some embedded seashell fragments, which they knew had to come out or there would be an infection.

"I feel awfully jittery," Daniel admitted. He stepped out of his pants before holding out his hand. It shook as if he was shivering. "It must be the adrenaline rush. Let's open a bottle of wine while we draw a bath. We should soak these abrasions, and the combination of wine and bath should calm us both down."

"Okay," Stephanie said. A bath might help her think more clearly. "I'll run the tub. You get the wine!" She turned on the hot water full-blast after adding some bath salts to the tub. The room quickly filled with steam. Within minutes, the aroma and the soothing sound of the rushing water had a calming effect on her. When she emerged from the bathroom in a hotel robe to tell Daniel the bath was ready, she felt significantly recovered. Daniel was sitting on the couch with the yellow pages open on his lap. There were two glasses of red wine on the coffee table. Stephanie picked one of them up and took a sip.

"I've had another thought," Daniel said. "Obviously, these Castigliano people were not as impressed as I hoped about the reassuring conversations you've been having with your mother."

"We can't be sure my brother told the Castiglianos what we wanted him to."

"Whatever," Daniel said with a wave of his hand. "The point is, they sent this thug down here to do me in and maybe you. They are unhappy people, to say the least. We don't know how long it will take for them to learn that their henchman isn't coming back. Nor can we guess what their reaction will be when they do learn it. For all we know, they'll think we killed him."

"What are you suggesting?"

"We use Butler's money to hire twenty-four-hour armed security. As far as I'm concerned, it's a legitimate expense, and it's only for a week and a half, two weeks tops."

Stephanie sighed with resignation. "Are there any listings in the phone book?"

"Yeah, there are quite a few. What do you think?"

"I don't know what to think," Stephanie admitted.

"I think we need some professional protection."

"All right, if you say so," Stephanie said. "But it might be more important for us to start being even more careful in general than we have been. No more walks in the dark. I mean, what were we thinking?"

"In retrospect, it was foolish, considering my having been beaten up and warned."

"What about the bath? Do you want to get in first? It's ready."

"No, you go ahead. I'll make some calls to these agencies. The sooner we have someone, the better I'll feel."

Ten minutes later, Daniel came into the bathroom to sit on the edge of the tub. He was still sipping his wine. Stephanie was up to her neck in sudsy water, and her wineglass was empty.

"Do you feel better?" Daniel asked.

"Much. How did you do on the phone?"

"Good. Someone will be here in a half hour to be interviewed. It's a company called First Security. They were recommended by the hotel."

"I've been trying to think of who could have

shot that guy. We haven't voiced it, but he was like our savior." Stephanie stood and wrapped herself in a towel and stepped out of the tub. "It had to be someone who was a damn good shot. And how did he happen to be there just when we needed him? It was like Father Maloney at the Turin airport but ten times more critical."

"Do you have any ideas?"

"Only one, but it is far-fetched."

"I'm listening." Daniel felt the bathwater and began adding more hot.

"Butler. Maybe he's had the FBI keep an eye on us for our own protection."

Daniel laughed as he got into the tub. "That would be ironic."

"Do you have any better ideas?"

"Not one," Daniel admitted. "Unless it had something to do with your brother. Maybe he sent someone down here to watch over you."

Now Stephanie laughed in spite of herself. "That's even more far-fetched than my idea!"

As the nighttime security supervisor, Bruno Debianco was accustomed to calls from his boss, Kurt Hermann. The man had no life other than as head of Wingate security, and since he lived on the grounds, he was always around hassling Bruno with all sorts of minor requests and orders. Some of them were unexpected and ridiculous, but tonight's took the cake. A little after ten, Kurt had called on his cell phone to instruct Bruno to drive one of the black Wingate vans out to Paradise Island. The destination was to be the Huntington Hartford cloister. Bruno was only supposed to stop if the road was clear, and if it was clear, he was to turn off his headlights before slowing down. Once stopped, he was supposed to walk up to the cloister but avoid stepping into the light. At that point, Kurt would accost him.

Bruno waited for the traffic light to turn green before accelerating up onto the bridge leading to Paradise Island. Never had he been ordered to leave the Wingate Clinic on a mystery mission, and what made it particularly strange was the request to bring a body bag. Bruno tried to think of what possibly could have happened, but nothing came to mind other than the trouble Kurt had gotten into in Okinawa. Bruno had served with Kurt in the Army's Special Forces and knew the man had a love-hate reaction to whores. It had been an obsession that had suddenly erupted into a personal vendetta on the

Japanese island. Bruno had never quite understood it, and he hoped he wasn't currently being drawn into a recrudescence of
that problem. He and Kurt had a good thing
going with Spencer Wingate and Paul Saunders, and Bruno didn't want it to get screwed
up. If Kurt had started up his old crusade, it
was going to be a problem.

The main east-west road that ran along
Paradise Island had moderate traffic, but it
dropped off after Bruno passed the shopping
areas. It dropped off even more after the first
few hotels, and after the turnoff to the Ocean
Club, it was deserted. Following orders,
Bruno switched off the lights as he neared
the cloister. With the moonlight and the white
stripe in the middle of the road, he had no
problem driving in the dark.

Passing the final coppice of trees, the illuminated cloister came into view on Bruno's
right. He pulled across the road into a shoulder parking area and stopped the car. He
turned off the engine and got out. To his left,
he could see down the hill to the Ocean
Club's lighted pool.

Bruno went around to the back of the van
and opened the rear door. He pulled out the
folded body bag, and with it under his arm,

he mounted the steps leading up to the cloister. Before he got into the light, he stopped. Ahead, the cloister was deserted. His eyes scanned the surrounding area, trying to peer into the darkness of the trees. He was about to call out Kurt's name when the man materialized out of the shadows to Bruno's right. Like Bruno, he was dressed in black and almost invisible. He waved for Bruno to follow him and said, "Move it!"

With the moonlight, it was fairly easy for Bruno to walk, but once they were within the trees, it was a different story. After a few steps, he stopped. "I can't see a blasted thing."

"You don't have to," Kurt said quietly. "We're here. Did you bring the body bag?"

"Yeah."

"Unzip it and help me load it up!"

Bruno did as he was told. Gradually his eyes adjusted, and he could make out Kurt's form. He also could see the vague outline of the body on the ground. Bruno extended the end of the body bag toward Kurt, who took it and stepped down the corpse's feet. Together they pulled it taut, placed it on the ground, and folded back the edges.

"On three," Kurt said. "But watch the head. It's a little messy."

Bruno got his hands under the corpse's armpits, and at the appropriate moment lifted the torso while Kurt lifted the legs.

"Good grief!" Bruno grunted. "Who is this guy, an ex-lineman for the Chicago Bears?"

Kurt didn't answer. The two of them got the body into the bag, and Kurt drew up the zipper from the foot.

"Don't tell me we have to carry this two-ton guy down to the van," Bruno said. The idea was daunting.

"We're not leaving him here. Run down and open the van's back door. When we get down there, I don't want there to be any delay getting him inside."

A few minutes later, they shoved Gaetano's upper body, encased in the body bag, into the van. To get the rest in, Bruno had to climb in himself and pull while Kurt pushed. Both were winded when they were finished.

"So far so good," Kurt commented, as he closed the door. "Let's get out of here before our luck runs out and someone drives by."

Bruno went around to the driver's side and got in. Kurt put his black rucksack in the backseat before climbing into the front passenger side. Bruno started the engine. "Where to?" he asked.

"The Ocean Club's parking lot," Kurt said. "The guy had keys to a rent-a-car Jeep in his pocket. I want to find it."

Bruno made a quick U-turn before switching on his headlights. They drove in silence. Bruno was dying to ask who in the hell the stiff in the back of the van was, but he knew better. Kurt had a habit of only telling him what he thought he needed to know and got pissed whenever Bruno asked questions. Ever since Bruno had known him, Kurt had been a man of few words. He was always tensed up and on edge, as if he was constantly angry about something.

It only took a few minutes to get to the parking lot, and when they did, it only took a few more minutes to find the car. It was the only Jeep in the lot and was positioned close to the exit, with nothing blocking it. Kurt had gotten out to check to see if the keys opened the doors. They did. The car's papers were in the glove compartment, and Gaetano's carry-on was on the backseat.

"I want you to follow me to the airport," Kurt said when he came back to Bruno's window.

"Needless to say, drive carefully. You don't want to get stopped and have them discover the body."

"That would be embarrassing," Bruno agreed. "Especially since I don't know a blasted thing."

Bruno thought he detected a glare in Kurt's eyes before he went back to climb into the rent-a-car. Bruno shrugged and started the van.

Kurt got the Cherokee started. He hated surprises, and the day had been nothing but surprises. With his Special Ops Army training, he prided himself in careful planning, as was necessary for any military mission. Accordingly, he had been observing the two doctors for more than a week, and he thought he understood their mindset and situation. Then the woman doctor had broken into the egg room; that had been totally unexpected and had caught him unprepared. Even worse was what had happened tonight.

As soon as they got through town and on open road, Kurt pulled out his cell phone and pressed the preprogrammed number for Paul Saunders. Although Spencer Wingate was the titular head of the clinic, Kurt preferred dealing with Paul. It had been Paul who had hired him back in Massachusetts. Besides, Paul, like Kurt, was always at the clinic, which was in sharp contrast to Spencer, who was always out looking for loose women.

As per usual, Paul answered after only a few rings.

"I'm on my cell," Kurt warned before saying anything else.

"Oh?" Paul questioned. "Don't tell me there is another problem."

"I'm afraid so."

"Is it related to our guests?"

"Very much so."

"Does it have anything to do with what happened today?"

"It's worse."

"I don't like the sound of this. Can you give me some idea what it is about?"

"I think it is better that we meet."

"When and where?"

"In three quarters of an hour in my office. Let's say twenty-three hundred hours." By force of habit, Kurt still used military time.

"Should we involve Spencer?"

"That's your call."

"See you then."

Kurt ended the call and slipped the phone into its holder on his belt. He glanced into the rearview mirror. Bruno was following at a comfortable distance. Events seemed to be back under control.

The airport was all but deserted, save for the cleaning crews. More specifically, the rent-a-car concessions were all closed. Kurt nosed the Cherokee into one of the appropriate rent-a-car slips. He locked the car and took the keys and the papers over to the after-hours deposit box. A moment later, he climbed back into Bruno's van. Bruno had kept the engine idling.

"Now what?" Bruno asked.

"You are going to drive me back to the Ocean Club to get my van. Then we are both going to drive out to Lyford Cay marina. You'll be taking a moonlight cruise on the company yacht."

"Aha! I'm starting to get the picture. My guess is that we'll soon be in the market for a new anchor. Am I right?"

"Just drive," Kurt said.

True to his word, Kurt pushed open the door to his office almost to the second of his eleven o'clock commitment. Both Spencer and Paul were already there, accustomed to his signature punctuality. Kurt brought his rucksack over to the desk and dropped it. It made a resounding thud against the desk's metal surface.

Spencer and Paul were sitting in the two chairs facing Kurt's utilitarian desk. Their eyes had followed Kurt from the moment the security chief had walked through the door. They were waiting for him to say something, but Kurt took his time. He took off his black silk jacket and draped it over the chair. Then he pulled out his gun from its holster in the small of his back and carefully placed it on the desk.

With obvious exasperation, Spencer exhaled noisily and rolled his eyes. "Mr. Hermann, I am forced to remind you that you work for us and not vice versa. What the hell is going on? And it better be good, for having dragged us in here in the middle of the night. I happened to have been pleasurably occupied."

Kurt peeled off his form-fitting gloves and put them next to his automatic. Only then did he sit down. He reached out and lifted his computer monitor and put it to the side to have an uninterrupted view of his visitors.

"I was forced in the line of duty to kill someone tonight."

Both Spencer and Paul's mouths slowly dropped open. They stared in consternation at their security supervisor, who calmly stared back at them. For a beat, no one moved and no one spoke. It was Paul who first found his voice. He spoke hesitantly, as if afraid to hear the answer: "Could you tell us who it was you killed?"

Kurt used one hand to open the buckle on his rucksack and the other to pull out a bill-fold. He pushed it across the desk at his bosses and then sat back. "His name is Gaetano Baresse."

Paul reached out and picked up the wallet. Before he could open it, Spencer slammed his palm down on the surface of the metal desk hard enough to make it sound like a kettledrum. Paul jumped and dropped the wallet. Kurt didn't visibly flinch, although all his honed muscles tensed.

After pounding the desk, Spencer leaped to his feet and began to pace with both hands clasped on top of his head. "I don't believe this," he wailed. "Before we know it, it will be Massachusetts all over again, with the Bahamian authorities instead of U.S. marshals knocking at our gate!"

"I don't think so," Kurt said simply.

"Oh, yeah?" Spencer questioned sarcastically. He stopped pacing. "How can you be so sure?"

"There's no body," Kurt said.

"How can that be?" Paul asked, as he bent over to retrieve the wallet.

"As we speak, Bruno is dumping the body and its effects into the deep. I returned the man's rent-a-car to the airport as if he left the island. The man is just going to disappear. Period! End of story."

"That sounds encouraging," Paul commented, as he opened the wallet and pulled out Gaetano's driver's license, which he examined.

"Encouraging, my ass!" Spencer shouted. "You promised me this . . ." Spencer pointed at Kurt while searching for the right descriptive word, " . . . This half-assed Green Beret wouldn't kill anybody, and here we are, barely with our doors open, and he's already iced somebody. This is a disaster in the making. We can't afford to move the clinic again."

"Spencer!" Paul said sharply. "Sit down!"

"I'll sit down when I feel like sitting down! I'm the head of this freaking clinic."

"Suit yourself," Paul said, gazing up at Spencer, "but let's hear the details before we fly off the handle and conjure up doomsday scenarios." Paul looked at Kurt. "You do owe us an explanation. Why was killing this Gaetano Baresse from Somerville, Massachusetts, in the line of duty?" Paul put both the wallet and the driver's license on the desk.

"I told you I got the bug in Dr. D'Agostino's phone. To monitor it, I had to stay close. After dinner, they took a walk in the Ocean Club's garden. As I followed at a distance, I realized this Gaetano Baresse was also following them, but much closer. So I closed in on them. It soon became apparent that Gaetano Baresse was a professional hit man, and he was about to do in the doctors. I had to make an instantaneous decision. I thought you would want the doctors alive."

Paul glanced back up at Spencer with arched eyebrows to question Spencer's reaction to what he had just heard. Spencer leaned over and picked up the driver's license. He stared at the photo for a second before flipping it back onto the desk. He yanked his chair back to where he was standing and sat down, slightly apart from the others.

"How are you so sure this Baresse guy was a professional hit man?" Spencer asked. His voice had lost most of its bluster.

Using his left hand, Kurt again opened his rucksack. Reaching in with his right, he pulled out Gaetano's gun. He pushed it across the desk as he had done with the wallet. "This is no Saturday night special, particularly not with a built-in laser and a suppressor."

Paul picked up the weapon gingerly, glanced at it, and extended it back toward Spencer. Spencer motioned that he didn't care to touch it. Paul put it back on Kurt's desk.

"With my mainland contacts, I may be able to learn more about this man," Kurt said. "But until then, there is no doubt in my mind he is a professional, and with a weapon like this, which he had to have gotten since his eight o'clock arrival, he's connected."

"Talk in English!" Spencer commanded.

"I'm talking about organized crime," Kurt said. "He was undoubtedly connected to organized crime, probably drug-related."

"Are you suggesting our doctor guests are into drugs?" Spencer asked with disbelief.

"No," Kurt said simply. He stared back at his bosses, challenging them to put it all together as he had while waiting for Bruno to show up at the cloister.

"Wait a minute!" Spencer said. "Why would a drug kingpin send a professional killer over here to the Bahamas to do away with a couple of researchers if the researchers weren't into drugs?"

Kurt stayed silent. He stared back at Paul.

Suddenly, Paul nodded a few times. "I think I'm getting Kurt's drift. Are you suggesting the mystery patient might not be connected with the Catholic Church?"

"I'm thinking he might be a rival drug lord," Kurt said. "Or at least some sort of Mob boss. Either way, his rivals do not want him to get better."

"Goddamn!" Paul remarked. "You know, it makes sense. It would certainly explain all the secrecy."

"It seems far-fetched to me," Spencer said skeptically. "Why would a couple of world-class researchers be willing to treat a drug lord?"

"Organized crime has many ways to put pressure on people," Paul said. "Who knows? Maybe some drug cartel laundered money by investing in Lowell's company. I think Kurt has something here. I mean, a sick drug lord from South America or a sick Mob boss from the Northeast would probably be Catholic, which could explain the Shroud of Turin part."

"Well, I can tell you one thing," Spencer said. "All this is souring me about finding out the patient's identity, and it's not just because of this killing. There's no way we would try to lean on some organized-crime figure. We'd be shooting ourselves in the foot."

"What about our involvement in general?" Paul asked. "Do we want to reconsider allowing the treatment to go forward?"

"I want that second payment," Spencer said. "We need it. We should just remain passive, so as not to anger anyone."

Paul turned to Kurt. "Was Dr. Lowell aware he was in danger?"

"Most definitely," Kurt said. "Gaetano had confronted him and had his gun aimed at Lowell's forehead. I took him out at the last second."

"Why do you ask that?" Spencer questioned.

"I'm hoping Lowell will look to his security," Paul responded. "Whoever sent Gaetano might send someone else when they learn Gaetano failed and is not coming back."

"That's not going to be for some time," Kurt said. "I went to great lengths to make the guy disappear for that very reason. And as far as Dr. Lowell is concerned, I can assure you he was scared shitless. Both of them were."

twenty-three

2:50 P.M., Saturday March 23, 2002

The clutch of people exited the Atlantis resort's Imperial Club elevator on the thirty-second floor of the Royal Towers west wing and started down the carpeted hallway. In the lead was Mr. Grant Halpern, the hotel manager on duty, followed by Ms. Connie Corey, the day-shift reception supervisor, and Harold Beardslee, Imperial Club director. Ashley Butler and Carol Manning were a few steps behind, slowed by Ashley's shuffling gait, which was more pronounced now than it had been a month earlier. Bringing up the rear were two bellmen; one pushed a hotel cart stacked with Ashley and Carol's checked suitcases, and the other carried their hand luggage and garment bags. It was like a miniature safari.

"Well, well, my dear Carol," Ashley voiced, drawing out the words in his Southern drawl but with a newly acquired monotone. "What is your first impression of this modest establishment?"

"*Modest* may be the last adjective that would come to my mind," Carol answered. She knew Ashley was merely playing to the hotel staff audience.

"Now, what adjective might you believe to be more befitting?"

"Whimsical but impressive," Carol said. "I wasn't prepared for such theatrical grandeur. The lobby downstairs is truly creative, particularly with its textured columns and golden, seashell-coffered dome. I would be hard put to guess how tall it is."

"It soars to seventy feet," Mr. Halpern said over his shoulder.

"Thank you, Mr. Halpern," Ashley called ahead. "You are so kind and admirably well-informed."

"At your service, Senator," Mr. Halpern said without slowing down.

"It pleases me that you are impressed with the lodging," Ashley said, lowering his voice and leaning toward his chief of staff. "I am sure you are equally impressed with the weather as compared with Washington at the end of March. I hope you are glad to be here. Truth be known, I feel guilty for not having had you accompany me here last year on my reconnaissance visit, when I was putting this whole endeavor together."

Carol shot a surprised glance at her boss. Never had he expressed any guilt in relation to her about anything, much less a trip to the tropics. It was another small but curious example of the unpredictability he had displayed on and off during the past year. "You needn't feel guilty, sir," she said. "I'm delighted to be here in Nassau. How about yourself? Are you glad to be here?"

"Most assuredly," Ashley said, without a trace of accent.

"Aren't you a little scared?"

"Me, scared?" Ashley questioned loudly, suddenly reverting back to his histrionics. "My daddy told me that the proper way to face adversity is to do your homework and everything else in your power to do, and then put yourself in the Good Lord's hands. And that's what I have done, plain and simple. I'm here to enjoy myself!"

Carol nodded but said nothing. She was sorry she had asked the question. If anyone felt guilty, it was she, since she was still conflicted about the outcome she hoped for the current visit. For Ashley's sake, she tried to convince herself she wanted a miraculous cure, while for herself, she knew she hoped for something less.

Mr. Halpern and the other hotel personnel stopped at a large double mahogany door decorated with carved mermaids in low relief. As Mr. Halpern fumbled in his pocket for a master keycard, Ashley and Carol arrived.

"Hold on here," Ashley said, with a quavering hand outstretched like he was making a point on the Senate floor. "This is not the room I occupied on my last sojourn here at the Atlantis. I specifically requested the same accommodations."

Mr. Halpern's suave expression faltered. "Senator, perhaps you didn't hear me earlier. When Ms. Corey brought you into my office, I mentioned that we had upgraded you. This is one of our few themed suites. It's the Poseidon Suite."

Ashley looked at Carol.

"He did say we were being upgraded," Carol said.

For a moment, Ashley appeared confused behind his heavy, thick-rimmed glasses. He was dressed as he always was, in a dark suit, generic white shirt, and conservative tie. A line of perspiration ringed his hairline. His doughy complexion appeared particularly pale as compared with the hotel staff's.

"This suite is larger, has a better view, and is far more elegant than the one you occupied last year," Mr. Halpern said. "It is one of our very best. Perhaps you'd like to see it?"

Ashley shrugged. "I suppose I'm just being a country boy, unaccustomed to being made a fuss over. Fine! Let's see the Poseidon Suite."

Ms. Corey, who had stepped ahead of Mr. Halpern, produced a keycard and opened the door. She stepped aside. Mr. Halpern gestured for Ashley to enter. "After you, Senator," he said.

Ashley walked through a small foyer into a large room, the walls of which were muraled with a surreal underwater view of an ancient submerged city, presumably the mythical Atlantis. The furniture consisted of a dining table for eight, a writing desk, an entertainment console, two club chairs, and two oversized couches. All the exposed wood was carved in the form of sea creatures, including the arms of the two facing couches, which were porpoises. The prints and colors of the fabrics and the design on the rugs continued the pelagic theme.

"My, my," Ashley voiced as he took it all in.

Ms. Corey went to the entertainment console to check on the minibar. Mr. Beardslee fluffed the pillows on the couches.

"The master bedroom is on your right, Senator," Mr. Halpern said, gesturing in the direction of an open door. "And Ms. Manning, as requested, there is a fine bedroom for you on your left."

The bellmen immediately began to distribute the luggage to the appropriate rooms.

"And now for the pièce de résistance," Mr. Halpern said. He had stepped around Ashley's blocky, stooped figure to a series of wall switches and now threw the first. With an electric whir, the drapes that covered the entire outside wall of the room began to pull apart, progressively revealing a stunning

scene of an emerald-and-sapphire sea beyond a balustraded, mosaic-tiled balcony.

"My word!" Carol exclaimed with a hand
clasped to her chest. From the vantage point
of thirty-two stories, the view was breathtak-
ingly commanding.

Mr. Halpern threw another switch, and the
sliding-glass-door ensemble retracted to
stack at each side. When the whirring
stopped, the balcony and the room were one
large, open space. He proudly gestured out
to the balcony. "If you'd care to step outside,
I can orient you to some of our many outdoor
attractions."

Ashley and Carol followed the manager's
suggestion. Ashley went right to the waist-
height, reddish-brown, stone balustrade.
Leaning on his hands on the wide rail, he
looked down. With a mild fear of heights,
Carol approached more slowly. Gingerly, she
touched the top of the rail before looking
down. It was as if she thought the balustrade
could fall over. Below was a bird's-eye view
of the extensive Atlantis beach and water-
park, dominated by the Paradise Lagoon.

Mr. Halpern moved to stand next to Carol.
He began pointing out the landmarks, including the jewellike Royal Baths Pool, al-

most directly in front of where they were standing.

"What's that to the left?" Carol asked. She pointed. It looked to her like a displaced archeological monument.

"That's our Mayan Temple," Mr. Halpern said. "If you are feeling courageous, there is a heart-stopping waterslide that takes you down from its six-story summit through a Plexiglas tube submerged in the shark-filled Predator Lagoon."

"Carol, my dear," Ashley gushed. "That sounds like the perfect activity for someone like yourself, seriously contemplating the pursuit of a Washington political career."

Carol glanced at her boss with the fear that there was more to his comment than humor, but he was blankly staring out at the view over the ocean, as if his mind had already moved on.

"Mr. Halpern," Ms. Corey called from inside the room. "All seems to be in order, and the senator's keycards are on the desk. I should be getting back to the reception desk."

"I'll be going as well," Mr. Beardslee said. "Senator, if there is anything you need, just let my staff know."

"Now, I want to thank you folks for being so

very kind to us," Ashley exuded. "You are all a tribute to this fine organization."

"I too should leave so you folks can get settled," Mr. Halpern said, as he started to follow the others.

Ashley lightly gripped the manager's arm. "I would be most appreciative if you would wait for just a moment," he said.

"Of course," Mr. Halpern responded.

Ashley waved as the others departed, then let his gaze return out to the expansive ocean. "Mr. Halpern, my being here in Nassau is no secret, nor could it be, having arrived on public transport. But that does not mean I wouldn't look kindly on respect for my privacy. I would prefer the room be registered solely under Ms. Manning's name."

"As you wish, sir."

"Thank you kindly, Mr. Halpern. I shall count on your discretion to avoid publicity. I want to feel I can enjoy the pleasures of your casino without fear of offending the more righteous of my constituents."

"You have my word we will make every effort in that regard. But, like last year, we cannot prevent your being approached in the casino by any of your many fans."

"My fear is reading about my presence in

the newspapers or that someone could merely call the hotel to ascertain that I am here."

"I assure you we will do everything in our power to protect your privacy," Mr. Halpern said. "Now, I should leave you folks to un-pack and unwind. Some complimentary champagne should be on its way, with our wishes for a most relaxing stay."

"One more question," Ashley said. "Reser-vations were made for our friends at the same time as ours. Has there been any word from Dr. Lowell and Dr. D'Agostino?"

"Indeed! They are already here, having checked in less than an hour ago. They are in 3208, one of our Superior Suites, just down the hall."

"How very convenient! It seems to me you have admirably taken care of all our needs."

"We try our best," Mr. Halpern said, as he bowed briefly before stepping back into the room on his way to the door.

Ashley switched his attention to his chief of staff, who had become progressively accli-mated to the height and was mesmerized by the view. "Carol, dear! Perhaps you can be so kind as to see if the doctors are in their room and, if so, whether they would care to join us."

Carol turned and blinked as if waking from a trance. "Certainly," she said quickly, remembering her role.

Maybe you should go in by yourself," Stephanie suggested. She and Daniel were standing outside the mermaid-carved door of the Poseidon Suite. Daniel's hand was poised over the doorbell.

Daniel breathed out in frustration, letting his arm fall limply to his sides. "What can possibly be the matter now?"

"I don't want to see Ashley. I haven't been wild about this affair from day one, and after all that has happened, I'm even less wild about it now."

"But we're so close to finishing it. The treatment cells are ready. All that's left is the implantation, which is the easy part."

"So you believe, and hopefully you'll be right. But I haven't shared your optimism from the beginning, and I can't imagine my negativity now can serve any constructive purpose."

"You didn't think we could have treatment cells in a month, and we do."

"That's true, but the cellular work is the only part that has gone smoothly."

Daniel rolled his head and his eyes around to relieve the sudden tension. He was exasperated. "Why are you doing this now?" he questioned rhetorically. He took a breath and looked at Stephanie. "Are you trying to sabotage the project here in the eleventh hour?"

Stephanie gave a short, pretend laugh, as color rose to her cheeks. "Quite the contrary! After all this effort, I don't want to ruin things. That's the point! That's why I'm suggesting you go in alone."

"Carol Manning specifically said Ashley wanted to see both of us, and I said we'd be right there. For God's sake, if you don't come in, he's apt to think something is wrong. Please! You don't have to say or do anything. Just be your charming self and smile. Surely that's not asking too much!"

Stephanie fidgeted and looked down at her feet and then back at their bodyguard, lounging against the wall outside their room, where they had told him to stay. For Stephanie, his presence was a stark reminder of everything that had gone awry. The whole ghastly affair had come down to the wire, and her intuitive misgivings were again driving her crazy. On the other hand, Daniel was right about the implantation. With

their mouse experiments, the actual treatment phase, once they got it right, had been
problem-free.

"All right!" Stephanie said with resignation.
"Let's get this over with, but you are doing
the talking."

"Good girl!" Daniel said as he rang the
bell.

It was Stephanie's turn to roll her eyes.
Under normal circumstances, she would
never tolerate such a condescending, sexist
appellation.

Carol Manning opened the door. She
smiled and was superficially friendly, yet
Stephanie sensed an underlying nervousness and distraction, as if she was a kindred
spirit in their present situation.

Ashley was sitting on one of the couches
with porpoise arms, although Daniel and
Stephanie didn't immediately recognize him.
Gone were the dark suit, plain white shirt,
and conservative tie. Even the signature
dark-rimmed glasses had been abandoned.
He was wearing a short-sleeve, bright green,
Bahamian-print shirt, yellow pants, and
white leather walking shoes with a matching
belt. With his pasty, pale, hairy arms, which
suggested they had never seen the light of

day, much less the sun, he was a caricature of a tourist. His blue-tinted, trendy sunglasses curved around the side of his face like those of a professional cyclist. Also unique was a fixity of facial expression that Daniel and Stephanie had not seen before.

"Welcome, my dear, dear friends," Ashley spouted in his familiar accent but with an unfamiliar, less modulated voice. "You are a sight for sore eyes, like the cavalry charge in the nick of time. I cannot describe the joy I feel seeing your handsome, intelligent faces. Excuse my not leaping to my feet to greet you appropriately, as my emotions dictate. Unfortunately, the clinical benefit of my medication wears off decidedly more quickly since we last met."

"Stay where you are," Daniel said. "We are glad to see you as well." He stepped over to shake hands with Ashley before taking a seat on the couch across from him.

After some indecision, Stephanie sat next to Daniel and tried to smile. Carol Manning preferred to sit apart, having turned the desk chair around to face into the room.

"After such limited communication during the past month, my belief in your ultimate appearance here was based mostly on faith,"

Ashley admitted. "The only encouraging clue that progress was being made was the considerable and relentless drain on the funds I put at your disposal."

"It has been a Herculean effort in more ways than we would care to explain," Daniel responded.

"I hope the implication is that you are prepared to proceed."

"Most definitely," Daniel said. "In fact, we have made all the arrangements for the implantation to take place tomorrow morning at ten A.M. at the Wingate Clinic. We hope you are prepared to move ahead so quickly."

"It can't be too soon, as far as this old country boy is concerned," Ashley said, becoming more serious, with only a vestige of his usual Southern accent. "I'm afraid I'm on borrowed time, keeping my degenerative infirmity from the media."

"Then it is in our mutual interest to get the implantation done."

"I am to assume you have been able to complete the arduous process of making the treatment cells you described a month ago."

"We have," Daniel said. "Mostly thanks to the skill of Dr. D'Agostino." Daniel gave Stephanie's knee a squeeze.

Stephanie temporarily managed a slightly broader smile.

"In fact," Daniel continued, "over the last week, we have created four separate cell lines of dopaminergic neurons that are clones of your cells."

"Four?" Ashley questioned with no accent whatsoever. He was regarding Daniel with an unblinking stare. "Why so many?"

"The redundancy is merely a safety net. We wanted to be absolutely certain we at least had one. Now we can choose, since all would be equally efficacious to treat you."

"Is there anything I need to know about the morning, other than getting my sad body out to the Wingate Clinic?"

"Only the usual preoperative restrictions, like no solid food after midnight. We would also prefer you not to take any of your medication in the morning, if it is at all possible. With our mouse studies, we saw rapid therapeutic effects after implantation, and we anticipate the same for you. Your Parkinson's drugs would mask this."

"Fine by me," Ashley said agreeably. "The last thing I want to do is confuse the issue. Of course, the burden will be on Carol to bear the brunt of getting me dressed and down to the limo."

"I'm certain the hotel will have a wheel-chair we can borrow," Carol said.

"Am I to assume from the proscription of food after midnight that I will be having anesthesia?" Ashley asked, ignoring Carol.

"I have been told the anesthesia will be local, with heavy sedation," Daniel said. "An anesthesiologist will be in attendance, with the option of deeper anesthesia if it is needed. I should tell you we have retained the services of a local neurosurgeon who has experience doing this kind of implant, although certainly not with cloned cells. His name is Dr. Rashid Nawaz. He knows you as John Smith, as does the Wingate Clinic, and both have been apprised of the need for discretion, and both are fine with that."

"It seems you have attended most admirably to all the details."

"That was our intention," Daniel said. "Following the procedure, we will recommend you remain in the Wingate Clinic's inpatient facility so we can closely monitor you."

"Oh?" Ashley questioned, as if surprised. "For how long?"

"At least overnight. After that, it will be as your clinical course dictates."

"I have counted on returning here to the Atlantis resort," Ashley said. "That is why I made arrangements for you all to stay here as well. You can monitor me to your hearts' content. You are just down the hall."

"But the hotel lacks medical diagnostic equipment."

"Like what?"

"What a normal inpatient facility has, like laboratory services and an X ray."

"X ray? Why an X ray? Are you expecting complications?"

"Absolutely not, but it is only prudent to be careful. Remember, for lack of a better word, what we are doing tomorrow is experimental."

Daniel cast a quick glance at Stephanie to see if she wanted to add anything. Instead, she briefly rolled her eyes.

Acutely sensitive under the circumstances to any nuances, Ashley caught Stephanie's reaction. "Do you have a more appropriate term, Dr. D'Agostino?" he asked her.

Stephanie hesitated a moment. "No. I think experimental is quite accurate," she said, while in reality, she thought *foolhardy* would be closer to the truth.

"I hope I'm not detecting a subtle negative undercurrent here," Ashley said, as his eyes switched back and forth between Daniel and Stephanie. "It is important to me that I feel you researchers are as positive about this procedure as you were in my hearing room."

"Absolutely," Daniel declared. "Our experience with our animal models has been nothing short of amazing. We could not be more excited and eager to bring this godsend to humankind. We are looking forward to treating you in the morning."

"Good," Ashley said, but his unblinking eyes zeroed in on Stephanie. "And you, Dr. D'Agostino? Are you in a like mind? You seem rather quiet."

There was a brief silence in the room, broken only by the distant squeals of delight from children rising from the crowded pools and waterslides thirty-two stories below.

"Yes," Stephanie said finally. She then took a breath to give her time to pick her words carefully. "I'm sorry if I seem quiet. I suppose I am a bit tired after all that we have gone through to create your treatment cells. But, to answer your question, I am of a like mind in that I can say without qualification I'm excited to finish the project."

"I am relieved to hear you say so," Ashley remarked. "That means you are happy with these four cell lines you have cloned from my skin cells?"

"I am," Stephanie said. "They are definitely dopamine-producing neurons, and they are . . . " She paused as if searching for the right word, " . . . vigorous."

"Vigorous?" Ashley questioned. "Hmmm. I'll assume that is advantageous, although it sounds rather vague to this layman. But tell me: Do they all contain genes from the Shroud of Turin?"

"Most assuredly!" Daniel answered. "But it was not without considerable effort on our part to get the shroud sample, extract the DNA, and reconstruct the necessary genes from fragments. Yet we did it."

"I want to be sure about this," Ashley said. "I know there is no way for me to check, but I want to be certain. It is important to me."

"The genes we used for HTSR are from the blood on the Shroud of Turin," Daniel said. "I give you my solemn oath."

"I will take your word as a true gentleman," Ashley said, his accent suddenly returning.

With great effort, he got his bulky, stiff body up from the couch to a standing position. He extended his hand toward Daniel, who had also gotten to his feet. Once again they shook hands.

"For the rest of my life, I shall be beholden to your efforts and scientific creativity," Ashley said.

"As I shall be to your leadership and political genius in not banning HTSR," Daniel responded.

A wry smile slowly spread across Ashley's otherwise expressionless face. "I like a man with a sense of humor." He let go of Daniel's hand and then extended his toward Stephanie, who'd stood when Daniel had.

Stephanie regarded the proffered hand for a moment, as if debating whether to take it or not. Ultimately, she did and felt her own hand enveloped by Ashley's in a surprisingly powerful grip. After a stiff, prolonged shake and an extended moment of staring into the senator's unblinking eyes, she tried to retrieve her hand, without success. Ashley held on firmly. Although Stephanie could have guessed the episode was a reflection of the senator's Parkinson's disease, her immediate reaction was sudden, irrational fear of being permanently ensnared by the man as a metaphor of her involvement in the whole madcap affair.

"My heartfelt gratitude for your efforts as well, Dr. D'Agostino," Ashley said. "And, as a gentleman, I feel I must make a confession of being enchanted by your considerable beauty from the first moment I had the pleasure of seeing you." Only then did his sausage-shaped fingers slowly release their formidable hold on Stephanie's hand.

Stephanie clasped her now closed fist against her chest, lest Ashley try to grab her again. She knew she was continuing to be irrational, but she couldn't help herself. At least she managed a nod and a half smile in acknowledgment of the senator's compliment and professed gratitude.

"Now," Ashley stated. "I demand you doctors get a good night's rest. I want you both well rested for tomorrow's procedure, which you have led me to assume will not be a lengthy affair. Is that a fair assumption?"

"My guess would be an hour, perhaps a little more," Daniel said.

"Glory be! A little more than an hour is all that modern biotechnology needs to bring this boy back from the precipice and career disaster. I am impressed. Praise be to the Lord on high!"

"Most of the time will be spent fitting you with the stereotaxic frame," Daniel explained. "The actual implantation will only take a few minutes."

"There you go again," Ashley complained. "More incomprehensible doctor's jargon. What in heaven's name is a stereotaxic frame?"

"It is a calibrated frame that fits over your head like a crown. It will enable Dr. Nawaz to inject the treatment cells into the exact location where you have lost your own dopamine-producing cells."

"I'm not at all certain I should be asking this," Ashley said hesitantly. "Am I to believe you will be injecting the treatment cells directly into my brain and not into a vein?"

"That's correct," Daniel started to explain.

"Hold it right there!" Ashley interrupted. "I'm afraid at this point the less I know, the better. I am an admittedly squeamish patient, especially without being put to sleep. Pain and I have never been compatible bedfellows."

"There will be no pain," Daniel assured the senator. "The brain has no sensation itself."

"But a needle has to go into my brain?" Ashley asked in disbelief.

"A blunt needle, to avoid any damage."

"How in God's name do you get a needle into someone's brain?"

"A little hole will be made through the bone. The approach in your case will be prefrontal."

"Prefrontal? That's more doctor gobbledygook."

"It means through the forehead," Daniel explained, pointing to his own forehead just above his eyebrow. "Remember, there will be no pain. You will feel vibration when the hole is made, somewhat like an old-fashioned dental drill, provided you are not asleep from the sedation, which happens to be a strong possibility."

"Why aren't I going to be definitely asleep through all this?"

"The neurosurgeon wants you awake during the actual implantation."

Ashley sighed. "That's quite enough!" he remarked, raising a trembling hand protectively. "I felt better laboring under the delusion the treatment cells went into a vein like a bone-marrow implant."

"It would not work for neurons."

"That's unfortunate, but I will deal with it. Meanwhile, tell me my alias again!"

"John Smith," Daniel said.

"Of course! How could I have forgotten? And you, Dr. D'Agostino, shall be my Pocahontas."

Stephanie managed another weak smile.

"Now!" Ashley said, marshaling his enthusiasm. "It's time for this old country boy to put the concerns of his infirmity aside and head down to the casino. I have an important date with a group of one-armed bandits."

A few minutes later, Daniel and Stephanie were on their way down the hall en route to their room. Stephanie acknowledged their bodyguard as they passed, but Daniel didn't. Daniel was demonstrably irritated, as evidenced by the way he slammed the door when they entered. Their suite was half the size of Ashley's. It had the same view but without the balcony.

"Vigorous! Give me a break!" Daniel snapped. He'd stopped just inside the door with his hands on his hips. "You couldn't think of some better description of our treatment cells than 'vigorous'? What were you doing in there—trying to get him to back out at this juncture? To top it off, you acted like you didn't even want to shake his hand."

"I didn't," Stephanie said. She went over to their single couch and sat down.

"And why the hell not? Good God!"

"I don't respect him, and as I've said ad nauseam, I don't have a good feeling about all of this."

"It was like you were being passive-aggressive in there, pausing before answering simple questions."

"Look! I did my best. I didn't want to lie. Remember, I didn't even want to go in there. You insisted."

Daniel breathed out noisily. He stared at Stephanie. "Sometimes you can be aggravating."

"I'm sorry," Stephanie said. "It's hard for me to pretend. And on the subject of aggravation, you don't do so bad yourself. Next time you are tempted to say 'good girl' to me, restrain yourself."

twenty-four

10:22 A.M., Sunday, March 24, 2002

If, over the years, going to a physician had become emotionally difficult for Ashley Butler because of its unwanted reminder of his mortality, going into a hospital was worse, and his arrival at the Wingate Clinic had been no exception. As much as he joked about his generic alias with Carol in the limo en route and used his Southern charm on the nurses and technicians during admission, he was terrified. The thin veneer of his apparent insouciance was particularly challenged when he met the neurosurgeon, Dr.

Rashid Nawaz. He was not as Ashley had pictured, despite having been told his plainly ethnic name. Prejudice had always played a role in Ashley's thinking, and it was operative now. In his mind, brain surgeons were supposed to be tall, serious, and commanding figures, preferably of Nordic heritage. Instead, he was confronted by a short, slight, dark-skinned individual with even darker lips and eyes. On the positive side was a lilting English accent that reflected his Oxford training. Also on the positive side was an aura of confidence and professionalism leavened with compassion. The man recognized and sympathized with Ashley's plight as a patient facing an unorthodox treatment and was gently reassuring, telling Ashley the upcoming procedure was not at all difficult.

Dr. Carl Newhouse, the anesthesiologist, was more in keeping with Ashley's expectations. As a mildly overweight Englishman with ruddy cheeks, he looked like the Caucasian doctors Ashley had encountered in the past. He was dressed in OR scrubs complete with a hat and a facemask. The facemask was tied around his neck but dangled over his chest. A stethoscope was draped around his neck, and a collection of pens

protruded from his breast pocket. A tourniquet of brown rubber tubing was coiled
around his pants' tie.

With exhaustive thoroughness, Dr. Newhouse had gone over Ashley's medical history, particularly in relation to allergies, drug
reactions, and episodes of anesthesia. While
Dr. Newhouse auscultated and thumped
Ashley's chest as part of a cursory physical
examination, he also started an IV with such
practiced ease that Ashley hardly felt it.
Once it was flowing to Dr. Newhouse's satisfaction, he told Ashley that he'd be giving
him a powerful intravenous cocktail that
would make him feel calm, content, possibly
euphoric, and definitely drowsy.

"The sooner the better," Ashley had
silently voiced. He was more than ready to
feel calm. With his fears about the upcoming
procedure, he'd had difficulty falling asleep
the night before. And on top of the psychological stress, it had not been an easy morning. Following Daniel's advice, he'd avoided
his Parkinson's medication, with consequences more severe than he'd anticipated.
He hadn't appreciated the extent to which
the drugs had been controlling his symptoms. He'd not been able to stop his fingers

from an involuntary rhythmical motion as if he were trying to roll objects in his palms. Worse yet was the stiffness, which he likened to trying to move while totally immersed in gelatin. Carol had to get a wheelchair to get him down to the waiting limo, and two doormen had to struggle to get him from the wheelchair into the car. The arrival at the Wingate had been equally difficult, with equivalent indignity. The only good part of the ordeal was that no one seemed to have recognized him, thanks to his tourist disguise.

Dr. Newhouse's intravenous cocktail had been everything he'd promised and then some. Currently, Ashley felt considerably more content and calm than if he'd downed several tall tumblers of his favorite bourbon, and this was in spite of being seated in a tiled operating room on an operating table cranked up to a sitting position with both arms splayed out to the sides and secured to armboards. Even his tremor was better, or if it wasn't, at least he wasn't aware of it. He was clothed in a skimpy hospital johnny with his stocky, pasty white legs thrust out in front of him. His bare, dry, and bunioned feet with curling yellow toenails pointed up at the ceiling. The IV was in one arm and a blood-pressure cuff around the other. EKG leads were attached to his chest, and the beeping of the readout echoed about the room.

Dr. Nawaz was busy with a tape measure, a marking pen, and a razor, as he prepared Ashley's head for the stereotaxic frame, which Ashley could see next to a collection of sterile instruments on a draped table off to the side. Despite the frame appearing like a torture device, Ashley, in his drugged state, was unconcerned. Nor was he bothered about Dr. Lowell and Dr. D'Agostino, who had appeared with Dr. Spencer Wingate and Dr. Paul Saunders at a window looking out into the operating suite hallway. Dressed in scrubs, the foursome seemed to be watching the preparations as if it were entertainment. Ashley would have liked to wave, but he couldn't with his hands tied. Besides, it was hard to keep his eyes open, much less lift his arms.

"I'll be shaving and prepping small areas on the sides and back of your head," Dr. Nawaz announced, while handing the marking pen and tape measure to Marjorie Hickam, the circulating nurse. "These will be the sites where the frame will be secured to your head, as I explained earlier. Do you understand, Mr. Smith?"

It took a moment for Ashley to remember his assumed name was Mr. Smith and that he was being addressed. "I believe I do," he announced in a slurred monotone. "Perhaps you could shave my face while you're at it. Without my medication, I'm afraid I did less than a commendable job this morning."

Dr. Nawaz laughed at this unexpected humor, as did the other occupants in the room, which included a scrub nurse by the name of Constance Bartolo. She was already gowned and gloved, and stood next to the table with the frame and the instruments as if on guard.

A few minutes later, Dr. Nawaz stepped back and eyed his handiwork. "I'd say that looks rather good. I'll duck out to scrub, then we'll drape, and we can begin."

Despite what should have been a terrifying circumstance of waiting to have a hole drilled into his skull, Ashley fell into a peaceful, dreamless slumber. He was soon partially awakened by the sensation of sterile drapes settling over him, but he rapidly fell back asleep. What succeeded in waking him a few minutes later was a sudden, searing scalp pain on the right side of his head. With great effort, he partially pulled up his heavy eyelids. He even tried to lift his right arm against its restraint.

"Easy!" Dr. Newhouse said. He was standing behind and to the side of Ashley. "Everything is okay!" He laid a restraining hand on Ashley's arm.

"I'm just injecting some local anesthesia," Dr. Nawaz explained. "You might feel a stinging sensation. There are going to be four locations."

"Stinging sensation!" Ashley marveled silently in his stupor. It was just like a doctor to downplay the symptom, because the pain was more like a white-hot knife cutting his scalp away from his skull. Yet Ashley was strangely detached, as if the pain involved someone else and he was a mere observer. It also helped that in each instance, the pain was fleeting, to be replaced by absolute numbness in the area.

Ashley was only vaguely aware of the process of being fitted with the stereotaxic frame. He floated effortlessly in and out of consciousness during the more than half hour of manipulations and adjustments it took to anchor the frame with pins attached firmly to the outer table of his skull. He had no awareness of the past, the future, or the passage of time.

"That should do it," Dr. Nawaz said. He reached up and grasped the calibrated semicircular arms that arched over Ashley's head and gently tested the frame's stability by trying to move it in any direction. It held solidly, with its four setscrews rooted into the senator's cranium. Pleased with the result, Dr. Nawaz stepped back, clasped his sterile, gloved hands against his gowned chest, and cleared his throat. "Miss Hickman, if you would be so kind, please let X ray know we are ready for them."

The circulating nurse stopped in her tracks en route to getting another bottle of IV fluid for Dr. Newhouse. Her gray-blue eyes first looked at her colleague Constance for a modicum of support before meeting Dr. Nawaz's gaze. For the moment, Marjorie was at a loss for words, since she'd had experience during her training with neurosurgeons' short fuses and operating-room tantrums, and she expected the worst.

"I say," Dr. Nawaz announced with an edge to his voice, "let's not dally. It is time for the X ray."

"But we don't have any X ray," Marjorie said hesitantly. She switched her attention to Dr. Newhouse for corroboration, lest she bear the full brunt of responsibility for the current problem.

"What do you mean there's no X ray?" Dr. Nawaz demanded. "You bloody well better have an X ray, or we'll be wrapping up and going home! There's no way I can do an intracranial implantation without an X ray."

"What Majorie means is that these two operating rooms were not set up for X ray," Dr. Newhouse explained. "They were designed primarily for infertility procedures, so they have state-of-the-art ultrasound available. Would that be of assistance?"

"Absolutely not!" Dr. Nawaz snapped. "Ultrasound would be no help whatsoever. I need a full size X ray to get accurate measurements. The frame's three-dimensional reference grid has to be related to the patient's brain. Otherwise, it would be like shooting in the dark. I need some bloody X rays! You mean to tell me you don't even have a portable machine?"

"Unfortunately, no!" Dr. Newhouse said. He waved through the window for Paul Saunders to come into the room.

Paul poked his head through the door while holding a mask to his face. "Is there a problem?"

"You'd better believe there's a bloody problem," Dr. Nawaz complained angrily. "I've been informed belatedly that there is no X ray."

"We have X ray," Paul said. "We even have MRI."

"Well, get the blasted X ray in here!" Dr. Nawaz commanded impatiently.

Paul stepped into the room and looked back out at the others through the window. He waved for them to come in, which they did, holding masks to their faces like he was.

"There is a problem no one thought of," Paul said. "Rashid needs X ray, but the room is not set up for it, and we have no portable unit."

"Oh, for Christ's sake! After all this effort, is it going to come down to this?" Daniel asked rhetorically. Then, looking directly at the neurosurgeon, he said, "Why didn't you mention you needed an X ray?"

"Why didn't you tell me it wasn't available?" Dr. Nawaz retorted. "I've never had the dubious honor of working in a modern OR that didn't have access to X ray."

"Let's think about this a moment and let cooler minds prevail!" Paul suggested. "There has to be a solution here."

"There's nothing to think about," Dr. Nawaz snapped. "I cannot localize an injection into the brain without X rays. It is as simple as that."

Except for the metronomic beeping of the cardiac monitor, the room sank into a strained silence. Everyone avoided locking eyes with anyone else. No one moved.

"Why not take the patient to the X-ray room," Spencer suggested suddenly. "It's not that far."

The others had thought of the idea but dismissed it. Now they reconsidered the suggestion. Taking a patient from the OR to the X-ray room in the middle of a procedure was hardly routine, yet it wasn't out of the question in the current circumstance. The facility was brand-new and practically empty, so contamination was less of an issue than it would have been normally, especially since the craniotomy had not yet been made.

"I have to say it sounds reasonable to me," Daniel said optimistically. "We've got enough hands. We can all help."

"What's your opinion, Rashid?" Paul asked.

Dr. Nawaz shrugged. "I suppose it would work, provided we keep the patient on the OR table. With him sitting up and the stereotaxic frame in place, it would be ill-advised to move him on and off a gurney."

"The OR table is on wheels," Dr. Newhouse reminded everyone.

"Let's do it!" Paul said. "Marjorie, alert our imaging tech we're on our way to X ray."

It took a few minutes for Dr. Newhouse to detach Ashley from the cardiac monitor as well as untie his arms from the armboards. With them sticking out laterally, it would have been impossible to get out through the door. When all was ready and Ashley's hands were safely in his lap, Dr. Newhouse released the wheel lock with his foot. Then, with Dr. Newhouse pushing and Marjorie and Paul pulling, they rolled the OR table into the hallway. Except for the scrub nurse, who remained in the OR, everyone else trooped behind. Ashley stayed asleep and completely oblivious to the unfolding drama, despite his being in a sitting position and being jostled. With his head locked into the futuristic-appearing stereotaxic frame, he could have been a slumbering actor in a science-fiction movie.

Once in the corridor, everyone but Dr. Nawaz lent a hand pushing, although it was hardly necessary. The OR table rolled easily across the composite flooring, with only a quiet rumble from its considerable weight. When the group arrived in X ray, a discussion ensued whether to move Ashley from the OR table to the X-ray table. After weighing the pros and cons, it was decided it was best to leave him on the OR table.

Dr. Nawaz donned a heavy lead apron, as he insisted on personally aligning and supporting Ashley's head while the films were taken. Everyone else retreated back out into the hallway. Ashley never awoke.

"I want the films developed before we move him back," Dr. Nawaz told the technician, when she came in to retrieve the exposed plates. "I want to be absolutely certain they are adequate."

"I'll have them back in a jiffy," the technician said brightly.

Dr. Newhouse returned inside the X-ray room to check Ashley's vital signs. Paul and Spencer accompanied the X-ray technician to await the emergence of the X-ray film from the developer. Daniel and Stephanie found themselves momentarily alone.

"This is like a comedy of errors that's not at all funny," Stephanie whispered, with a disgusted shake of her head.

"That's not fair," Daniel whispered back. "The X-ray misunderstanding was nobody's fault. I can see both sides, and it's already water under the bridge. The X rays have been taken, so the implantation is back on track."

"It doesn't matter if it's anyone's fault or not," Stephanie retorted with a *pshaw.* "It's still a screw-up, and it's been one thing after another from that fateful, rainy night in Washington until now. I keep asking myself what else can go wrong."

"Let's try to be a bit more optimistic," Daniel snapped. "The end is in sight."

Paul and Spencer emerged from the processing room with the technician a few steps behind. Paul clutched the X rays in his hands. "They look good to me," he remarked, as he passed Daniel and Stephanie and went into the X-ray room. The others followed. Paul snapped the films up on the viewing box, switched on the light, and stepped to the side. The images were of Ashley's skull surmounted by the opaque image of the stereotaxic frame.

Dr. Nawaz moved over, and with his nose close to the films, he carefully examined each in turn, orienting himself mostly by the indistinct shadows of fluid-filled ventricles in Ashley's brain. For a moment, no one spoke. The only sound was Ashley's deep breathing briefly obscured by the noise of Dr. Newhouse inflating the blood-pressure cuff on Ashley's arm.

"Well?" Paul questioned.

Dr. Nawaz nodded reluctant approval. "They look okay. They should work." He took out a marking pen, a protractor, and a precision metal ruler. With great care, he located a specific location on each film and marked it with a small X. "That is our target: the pars compacta of the substantia nigra on the right side of the midbrain. Now I have to figure out the x, y, and z coordinates." He set to work drawing lines on the X rays and measuring angles.

"Are you going to do that here?" Paul asked.

"This is a good light box," Dr. Nawaz said. He was preoccupied.

"We should get the patient back to the OR," Dr. Newhouse said. "I'll feel more comfortable with him reattached to the cardiac monitor."

"Good idea," Paul said. He immediately went to the foot of the OR table to lend a hand. Dr. Newhouse released the brake on the wheels.

Both Daniel and Stephanie peered over Dr. Nawaz's shoulder and watched in rapt attention as he plotted the coordinates for the implantation needle, the guide of which would be firmly affixed to the frame.

With Paul pulling and Dr. Newhouse pushing, they maneuvered the OR table out of the X-ray room. Dr. Newhouse kept one hand on Ashley's shoulder to help stabilize him as they moved. It probably wasn't necessary, since Dr. Newhouse had taped Ashley's chest to the cranked-up part of the OR table earlier, but he wanted to be certain.

Once in the hallway, Paul turned to face forward while holding on to the foot of the OR table behind his back. It was easier than trying to walk backward. He continued pulling, but his contribution was more for steering, since the OR table, with its four casters, had a tendency to yaw. Marjorie walked alongside, holding up the IV bottle but also ready to help support Ashley if need be. Spencer brought up the rear, giving occasional orders, which everyone ignored.

"His color is not great," Dr. Newhouse complained in the bright fluorescent illumination of the hallway. "Let's move it!"

Everyone upped the pace.

"His color was pasty from the moment he entered the front door," Spencer said. "I don't think it has changed."

"I want him back on the monitor," Dr. Newhouse said.

"We're here!" Paul announced, as he thrust open the OR door and entered without turning around to face the OR table. In his haste, he failed to align the table with the doorway, causing the table to come in at an angle. The result was that one of the front corners thumped into the metal doorjamb with enough force to cause Ashley's body to jolt against the tape that bound his chest to the table. The inertia of the stereotaxic frame caused a mild whiplash effect, snapping Ashley's head forward obliquely. Both Dr. Newhouse and Marjorie reacted swiftly and caught Ashley's arms, which had also flopped up from the impact.

"Good grief!" Dr. Newhouse blurted.

"Sorry," Paul said guiltily. Since he was mostly responsible for the steering, the collision was his fault more than anyone else's.

"Did the frame hit the doorjamb?" Dr. Newhouse questioned, as he patted Ashley's hand down into his lap.

"No, it missed," said Marjorie, who was on the side of the collision and might have been able to avert it had she seen it coming. It just happened too quickly. She let go of Ashley's arm to push the front of the OR table away from the doorjamb.

"Thank goodness for small favors," Dr. Newhouse said. "At least we didn't contaminate it. If we had, we would have had to start from the beginning."

Constance hurried over from where she was standing at the scrub table. Since she had remained gowned and gloved while everyone had gone down to X ray, she was able to grasp the frame without threatening its sterility, straighten it up along with Ashley's head, and support it.

"Am I finished already?" Ashley asked, sounding inebriated. The collision had jarred him from his drugged repose. He tried to open his eyes, with little success. His lids were only able to struggle to less than halfway open. Sensing the strange weight on his head, he strained to reach up and feel what it was. Dr. Newhouse grabbed his raised arm; Marjorie restrained the other.

"Get the table into position," Dr. Newhouse ordered.

Paul pulled the table to the center of the room. He helped Dr. Newhouse get the arm-boards in place. A moment later, Ashley's arms were appropriately restrained. Ashley helped by immediately falling back asleep. Dr. Newhouse handed the EKG leads to Marjorie, who connected them to the electronic unit. Soon the regular and reassuring beeping of the cardiac monitor replaced the tense silence in the room. Dr. Newhouse took the stethoscope from his ears after taking the blood pressure. "Everything is fine," he announced.

"I should have been more careful," Paul said.

"No harm done," Dr. Newhouse responded. "The frame wasn't compromised. We'll let Dr. Nawaz know so he can check it. Does it feel stable, Constance?"

"Rock-solid," said Constance, who was still supporting the frame.

"Good," Dr. Newhouse said. "I think you can let go now. Thanks for your help."

Constance released her grip tentatively. The frame's position did not change. She returned to stand by the scrub table.

"I guess you were right about the patient's color," Dr. Newhouse called over to Spencer. "There's been no change in his cardiovascular status. At the same time, I think I'll set up a pulse oximeter. Marjorie, could you get one for me from the anesthesia room?"

"No problem," Marjorie said, before disappearing through the door into the adjoining space.

A figure appeared at the window to the hallway and caught Paul's attention. Although the man was dressed in scrubs and was wearing a mask, Paul instantly recognized Kurt Hermann. Paul's pulse rate shot up again after having recovered from the collision with the OR table against the doorjamb. He was nervous, since it was highly unusual for Kurt Hermann to be seen in any building other than admin, where his office was located, and particularly unlikely in the OR suite. Something had to be seriously wrong, especially with the typically restrained Kurt waving for Paul to come out into the hall.

Paul made a beeline for the door and stepped out into the corridor. "What's up?" he asked anxiously.

"I need to talk with you and Dr. Wingate in private."

"What about?"

"The patient's identity. He's not Mob-related."

"Oh, really?" Paul voiced with relief. The last thing he expected was good news. "Who is he?"

"Why don't you get Dr. Wingate."

"Okay! Just a moment!"

Paul returned to the OR and whispered into Spencer's ear. Spencer's eyebrows arched. He made a point to look out the window at Kurt, as if he didn't believe what Paul had just told him. With alacrity, he followed Paul back out into the hallway. Kurt motioned for them to follow him across the corridor and into the OR storeroom. Once there, he made sure the door was closed before turning to stare at his bosses. He didn't have a high regard for either one of them, especially since he was never quite sure who was in control.

"Well?" Spencer questioned. He didn't have the patience with Kurt that Paul had.

"Are you going to tell us or what? Who is he?"

"First, a bit of background," Kurt said in his clipped military style. "I learned from the limo driver that he'd picked up the patient and his woman companion from the Atlantis resort. Through employee contacts at the resort that I'd been provided by the local police, I found out they are staying in the Poseidon Suite, registered to Carol Manning of Washington, D.C."

"Carroll Manning?" Spencer questioned. "I never heard of him. Who the devil is he?"

"Carol Manning is a she," Kurt said. "I had a friend run the name on the mainland. She's the chief of staff of Senator Ashley Butler. I checked with the Bahamian immigration authorities; Senator Butler arrived on the island yesterday. It is my belief the patient is the senator."

"Senator Butler! Of course!" Spencer said, while slapping the top of his head. "You know, I thought I recognized him this morning, but I just couldn't put the face and the name together, at least not with him in that ridiculous tourist outfit."

"Crap!" Paul swore. He jammed his hands

onto his hips and paced in the small area the storeroom afforded. "All this trouble to find out who he is, and he turns out to be a freaking politician. There goes our big payoff."

"Let's not be too hasty here," Spencer said.

"And why the hell not?" Paul said. He stopped and looked at Spencer. "We were counting on the mystery man to be rich and famous. That meant a celebrity like a movie star, a rock star, or sports hero, or at the very least, a prominent CEO. Certainly not a politician!"

"There are politicians and there are politicians," Spencer said. "What could be important to us is that there's been considerable talk of Butler running for the '04 Democratic nomination for President along with everyone else."

"But politicians don't have any money," Paul said. "At least, not any of their own."

"But they have access to people with a lot of money," Spencer said. "That's what's important, particularly with serious Presidential contenders. When the field of Democratic Presidential hopefuls gets whittled down, which it undoubtedly will, there will be lots of money. If Butler runs, and if he does well in the early going, we could get that monetary windfall yet."

"That's a number of big ifs," Paul said with a wry, disbelieving expression. "But regardless, I'm happy with what we've got already. Windfall or not, I got great exposure to HTSR, which we'll profit from greatly, and that's in addition to the forty-five K, which isn't chicken feed. So I'm happy, especially getting Dr. Lowell to sign that statement. He's not going to be able to deny what he's done here, and I'm going to push for that article with the Shroud of Turin twist in the *NEJM*. Publicity will be our big long-term payoff, and for that, a politician is as good or better than any other celebrity."

"I'll be getting back to my normal security duties," Kurt said. He wasn't going to stand there and listen to the drivel of these two buffoons. He stepped to the door and pulled it open.

"Thanks for getting the name," Paul said.

"Yeah, thanks," Spencer added. "We'll try to forget it took you a month and you had to kill someone in the process."

Kurt glared back at Spencer for a moment, then he was gone. The automatic closer pulled the door shut.

"That last comment wasn't fair," Paul complained.

"I know," Spencer said, with a wave of dismissal. "I'm trying to be funny."

"You don't appreciate his contribution around here."

"I guess I don't," Spencer agreed.

"You will when we get up and running at full capacity. Security is going to be a big issue. Trust me!"

"Maybe so, but for now let's get back to the implantation, and let's hope it goes better than it has so far." Spencer pulled open the door and started out.

"Wait a second," Paul said, grabbing Spencer's arm. "Something just occurred to me: Ashley Butler is the senator who has been spearheading the movement to ban Lowell's HTSR. Now that's ironic, since he is now going to be the beneficiary!"

"It's more hypocritical than ironic, if you ask me," Spencer said. "He and Lowell must have come up with some kind of clandestine deal."

"That has to be the case, and if it is, it bodes well for our financial windfall, since both would be committed to keeping it a deep, dark secret."

"I think we're in the driver's seat," Spencer said with a nod. "Now, let's get back in that OR to make sure there are no more problems, so the implantation actually takes place. It was a damn good thing we were around for that X-ray muddle."

"We're going to have to get a portable X-ray machine."

"Let's hold off until we get some cash flow, if you don't mind."

Spencer hesitated just outside the OR door. He turned back to Paul. "I think it is important we don't let on about knowing the senator's true identity."

"Of course," Paul said. "That goes without saying."

twenty-five

11:45 A.M., Sunday, March 24, 2002

For Tony D'Agostino, it was like being caught in a bad dream, unable to wake up, as once again he found himself pulling up to the front of the Castigliano brothers' plumbing supply store. To make matters worse, it was a cold, rainy late March Sunday morning, and there were a thousand other things he'd prefer to be doing, like having a cappuccino and a cannoli in cozy Café Cosenza on Hanover Street.

After opening the car door, Tony first stuck out his umbrella and got it open. Only then did he climb from the car. But his efforts were to no avail. He still got wet. The wind was whipping the rain around so that it was going every which way. It was even a struggle to hold on to the umbrella to keep it from being yanked out of his hand.

Just inside the door, Tony stomped the moisture off his feet, wiped his forehead with the back of his hand, and leaned the umbrella up against the wall. As he passed the counter where Gaetano usually worked, he swore under his breath. There was no doubt in his mind that Gaetano was the one who had screwed up yet again, and he had hoped the hulk would be there so he could give him a piece of his mind.

As usual, the door to the inner office was unlocked, and Tony entered after a cursory knock without waiting for a reply. Both the Castiglianos were at their respective desks, the cluttered surfaces of which were illuminated by the matching desk lamps with green glass shades. With the heavy cloud cover, very little light was coming in through the dirty, small-paned windows facing out over the marsh.

The Castiglianos looked up in unison. Sal had been busy making entries into an old-fashioned ledger book from a stack of crinkled notes. Lou was playing solitaire. Unfortunately, Gaetano was nowhere to be seen.

Following the usual ritual, Tony gave each twin a slapping handshake before sitting down on the sofa. He didn't sit back or even open his coat. He planned on making the visit as short as possible. He cleared his throat. No one had said a word, which was a little strange, especially since he was the one planning to act irritated.

"My mother talked to my sister last night," Tony began. "I want you people to know I'm confused."

"Oh, really?" Lou questioned with a touch of scorn. "Welcome to the club!"

Tony looked from one twin to the other. It was suddenly obvious that both the Castiglianos were in as ugly a mood as he, especially with Lou showing the disrespect of immediately going back to his game of solitaire, snapping his cards on the desktop as he played. Tony looked at Sal, and Sal glared back. Sal appeared more sinister than usual, with his gaunt face illuminated from below with sickly green light. He could have been a corpse.

"Why don't you tell us what you're confused about?" Sal suggested superciliously.

"Yeah, we'd like to hear," Lou added, without interrupting his card playing. "Especially since you're the one who twisted our arms to come up with the hundred K for your sister's scam."

Mildly alarmed at this unexpected cool reception, Tony sat back. Feeling suddenly warm all over, he opened his coat. "I didn't twist anybody's arm," he said indignantly, but as the words escaped his lips, he felt an unpleasant sense of vulnerability wash over him. Belatedly, he questioned the wisdom of coming out to the twin's isolated office without any protection or backup whatsoever. He wasn't packing, but that wasn't unusual. He almost never did, which the twins knew. Yet he certainly had muscle as part of his organization just like the Castiglianos, and he should have brought it along.

"You're not telling us what you are confused about," Sal said, ignoring Tony's rebuttal.

Tony cleared his throat again. With his mounting uneasiness, he decided it best to mellow his anger. "I'm a bit confused about what Gaetano did on his second trip to Nassau. A week ago, my mother told me she'd had difficulty getting ahold of my sister. She said that when she did, my sister acted weird, like something bad had happened that she didn't want to talk about until she got home, which was going to be soon. Obviously, I thought Gaetano had done his job and the professor was history. Well, last night my mother managed to get my sister again, since she hadn't shown up. This time she was, in my mother's words, 'back to her old self,' saying she and the professor were still in Nassau, but that they were coming home in just a few days. I mean, what gives?"

For a few tense minutes, no one said anything. The only noise in the room was Lou's cards intermittently snapping on the desktop, combined with the sound of seagulls squawking out in the marsh.

Tony made a point of looking around the room, which was mostly lost in shadow despite the hour. "Speaking of Gaetano, where is he?" The last thing Tony wanted was a surprise coming from the twins' enforcer.

"That's a question we've been asking ourselves," Sal said.

"What the hell do you mean?"

"Gaetano has yet to come back from Nassau," Sal said. "He's AWOL. We haven't heard boo since he left the last time you came over here, nor has his brother and sister-in-law, who he's close to. Nobody has heard a goddamn thing. Not a peep."

If Tony thought he was confused before, now he was dumbfounded. Although he had been complaining about Gaetano recently, he respected the man as an experienced professional, and, as a connected man, Tony assumed Gaetano would be unquestionably loyal. His going AWOL didn't make any sense.

"Needless to say, we're a tiny bit baffled ourselves," Sal added.

"Have you made any inquiries?" Tony asked.

"Inquiries?" Lou questioned sarcastically, finally looking up from his solitaire. "Why would we do a crazy thing like that? Hell, no! We've just been sitting here day after day, chewing our fingernails, waiting for the phone to ring."

"We called the Spriano family in New York," Sal said, ignoring his brother's sarcasm. "In case you didn't know, we're distantly related. They're checking into it for us. Meanwhile, they're in the process of sending us another assistant, who should be getting here in a day or so. They were the ones that sent us Gaetano in the first place."

A shiver of fear creeped up Tony's spine. He knew the Spriano organization was one of the most powerful and ruthless families on the East Coast. He'd had no idea the twins were associated, which put everything in a more serious and worrisome category. "What about the Miami Colombians who were to supply the gun?" he asked to change the topic.

"We called them too," Sal said. "They're never overly cooperative, as you know, but they said they'd check it out. So there are feelers out there. Obviously, we want to know where the moron is holed up and why."

"Is any of your money missing?" Tony asked.

"Nothing Gaetano could have taken," Sal said enigmatically.

"Weird," Tony remarked, for a lack of anything else to say. He didn't know what Sal meant, but he wasn't about to ask. "I'm sorry you're having this problem." He moved forward on the couch as if he were about to get to his feet.

"It's more than weird." Lou sneered. "And

sorry ain't good enough. We've been talking about all this over the last few days, and I think you should know how we feel. Ultimately, we hold you responsible for this foul-up with Gaetano, however it plays out, and also for our one hundred K, which we're going to want back with interest. The interest will be at our usual rate from the day we handed it over and is nonnegotiable. And one last thing: We now consider the loan overdue."

Tony abruptly stood up. His rising anxiety had reached a critical point after hearing Lou's comments and thinly veiled threat. "Let me know if you hear anything," he said, heading for the door. "Meanwhile, I'll make a few inquiries myself."

"You better start making inquiries about how you are going to raise the hundred grand," Sal said, "because we're not going to be all that patient."

Tony hurried out of the store, oblivious to the rain. He was perspiring, despite the chill. It was only after he'd leaped into his car that he remembered his umbrella. "Screw it!" he said out loud. He got the Caddy going, and with his arm hooked over the back of the front seat, he looked out the rear window and gunned the engine. With a shower of pebbles, the car lurched out into the street. A moment later, he had the Cadillac up to almost fifty miles per hour, heading back into the city.

Tony relaxed to a degree and dried each palm off in turn on his pant legs. The immediate threat was over, but he knew intuitively that a much larger long-term threat was looming on the horizon, especially if the Sprianos became involved, no matter how tangentially. It was all very discouraging, if not frightening. Just when he was mobilizing his resources to fight his indictment, he was now facing a possible turf war.

John! Can you hear me?" Dr. Nawaz called. He had leaned over while holding up the edge of the sterile drapes hanging down over Ashley's face. Most of the stereotaxic frame anchored to Ashley's skull as well as Ashley himself was covered by drapes, exposing only a portion of the right side of the senator's forehead. There, Dr. Nawaz had made a small skin incision, now held open with a clamped skin retractor.

After exposing the bare bone, Dr. Nawaz had used a special power drill to make a small, eleven-sixteenth-inch-diameter craniotomy hole to expose the grayish-white fascial coverings of the brain. Directly aligned with the hole and firmly attached to one of the arches of the stereotaxic frame was the implantation needle. With the help of the X rays, the correct angles had been determined, and already the needle had been inserted through the brain's coverings, into the outer part of the brain itself. At this point, it was only necessary to advance the needle to the exact, predetermined depth to reach the targeted substantia nigra.

"Dr. Newhouse, perhaps you could nudge the patient for me," Dr. Nawaz said in his melodious, Pakistani-English accent. "At this point, I would prefer the patient to be awake."

"Of course," Dr. Newhouse said, getting to his feet and putting aside a magazine he was reading. He reached under the drapes and gave Ashley's shoulder a shake.

Ashley's heavily lidded eyes struggled open.

"Can you hear me now, John?" Dr. Nawaz asked again. "We need your help."

"Of course I can hear you," Ashley said, his voice thick with sleep.

"I want you to tell me if you have any sen-

sations whatsoever over the next few minutes. Can you do that?"

"What do you mean 'sensations'?"

"Like images, thoughts, sounds, odors, or
sense of movement: anything at all you notice."

"I'm very sleepy."

"I appreciate that, but try to stay awake for
just these few minutes. As I said, we need
your help."

"I'll try."

"That's all we can ask," Dr. Nawaz said. He
lowered the drape, obscuring Ashley's face.
He turned and gave a thumbs-up to the
group standing outside the window in the
hall. Then, after flexing his latex-gloved fingers, he used the micromanipulator wheel
on the guide holding the implantation needle. Slowly, millimeter by millimeter, he advanced the blunt implantation needle into the
depths of Ashley's brain. When the needle
was halfway in, he again lifted the edge of
the drape. He was pleased to see Ashley's
eyes still open, although barely. "Are you doing okay?" he asked the senator.

"Lovely," Ashley said, with a trace of
Southern accent. "As happy as a pig in a
poke."

"You are doing fine," Dr. Nawaz said. "It won't be much longer."

"Take your time. The important thing is that it is done right."

"There's never a question about that," Dr. Nawaz responded. He smiled beneath his surgical mask as he lowered the drape and returned to advancing the needle. He was impressed with Ashley's courage and good humor. A few minutes later and with a final twist of the micromanipulator, he stopped at the exact measured depth. After a final check of Ashley's status, he told Marjorie to ask Dr. Lowell to come into the room. Meanwhile, he readied the syringe that was to deliver the treatment cells.

"Everything going okay?" Daniel asked. He had donned a facemask as he entered. With his hands clasped behind his back, he bent over to look into the craniotomy hole with its imbedded needle.

"Very well," Dr. Nawaz said. "But there is a problem I admit slipped my mind in the earlier fracas. At this stage, it is customary to take another corroborating X ray to be one hundred percent certain of the needle tip's location. However, without X ray here in the OR, that is not possible. With the craniotomy open and the needle inserted, the patient cannot be safely moved."

"Are you asking for my opinion whether to proceed?"

"Precisely. Ultimately, he is your patient. In this rather unique situation, I am, as you Americans say, only a hired gun."

"How confident are you of your needle's position?"

"Very confident. In all my experience with the stereotaxic frame, I have never not been where I targeted. There is also another reassuring factor in this case. We are adding cells, not doing ablative surgery, which is what I am usually doing with this procedure and which would cause far more problems if the needle were to be slightly off."

"It is hard to argue with a one hundred percent record. I'm confident we're in good hands. Let's do it!"

"Right you are!" Dr. Nawaz said. He picked up the syringe, now loaded with the predetermined aliquot of treatment cells. After removing the trocar from the lumen of the imbedded implantation needle, he attached the syringe. "Dr. Newhouse, I'm ready to begin the implantation."

"Thank you," Dr. Newhouse said. He liked

to be informed at critical stages of a procedure, and he quickly rechecked the vital signs. When he was done and had taken the stethoscope from his ears, he motioned for Dr. Nawaz to go ahead.

After raising the drape and having Dr. Newhouse give Ashley another nudge to wake him, Dr. Nawaz repeated the same instructions he'd given Ashley before inserting the needle. Only then did he start the implantation, utilizing another manual mechanical-assist device to depress the syringe's plunger in a slow, even fashion.

Daniel felt a chill of excitement as he watched the implantation proceed. As the cloned dopamine-producing neurons augmented with genes from the blood on the Shroud of Turin were being slowly deposited in Ashley's brain, he was confident medical history was in the making. In one fell swoop, the promise of stem cells, therapeutic cloning, and HTSR was being realized to cure a major human degenerative disease for the first time. With a sense of mounting exhilaration, he turned and flashed Stephanie a victory sign with his index and middle fingers. Self-consciously, Stephanie returned the gesture, with hardly the same alacrity. Daniel assumed it was because she was uncomfortable having to stand alongside Paul Saunders and Spencer Wingate and make small talk.

Midway through the implantation, Dr. Nawaz stopped as he'd done during the needle insertion. When he lifted the edge of the drape, he discovered that Ashley had fallen back asleep.

"Do you want me to wake him?" Dr. Newhouse questioned.

"Please," Dr. Nawaz responded. "And maybe you could try to keep him awake for the next few minutes."

Ashley's eyes struggled open in response to being jostled. Dr. Newhouse's hand was gripping his shoulder.

"Are you okay, Mr. Smith?" Dr. Nawaz asked.

"Delightful," Ashley mumbled. "Are we finished?"

"Almost! Just a moment longer!" Dr. Nawaz said. After letting go of the drape, he looked at Dr. Newhouse. "Is everything stable?"

"Rock solid."

Dr. Nawaz went back to depressing the syringe's plunger. He continued at the same slow, controlled rate. At the moment he was about to give the mechanical-assist device the final twist, which would have delivered the last bit of treatment cells, Ashley mumbled something unintelligible beneath the drapes. Dr. Nawaz stopped, glanced at Dr. Newhouse, and asked if he'd understood what Ashley had said.

"I couldn't hear it either," Dr. Newhouse admitted.

"Is everything still stable?"

"There's been no change," Dr. Newhouse said. He put the earpieces of the stethoscope back in his ears to recheck the blood pressure. Meanwhile, Dr. Nawaz raised the edge of the drape and peered in at Ashley. The appearance of his face, which was visible only to the level of his eyebrows because of the frame, had changed rather dramatically. Curiously, the corners of his mouth were drawn up, and his nose was wrinkled in an expression that suggested disgust. This was even more surprising, because earlier his face had been demonstrably blank, a symptom of his disease.

"Is there something bothering you?" Dr. Nawaz asked.

"What is that awful stink?" Ashley questioned. He still sounded drunk, with his words running together.

"You tell us!" Dr. Nawaz said, with the stirrings of concern. "What does it smell like?"

"Pig shit, if I had to guess. What the hell are you people doing?"

An intuition of potential disaster spread through Dr. Nawaz like a faint, unpleasant electric current leaving a weak feeling in his stomach that only experienced surgeons know. He glanced at Daniel for consolation, but Daniel merely shrugged. With limited personal surgical experience, Daniel was only confused. "Pig manure? What's that about?" he asked.

"Since there are no pigs in here, I'm afraid he's having an olfactory hallucination," Dr. Nawaz said, as if angry.

"Is that a problem?"

"Let's put it this way," Dr. Nawaz snapped. "It worries me. We can all hope it's nothing, but I recommend we forego the last bit of implantation cells. Do you agree? We've given well over ninety percent."

"If there is any question, absolutely," Daniel said. He didn't care about the last of the treatment cells. The amount he had decided on had been a mere educated guess, based on the mouse experiments. What bothered him was Dr. Nawaz's reaction. He could tell the man was concerned, but he had no idea why a bad smell would be so worrisome. But the last thing Daniel needed was a complication of any sort, especially not when they were this close to success.

"I'm withdrawing the needle," Dr. Nawaz said for Dr. Newhouse's benefit, although there was no inhalation anesthesia to lighten up. With the same amount of care Dr. Nawaz had used for the insertion, he slowly extracted the implantation needle. Once its tip cleared the brain, Dr. Nawaz checked for any sign of bleeding from the site. Thankfully, there was none.

"Needle out!" Dr. Nawaz announced and handed it over to Constance. He took a deep breath and then lifted the edge of the drape to look in at Ashley. He could sense Daniel was looking over his shoulder. Ashley's expression of revulsion had changed to irritation. His mouth was now set, with his lips pressed together in a thin line. His eyes were open wider and his nares flared.

"Are you all right, Mr. Smith?" Dr. Nawaz asked.

"I want to get the hell out of here," Ashley snapped.

"Do you still smell that odor?"

"What odor?"

"You complained about a bad smell just a moment ago."

"I don't know what the hell you are talking about. All I know is I want out of here!" Suddenly intent on standing up, Ashley strained against the tape holding his torso to the cranked-up operating table and against the tape on his wrists. At the same time, he drew his legs up, bringing his knees to his chest.

"Hold him down!" Dr. Nawaz shouted. He leaned across Ashley's lap, trying to force Ashley's legs back down flat with the weight of his body. Dr. Nawaz was still holding up the edge of the drape, watching Ashley's face turn red with effort.

Daniel dashed to the foot of the operating table and reached in under the drapes to grasp Ashley's ankles. He tried to pull them down and was surprised at Ashley's strength of resistance. Dr. Newhouse had released the hold he had on Ashley's shoulder to grab his wrist, which Ashley had succeeded in freeing from its taped restraint. Marjorie leapt around the table to grab Ashley's other arm, which was also coming free.

"Mr. Smith, calm down!" Dr. Nawaz shouted. "Everything is okay!"

"Get off me, you freaking animals," Ashley shouted back. He sounded like the quintessential belligerent drunk, resisting all efforts to be constrained.

Stephanie, Paul, and Spencer came flying into the operating room while struggling to get their facemasks in place. They lent a hand holding Ashley down, giving Marjorie a chance to reinforce the wrist restraints and helping Daniel get Ashley's legs flat again. With his hands free, Dr. Newhouse rechecked Ashley's blood pressure. The beeping of the cardiac monitor had increased its tempo considerably. Marjorie briefly left the room to get a pair of leather ankle restraints.

"Everything is okay," Dr. Nawaz repeated to Ashley once they had him under control. He stared at the man's defiant, enraged face, which was beet-red from exertion. "You must calm down! We have to close your little incision, and we will be done. Then you can get up. Do you understand?"

"You're all a bunch of perverts. Get the fuck off me!"

Ashley's use of such inappropriate and objectionable language in the operating room stunned everyone almost as much as his sudden physical struggling. For a beat, no one moved or said a word.

Dr. Nawaz was the first to recover. Now that he was confident Ashley was restrained, he raised himself from lying across Ashley's lap. As he did so, everyone noticed Ashley had a full penile erection that tented up the drapes.

"Please let go of my hands and feet!" Ashley said tearfully, as he began to cry. "They are bleeding."

Everyone's eyes immediately looked at Ashley's hands and feet, particularly Daniel, who was still holding Ashley's ankles as Marjorie struggled to put on the restraints.

"There's no blood," Paul said, speaking for the group. "What's he talking about?"

"John, listen to me!" Dr. Nawaz said. He was still holding up the flap of drape to expose Ashley's face from the eyebrows down. "Your hands and feet are not bleeding. You are fine. You just have to relax for a few more minutes to allow me to finish."

"My name is not John," Ashley said softly. The tears had disappeared as quickly as they had appeared. Although he still sounded inebriated, he seemed suddenly at peace.

"If it is not John, what is it?" Dr. Nawaz asked.

Daniel shot a worried glance at Stephanie, who had taken a step back from the OR table after having helped restrain one of Ashley's hands. On top of Daniel's bewilderment, he was now concerned that Ashley was about to reveal his true identity in his drugged state. What that would do to the final outcome of the project he had no idea, but it couldn't be good, not with all the requisite secrecy so far.

"My name is Jesus," Ashley said softly, as he beatifically closed his eyes.

Most everyone in the room was again dumbfounded and exchanged bemused glances, but not Dr. Nawaz. His response was to ask Dr. Newhouse what he had given the patient as a sedative before the procedure.

"Intravenous diazepam and fentanyl," Dr. Newhouse answered.

"Do you feel comfortable giving him another dose immediately?"

"Sure," Dr. Newhouse said. "Do you want me to?"

"Please," Dr. Nawaz said.

Dr. Newhouse pulled out the drawer on his anesthesia cart, took out a fresh syringe, and tore open the packaging. With practiced hands, he drew up the medication and injected it into the intravenous port on the IV line.

"Forgive them, Father," Ashley said without opening his eyes, "for they know not what they do."

"What's going on here?" Paul asked in a forced whisper. "Does this guy think he's Jesus Christ being crucified?"

"Is this some kind of weird drug reaction?" Spencer asked.

"I doubt it," Dr. Nawaz said. "But whatever its cause, it is certainly a seizure!"

"Seizure?" Paul questioned with incredulity. "This is like no seizure I've ever seen."

"It's called a complex partial seizure," Dr. Nawaz said. "Better known as a temporal lobe seizure."

"What caused it, if not the drugs?" Paul asked. "Sticking the needle into his brain?"

"If it had been the needle, I think it would

have occurred earlier," Dr. Nawaz said. "Since it occurred near the end of the implantation, I think we have to assume it was that." He looked at Dr. Newhouse. "Check to see if he is asleep?"

Dr. Newhouse reached under the drape and gave Ashley's shoulder a gentle shake. "Any response?" he asked Dr. Nawaz.

Dr. Nawaz shook his head and lowered the drape over Ashley's face. He sighed beneath his face mask and turned to look at Daniel. He crossed his still sterile and gloved hands across his gowned chest.

Daniel felt his legs turn rubbery as he looked into the neurosurgeon's dark, unblinking eyes. Daniel could tell he was troubled, which undermined the composure Daniel had been strenuously maintaining. The fear of a complication, which had been floating in the background of his mind since Ashley's complaint about a smell, came flooding back with the force of a burst dam.

"I believe you can let go of the patient's ankles," Dr. Nawaz said.

Daniel released his grip, which he had been absently maintaining, even after Marjorie had secured the ankle restraints.

"This seizure has me concerned," Dr.

Nawaz said. "Not only do I believe it was not caused by the drugs, the fact that it occurred with the drugs on board suggests it was a particularly violent focal brain disturbance."

"Why couldn't it be drug-related?" Daniel asked, with more hope than reason. "Couldn't it just be like a drug-induced dream? I mean, intravenous diazepam and fentanyl is a potent mix. Combining such a concoction with the suggestively emotive power of the Shroud of Turin is bound to cause wild flights of fancy."

"What does the Shroud of Turin have to do with this?" Dr. Nawaz asked.

"It has to do with the treatment cells," Daniel said. "It's a long story, but prior to the cloning process, a few of the patient's genes were replaced with genes obtained from the blood on the Shroud of Turin. It was a specific request by the patient, who believes in the shroud's authenticity. He even said he was hoping for divine intervention."

"I suppose such ideation could play a role in the patient's delusion," Dr. Nawaz said. "But the fact that this was a seizure that occurred with the implantation cannot be denied."

"But how can you be so sure?" Daniel asked.

"Because of the timing and because of the olfactory hallucination," Dr. Nawaz said. "The smell he reported was an aura, and a characteristic of a temporal lobe seizure is that it begins with an aura. Other characteristics are hyperreligiosity, profound mood changes, intense libidinal urges, and aggressive behavior, all of which the patient demonstrated in the short time he was awake. It was a classic example."

"What should we do?" Daniel asked, although he was afraid to hear the answer.

"Pray that it was a one-time phenomenon," Dr. Nawaz said. "Unfortunately, with the intensity the focus undoubtedly had, I would be surprised if he doesn't develop full-blown temporal lobe epilepsy."

"There isn't anything that can be done prophylacticlly?" Stephanie asked.

"What I'd like to do but know I can't is image the treatment cells," Dr. Nawaz said. "I'd like to see where they went. Maybe then we could do something."

"What do you mean where they went?" Daniel demanded. "You told me with your experience using the stereotaxic frame for injections, you have never had a problem of not being where you were supposed to be."

"True, but I have also never had a patient develop a seizure during a procedure like this," Dr. Nawaz said. "Something is amiss."

"Are you suggesting the cells might not be in the substantia nigra?" Daniel protested. "If so, I don't want to hear it."

"Listen!" Dr. Nawaz shot back. "You're the one who encouraged me to go ahead with this procedure without the appropriate X-ray capability."

"Let's not argue," Stephanie interjected. "The treatment cells can be imaged."

All eyes turned to her.

"We incorporated a gene for an insect cell surface receptor in the treatment cells," Stephanie explained. "We did the same thing with our mouse experiments, specifically for imaging purposes. We have a monoclonal antibody containing a radiopaque heavy metal devised by a contributing radiologist. It's sterile and ready for use. It just has to be injected into the cerebrospinal fluid in the subarachnoid space. With the mice, it worked perfectly."

"Where is it?" Dr. Nawaz asked.

"Over in the lab in building one," Stephanie said. "It is sitting on our desk in our assigned office."

"Marjorie," Paul said. "Call over to Megan Finnigan in the lab! Have her get the antibody and bring it over here on the double."

twenty-six

2:15 P.M., Sunday, March 24, 2002

Dr. Jeffrey Marcus was a local radiologist on the staff at Doctors Hospital on Shirley Street in downtown Nassau. Spencer had made a deal with him that he would cover the Wingate Clinic's radiological needs on an ad hoc basis until a full-time radiologist could be justified. As soon as it was decided a CAT scan was needed for Ashley, Spencer had a nurse call Jeffrey. Since it was a Saturday afternoon, he was able to come immediately. Dr. Nawaz had been pleased because he was acquainted with Jeffrey from Oxford and knew him to have significant neuroradiological experience.

"These are transverse sections of the brain, starting at the dorsal edge of the pons," Jeffrey said, pointing at the computer monitor with the eraser end of an old-fashioned, yellow number-two Dixon pencil. Jeffrey Marcus was an English expatriate who had fled to the Bahamas to escape England's weather, just like Dr. Carl New-house. "We'll be traveling cephalad in one-centimeter increments and should be at the level of the substantia nigra in one or two frames, at most."

Jeffrey was sitting in front of the computer. Standing to his right and bending over for a better view was Dr. Nawaz. Daniel stood immediately to Jeffrey's left. By the window facing into the CAT-scan room stood Paul, Spencer, and Carl. Carl was holding a syringe loaded with another dose of sedative, but it had not been necessary. Ashley had not awakened since the second dose and had slept through his craniotomy hole being stitched closed over a metal button, the stereotaxic frame being removed, and his being transferred to the CAT-scan table. At the moment, Ashley was lying supine with his head inside the opening of the giant, donut-shaped machine. His hands were crossed on his chest with the wrist restraints in place but not secured. The IV was still running. He appeared to be the picture of peaceful slumber.

Stephanie was in the background, away from the others and leaning against a countertop with her arms crossed. Unbeknownst to anyone, she was fighting back tears. She hoped no one would address her, because if they did, she feared that she would lose control. She thought about walking out of the room but then worried that doing so would draw too much attention, so she stayed where she was and suffered in silence. Without even looking at the upcoming CAT scan, her intuition told her there had been a major complication with the implantation, and it had broken the back of her emotional control, which had been strained by everything that had happened during the last month. She berated herself for not listening to her intuition back at the beginning of this farcical and now potentially tragic affair.

"Okay, here we go!" Jeffrey said, pointing again at the image on the monitor. "This is the midbrain, and this is the area of the substantia nigra, and I'm afraid there is no radiolucency one would expect from a heavy-metal-tagged monoclonal antibody."

"Maybe the antibody has yet to diffuse from the cerebrospinal fluid into the brain," Dr. Nawaz suggested. "Or maybe there is no unique surface antigen on the treatment cells. Are you sure the gene you inserted was expressed?"

"I'm certain," Daniel said. "Dr. D'Agostino checked."

"Maybe we should repeat this in a few hours," Dr. Nawaz said.

"With our mice, we saw it within thirty minutes and maximum at forty-five minutes," Daniel said. He looked at his watch. "The human brain is bigger, but we used more antibody, and it's been an hour. We should see it. It's got to be there."

"Wait!" Jeffrey said. "Here's some diffuse radiolucency laterally." He moved the tip of the eraser a centimeter to the right. The spots of lucency were subtle, like tiny flakes of snow on a ground-glass background.

"Oh my God!" Dr. Nawaz blurted. "That's in the mesial part of the temporal lobe. No wonder he had a seizure."

"Let's look at the next slice," Jeffrey said,

as the new image started to wipe out the old from the top, moving down the screen as if unrolling.

"Now it is even more apparent," Jeffrey said. He tapped the screen with his eraser. "I'd say it is in the area of the hippocampus, but to precisely locate it, we'd have to get some air into the temporal horn of the lateral ventricle. Do you want to do that?"

"No!" Dr. Nawaz snapped. He straightened up, clasping his hands to his head. "How the bloody hell could the needle have been so far off? I don't believe this. I even went back and looked at the X rays, remeasured, and then checked the settings on the guide. They were all absolutely correct." He lifted his hands from his head and spread them in the air as if pleading for someone to explain what had happened.

"Maybe the frame moved a bit when we hit the doorframe with the OR table?" Carl Newhouse suggested.

"What are you saying?" Dr. Nawaz demanded. "You told me the table brushed the doorframe. What exactly do you mean by 'hit'?"

"When did the OR table touch the doorframe?" Daniel asked. It was the first time he had heard anything about it. "And what door-frame are you talking about?"

"Dr. Saunders said it brushed," Carl said, ignoring Daniel. "Not me."

Dr. Nawaz looked over at Paul questioningly. Paul reluctantly nodded. "I suppose it was more of a hit than a brush, but it doesn't matter. Constance said the frame was anchored solidly when she grabbed ahold of it."

"Grabbed it?" Dr. Nawaz yelled. "What necessitated her having to grab the frame?"

There was an uncomfortable pause as Paul and Carl exchanged glances.

"What is this, a conspiracy?" Dr. Nawaz demanded. "Somebody answer me!"

"There was kind of a whiplash effect," Carl said. "I was in a hurry to get the patient back on the monitor, so we were pushing the table rather quickly. Unfortunately, it wasn't aligned with the OR doorway. After the bump occurred, Constance came over to support the frame. She was still gowned and gloved. At that point, we were concerned about contamination, since the patient had awakened and his hands weren't restrained. But there wasn't any contamination."

"Why didn't you tell me all this when it happened?" Dr. Nawaz snapped.

"We did tell you," Paul said.

"You told me the table brushed the door frame. That is a far cry from hitting it hard enough to cause whiplash."

"Well, whiplash might be an exaggeration," Carl said, correcting himself. "The patient's head fell forward. It didn't snap back or anything like that."

"Good God!" Dr. Nawaz mumbled with discouragement. He sat down heavily in a desk chair. He pulled off his surgical hat with one hand and gripped his scalp with the other while he shook his head in frustration. He couldn't believe he'd allowed himself to get caught up in such a burlesque affair. It was now clear to him that the stereotaxic frame had to have slightly rotated as well as tipped down, either on impact or when the scrub nurse grasped it.

"We've got to do something!" Daniel said. It had taken him a moment to recover from the revelation about the OR table's collision with the doorframe and its possible tragic consequences.

"And what do you suggest?" Dr. Nawaz questioned derisively. "We've mistakenly implanted a host of rogue, dopamine-producing cells in the man's temporal lobe.

It's not like we can go back in there and suck them out."

"No, but we can destroy them before they arborize," Daniel said, with a flicker of hope beginning to crackle like a fire in his imagination. "We have the monoclonal antibody to the cell's unique surface antigen. Instead of attaching the antibody to a heavy metal like we did for X-ray visualization, we bind it to a cytotoxic agent. Once we inject this combination into the cerebrospinal fluid, bam! The misplaced neurons are annihilated. Then we merely do another implantation on the patient's left side, and we're home free."

Dr. Nawaz smoothed back his shiny black hair and gave Daniel's idea a moment of thought. On the one hand, the idea of potentially rectifying a disaster for which he shared a significant responsibility was enticing, even if the method was unorthodox, but on the other hand, his intuition told him he shouldn't allow himself to be dragged in any further by doing yet another highly experimental procedure.

"Do you have this cytotoxic antibody combination on hand?" Dr. Nawaz asked. There was no harm in asking.

"No," Daniel admitted. "But I'm certain we

could get it concocted on a rush basis by the same firm that supplied us with the antibody heavy-metal combination, and then have it overnighted."

"Well, you let me know if and when you get it," Dr. Nawaz railed as he stood up. "I said a second ago that we couldn't go back in and suck out the misplaced treatment cells. The unfortunate irony is that if nothing is done and the patient ends up with the kind of temporal lobe epilepsy he most likely will, he'll probably have to undergo something along those lines in the future. But it would be serious, ablative neurosurgery, requiring the removal of a lot of brain tissue with high attendant risk."

"That strengthens the rationale for doing what I have proposed," Daniel said, progressively warming to the idea.

Stephanie abruptly pushed away from the countertop and headed for the door. Her fragile emotions and fear of calling attention to herself notwithstanding, she couldn't bear to hear another word of this exchange. It was as if the conversation involved an inanimate object rather than an iatrogenically stricken fellow human being. She was particularly appalled at Daniel, because she could tell that despite the dreadful complication, he was still maneuvering like a modern medical Machiavelli, in blind pursuit of his own entrepreneurial interests despite the moral consequences.

"Stephanie!" Daniel called, seeing her heading for the door. "Stephanie, why don't you call Peter up in Cambridge and have him . . ."

The door closed behind Stephanie, cutting Daniel's voice off. She began to run down the hall. She fled toward the ladies' room, where she hoped she could cry in peace. She was upset about a lot of things, but mainly because she knew that she was as responsible as anyone for what had happened.

twenty-seven

7:42 P.M., Sunday, March 24, 2002

"Now, I do not mean to be a bother to you talented folks," Ashley said, drawing out the words in his prototypal drawl. "And I do not mean to seem unappreciative of all your efforts. I apologize from the bottom of my heart if it distresses you, but there is no way I can stay here tonight."

Ashley was sitting up in a hospital bed with the back cranked up as high as it would go. Gone was the hospital johnny, and in its place was his wacky tourist outfit. The only evidence of his recent surgery was a double-wide bandage on his forehead.

The room was one of the Wingate's inpatient rooms, and it appeared more like a hotel than a hospital. The colors were all bright tropical hues, particularly the walls, which were peach, and the drapes, which were a combination of seafoam green and hot pink. Daniel was standing to Ashley's immediate right in his efforts to dissuade the senator from leaving the clinic. Stephanie was standing at the foot of the bed. Carol Manning was ensconced in a purple club chair near the window with her shoes on the floor and her feet tucked in underneath her.

After the CAT scan, Ashley had been brought to the room and put in the bed to sleep off his sedation. Both Dr. Nawaz and Dr. Newhouse had left after they were certain Ashley was stable. Both had given Daniel cell phone numbers to be called if and when there was a problem, particularly a seizure recurrence. Dr. Newhouse had also left a vial of the fentanyl and diazepam combination that had been so effective, with the instructions that two cc's should be given either intramuscularly or intravenously if the need arose.

Technically, Ashley was under the care of an impeccably groomed nurse by the name of Myron Hanna, who had been the Wingate Clinic's recovery room nurse back in Massachusetts. But Daniel and Stephanie had stayed at the bedside, along with Carol Manning, for the four hours it had taken Ashley to wake up. Paul Saunders and Spencer Wingate had stayed for a while as well, but they had left after an hour with assurances that they too could be reached if needed.

"Senator, you are forgetting what I told you," Daniel said with as much patience as he could muster. At times, it seemed that dealing with the senator was like dealing with a three-year-old.

"No, I understand there was a little problem during the procedure," Ashley said, quieting Daniel by laying his hand on Daniel's folded arms. "But I feel fine now. In fact, I feel like the spring chicken that I know I'm not, which is a tribute to your Aesculapian powers. You told me before the implantation that I might not notice much change for a few days, and even then it might be gradual, but that is clearly not the case. In comparison to how I felt this morning, I'm already cured. My tremor is almost gone, and I am moving with considerably more ease."

"I'm glad you feel that way," Daniel said with a shake of his head. "But it's probably due more to your positive attitude or to the strong sedatives you were given than anything else. Senator, we believe you need more treatment, as I told you, and it is safer to remain here in the clinic, with all the medical resources at our fingertips. Remember, you had a seizure during the procedure, and while you were having the seizure, you acted like a completely different person."

"How could I act like someone else? I have trouble enough being myself." Ashley laughed, although no one else did. He looked around at the others. "What is wrong with you people? You all are behaving like this is a funeral rather than a celebration. Is it truly hard for you to believe how good I feel?"

Daniel had told Carol that the treatment cells had been placed inadvertently in an area slightly wide of where they were intended. Although he had downplayed the seriousness of the complication, he did tell her about the seizure episode and his worry that there might be more, and he admitted to the need for more treatment. Because of the presence of the restraints on Ashley's wrists and ankles, he had even acknowledged the collective concern about what was going to happen when Ashley woke up. Luckily, such worries were proved to be unfounded, since Ashley awakened with his normal, histrionic personality as if nothing had happened. The first thing he did was insist the restraints be removed so he could get out of bed. Once that was accomplished and the slight dizziness went away, he demanded to put on his street clothes. At that point, he was ready to go back to the hotel.

Sensing he was losing the argument, Daniel glanced at Stephanie and then at Carol, but neither elected to come to his aid. Daniel looked back at Ashley. "How about we negotiate," he said. "You stay here in the clinic for twenty-four hours, and then we'll talk again."

"Obviously you've had scant experience negotiating," Ashley said with another laugh. "But I will not hold that against you. The fact of the matter is that you cannot keep me here against my will. It is my desire to go back to the hotel, as I informed you yesterday. Bring whatever kind of medication you think I might need, and we can always come back here if need be. Remember, you and the ravishing Dr. D'Agostino will be conveniently right down the hall."

Daniel glanced up at the ceiling. "I tried," he said with a sigh and a shrug.

"Indeed you did, Doctor," Ashley admitted. "Carol, dear, I trust our limo driver is still outside, waiting for us?"

"As far as I know," Carol said. "He was when I checked an hour ago, and I told him to stay until he heard from me."

"Excellent," Ashley said. He swung his legs over the side of the bed in a manner that surprised everyone, including himself. "Glory be! I do not think I could have done that this morning." He stood up. "Well then, this country boy is ready to return to the pleasures of the Atlantis and the splendor of the Poseidon Suite."

Fifteen minutes later in parking area in front of the Wingate Clinic, a discussion ensued about the travel arrangements. Eventually, it was decided that Daniel would ride with Ashley and Carol in the limo while Stephanie would drive the rent-a-car. Carol had offered to ride with Stephanie, but Stephanie assured her she would be fine and actually preferred to be alone. Daniel had the vial of the sedative combination, several syringes, a handful of sealed individual alcohol pledgets, and a tourniquet in a small, black, zippered pouch compliments of Myron. Armed with the medication, Daniel felt it was imperative for him to remain in Ashley's presence in case of a problem, at least until Ashley was safely in his suite.

Daniel sat in the seat facing the rear directly behind the glass shield separating the driver's compartment from the passenger section. Ashley and Carol were sitting in the back, their faces intermittently illuminated by the flickering light of oncoming vehicles. With his procedure behind him, Ashley was ostensibly euphoric, carrying on an animated conversation with Carol about his political agenda after the Congressional recess. In reality, the discourse was more like a monologue, since Carol merely nodded or said yes at infrequent intervals.

As Ashley talked and carried on, Daniel began to relax from the tension engendered by his worry that Ashley was about to have a seizure and the associated concern of having to give a dose of the sedative. If the seizure was anything like what had occurred in the OR, Daniel knew the intravenous route would be close to impossible, and he'd be reduced to giving it intramuscularly. The problem with the IM route was that it took longer for the drugs to cause an effect, and any delay could be problematic if aggression was an issue, as Dr. Nawaz had strenuously warned. Considering Ashley's size and surprising strength, Daniel knew that wrestling with him within the confines of the limo would be a nightmare.

The more relaxed Daniel became, the more his mind was able to go beyond the seizure concern. He became progressively amazed at the degree of mobility Ashley was displaying with his gestures and how normal his facial expressions and voice modulation were. He was a far cry from the semifrozen individual Daniel had seen that morning. Daniel was puzzled, since the treatment cells were not in their proper location, as was shown all too clearly on the CAT scan. But the effect he was observing could not be the result of the sedative or placebo, as he'd so blithely suggested earlier. There had to be some other explanation.

Like all scientists, Daniel was aware that science occasionally leapt ahead not by hard work alone but also by serendipity. He started to wonder if the errant site the treatment cells now occupied might prove to be particularly appropriate for dopamine-producing cells. It didn't make sense, because Daniel knew that the area of the limbic system where the cells now resided was not a modulator of motion, but rather was involved with olfaction, autonomic behaviors like sex, and emotion. Yet there was a lot about the human brain and its function that was still a mystery, and at the moment Daniel was enjoying seeing such a positive result from his efforts.

When they arrived at the Atlantis, Ashley made it a point that he did not need assistance from the doormen as he climbed from the car. Although he had another bout of dizziness when he got to his feet, requiring him to hold on to Carol for a moment, it passed quickly, and he was able to walk reasonably normally into the lobby and to the elevators.

"Where is that gorgeous Dr. D'Agostino?" Ashley asked as they waited.

Daniel shrugged. "She either got here before us or will be here shortly. I'm not concerned. She's a big girl."

"Indeed!" Ashley agreed. "And smart as a whip."

In the hallway of the thirty-second floor, Ashley walked ahead as if showing off his new capabilities. Although he was still hunched over to a degree, he was moving much more normally, including his arm swing, which had been almost negligent that morning.

Carol used her keycard when they got to the mermaid door. She opened it and stepped aside for Ashley to enter. As he did so, he turned on the lights. "Every time they make up the room, they close everything to make the place look like a root cellar," he complained. He walked over to the wall switches and activated the curtains and the sliding-glass panels simultaneously.

At night, the view from inside the suite was nowhere near as dramatic as it was in the day, since the expanse of ocean was as dark as crude oil. But that was not the case from the balcony, where Ashley immediately went. He put his hands down on the cool stone balustrade, leaned forward, and surveyed the vast semicircular Atlantis water park splayed out in front of him. With its profusion of pools, waterfalls, walkways, and aquariums, all creatively illuminated, it was a feast for his eyes after the stress of the day.

Carol disappeared into her room while Daniel advanced to the balcony's threshold. For a moment he watched Ashley as the senator closed his eyes and raised his head into the cool tropical breeze coming off the ocean. The wind rustled his hair and the sleeves of his Bahamian print shirt, but he was otherwise motionless. Daniel wondered if Ashley was praying or communicating with his God in some personal fashion now that he thought he had genes from Jesus Christ embedded in his brain.

A slight smile appeared on Daniel's face. Suddenly he had more optimism about the outcome of treating Ashley than he had since the seizure in the operating room and more optimism than he thought possible after seeing the CAT scan. He began to think there was something of a miracle involved.

"Senator!" Daniel called after five minutes had passed and Ashley had not moved a muscle. "I don't mean to bother you, but I think I will go to my own room."

Ashley turned around and acted as if he was surprised to see Daniel standing there. "Why, Dr. Lowell!" he called out. "How nice to see you!" He pushed away from the balustrade and walked directly up to Daniel. Before Daniel knew what was happening, he was enveloped in a bear hug that kept his own arms pinned to his sides.

Self-consciously, Daniel allowed himself to be hugged, although he wondered if he had any choice in the matter. It was a testament to how much bigger and heavier the stocky Ashley was in comparison to Daniel's spare and comparatively bony frame. The hugging continued beyond what Daniel thought reasonable, and just when he was about to voice impatience, Ashley let up and stepped back but kept one hand gripping Daniel's shoulder.

"My dear, dear friend," Ashley oozed. "I want to thank you for all you have done from the bottom of my heart. You are a tribute to your profession."

"Well, thank you for saying so," Daniel murmured. Feeling himself blush, he was embarrassed.

Carol reappeared from her bedroom and her presence rescued Daniel from Ashley's clutches. "I'm on my way back to my room," Daniel called out to her.

"You get a good rest!" Ashley ordered, as if

he were the doctor. He gave Daniel a pat on the back, which was strong enough to cause Daniel to take a step forward to keep from losing his balance. Ashley then turned around to retreat back to his place at the balustrade, where he assumed the same meditative pose he'd struck earlier.

Carol accompanied Daniel to the door. "Is there anything I should know or do?" she asked.

"Not that I haven't already told you," Daniel said. "He seems to be doing okay, and certainly better than I expected."

"You should be very proud."

"Well, yeah, I suppose," Daniel stammered. He wasn't sure if she was referring to how Ashley was doing at the moment or sarcastically to the complication. Her tone, like her broad expressionless face, was hard to read.

"What exactly should I be watching for?" Carol asked.

"Any change in his health status or his behavior. I know you have no medical training, so you'll just have to do the best you can. I would have preferred he stay in the clinic tonight so his vital signs could have been

checked through the night, but that didn't
happen. He's a strong-willed individual."

"That is an understatement," Carol said.
"I'll watch over him as I usually do. Am I supposed to wake him during the night? Anything like that?"

"No, I don't think that is necessary, with
him doing as well as he is. But if there is any
problem whatsoever or you have any questions, call me, no matter what the time."

Carol opened the door for Daniel and then
closed it behind him without another word.
For a moment, Daniel stared at the carved
mermaids. Trained as a hard scientist, he
knew psychology was far from his forte, and
people like Carol Manning confirmed it. She
confused him. One minute she seemed the
perfect, dedicated assistant; the next she
seemed as if she was mad about her sub-
servient role. Daniel sighed. At least it wasn't
his problem, provided she watched the senator through the night.

On the short walk to the suite he shared
with Stephanie, Daniel's attention switched
back to the shocking improvement in Ashley's Parkinson's. He was mystified on many
counts but enormously pleased, and he

couldn't wait to share the news with Stephanie. He opened the door and was surprised not to see her, especially when she wasn't in the bedroom either. Then he heard the shower going.

When Daniel entered the bathroom, he found himself enveloped in a fog as if Stephanie had been in there for a half hour. He put the toilet seat down and sat. With his line of sight at a lower level, he could now make out Stephanie's form behind the frosted and fogged shower door. It appeared as if she weren't moving beneath the full force of the spray.

"Are you all right in there?" Daniel yelled out.

"I'm better," Stephanie answered.

"Better?" Daniel questioned silently. He had no idea what she meant, although it reminded him that she had been rather silent all afternoon. It also reminded him of her seemingly insensitive response to Carol's offer to ride with her, although he admitted if the situation had been reversed, he would have responded similarly. The difference was, in contrast to him, Stephanie ordinarily concerned herself about other people's feelings. Daniel didn't consider himself base or even rude, but rather he just couldn't be bothered. People had to understand that there were too many more important things for him to think about than social niceties.

Daniel debated with himself whether or not to go out to the minibar to get something to drink. In many ways, it had been one of the most stressful days of his life. Ultimately, he decided to stay put. He was eager to tell Stephanie about Ashley; the drink could wait. But Stephanie didn't budge.

"Hey, in there!" Daniel yelled at length. "Are you coming out or what?"

Stephanie cracked open the door, and steam billowed out. "I'm sorry. Are you waiting to get in here?"

Daniel waved the vapor away from his face. The bathroom had become a Turkish bath. "No, I'm waiting to talk to you."

"Well, maybe you shouldn't wait. I'm not sure I'm up to talking much."

Daniel felt a wave of irritation course through him. Stephanie's response was not what he wanted to hear. With the day's events, he needed and deserved a bit of support, which he certainly did not believe was asking too much. Abruptly, he stood up, left the bathroom, and slammed the door.

While he got himself a cold beer, he brooded. He didn't need any more aggravation. He plopped himself down on the couch and concentrated on sipping his beer. By the time Stephanie appeared, wrapped in a towel, he had recovered.

"I can tell by the way you slammed the door you're mad," Stephanie said in a calm voice. She was standing in the doorway to the bedroom. "I just want to let you know I'm emotionally and physically exhausted. I need some sleep. We did wake up at five this morning to make sure everything was ready."

"I'm tired too," Daniel said. "I just wanted to tell you that Ashley is doing unbelievably. Most of his Parkinson's symptoms have already mysteriously improved."

"That's nice," Stephanie said. "Unfortunately, it does not alter the fact that the implantation went awry."

"Maybe it didn't go awry!" Daniel responded. "I'm telling you that you will be amazed. He's a different man."

"He certainly is a different man. We've inadvertently crammed a horde of aberrant dopamine-producing cells someplace into his temporal lobe. An experienced neurosurgeon strongly believes he'll be saddled with the hell of temporal lobe epilepsy. For Ashley, that will be even worse than the Parkinsonism."

"But he's not had a seizure since the one in the OR. I'm telling you, he's is doing marvelously."

"He's not had a seizure *yet.*"

"If he has a problem, we can deal with it the way I suggested to Dr. Nawaz."

"You mean with the cytotoxic agent attached to the monoclonal antibody?"

"Exactly."

"You can do that if you are so inclined and if you can talk Ashley into subjecting himself to such a foolhardy experiment, but it is not going to be 'we.' I'll have no part of it. We haven't even tried it in cell culture, much less animals, and as such, it is a quantum leap more unethical than what we have already done."

Daniel stared at Stephanie. He could feel his irritation sweeping back over him. "Whose side are you on, anyway?" he demanded. "We decided on a goal to cure Ashley to save HTSR and CURE, and by God, we are going to get there."

"I'd like to think that I am crossing over to the side less motivated by self-interest,"

Stephanie said. "Today, when we realized the OR was not equipped with the necessary X ray, we should have stopped the procedure. We were gambling with someone else's life for our own benefit." Then she held up her hands as Daniel's face flushed and his mouth opened to respond. "If you don't mind, let's cut it off right here," she added. "I'm sorry, but this has become exactly the kind of discussion I did not feel capable of having tonight. I told you I'm drained. Maybe I'll feel differently after a night's sleep. Who knows?"

"Fine!" Daniel said sarcastically, with a wave of his hand. "Go to bed!"

"Are you coming?"

"Yeah, maybe," Daniel said angrily. He got up and went to the minibar. He needed another beer.

Daniel wasn't sure how many times the phone had rung since his exhausted mind had incorporated the jangle into the nightmare he was having. In his dream, he was a medical student again, and the phone was something to fear. Back then, it was often a call to an emergency he was untrained to handle.

By the time Daniel's eyes popped open, the ringing had stopped. He sat up and looked over at the now silent phone on the side table and wondered if it had rung or if he'd just dreamed it. Then his eyes darted around the room to orient himself. He was in the living room, still in his clothes, with all the lights on. After two beers, he'd fallen fast asleep.

The door to the bedroom opened. Stephanie appeared in her silk shorty pajamas, squinting and blinking in the bright light. "Carol Manning is on the phone," she said, in a voice thick with sleep. "She's upset and needs to talk with you."

"Oh, no!" Daniel said worrisomely. He swung his legs off the coffee table. He even still had his shoes on. Without standing up, he leaned across the length of the couch and picked up the phone. Stephanie stayed in the doorway to listen.

"Ashley is acting strangely," Carol blurted into the phone after Daniel identified himself.

"What's he doing?" Daniel asked. The old medical school fear of incompetence in the face of an emergency came flooding back. With as many years as Daniel had been away from clinical medicine, he had forgotten most of his doctoring skills.

"It's not so much what he is doing, it's what he's complaining about. Excuse my language, but he says he smells pig shit. You told me that if he smelled something strange, it might be important."

Daniel felt his heart skip a beat and the optimism he'd felt earlier vanish. Immediately, there was not a modicum of doubt in his mind that Ashley was having an aura heralding the onset of another temporal lobe seizure. At the same time, the last vestiges of clinical confidence Daniel was holding on to crumbled as he acknowledged he was about to face handling an episode of what Dr. Nawaz predicted would be worse than the first. "Has he been aggressive or is he acting out in any way?" Daniel asked nervously. Frantically, he looked around the room for the black pouch containing the sedative and syringes. Thankfully, he spotted it on the table in the foyer.

"Acting out is a little strong, but he has been irritable. Then again, he's been irritable for the last year."

"Okay, be calm!" Daniel said, as much for his own benefit as for Carol's. "I'll be right down to the room." He looked at his watch. It was two-thirty in the morning.

"We're not in the room," Carol said.

"Where the hell are you?"

"We're in the casino," Carol admitted. "Ashley insisted. There was nothing I could do, and I tried. I didn't call you because I knew there was nothing you could do either. When he makes up his mind, that's it. I mean, he's a senator."

"Good God!" Daniel complained. He slapped a hand to his forehead. "Did you try to get him to come back to the room when he smelled the pig poop?"

"I suggested it, but he told me to go out and jump in the shark tank."

"Okay! Where in the casino are you?"

"We're at a bank of slot machines on the ocean side of the room, beyond the roulette tables."

"I'll be right down. We've got to get him back to the room!"

Daniel got to his feet and glanced at Stephanie, but she had disappeared back into the bedroom. He dashed over and looked in. Stephanie was tearing off her pajamas and pulling on her clothes.

"Wait!" she called out. "I'll come with you. If

Ashley is going to have a seizure anything like what he had in the OR, you'll need all the help you can get."

"Okay," Daniel said. "Where's the cell phone?"

Stephanie nodded toward the bureau as she hastened to button her blouse.

"Bring it along! Where are the numbers for Newhouse and Nawaz?"

"I've got the numbers already," Stephanie said, stepping into her pants. "They're in my pocket."

Daniel ran to the medical pouch. Just to be sure, he pulled open the zipper. He felt some reassurance after seeing the vial and the syringes. The trick was going to be getting the medicine into Ashley before all hell broke loose.

Stephanie appeared at the bedroom doorway, still struggling to get into her loafers and tuck in her blouse. By the time she got over to Daniel, he had the door to the hall open. Together, they flew toward the elevators.

After hitting the down button, Daniel took the cell phone from Stephanie, handed her the medical pouch, and dialed Dr. Nawaz's number.

"Come on!" Daniel urged, as the phone

rang and rang. Just as the elevator arrived, Dr. Nawaz answered sleepily.

"It's Dr. Lowell," Daniel said. "We might get cut off. I'm stepping into an elevator." In response to Stephanie pressing the lobby button, the doors closed. "Can you still hear me?"

"Just barely," Dr. Nawaz said. "What's the problem?"

"Ashley is having an olfactory aura," Daniel said. He was watching the floor indicator. It was supposed to be a high-speed elevator, but the numbers seemed to be decreasing agonizingly slowly.

"Who is Ashley?" Dr. Nawaz questioned.

"I mean Mr. Smith," Daniel said. He glanced at Stephanie, who rolled her eyes. For her, it was another small episode in the continuously unfolding and unfunny comedy.

"It will take me about twenty minutes to get to the clinic. I advise you to call Dr. Newhouse. As I said earlier, I suspect this seizure might be worse than the first, especially considering where those cells are. We might as well have the same team."

"I'll call Dr. Newhouse, but we are not at the clinic."

"Where are you?"

"We're at the Atlantis resort on Paradise

Island. At the moment, the patient is in the casino, but we are going to try to get him back to his room, which is registered under a Carol Manning. It's called the Poseidon Suite."

There was a silence that lasted for several floors.

"Are you still there?" Daniel said into the phone.

"I'm not certain I'm believing what I am hearing. This man had a craniotomy some twelve hours ago. What the hell is he doing in the casino?"

"It would take too long to explain."

"What time is it?"

"It's two-thirty-five. I know it sounds like a lame excuse, but we had no idea Mr. Smith would go to the casino when we brought him back here, but he is extremely strong-willed, with a mind of his own."

"Has there been any progression beyond the aura?"

"I haven't seen him yet, but I don't think so."

"You'd better get him out of that casino. Otherwise, there could be one hell of a scene."

"We're on our way down to the casino as we speak."

"I'll be there as soon as I can. I'll check the casino first. If you're not there, I'll assume you are in the room."

Daniel ended the call and then dialed Newhouse's number. Like with Dr. Nawaz, the phone had to ring multiple times before it was picked up. But in contrast to Dr. Nawaz, Dr. Newhouse sounded chipper, as if he'd been awake.

"Sorry to bother you," Daniel said, as the elevator doors opened on the lobby level.

"No bother. As an anesthesiologist frequently on call, I'm accustomed to calls in the middle of the night. What's the problem?"

Daniel explained the situation as he jogged down the main hall toward the casino, which was centrally located in the huge complex. Dr. Newhouse's reaction mirrored Dr. Nawaz's in all respects, and he too said he would be there imminently. After disconnecting, Daniel exchanged the phone for the black medical pouch.

Upon reaching the casino, Daniel and Stephanie slowed to a fast walk. The facility was in full swing and significantly more crowded than either anticipated, despite the hour. It was a colorful sight with its rich, red-and-black carpet, huge crystal chandeliers, and snappily dressed croupiers. Daniel and Stephanie made a beeline through the clutter of activity and past the roulette tables grouped in the middle of the spacious room. It didn't take them long to find the bank of slot machines Carol had described and, once there, even less time to find Ashley. Carol was standing right behind him and was ostensibly glad to see help arrive.

Ashley was sitting in front of one of the slot machines with a considerable pile of coins on the counter. He was still dressed in his laughable tourist outfit. His bandage was still in place on his forehead. His paleness wasn't as apparent with the red glow reflecting off the carpet. There was no one at the machines immediately neighboring his.

Ashley was relentlessly feeding his machine in a manner he clearly wouldn't have been able to do the day before. The instant the inner wheels stopped, another coin dropped into the slot and the arm was pulled. Ashley appeared mesmerized by the blurred images of fruit.

Without a moment's hesitation, Daniel went directly up to Ashley and pulled him around with a hand on his left shoulder. "Senator! How nice to see you!"

Ashley squinted up into Daniel's face. His eyes were unblinking, his pupils dilated. His normally carefully combed hair was tousled as if someone had deliberately messed it up, giving him a wild appearance.

"Take your hands off me, you skinny shit," Ashley growled, without a trace of his normal accent.

Daniel obeyed instantly, shocked and terrified by Ashley's uncharacteristic profanity, which recalled a similar outburst in the operating room. The last thing he wanted to do was provoke the man and thereby incite a more rapid progression of the seizure symptoms. He stared into Ashley's eyes, which reflected a kind of disconnect, since Ashley evidenced no signs of recognition. For a beat, neither moved as Daniel rapidly debated whether to attempt to medicate him on the spot. He decided against it, for fear he'd be unsuccessful and make things worse in the process.

"Carol tells me you smelled a disagreeable odor," Daniel remarked, unsure of what to say or how to proceed.

Ashley gave a wave of dismissal before nodding his head. "I think it was that whore over there in the sexy red dress. That's why I moved to this machine."

Daniel glanced down the row of slot machines. There was a young woman in a red dress showing significant cleavage, especially when she worked the slot machine's arm. Daniel redirected his attention to Ashley, who had gone back to feeding the machine in front of him.

"So you don't smell the odor any longer?"

"Just a little, now that I moved away from that bitch."

"Well, good," Daniel said, allowing himself a ray of hope that the aura might resolve without progression. Regardless, he wanted Ashley back in the Poseidon Suite. If there were a scene in the casino, undoubtedly the whole affair would unravel in the media.

"Senator, I have something I want to show you up in your room."

"Piss off, I'm busy."

Daniel swallowed nervously. His nascent ray of hope began to fade as he acknowledged that Ashley's mood and behavior were obviously already significantly abnormal, even if not yet outrageous. Frantically he tried to think of something to get Ashley up to his suite, but nothing came to mind.

All at once, Carol gave Daniel's shirt sleeve a tug and whispered in his ear. Daniel shrugged. He was willing to try anything, no matter how ridiculous. "Senator. There's a full case of bourbon in your room."

With encouraging rapidity, Ashley let go of the slot machine's arm, turned, and looked up at Daniel. "Why, Doctor, fancy seeing you down here," he said, with his accent returning.

"Good to see you as well, sir. I came down to tell you about the case of bourbon that arrived in your room. You have to come up and sign for it."

To Daniel's relief, Ashley immediately slid off the stool attached to the floor in front of the slot machine and stood. He must have had a wave of dizziness, because he tottered for a moment before grasping the edge of the counter. Daniel grabbed his arm just above his elbow for additional support. Ashley blinked, looked at Daniel, and for the first time smiled.

"Let's proceed, young man," Ashley said. "Signing for a case of bourbon sounds like a worthy cause to this old country boy. Carol, dear, see to my loot, if you please!"

With his hand still gripping Ashley's upper arm, Daniel guided the man away from the slot machines. In appreciation of Carol's suggestion, which he never would have thought of on his own, Daniel winked at her as their eyes briefly met. While Carol quickly gathered up Ashley's coins, Daniel and Stephanie accompanied the senator across the floor and through the milling crowd of gamblers.

The journey went smoothly until they got to the elevators, where they had to wait briefly. Like a cloud passing in front of the sun, Ashley's smile suddenly disappeared and was replaced by a scowl. Having been watching his face and seeing the transition, Daniel was tempted to ask the senator what he was thinking. But he didn't, for fear of undermining the status quo. Daniel's intuition told him that a mere tendril of reality was maintaining Ashley's control of his mind.

Unfortunately, two couples that Ashley had spotted over Daniel's shoulder boarded the same elevator behind them. One of them pressed the button for the thirtieth floor. Daniel swore under his breath. He had hoped to have the car to themselves, and the tension of worrying about an explosion of Ashley's behavior in the presence of strangers caused his pulse to race and perspiration to appear on his forehead. For a split second he looked at Stephanie, who appeared as terrified as he. Returning his attention to Ashley, he could tell the senator was glaring at the couples who were tipsy and carrying on in a boisterous and provocative manner.

Daniel unzipped the medical pouch. He looked in at the vial and syringes, and considered whether he should fill one of the syringes. The problem was that the strangers would see what he was doing and might become alarmed.

"What's the matter, Papa?" one of the women questioned teasingly after noticing Ashley's truculent, unblinking stare. "Are you jealous, old man? You need a little action?"

"Screw you, bitch!" Ashley snapped.

"Hey, that's no way to talk to a lady," the woman's companion blurted. He pushed the woman to the side and stepped forward to confront Ashley.

Without thinking of the consequences, Daniel sandwiched himself between the two. He could smell the man's garlic-and-alcohol breath and feel Ashley's stare on the back of his head.

"I apologize for my patient," Daniel said. "I'm a doctor, and the gentleman is ill."

"He's going to be a lot sicker if he doesn't apologize to my wife," the man threatened. "And what's he ill with, loss of marbles?" The man laughed mockingly as he tried to peer around Daniel for a better look at Ashley.

"Something like that," Daniel agreed.

"Whore!" Ashley shouted, while making a lewd gesture toward the woman.

"Oh, that's it!" the man snapped. He reached out and tried to move Daniel aside while making a fist with his other hand.

Stephanie grabbed the man's arm. "The doctor is telling the truth," she asserted. "The gentleman is not acting like himself. We're taking him back to his room to give him some medication."

The elevator stopped at the thirtieth floor, and the doors opened.

"Maybe you'd better give him a new brain," the man said, as his laughing companions pulled him off the elevator. He yanked his arms free and stood, glaring in at Ashley, until the doors closed in front of him.

Daniel and Stephanie exchanged a nervous glance. A potential disaster had been averted. Daniel looked at Ashley, who was smacking his lips as if tasting something disagreeable. The elevator doors opened on the thirty-second floor.

With Carol on one arm and Daniel on the other, they managed to get Ashley off the elevator and down the hall. He did not resist but rather walked like an automaton. At the mermaid door, Carol let go of Ashley long enough to get out her keycard and hand it to Stephanie, who got the door open. As Daniel and Carol started to urge Ashley forward, he shook off their hands and walked in freely.

"Thank heavens," Stephanie said, as she closed the door behind the group.

The chandelier in the foyer was turned on, as was a lamp on the desk in the great room. Otherwise, the suite was lost in shadow. The drapes were pulled to the side, along with the glass panels. Beyond the balcony, a star-strewn sky arched over a dark sea. Freshly cut flowers rustled softly on the coffee table from the night breeze.

Ashley continued walking until he reached a point a few steps away from the coffee table. There he stopped and remained motionless while staring out at the balcony. Carol turned on more lights to fill the room

with illumination, then went to Ashley to see
if she could get him to sit down.

Daniel dumped the contents of the medical pouch on one of the small matching console tables in the foyer. He fumbled, trying to
tear open a syringe packet, while Stephanie
removed the cap covering the rubber stopper on the parenteral medication vial.

"How are you going to do this if he re-
sists?" Stephanie whispered.

"I haven't the slightest idea," Daniel admitted. "Hopefully, Dr. Nawaz and Dr. Newhouse
will be here to lend a hand." He had to use
his teeth on the cellophane.

"The senator is grimacing like he did when
he smelled the pig excrement," Carol called
from the other room.

"Try to get him to sit down," Daniel yelled
back. He finally got the syringe out of its
packaging and threw the wrapper to the side.

"I already tried," Carol said. "He refuses."

A loud crash of furniture in the other room
snapped Daniel and Stephanie's heads
around. Carol was picking herself up from
the floor after having been shoved into one
of the end tables, knocking its lamp over. The
ceramic lamp had shattered into a thousand

pieces. Ashley was tearing off his clothes and throwing them around the room.

"Oh God!" Daniel cried. "The senator is going off the deep end." Daniel grabbed one of the alcohol pledgets and tore it open, but the moment he got the pledget itself out, he dropped it. He grabbed another.

"Can I help?" Stephanie asked.

"I'm all thumbs," Daniel admitted. He got another pledget out and swabbed the rubber stopper of the medication vial. But before he could insert the needle, Ashley let out a shriek. In a panic, Daniel thrust the vial and the syringe into Stephanie's hands before dashing into the room to see what was happening. Carol was standing behind one of the couches with her hands clasped alongside her face. Ashley was still in the same place but naked save for calf-length black socks. He was slightly hunched over and staring at his hands, which he had cupped close to his face.

"What's the trouble?" Daniel cried, as he came around to look at Ashley.

"My palms are bleeding," Ashley said with horror. He was shaking. Slowly, he lowered his trembling hands palm-up, spreading his fingers widely.

Daniel looked at Ashley's hands and back up into his face. "Your hands are fine, Senator. You have to calm yourself. Everything is going to be all right. Why don't you sit down? We have some medicine for you, which will make you feel relaxed."

"I am sorry for you that you cannot see the wounds on my hands," Ashley snapped. "Perhaps you can see them on my feet."

Daniel looked down and then back up at Ashley. "You're wearing socks, but your feet look fine. Let's sit you down on the couch." Daniel reached out to take Ashley's arm, but before he could, Ashley slapped his hands against Daniel's chest and viciously shoved him away. Completely caught off guard, Daniel stumbled into the coffee table, falling over backward onto it and smashing the flower vase in the process. Water and cut flowers splayed out in an arc on the thick carpet. Daniel rolled off the table face-first, falling between it and one of the couches. Carol screamed.

Mindless of the havoc he'd caused, Ashley skirted around the other side of the coffee table and ran toward the balcony. He stopped abruptly just over the threshold and lifted his hands horizontally with his palms facing forward. The night breeze off the ocean fluttered his disheveled hair.

"Good grief! He's out on the balcony!" Stephanie yelled. She was clutching the syringe, alcohol pledget, and vial to her chest.

Wincing from the pain in his back from the collision with the flower vase, Daniel struggled to his feet. He ran out onto the balcony, skirting Ashley, to put himself between Ashley and the balustrade.

"Senator!" Daniel yelled, holding up his hands. "Get back in the room!"

Ashley did not move. His eyes were closed, and a look of serenity had replaced the earlier horror.

Daniel snapped his fingers to get Stephanie's attention. She had stopped just inside the room with a look of dismay on her face. "Is the syringe filled?" he asked, without taking his eyes off Ashley.

"No!"

"Fill it fast!"

"How much?"

"Two cc's. Quick!"

Stephanie drew up the fluid, pocketed the vial, and snapped the syringe with the nail of her index finger to get rid of any bubbles. She dashed out onto the balcony and handed the syringe to Daniel. She looked into Ashley's placid face. The man was like a statue. He didn't move. He didn't even seem to be breathing.

"It's like he is frozen," Stephanie said.

"I don't know whether to try to give this IV or just settle for IM," Daniel debated. He took a step forward, still not having decided what he was going to do, when Ashley's eyes popped open. Without the slightest warning, Ashley bolted forward. Daniel reacted by throwing his arms around Ashley's chest while trying to brace himself against the floor tiles. But it was like trying to hold back a charging bull. Daniel's shoes slid easily across the ceramic floor, and when the two men collided with the balustrade, Ashley's momentum caused them to flip over the top and out into the night.

Stephanie screamed "No!" as she raced to the railing and looked down. To her utter horror, Ashley and Daniel were locked in a slow-motion, tumbling embrace, like two lovers falling into the abyss. In the next instant, Stephanie averted her gaze, and with a sick feeling, she slumped down with her back against the cold stone balustrade.

Epilogue

6:15 A.M., Monday, March 25, 2002

The faint brightening of the sky, which had been almost imperceptible a half hour earlier, was now definite. The stars had faded, and in their place was a soft, rosy glow heralding the imminent sunrise. The night breeze had quieted. Incessant chatter of songbirds could now be heard, even thirty-two stories up from the ground.

Stephanie and Carol were sitting on opposite couches in the main room of a suite similar in size but not quite as luxurious as the

Poseidon Suite. They had been sitting there for hours without moving or speaking, in near catatonia, after having been emotionally traumatized by Ashley and Daniel's shocking somersault over the balustrade. Carol had been the first to react after the event. She'd dashed for the phone and blurted to the operator that two people had fallen from the Poseidon Suite balcony.

Carol's panicked voice had mobilized Stephanie to clamber to her feet. She avoided looking over the railing again but rather rushed for the door and ran headlong down the corridor. As she waited breathlessly at the elevator, Carol had joined her. On the elevator, neither spoke, but they stared at each other in total disbelief of what they had witnessed. Both nursed a wisp of hope for a miracle. It had all happened so quickly that there was a sense of unreality.

The two women descended to the level of what was called the Dig, requiring them to run past huge illuminated aquariums filled with all manner of sea creatures, as well as fanciful ruins of the mythical city of Atlantis, in order to reach the ground level in front of the hotel complex. They both guessed that there was a shorter route, but this was the only way Carol knew to get there, and time was of the essence.

On emerging into the night, they veered left, skirting the Royal Baths Pool, illuminated with its underwater lights. Reaching a narrower walkway that wasn't as well lighted, they had to slow. They crossed a bridge over the Stingray Lagoon to arrive at the darkened, carefully landscaped area at the foot of the Royal Towers' west wing. Both women were winded.

A contingent of the hotel security had reacted swiftly to the alarm initiated by Carol's call and was already on the scene. Several were busy roping off the area with yellow caution tape stretched between palm trees. A large African-Bahamian man dressed in a dark suit stepped from the shadows and intercepted the women.

"I'm sorry," he said, blocking their path as well as their view. "There's been an accident."

"We're staying with the victims," Stephanie blurted. She tried to see around the sizable man.

"I'm sorry, but it is still best you remain here," the man said. "Ambulances are on the way."

"Ambulances?" Stephanie questioned, desperately maintaining her ray of hope.

"And the police," the man added.

"Are they all right?" Stephanie hesitantly asked. "Are they still alive? We have to see them!"

"Ma'am," the man said gently. "They fell from the thirty-second floor. It's not a pretty sight."

Ambulances had come to remove the bodies. The police arrived as well and conducted a preliminary investigation. They found the syringe, and it initially caused an excitement until Stephanie explained it was medication prescribed by a local doctor. This was confirmed by both Dr. Nawaz and Dr. Newhouse, who arrived soon after the tragedy. The police had accompanied the women and the doctors back up to the Poseidon Suite to check the balcony and the balustrade. The Chief Inspector then confiscated the women's passports and told them they would be required to remain in the Bahamas until an inquest had been held. He also had the Poseidon Suite and Stephanie's suite sealed for further investigation.

The hotel night manager had been a paragon of composure, efficiency, and empathy. Immediately and without question, he had transferred the women to a suite in the Royal Towers' east wing, where they were now sitting. He also provided them with all sorts of personal care products to ease their short-term inability to use their own. Dr. Nawaz and Dr. Newhouse had remained for a time. Dr. Newhouse had provided a sedative for the women, which they could use if they so chose. Neither did. The small plastic container sat untouched on the coffee table between them.

Stephanie had been mulling over and over in her mind the entire affair, from the rainy night in Washington until the tragedy that morning. With hindsight, she had trouble believing that she and Daniel could have allowed themselves to be drawn into such a foolhardy business. Even stranger was their inability to recognize their folly, despite multiple setbacks that should have been hints that their decision-making was terribly flawed. They had truly confused ends and means. The fact that she had on occasion questioned what they were doing was scant comfort, because she had never acted on her intuitions.

Finally, Stephanie took her feet off the coffee table and sat up. She had exhausted her ability to introspect. With her fingers entwined, she stretched out her arms. She was stiff from inaction. After running her fingers through her hair and taking a deep breath, which she let out forcibly, she looked at Carol.

"You must be exhausted," Stephanie said. "At least I got a few hours of sleep."

"As strange as it may sound, I'm not," Carol said. Following Stephanie's lead, she too stretched. "I feel like I've had ten cups of coffee. I can't stop thinking about how ridiculous this whole episode has been, from the night of that fateful meeting in my car until this current catastrophe."

"You were against it?" Stephanie asked.

"Of course! I tried to talk Ashley out of it from the start."

"I'm surprised."

"Why?"

Stephanie shrugged. "I don't know exactly, but I guess it's because it means you and I felt similarly. I was against it too. I tried to talk Daniel out of it as well but unfortunately not stridently enough."

"Apparently, we both were fated to be a Cassandra of sorts," Carol said. "I suppose that is metaphysically apropos, since the whole affair has turned out to be a Greek tragedy."

"How so?"

Carol gave a short, exhausted laugh. "Don't mind me. I was a literature major in college, and sometimes I get carried away with my metaphors."

"I'm interested," Stephanie said. "How was it a Greek tragedy?"

Carol was silent for a moment, organizing her thoughts. "It's because of the characters of the protagonists," she said. "It's the story of two titans, in their own separate arenas yet strangely similar in their hubris, who had achieved greatness but suffered tragic faults. Senator Butler's was a love of power, which had evolved from a means to an end to an end in and of itself. Dr. Lowell's, I'd guess, was a desire for financial recognition and celebrity status appropriate in his mind to his intellect and contribution. When these two men collided by conspiring to use each other for their own purposes, their tragic faults literally brought them down."

Stephanie stared at Carol. She'd always thought of the self-contained woman as a colorless, rather dull, quintessential subordinate. Suddenly she felt differently and by comparison distinctly less intelligent and less educated than she had earlier. "What does it mean to be a Cassandra?"

"In Greek mythology, Cassandra was endowed with the gift of prophecy but fated not to be believed."

"Interesting," Stephanie said lamely. "At one point, I teased Daniel about being similar to Ashley."

"In some respects, they were, at least in respect to their egos. But tell me, what was Dr. Lowell's response to your teasing?"

"Anger."

"I'm not surprised. Senator Butler's response would have been the same if I had had the courage to say anything equivalent. Actually I believe they admired, despised, and were jealous of each other all at the same time. They were competitors in a distorted masculine sort of way."

"Maybe so," Stephanie said, as she mulled the idea. She wasn't immediately convinced Daniel had admired much about Ashley Butler, but she recognized that her contemplative abilities were hardly at their sharpest. "Are you hungry?" she asked, to change the subject.

Carol shook her head. "Not in the slightest."

"Nor am I," Stephanie said. She was exhausted, but she knew she couldn't sleep. What she wanted was human contact and conversation to keep her mind from going over and over the same issues. "What are you going to do when we can finally leave the Bahamas after the inquest?"

"I'm not sure there will be an inquest, or if there is, it will be quick, pro forma, and behind closed doors."

"Oh? Why do you say that?"

"Ashley Butler was a senior U.S. Senator in a Congress with a slim majority. The United States government is going to be immediately and aggressively involved at a high level. I think this will all be resolved very, very quickly, because it will be in everybody's interest. I even believe there will be powerful impetus to keep the affair from the media, if at all possible."

"My word!" Stephanie muttered, as she pondered such a scenario. The idea had not occurred to her. In fact, in her mind's eye she had already seen the headlines in *The Boston Globe* as the final coup de grace for CURE. Yet she had not considered the political ramifications due to Ashley's notoriety.

"As for me," Carol said, "I'm going to head home and arrange to see the governor. He'll be making an appointment to Senator Butler's seat, and I'll make the case that I am the most qualified and should be selected. If that doesn't happen or even if it does, I'll start making the arrangements to run for the seat in the next election."

"What do you think will happen to Senate Bill 1103?"

"Without Senator Butler, it will probably just languish," Carol said. "Your worry should reside across the aisle, where the hard right Republicans might pick up the banner."

"That was our concern from the start," Stephanie admitted. "We were surprised when we were blindsided by your boss."

"You shouldn't have been. That was the kind of populist issue he always championed. It was the way he maintained his power base. I suppose his hypocrisy in regard to Dr. Lowell's procedure was not lost on you."

"Hardly."

"And what about you?" Carol asked. "What are you going to do when you leave Nassau?"

Stephanie thought for a moment. "First, I

have to deal with a problem with my brother. It's a long story, but our relationship is another casualty of this regrettable affair. Then I guess I'll see about picking up the pieces of CURE. I hadn't thought it possible until you suggested that the media might not get ahold of this regrettable story and that Senate Bill 1103 might languish in committee. I'm not much of a businessperson, but I suppose I could give it a try. I think it is what Daniel would want, especially if it brings HTSR to the people."

"Well I have to say I've become a believer in Dr. Lowell's procedure, as well as therapeutic cloning. I know there was a technical complication with Senator Butler's implantation, but there was no doubt his Parkinson's was miraculously helped."

"Such an immediate positive effect surprised us," Stephanie admitted. "We never saw such quick resolution of symptoms with our mice. Why it happened to Ashley I can't explain, but there's no doubt in my mind had the implantation gone as planned in an appropriate Stateside medical center, the senator would have been cured, or close to it."

"I was impressed," Carol said.

"Even in the face of this tragedy, it proves

how promising this technology is. I'm convinced it is the future of medicine for a host of diseases, provided a handful of politicians don't manage to keep it from the American people for political reasons."

"Well, I hope I get a chance to keep that from happening," Carol said. "If I get to fill Ashley Butler's seat, I'll make it my crusade."

Author's Note

I think of my novels as "faction," a coined word meaning that the fact and fiction are so mixed that the dividing line between the two is often hard to discern. What does this mean for *Seizure*? Certainly the characters are all fictional, as is the storyline. Also, unfortunately, the HTSR procedure is not yet part of the biomedical armamentarium. But just about everything else is factual, including the parts about the Shroud of Turin, from which specific genes have been isolated from its bloodstains. I must admit, like Daniel and Stephanie, I became fascinated by the shroud. The reference Stephanie cites is also real, and for those interested in pursuing the subject further, I recommend it as a start.

It is also fact that a number of U.S. politicians have involved themselves in the debate about bioscience, a field whose rate of discovery has become geometric. Indeed, it seems as if the twenty-first century will belong to biology, just as the twentieth century belonged to physics and the nineteenth century belonged to chemistry. Unfortunately, in my opinion, some of the politicians have been drawn into the debate, like my fictional Senator Ashley Butler, for demagogic purposes rather than as true leaders with the public weal at heart. And even those politicians, who seek to ban research of these twenty-first century therapeutic technologies in the United States for what they believe to be legitimate moral reasons, I suspect would not hesitate to fly to another country where such treatments were allowed to develop if they or a member of their family were stricken with an illness capable of being cured.

In the congressional hearing room scene in *Seizure* (Chapter Two), Senator Ashley Butler shows his true colors by playing to public fears about embryo farms and ata-vistic Frankenstein mythologies. The sena-tor also refuses to separate reproductive cloning (cloning a person, about which there is almost universal repugnance) from therapeutic cloning (cloning cells from an individual for the purpose of treating that in-dividual). Senator Butler, like other oppo-nents of stem-cell and therapeutic cloning research, suggests that the procedure re-quires the dismemberment of embryos. As Daniel points out to little avail, this is false. The cloned stem cells in therapeutic cloning are harvested from the blastocyst stage well before any embryo forms. The fact is that in therapeutic cloning, an embryo is never al-lowed to form and nothing is ever implanted in a uterus.

Most of my readers are aware that my medical thriller stories have significant socio-logical issues at their core. *Seizure* is no ex-ception, and obviously the issue here is the regrettable collision of politics and rapidly advancing bioscience. But it is one thing to use a cautionary tale to delineate a problem and quite another to suggest a solution. However, Daniel does allude to one, and it is one I personally would like our country to adopt. As Daniel questions in Chapter Six, "We [meaning the United States] took a lot of our ideas about individual rights, government, and certainly our common law from England. Why couldn't we have followed England's lead in how best to deal with the ethics of reproductive bioscience?"

In response to the often difficult and disturbing ethical issues arising from molecular genetics and human reproductive research underscored by the birth of the world's first in vitro fertilization baby in 1978, the British Parliament in their wisdom created the Human Fertilisation and Embryology Authority (HFEA), which has been operational since 1991. This organization, among other functions, licenses and monitors infertility clinics (something lacking in the U.S.) as well as debates and recommends policy to Parliament in regard to reproductive technologies and research. Interestingly enough, the chairman, deputy chairman, and at least one half the general membership are statutorily neither doctors nor scientists involved in reproductive technology. The point is that the English have managed to form a truly representative body whose members reflect a wide range of the general public's interests and which can debate the issues in an apolitical environment. Of note, the HFEA issued a report in 1998 that clearly differentiated between reproductive cloning, which it recommended be banned, and therapeutic cloning, which it recommended as holding promise for the therapy of serious illnesses.

The fact that bioscience in general and reproductive bioscience in particular is advancing so quickly begs the issue that the field needs some form of oversight. There is no doubt that completely unfettered bioscience can be a threat to human dignity, if not our identity, as Dr. Leon Kass, the current chairman of the President's Council on Bioethics has suggested. But partisan politics is not the appropriate arena to deal with this problem. In such a setting, any committees formed would invariably become stacked with members of a particular political bent.

It is my belief that if the U.S. Congress were to set up a nonpartisan standing commission like the English HFEA to recommend policy, the U.S. public would be well served. Not only could the current debate about therapeutic cloning be resolved in an intelligent, apolitical, and democratic fashion (there is already consensus against reproductive cloning), but also infertility clinics could be monitored appropriately. It is even conceivable that the related abortion issue could be taken out of politics, to our collective benefit.

Robin Cook, M.D.
March 12, 2003
Naples, Florida